MW00388407

Deadly Enterprise

A Mike Stoneman Thriller

Deadly Enterprise

A Mike Stoneman Thriller

Kevin G. Chapman

Copyright © 2019 by Kevin G. Chapman

ISBN: 9781700401083
Kindle Direct Publishing

   This is a work of fiction. The events and characters depicted here are the products of the author's imagination and any connection or similarity to any actual people, living or dead, is purely coincidental.

   All rights reserved. Copyright under Berne Copyright Convention, Universal Copyright Convention, and Pan-American Copyright Convention. No part of this book may be reproduced, stored in a retrieval system, or transmitted in any form, or by any means, electronic, mechanical, photocopying, recording or otherwise, without prior permission of the author.

   Cover image: Ryan McGrady

   Cover design: Bespoke Book Covers

   .

Other novels by Kevin G. Chapman

Identity Crisis: A Rick LaBlonde Mystery

A Legacy of One

Righteous Assassin (Mike Stoneman #1)

Visit me at www.KevinGChapman.com

For Sharon, who cares as much about my characters as I do, and who never lets me get away with lazy writing. She's also a runner, which helped substantially with parts of this story.

Table of Contents

Chapter 1 – A Very Bad Date

THE GIRL ON THE FLOOR in the skimpy red dress groaned softly and rolled her head to the side. The corner of her right eye was caked with dried blood. A gooey scarlet trickle ran down toward the dirty blonde hair hanging in unkempt wisps around her ear. One of the thin shoulder straps of her dress was snapped off, allowing the shiny material to peel down, exposing the top half of her small breast. A knot on her forehead the size of a golf ball throbbed an angry shade of red with each heartbeat.

"I'm not so sure about dumping her in the river," a male voice said, without a hint of anxiety. He sat casually on the edge of a bare wooden desk in a Spartan room lacking any semblance of charm. The bed, covered with a drab brown comforter, was pushed up against the wall in front of an imitation leather headboard with large buttons holding in the padded surface. Next to it, a nondescript lamp glowed on a stained nightstand. There was no art on the walls and the floor was industrial-grade carpet with a swirling pattern that hid most of the

1

remnants of prior visitors. The air smelled of musty sweat and industrial-strength disinfectant. The calm man, by contrast, wore an expensive suit and a gold Citizen watch. He was tall and fit, with graying black hair that was carefully groomed. He looked decidedly out of place in the dumpy room.

"We gotta make sure," a different voice replied. "She's not hurt that bad. Look, she's coming around." This second voice was agitated and came from a much shorter man, who paced within the cramped space. He was thin and wiry. He ran his hand through a head of brown curls, pondering his next move. He wore blue jeans and a plaid button-down shirt. His gaunt face looked like it was pushed together from the sides, with large bulging eyes and a bent nose. "We'll make it look like an overdose, but make sure she's dead. We don't want her ending up in an ambulance like the last one."

"Not many people accidentally go in the river, Eddie," the first man said, still without emotion.

"She's an addict. She can OD, then there's lots of reasons somebody might toss the body in the river."

"All of those reasons involve somebody trying to hide something."

"Yeah, I know, but what other options have we got? She was gonna run. She knows who you are, so sending her into lockup ain't gonna be safe."

The first man stood up, stretching his arms above his head. He was much bigger than his companion and thick, like the trunk of a sturdy tree. He looked down at the woman, who had brought one arm up to her head. She was clearly going to open her eyes in a few moments, but she was no threat to jump up and run away. "I don't want to get in the habit of just shooting up every girl who gets out of line."

"Nobody has said boo about the others," replied Eddie, who stopped pacing. "I can go upstairs and get it from the doc." He glanced nervously down at the figure still sprawled on the floor, then back up at his comrade. "I'll go right now." The taller man nodded, and then Eddie scurried to the door and disappeared into the dimly lit hallway beyond. The heavy door slammed behind him with a loud thump.

The woman partially opened her eyes, then blinked several times. Once she focused on the tall man, a shadow of fear passed over her expression and she started to cry. "I'm sorry," she sobbed, her body shaking, causing the remaining fabric of her dress to fall completely off her left breast. "Please. I won't say anything. I promise. I'll be good. I'll be—"

Her voice was snuffed out by the man's vicious kick to the side of her head, which then lolled in the opposite direction as her eyes re-closed and she sank back into unconsciousness.

The tall man looked down, dispassionately. "You'll be dead, Sweetheart."

Chapter 2 – Physical Torture

Wednesday, Feb. 6

MIKE STONEMAN'S FACE was contorted in a mask of pain. "Aaaahhoooww! No more!" he groaned, a tear forming in his right eye as he turned his head to that side. He was lying on his back on an elevated table; his feet were strapped down to prevent movement. The man on his left, wearing a plain white t-shirt and sweat pants, held Mike's left wrist in a vice-like grip with his left hand and pressed his right hand into Mike's elbow, keeping the arm straight and pushing upwards. Pain shot through Mike's shoulder and down his arm, making his fingers tingle. He could feel the sinew in his labrum stretch to the breaking point and heard the pop and crunch of scar tissue ripping. He gritted his teeth and held his breath as long as he could stand it, before shouting out again, "Stop!"

Mike felt the pressure relax slightly, allowing him to catch his breath. He blew out three quick puffs of air as he looked up at Terry Kramer with malice in his eyes. Then the pressure returned as the man once again pushed against the limits of Mike's flexibility.

"You can take more," Terry said, pushing a little harder this time. "What's the PIN to your ATM card?!"

"You'll never get me to . . . Aahhh . . . talk, you bastard!" Mike grunted out. Then the pain subsided slightly as the big man eased his grip on Mike's wrist and relaxed the pressure. Mike sighed, then cried out in pain again as his arm retracted down toward his side. He panted as he lay on the soft tabletop, sweat running down his forehead and dripping onto the vinyl surface. "I hate you," Mike said softly, slowly regaining his regular breathing.

"Good," Terry replied as he released Mike's legs from their straps. Mike struggled to a sitting position, careful to keep his left arm immobile as much as possible at his side. He swung his legs over the edge of the table and looked across the therapy room, where his recovery partner, Dolores, was doing arm curls with a giant blue rubber band while standing against a full-length mirror. Terry smiled. "You got up to sixty degrees today, Mike. I'm proud of you."

"Hmmff," Mike grunted. "You're going to rip all my pins out and send me back to surgery."

Terry laughed robustly and slapped Mike on the back with a solid open palm. "Like I don't know how far I can push you without doing damage? C'mon, Mike. Trust me."

Mike was now fourteen weeks removed from being stabbed in the shoulder in a Queens warehouse by former Army lieutenant Ronald Randall, dubbed the "Righteous Assassin" by the New York press. After his surgery, he spent six weeks in a brace to keep his arm immobile, and then started physical therapy in mid-December. Now it was the middle of February and struggling into his parka was an ordeal, but the New York winter would not permit Mike to get away with just a light jacket or a zip-up hoodie. At least the abdominal knife wound was fully healed. He had a scar that looked like he had given birth by Caesarian section through his belly button, but his abs looked pretty decent due to the exercises he had to do for his post-operative recovery. Overall, he was down fifteen pounds since the fall. At least that was a plus.

"I'm gonna shoot you," Mike replied with a smile. He took a deep breath, then hoisted himself off the table and walked slowly toward the far wall, where Dolores had finished her arm work. She was a traffic enforcement agent who had injured her shoulder in a kayaking accident while on vacation in Florida. She was a thick Black woman just over five feet tall, but she had disproportionately slender calves and ankles. Her upper body was dominated by a huge bosom and a pile of black hair mounted on her head in a never-ending variety of styles. Today she wore a 70's afro that increased her apparent height by a good six inches. She also sported a set of bright white teeth that were nearly always smiling. Her perpetual good mood sometimes caused Mike to be even more curmudgeonly than normal, as if it were a competition to see whether Dolores could get him to smile back. She had a torn labrum and a torn rotator cuff and had her surgery one week after Mike's. They had been in rehab together since just before Christmas and were basically on the same regimen of exercises.

Terry, the physical therapist at the NYPD athletic and medical facility, had scheduled them for simultaneous sessions so that he could maximize his efficiency as the two patients traded off time on the table with time on the exercise equipment. Mike and Dolores had a running wager on who would complete rehab and get to a full range of motion first. As Dolores sauntered past, Mike whispered, "Sixty."

"Ooohh," Dolores said with a twinkle in her eye. "You are making progress. I better get busy!" She laughed and hopped up on the table so that Terry could manipulate her arm and shoulder, as he had done with Mike moments before. The therapy included strengthening exercises and also manual stretching to push the now ultra-tight muscles, ligaments, tendons, and cartilage back to their normal range of motion and flexibility. Terry forced the joints to move despite the fact that the surrounding muscles and tissue had been sewn together and locked down tight during surgery, then allowed to sit immobile for six weeks while the cuts healed. Now, stretching the joints back out involved more pain than the original injuries. Dolores took it all with her usual smile and good cheer. Mike was just sore.

Mike went to work on the rubber bands, lifting his arm up in front of his body as far as he could before the pain stopped him, then down. Ten reps with his injured left arm, then ten with the right, just to keep both arms in shape. This was his eighth week of physical therapy. He could see the progress. When he started, he could not lift his arm more than ten degrees, even without weights or resistance from the rubber band. Now he was at sixty degrees. He still had a long way to go, and progress was agonizingly slow. He was sure that if he were twenty years younger, he would be recovering faster. As always, he thought, it sucks to get old.

Dolores hopped off the table, fresh off her torture at Terry's hands, but Mike did not recall her screaming even once. She flashed him her bright teeth and whispered "Sixty-five," as she passed him by, on her way to grab her coat and purse from a hook on the wall. Mike congratulated her as sincerely as he could, dropped his last resistance band, and waved to Terry that he was also calling it a day. They were actually several minutes beyond the official end of their time, but Terry always allowed them to stay as long as they wanted to keep stretching.

Mike grabbed his workout towel and pushed through the glass doors of the PT room. He waved at the elderly receptionist who scheduled the appointments and exited out into the general gym portion of the facility. Mike thought that, on the one hand, it was great that the NYPD had its own physical therapy facility so that the recovering cops did not have to fight with the general public for appointment times. On the other hand, it was unfortunate that the police had so many injuries that its officers could fully book an entire physical therapy operation, to the point that it was difficult finding open time slots and officers had to double up with the therapists. At least he had been able to set up a reasonable schedule.

After changing in the locker room, Mike headed south down Amsterdam Avenue, bending his head down against the chilly wind. He fished a knit hat out of the pocket of his jacket with his right hand and managed to get it on his head one-handed, since he could not get his left arm up that high. He had twenty blocks to walk, but he needed to keep up the exercise. It was still impossible for him to jog because the pounding jarred his injured shoulder too much, but walking was fine, so he had been walking everywhere, even through the snow and slush of the city. His plan was to stop by the precinct on 94th Street for a while, then continue on to his apartment on 68th Street. That would be close to fifty blocks of walking by the end of the afternoon. He wished he were back on active duty, but he was mollified somewhat by Captain Sullivan's willingness to let him visit the precinct, consult on pending cases, and work on his training class materials while he was drawing disability pay. This was not strictly permitted under departmental rules, but as long as nobody from the downtown brass or the benefits consultants came in to check on him, Sully would swear he was never there. Mike limited his appearances to about once per week, just in case.

After several weeks of bitterly cold weather, which the reports had referred to as the "polar vortex," the temperature had shot up into the low 40s, which seemed like spring. It was nearly 4:00 p.m. when Mike turned west on 94th Street and saw the line of black and white cruisers lined up in the parking spaces in front of the precinct house. He climbed up the four steps of the building that was once a brownstone residence and pushed open the heavy wooden door with his right arm, nodding in greeting at two uniformed officers who were exiting. He climbed the stairs to the third-floor bullpen, where the detectives had their desks, and waved at his comrades. He scanned the room for his partner, Jason Dickson, but didn't see the big man anywhere. Jason was the only Black detective in the Homicide division and he was also always the best dressed cop in the room, so he stood out in the crowd. Mike called out a greeting to Detective Steve Berkowitz, who grinned widely and yelled back that Mike should demand a new contract with the Mets, now that he had a surgically repaired left arm.

"I'm leaving for Spring Training in the morning," Mike quipped back.

"Hey, Mike!" came the booming voice of Jason Dickson from the foot of the stairs. Jason came bounding into the bullpen and charged toward Mike with his arms extended as if he were going to tackle the older detective, or put him in a bear hug. Mike crouched quickly and held out his right palm, signaling for Jason to stop. Jason kept running right up to the point of contact before stopping short and softly giving Mike's right hand a high-five. Jason towered five inches and easily fifty pounds of muscle over Mike's five-foot-ten frame. "A little late for work, aren't you, Detective?"

"I make my own hours now," Mike deadpanned.

"While you're here, do you have a minute?"

"Sure. I got nowhere to be."

Jason turned and yelled across the room, "Hey, Ray!" as he waved at Detective Raymond McMillian, who was filling in as Jason's partner while Mike was out on disability. Ray rose from his desk and slowly walked in Jason's direction. Ray was in his early thirties and tried to look even younger, sporting a Fu-Manchu beard and moustache combination and combing back his flowing brown curls into a wave. He was shorter than Jason and stockier, but still bigger than Mike. He swaggered across the room with an attitude not generally seen from the newest detective in the group.

"Hey, old man," Ray said with a smile. "How's the broken wing?"

Mike scowled at the man's familiarity. "It wasn't broken, Kid. If you survive in this job long enough to reach my advanced age, you can tell me how your body's doing."

"OK," Ray said, only slightly chastised, "I'll be sure to look you up in the rest home to tell you."

"Great. Maybe you'll pass my evidence handling class by then."

That shut Ray up for a moment and let Jason insert himself between the two of them. "Ray, I want Mike to join us on the call with the M.E. on the floater. Let's go into the conference room." Mike raised an eyebrow at the mention of the medical examiner, Dr. Michelle McNeill, who was a veteran of many homicide investigations and a frequent witness in high-profile trials. She was also the woman with whom Mike was spending most of his nights, now that he was able to sleep in a reclining position again after his surgery. Dr. McNeill had been present in the Queens warehouse when Mike was injured. Mike and Jason exchanged a knowing look, passing between them the understanding that Ray was not clued in to Mike's relationship with the doctor.

The three men huddled around a small wooden table in a cramped, windowless room, which passed for a conference area in a Manhattan precinct where space was always at a premium. An ancient telephone with a black cord snaking to a large silver speaker box sat in the center of the pock-marked tabletop. Mike glanced toward a credenza at the far side of the room where an urn of coffee sat next to a stack of paper cups and a bowl of sweetener and creamer packets. A red light glowed over the black spigot, indicating that the coffee was brewed and ready to drink. There was a small pile of paper plates on the opposite side of the wooden surface, along with a leaning tower of white paper napkins, but the rest of the space was bare. Mike raised an eyebrow and asked, "No donuts today?"

"He hasn't heard?" Ray asked.

"I guess not," Jason replied. "No donuts, Mike. No food at all. We've got a rat issue."

"Issue?" Mike said with another raise of his brow.

"Yeah. We had one running around the bullpen a few days ago. The exterminators came in and said they found droppings all over the place and a bunch of bags of candy and crackers had been chewed open. They say we have to clear out all the food in the building until they get the infestation under control, so Sully has banned all food. We can have coffee, but that's it. Anybody caught eating in the building will do hard time."

"That sucks," Mike said, stating the obvious. "What about lunch?"

"We have to go out of the building to eat. We've turned the squad cars into makeshift food trucks, since it's too damned cold to stand around outside."

"I guess you do what you gotta do."

"It's a pretty poor reflection on the city's building maintenance program," Ray cut in.

Mike and Jason just stared at him without speaking. Jason shot Mike a look to say, "This is what I have to put up with from this guy," then reached for the phone without further comment. He picked up the receiver, then paused.

"Ray, please brief Detective Stoneman on the case before we call the M.E."

Ray looked up, slightly flustered at being put on the spot. He quickly recovered his composure, sat back in his chair, and began his summary. "Well, Mike, it's pretty routine, I think. Some jogger reported seeing a body floating in the East River. The uniforms and the EMTs fished her out, but she was way dead. We got prints and we're running them through the national database, but her fingers were pretty bloated, so we're not sure about getting a match. She was naked except for a pair of red silk panties. Looked to be early 20s. Bruise on her head, but other than that no obvious signs of injury." Ray looked at Jason, seeking approval for his recitation.

Jason looked at Mike. "Any questions?"

"Not yet."

Jason dialed the phone and punched a button at the bottom of the ancient device, which blinked once, then stayed lit. The line connected and rang several times before being answered.

"Medical examiner," came the voice through the tinny speaker.

"Doctor McNeill, it's Jason Dickson from Homicide. I'm here with Detective Raymond McMillian and Detective Mike Stoneman. You sent me a note that you wanted to talk about the Jane Doe that you've been examining."

There was a pause on the line and the detectives could hear the sound of footfalls. Mike pictured Michelle walking across her examination room to her neatly organized desk, extracting a file from her desktop, and then walking back to the phone. He smiled at the thought, and remembered that he needed to pick up something he could make for dinner at Michelle's downtown apartment later. "I have the file, gentlemen."

Mike said, "Go ahead, Doctor."

"We have a Caucasian female between eighteen and twenty-three. Cause of death is drowning. I'd say she was in the water between twenty-four and thirty-six hours. Deceased has a large contusion on her left forehead consistent with a blunt force blow, which occurred several hours before death. She has other assorted scratches and bruises that I can't say for sure existed before she went into the water. Most importantly, she had a large quantity of opiates in her system, and a single needle scar on her right arm consistent with an injection of heroin shortly before her death. When her system shut down, she stopped metabolizing the drug, so I was able to detect about how much she had in her at time of death, which was pretty significant. Her teeth and nose showed signs of recent use of crystal meth, but the tox screen didn't find any of that in her system. Her stomach was basically empty. She had semen in her vagina but no indication of trauma or tearing, so it does not look like sexual assault."

When Dr. McNeill stopped talking, Mike spoke up. "Anything else to suggest foul play, and not just an overdose and an accidental or intentional dive into the water?"

The doctor was silent for ten seconds before responding. "You know that I can't speculate. That's your job. But I've seldom seen an overdose case with just one needle mark."

"What do you mean?"

"This woman had one needle scar in her arm. Nothing in the other arm, and no other indication of heroin use. So, if she accidentally overdosed, she did it on the first hit, or at least the first hit in a very long time. That's not normal for a heroin addict, in my experience. The big bump on her head, which did not happen when she went into the water, suggests that she took a significant impact, and then a few hours later, high as a kite from a big dose of heroin, she ends up in the river. And it's February and freezing cold, so she's not skinny dipping. She may have been wearing something when she went in, but it wasn't anything warm, which would have stayed attached to her. So, either she walked in light clothing to the river while really high, after taking a serious blow to the head, and jumped or fell in, or somebody clubbed her in the head, before or after she took the drugs, and then helped her in where she was sure to drown."

"Thank you, Doctor," Mike said, determining that Michelle was done. He then looked at Jason. "Any other questions?" Jason shook his head. Mike turned to Ray, who leaned forward, but then waved a hand to indicate that he had nothing to say. "Okay, Doctor. Thanks for the report. We'll get back to you if we think of any other information we want. By the way, are her fingerprints more legible now than when she came in?"

"Yes, I think so. Her bloating has subsided some. I'll take another set of prints and send them up for processing."

"Thanks again." Mike reached out to punch the lighted button and end the call. "So," he said, looking at Jason, "you're treating this as a homicide?"

"We're treating it as a possible homicide," Jason responded. "Let's see what we get once we have an ID on her and take it from there. It's still possible that she went into the river because she was so high she didn't know any better. Stranger things have happened to junkies."

"The M.E. just told us that she doesn't think she was a heroin addict. I must say that I tend to agree – it's pretty rare for an addict to have no track marks."

"She can't know that for sure," Ray broke into the discussion. "The lady said there was evidence of crystal meth use, and she was high on the smack for sure at the time. Let's not make her out to be Cinderella yet."

Mike frowned, but chose not to respond. Ray was not wrong. Mike would have supported the M.E. loudly, but he didn't want to seem like he was too deferential. He was pretty sure that Jason got the message. "It's your case, gentlemen. What can I do to help?"

Ray started to say something but Jason cut him off. "What do you think, Mike? Where would you go from here?"

"Well, you don't know where she went into the river. It could have been anywhere on the Manhattan or Brooklyn side. Without an ID, you have no idea where to look or who to talk to. I'd say you work every angle you can to find out who she was and go from there. Until you have that, you have nothing."

"That's what I was gonna say," Ray blurted out.

"That's good, Detective McMillian," Mike said, nodding at Ray. "We're on the same page. Now see what you can do to get a positive ID."

"How would you suggest we do that?"

"You look like a smart guy, Detective. I'm sure you can figure it out." Mike stood up slowly, careful not to put weight on his left arm as he pushed up from his chair. He shook hands with Jason, then waved in the direction of Ray, who was sitting on the opposite side of the table and who did not stand up when Mike did. Jason walked Mike to the door of the precinct and watched as the older man climbed carefully down the four slippery stone steps to the sidewalk, turned left, and walked away toward Broadway.

When Jason went back inside, Ray was still sitting in the conference room. "Can we talk about the Sheffield case?" he asked when Jason came in.

"You think there's nothing else to do about our unidentified floater?"

"Nah. Let's wait to see if the fresh prints come back with an ID. No point spinning our wheels over this junkie until we know something."

"You've decided you don't like her already?"

"Hey, I see a lot of these strung-out losers on the street over in Robbery. They are suspects in a lot of the snatch-and-grab cases; just trying to snag enough for their next fix. They're disgusting. Maybe the crazy bitch wanted to kill herself. Maybe she fell in. Maybe she thought she could fly and jumped off the bridge. Maybe a lot of things. I'm not losing any sleep over her."

"Is there anything that makes you lose sleep, Ray?"

"Not really."

"I didn't think so." Jason turned toward the door to the conference room. "I tell you what. I'm going to go home. We can work Sheffield in the morning. You do what you want."

"I always do," Ray said, smiling and leaning back as he clasped his hands behind his head.

Jason turned and walked out, muttering, "I know."

Chapter 3 – Once a Partner

Friday, Feb 8

TWO DAYS LATER, Mike was back on the PT table. His sessions were scheduled for Mondays, Wednesdays, and Fridays and this was Friday, not that the days of the week mattered that much for someone who wasn't working. Terry stretched his arm, while Mike bit down and tried not to scream. Dolores had finished with the light weights and was sitting on a large exercise ball next to Mike's head, waiting for her turn on the table and taking great joy in tormenting Mike.

"You're a pansy-ass weenie," Terry teased. "Dolores here doesn't whine half as much as you, Stoneman."

"Yeah, well, she's given birth, so after that nothing really hurts, right, Dolores?" Mike turned toward his therapy companion for confirmation.

"You're damn right!" she agreed. "If you macho men had to go through that, you'd never complain about pain again in your life." The two men chuckled nervously in agreement.

Mike climbed down from the table and collected his coat before waving good-bye to Terry and wishing him and Dolores a pleasant weekend. He exited the PT room and walked through the general gym area toward the locker room. As he walked past the rows of weight machines and treadmills, lost in his own thoughts, Mike was startled by the sound of someone calling his name.

"Yo! Stoneman!"

Mike stopped and turned in the direction of the voice, then broke into a broad smile as he strode back toward a collection of weights and pulleys. Sitting on a low, padded seat with his right leg strapped into one of the machines was Mike's former partner, who had dark sweat stains around the collar of his gray NYPD t-shirt. "Hey, Darren!" Mike called out. He had been Mike's partner for two years. "Darren! How the hell are you?"

"You just couldn't stay away from me, could ya, Mike?"

"Hey, I'm here on legitimate police business."

"I heard you had a little scrape. Too bad your partner wasn't there to watch your back." Darren reached down to remove the strap holding his foot to the machine, then looked up at Mike, who had made his way to Darren's bench. "How's things working out with your new guy, anyway?"

"Are you doing anything after you're done here?" Mike asked.

Darren thought for a moment, then said, "I don't think so, why?"

"Want to step out for a beer, catch up a bit? It's been too long."

"Sure," Darren replied. "I'll be done in ten minutes."

"I'll wait for you by the front."

"Okay. I'll see you there," Darren grunted as he strained to lift his left leg against the resistance of the weight machine.

Ж Ж Ж

A half-hour later, the two men were seated at a dimly lit bar called One-Ten at 110th and Amsterdam, sipping their second round of beers. Darren was in his mid-thirties, with brown hair clipped short, but not quite a military buzz. His face was youthful, with round cheeks that looked as if he couldn't grow a beard if he tried. He wasn't tall, about the same as Mike's five foot ten, and was stocky without being at all overweight. Mike often envied Darren's metabolism. Now that he was exercising regularly at the gym as part of his rehab, he was even more buff than when he had been working. Mike remembered how Darren would always squeeze a spring-loaded pair of bicycle handles to build up his upper arms. Mike guessed that these days, Darren didn't have much to do besides work out.

"I'm sorry about the dig on your new partner, Mike."

"Don't worry about it. It wasn't his fault that I was alone. I went in by myself because I had to. Truth is that Jason acted quickly, found me, and saved my life by calling in the ambulance. I have no problems with how he handled it."

"Glad to hear it, Mike," Darren said without much enthusiasm. "Does that mean when I get back on my feet, my old chair won't be available?"

Mike looked up from his glass and scrutinized his old partner, who had limped his way from the gym to the bar in twice the time it would have taken Mike by himself. The injury was more than a year and a half old. "Are the doctors saying that you could get back to full strength again?"

Darren turned his head away. "The doctors don't always know everything."

"So, you're still in PT?"

"I'm seeing my therapist once a week. That's the minimum I need to do in order to stay in rehab status."

"Are you progressing at all?"

19

"I get a report every month that says I have 'not yet reached maximum medical recovery.' So, officially, yes. The reality is that I'm investigating some experimental treatment options. I haven't given up hope."

"Okay," Mike said, reaching over to give Darren a light punch in the shoulder. "If you get back, I'll make sure there's a place for you. Might not be with me, but you were due to rotate away from me anyway."

"Yeah, I know. I just feel like our tour was left unfinished."

"It was. But there's no point in crying over spilt milk. And speaking of spilt milk, how are Tony and Jenny doing? It's been a while since I saw them."

"Yeah. Marie was asking me whether you had called. But don't worry. I know how it is. It's not your job to look after me anymore. But thanks for asking. Tony and Jenny don't spill their milk much anymore." Darren broke into a grin. Mike noticed that his top row of teeth showed some brown blotches, and wondered if he had dropped his dental insurance because of the cost. "Tony's going to be in middle school next year."

"Really?" Mike said with genuine surprise. "Shit. The time gets away from me."

"Tell me about it."

"You need to have me over for dinner so I can say hello to Marie."

"Sure," Darren said, sipping his beer and avoiding eye contact with Mike. "I'll mention it to her and give you a call."

"I mean it. I feel awful about not keeping in touch more. Last time I saw you was, what, last June?"

"July, at the fireworks."

"Right. Well, it's too long. We spent a lot of time together for two years. We should stay in touch."

"Don't worry about me, Mike. I'm fine."

"Well, you should never have taken that bullet in the first place," Mike mumbled.

"Drop it, Mike."

"Fine. You keep working on your rehab. We'll worry about the rest when you get back to work. Is the Department taking care of you financially?"

"I'm fine," Darren responded. "I'm drawing disability."

"That's only seventy-five percent of pay."

"Sure, but I have no commuting expenses," Darren said with a wry smile.

"You let me know if you need anything."

"I will." Darren downed the last of his beer, reached into his pocket, and tossed a twenty-dollar bill on the bar as he carefully hopped down from his stool onto his right leg.

Mike quickly reached out and slid the bill back toward Darren. "I got this."

"It's not a problem, Mike. I'm not hurting for cash. I got it."

"Listen, you stubborn bastard, I invited you for a beer and I'm paying," Mike fixed a stern gaze on his friend.

"Fine. You got this one. I'll get the next one. You're at the rehab center a few times a week, right?" Mike nodded. "Great. Next time, then." Darren took back his twenty and put on his coat. Mike reminded Darren to talk to his wife about setting up a dinner. The two men shook hands at the door and Darren hopped off to the north, while Mike turned south. As he walked toward his apartment, Mike bent his head down against the cold wind and thought about the day that Darren had been shot and injured. Mike had alternated between being angry with Darren for being so careless and being angry with himself for not preventing it. Today was no different. He couldn't make up his mind. All he knew for sure was that it was a damned shame.

Chapter 4 – Racial Profiling

WHILE MIKE WAS SIPPING A BEER with his old partner, Jason Dickson and his temporary partner, Ray McMillian, were in a briefing with Captain Edward Sullivan. Sullivan had a ruddy face and a large nose that was perpetually red. He looked like a Central Casting model of an Irish cop. And, like every other cop in history named Sullivan, all his officers and detectives called him "Sully." He was a bulldog in supporting his detectives, but he would also call them out if they made him or his homicide unit look bad. In his police uniform, the detectives in the bullpen liked to joke that he looked like the Captain from Gilligan's Island. Dickson and McMillian were back in the cramped and donut-less conference room along with Sully, staring at the ancient speaker box hooked up to the telephone. On the other end of the line, Deputy Mayor Kendrick Williamson and the chief communications officer for Mayor Frederick Douglass were explaining the public relations issues and the consequential urgency of a new case.

"There is already a huge memorial springing up outside the bodega," Williamson said, clearly agitated but trying to hold it together. "The local TV stations are all over it and Al Sharpton has already implied that the police will not take the case seriously because the victim is Hispanic, and also that the police will be looking to pin the murder on a minority suspect even if there's no evidence. It's a shit show and we're only on day one."

Kim Martinez, the mayor's communications director, chimed in to agree with Williamson's assessment. "The only way to prevent this from becoming a racial issue, and a problem for the mayor, is if we find the culprits who did this and build a solid case, maybe with a confession or two, and do it fast."

"You make it sound like we don't try to do that except in politically sensitive cases," Sully observed, looking at Dickson and McMillian with a scornful expression.

"No, of course," Martinez said, trying to recover without admitting the implication of her original comment. "I just mean that whatever additional resources can be brought to bear on this investigation should be considered and the mayor will support you."

"Thanks," Sully responded. "I already have a detective team working the case. They responded to the scene last night – or early this morning – and they already made some progress during the day today. They had been on duty for thirteen straight hours, so I told them to go home and get some sleep, but I expect they will be working the weekend on it."

"That's Detectives Berkowitz and Mason, right, Captain?" Williamson said, more like a statement than a question.

"Yes," Sully responded curtly, knowing that Williamson already knew this; the deputy mayor had been part of the briefing on the case they had done just after noon that day. "They aren't here. I have Detectives Dickson and McMillian here, as you requested. Do you think we need two teams working in tandem on this so we can put on a full-court press?"

Williamson paused on the other end of the phone and the detectives could hear muffled conversation between him and Martinez, but could not determine what they were saying. After more than a full minute, Martinez spoke up. "Captain, we appreciate that Detectives Berkowitz and Mason have started the investigation and done a really fine job. But we are anticipating that this case could become a racial issue and we're concerned about the optics."

"So, you want a Black detective leading the team, is that it?" Sully snapped.

"In a word, yes."

Now it was Sully's turn to pause while he calmed down and told himself to avoid saying something he would regret. "Have you discussed this with Commissioner Ward?"

"Yes," Williamson cut in. "The mayor called him and discussed it this afternoon."

"Why was I not included in that discussion?" Sullivan said, his voice getting louder and his face starting to tinge pink as the blood rushed to his cheeks.

"The mayor and the commissioner felt that this decision was sensitive and needed to be made at a higher level."

"Then why isn't one of them on the phone to tell me that?" Sully was yelling now and all pretense of remaining calm had apparently gone out the window.

"That's not my call, Captain," Williamson said curtly. "I'm doing what I've been told to do and you need to do what you're being told to do."

"I'm going to call the commissioner when we're done here," Sully said threateningly.

"That's fine, Captain, but for now, can we complete our assignments?"

"Fine. Dickson, McMillian, you two are going to take over this case, at the direction of the mayor, and apparently the commissioner." Jason and Ray just nodded and stayed silent. Ray was too new to the unit to have a clue about what he should or should not say, and Jason had seen Sully in this kind of powder-keg mood often enough to know that he needed to keep his mouth shut. "Mr. Williamson, since you are apparently directing this operation, why don't you brief the new lead detective and his partner on where we stand?"

"I'll be happy to do that," Williamson said soothingly, hoping he could nudge the conversation back toward professional. Sully sat back in his chair and folded his arms across his chest, while Jason and Ray both pulled out notebooks and pens and started writing.

"Early this morning, about 1:00 a.m., a bodega owner and operator named Raul Rosario was locking up his store at East 193rd Street and Decatur Avenue. He never got the lock on the security door before he was assaulted, beaten, and presumably robbed. At some point, Rosario sustained a stab wound to the chest and subsequently died at the hospital, although we don't have the report from the medical examiner yet to say it was from the knife. We have one witness, a clerk at a 24-hour donut shop on the opposite side of the street, who called 9-1-1. She said she saw a group of figures who looked like young men of indeterminate age or race running away, perhaps four or five of them, according to the statement taken by the officer on the scene. We're checking the neighborhood businesses to see if there are any surveillance cameras that might have caught any images, but so far, we haven't found any. No traffic cams, either.

"Berkowitz and Mason responded to the scene and found a bartender at a pub halfway down the block, who said there was a group of basketball players from Fordham in the place late last night. They were celebrating after some big win or something. The college is just a few blocks away in the direction of the bodega. The bartender said that the group of guys had several pitchers of beer and staggered out about one o'clock. From the bar toward the college, they would have walked right in front of the donut shop and then made the right at the corner, so if there was anything going on while they were passing by, they would have seen it."

Dickson broke into the narrative. "Is it possible that the basketball players are the group of males that the donut shop clerk saw running away from the scene?"

"We tracked down three of the players today and we got somewhat different stories. Two of them said they saw a group that included a few big Black guys and a single white male in a dark jacket and dark hat across the street and moving in the opposite direction. One of them said he did see a shadow or a figure that was lying on the ground in front of the bodega, which was dark, but he figured it was just a homeless person so he didn't think much of it. We're still tracking down the rest of the group and we should have contact with them tonight, since they have another game that starts at seven o'clock. There are two uniformed officers at the gym waiting to interview them when they arrive. We'll see if the others tell any different stories, but for now we don't consider them suspects.

"But, a few of the local business owners who we spoke with today said that there has been a lot of activity in the area involving a local gang. There have been several muggings over the past month, although none of the victims wanted to identify the perp or perps. Most of the victims were Black or Hispanic, but none of them are similar to the bodega owner and no one involved got stabbed. Still, we think if it was the gang members who were fleeing the scene, they have to be considered prime suspects."

"What about the white guy the basketball players saw walking away from the scene?" Jason asked.

"Well, none of the basketball players saw him at the scene, he was just coming from that direction," Williamson replied. "He's a person of interest at this point because he might be a suspect and he might be a witness, but all we have is a vague description and nobody else has been able to confirm his existence or give us any leads on him. For now he's a secondary concern."

"Don't you think the detectives should be the ones deciding primary and secondary concerns?" Sully broke in, annoyed.

"Of course," Williamson soothed. "But we do want to move quickly here and the gang members seem to be the most immediately available lead."

"Let me get this straight," Jason said, and then paused. Now it was his turn to struggle to keep his anger under control. "You have decided that this murder was committed by these gangbangers, who are likely Black, and you need a Black detective to lead the investigation so that when we arrest them, the Black community won't be able to accuse the white cops of busting the Black dudes and so Al Sharpton will have a harder time making this into a racial and political issue. Have I got it right?"

"That's about right," Martinez answered for the deputy mayor.

"And the reason that neither the mayor nor the commissioner are on this call is so that they can have deniability about what's being discussed and planned?" Sully said, not trying to hide the disgust in his voice.

"I really can't answer that question," Martinez said softly.

"It doesn't matter," Jason cut in quickly. "There is a man dead and somebody is responsible, and we need to investigate it and do it quickly. If it turns out these gang members are responsible, we'll bust them and make it stick. But we'll be sure about it first. We're not busting anyone without good cause, and we're going to find this white guy and see what he knows."

"Fine," Williamson said dismissively, as if trying to end the discussion.

"Anything else?" Sully asked, motioning silently to Ray and Jason. When they both shook their heads, he said, "We'll take it from here."

He reached to punch the button to end the call. When he was sure they were disconnected, Sully threw his hands into the air. "I'm sorry about this, Dickson. They called and asked me to get you two for a conference call and told me not to brief you in advance. This is such political bullshit."

"It's bullshit," Jason responded calmly, "but there is a point to it. Plus, I might get more cooperation from the locals on this than Berkowitz or Mason."

"Are you saying they are the whitest cops in the city?" Ray quipped.

"You know any whiter?"

Ray laughed, and even Sully couldn't suppress a chuckle. "Okay, you clowns. I'll tell Berkowitz and Mason to send you all their notes and they can debrief you in person tomorrow."

Jason raised an eyebrow. "You're authorizing them to work overtime on a Saturday just to debrief us?"

"Yeah," Sully said, smiling. "The one good thing about this shit show is that we have authorization to spend money and I can assign you whatever manpower you need to assist in the investigation. The mayor really wants this cleared, as if that wasn't obvious."

"Do we have uniforms canvasing the area tonight to identify additional witnesses?" Jason asked.

"Only the two at the college who are meeting with the other basketball players," Sully said.

"Okay, well that's the first order of business. Captain, can you give us six or eight officers to help knock on doors and talk to the locals who may be able to help us find these gang-bangers, or point us toward our mystery white guy? Ray and I will get out there and coordinate the efforts. Since the media are already there, do you want to have someone from the communications office there to field questions?"

"That's a good idea, Detective," Sully agreed. "I'll call back Martinez and make sure we have someone."

"Looks like we're going to be logging some overtime," McMillian said with a smile as he rose from his chair.

"Yeah, but not the good kind. Something tells me we're going to be earning every penny on this one," Jason said, shooting a resigned look toward Sullivan.

Chapter 5 – Blood Brothers

Saturday, Feb. 9

THE NEXT DAY WAS SATURDAY and Jason and Ray were in the Bronx. They were still waiting on identification of their Jane Doe floater, so that case was on hold while they tracked down whoever killed Raul Rosario. They set up a makeshift command center inside the bodega, behind the crime scene tape and separated from the six local news crews who were set up for live remotes outside. The story was the lead on every local news channel and had been picked up by the national networks. Al Sharpton had, indeed, held a press conference that morning in which he accused the police of failing to give priority to the murder of a minority citizen. Apparently, a Black mayor in the city did not slow down Sharpton's willingness to play the race card before the investigation was two days old. The command center's location also had the advantage of being warm, while the press was relegated to the cold space outdoors.

Dickson and McMillian were debriefing pairs of uniformed officers about their interviews with local residents and the regulars at the local watering holes. They were hoping to find somebody who was willing to talk to the detectives about the local gang members. Dickson noted that every pair of uniforms included one that was either Black or Hispanic, which was statistically unlikely given the overall makeup of minorities within the department.

The two detectives were talking with one set of officers about their lack of progress canvassing the apartment building across the street when they were distracted by a commotion at the front door. Somebody was shouting and they could see a man through the glass, waving his arms and pushing against the officer who was guarding the door to make sure the press stayed outside. The man pushed the door halfway open, yelling, "This is my store!"

The officer pulled him back and the two continued wrestling as Jason and Ray both sprang up and rushed to the door to try to diffuse the situation, before the television news crews got video of a white cop beating up an unarmed Hispanic man. Jason was first through the door and immediately ordered the officer to stand down. He looked out toward the reporters and found himself staring into five high-definition video cameras. He smiled and waved as he patted the still-enraged man on the back and calmly escorted him inside the building. Once the door was closed, he lost the smile and demanded that the man explain why he was trying to push his way into a restricted crime scene.

"This is my store!" the man yelled as he glared up at the much taller Black man.

"Who are you?" Jason inquired as calmly as he could manage.

"Luis Rosario," the man shot back in a heavy Puerto Rican accent. He was short and stocky, with dark eyes and a thin moustache. He had on a bulky green parka and a black knit hat.

Jason furrowed his brows. "Are you related to Raul Rosario?"

"Yes. He's my brother. We own this store together." Mr. Rosario had calmed down slightly but was fidgeting and looking quickly back and forth at the two detectives, as if he was concerned that somebody was going to arrest him.

"Where have you been for the past two days?" Jason inquired skeptically.

"I was home in Puerto Rico. I saw the report on the news and flew back this morning." The man was upset, and still semi-shouting, but Jason believed him.

"I'm sorry," Jason soothed. "Please understand that we have a crime scene here and we're investigating a murder. Can you show me some identification?"

Rosario looked annoyed, but dug into his bulky coat and extracted his wallet, from which he pulled out a driver's license and handed it to Jason. After a few seconds of examination, Jason handed it back. "I'm very sorry for your loss, Mr. Rosario. I hope you understand that we will need to verify that you are really the brother of our deceased victim."

"Yeah, I guess," Rosario said reluctantly. "I'm just so angry!"

Jason shifted into treating this man as a potential witness. "Do you know of anyone who would want to kill your brother?"

"I know who killed him," Rosario responded quickly.

"Really? Who?"

Rosario looked down at the floor, then back up at Jason. "I don't care anymore. I'll tell you."

Jason and Ray looked at each other, then back at the dead man's brother.

"I told him not to take a stand. They said they would hurt us. But Raul wanted to organize the other store owners and fight back. He wanted to go to the police. They must have found out and came for him. They have no soul, these *bastardos*."

"Who?" both Jason and Ray said simultaneously.

"El jefe mafioso."

"Why do you think that?" Jason asked.

Over the next twenty minutes, Luis Rosario told Ray and Jason quite a story. Although they had not yet verified the man's identity, neither detective doubted his sincerity by the time he was through. He told them how he and his brother had come to New York in 2012 to work and eventually scraped together money to lease the bodega and open their own business. They worked eighty-hour weeks and built up a nice neighborhood clientele, then brought their wives from Puerto Rico. At one point, Ray asked whether Luis had applied for citizenship. Jason smacked him in the arm and reminded him that Puerto Rico is part of the United States.

Rosario then explained that they'd had a visit about a year ago from a man named Ricky, who told them that there was a lot of gang violence in the neighborhood and that they needed to purchase some security services to protect their property and customers.

"We didn't know about any gangs and never had any problems," he said, holding out his hands in a confused expression. "This *gringo* says we need to pay him and that he'll take care of our security. So, Raul tells him we'll think about it and he leaves. Then a few days later, somebody puts a big rock through our front window just before we close up. We had to pay six hundred dollars to fix it. Then Mr. Ricky comes back and asks if we made up our minds about his security services. He says it would be sad if somebody threw a brick through our window. We said we would have to think about it. A week later, we came to work and the metal gate on our door was bashed in like somebody drove a truck into it. The door was cracked, too.

"The next day, this group of gang thugs starts hanging around on the corner right outside the door, and they're hassling our customers and scaring people away. In comes Mr. Ricky and tells us that he thinks we have a problem, but he can make it go away. So, Raul asks how much and the guy says he just wants to do business with us, which we thought was bullshit. But he says he's going to give us a show of good faith, so he leaves and the gang guys leave right behind him.

"He comes back the next Monday and he tells us what he wants. He says he has people who need to buy things, so he will bring us packages and then, when his customers come in and ask for them, we'll take their money and give them the packages. We get to keep five percent of the money. He says it's all legal and he'll give us an invoice for the stuff. We'd pretend like we bought it from him and then sold it to the other guy and made a profit, so he gets his money and we get our money and everybody is happy. Raul thinks it sounds illegal, but Mr. Ricky smacks him on the face and says it's all legal and if he says anything like that again, he'll be making a visit to the hospital. So, we go along and we do it. We're not allowed to look inside the packages. We just take the money and turn over the boxes.

"He did the same thing to some of the other small business owners in the neighborhood. Then Raul got curious and opened up one of the boxes."

"Was it drugs?" Ray asked, interrupting the story.

"Shit yeah, it was drugs, man. We knew it was drugs all along, but we didn't need to know it. Raul just had to look. And then he started talking to the others and he wanted them all to agree to tell the truth and call the cops. Well, somebody must have gotten scared because we got a visit from Ricky and he was not happy. Raul tells him he don't know what he's talking about. I was scared, but Raul said not to worry and that I should go ahead and make my trip home to see my mother in the hospital. So, I went on Thursday, and then this happens."

Jason was sympathetic, but he knew that saying "I'm sorry," was not going to help, so he stayed in interrogation mode. "Could you identify Mr. Ricky if you saw him again?"

"Sure. I ain't afraid of him and his bullies."

"Do you know where he lives, or have a telephone number, or any way of getting in touch with him?"

"No, man. He never gave out any information. He just came around in person when he wanted to talk or collect his money. He had a few of his gang dudes with him most of the time. They're the ones who dropped off the boxes. We never tried to get to him. Why would we want to?"

"Fair enough," Jason said, hanging his head slightly. "Do you have any of the boxes now?"

"I don't think so. We did one on Wednesday and it's never more than one a week."

"When does Mr. Ricky usually come around to collect his money?"

"It's usually on Thursdays. That's when Raul got killed, so I guess they got their money."

"What time does he come around?"

"Well, usually pretty late – always after dark."

"Do you know if he visits any of the other local businesses on Thursday nights?" Jason asked.

"I don't know for sure. I don't go looking. I'm here in my store."

"Thank you, Mr. Rosario. I'm sure that this information will help us catch these guys."

Chapter 6 – Every Death is Tragic

Monday, Feb. 11

O N MONDAY MORNING, while he was still waking up with his first cup of oily coffee, Jason got an email from the crime lab and called for Ray to come over to his desk. They had a positive ID on their Jane Doe floater. The second set of fingerprints Dr. McNeill had extracted after her body had dried out a bit had come back as a match twice – once from the NYPD's own database, and once from the Seattle PD. Both reports identified her as Christine Barker. The local rap sheet showed her having been arrested and booked three times since November. Twice for petty theft and once for theft and drug possession. All three times she was processed and released on a bench summons, although she had blown off her hearing on the first charge and there was a pending warrant for her arrest, which could now be removed. She had been identified as a drug addict and referred to a city-funded rehab clinic, but there were no records of her attending any program activities.

The Seattle report was pretty similar.

Jason looked up the email address for the Seattle PD to see if they could shine some additional light on Miss Barker's past and fired off an inquiry, not expecting a quick response. He also sent a note to Mike and forwarded him the reports. He figured Mike would have more interest, and time, than he had at that moment.

Ten minutes later, Jason, Ray, and Captain Sullivan were huddled in the conference room. Sully gazed longingly at the empty credenza against the far wall where a plate of bagels would normally sit. Its absence made him even grumpier than normal.

"The dead girl, Christine Barker, was 20 years old," Jason explained. "According to the Seattle PD file, Christine was from a small town in Northwest Washington called Port Angeles. She was a known drug addict who had been arrested multiple times for drug possession, petty theft, and solicitation. She had been referred to rehab in Seattle once but may not have actually attended. She fell off the radar in Seattle about three months ago after she failed to appear for a desk warrant."

"Well, that's about that, then," Sully said dismissively. "She's a druggie and a hooker and she OD'd and ended up in the river. I don't want you to spend any more time on this, Dickson. You and Ray are on this bodega killing. That's your priority."

"We understand, Captain. But—"

"But nothing! Don't get distracted. That's an order."

"So, are you closing the Christine Barker case, Sully?"

Sullivan scowled, but knew that if he ordered Dickson to close the case, Dickson would include that in his report and his case disposition summary. Sullivan's boss would ask him about it, and Sully did not really want to explain why he ordered a case closed one day after they got an ID on the victim. "No, Detective Dickson, I am not closing it. But you should be able to get it closed without much more time or effort, right?"

Dickson nodded, but said nothing as Sullivan rose and stomped out of the conference room. Jason looked at Ray and shrugged. "The M.E. thinks the death is suspicious and that's good enough for me to do at least a little digging. You have any problem with that?"

"None at all, Jason."

"Good. Like the captain said, this is not a priority compared to the Rosario case, but let's see if we have anything on Miss Barker since she arrived in the city. Ask records to take a look for us."

Ray nodded as he picked up his Starbucks cup and left the room. Jason sat for a moment, trying to put a finger on why the dead woman's case bothered him. She was nobody, a runaway from Seattle who had landed in the Big Apple, into the drug and vice culture which eventually killed her. It was not an unusual story, and did not merit much attention, just like Sully said. That was what bothered him – that she was getting the brush-off because her death was routine. The death of a twenty-year-old woman should never be routine.

Jason didn't have much time to wax philosophical. When he got back to his desk, he had a message waiting for him. He didn't immediately recognize the name, Manuel Hwong, but as soon as he returned the call, he remembered that the man was one of the store owners near the Bronx bodega where Raul Rosario was killed. He was reluctant to talk on the phone, but was willing to meet Jason at the precinct house. While Jason waited for Mr. Hwong, he reviewed reports from the Vice department on drug cases that involved prostitution and deaths. He was discouraged by the number of hits for his search, but after narrowing down the cases to exclude Staten Island and the Bronx and looking only at the past two years, the number was a manageable, if still discouraging, twenty-three. He scanned each of the cases once, hoping that something would stand out. After finishing his first pass through the files, he went back and started again, this time reading much more carefully and making notes on a notepad.

After three hours and no real progress, Jason's desk phone rang and the sergeant at the front reception desk informed him that Mr. Hwong was there to see him. Jason brought him up to the fifth-floor conference room, where they would have a little privacy. The conference room featured a large whiteboard that took up most of the wall opposite the door. In the upper right-hand corner, Jason noticed the outline of a black square that had been drawn there so many times that the dry eraser could not entirely eliminate the remnants.

Mr. Hwong sat down hesitantly and clasped his hands in front of him on the conference table. He looked tired and somewhat withered, with silver hair and deep wrinkles on his face and hands. His dark, almond-shaped eyes were set deep into their sockets, but he managed to appear alert even while the rest of his body sagged. Jason figured him to be over seventy.

"Can I get you some coffee or soda?" Jason offered. The man shook his head silently. "What kind of shop do you have?" Jason asked.

"Dry cleaner," Hwong responded. "An officer came to the store and interviewed me. That's how I got your number – he gave me your card and asked me to call if I remembered anything important."

"Of course," Jason said calmly, trying to make the old man feel comfortable. "So, what prompted you to call today? What did you want to tell me?"

The man ran his fingers through his white hair and pursed his lips, as if reluctant to start. "I – well, I just – I don't want you to think that Mr. Rosario was the only one."

"Only one of what?" Jason asked.

"The only one of us who he came to."

"He? Who is he? Who do you mean?"

The dry cleaner looked at Jason with a puzzled expression. "Him, the guy who came around. The guy who killed Mr. Rosario."

Jason stared at the man, trying to figure out whether he could be lying. He could not imagine a reason why he would leave his dry cleaning shop, come to the police station in Manhattan, and tell this kind of story, which could get him into a heap of trouble if the guys who killed his fellow business owner were the kind of bad guys that Jason suspected. No, there didn't seem to be any reason for the man to lie, and nothing about his demeanor or body language suggested he was. Jason sat forward in his chair and looked directly into Mr. Hwong's eyes as he asked his next question. "Did that guy come to visit you, too?"

The dry cleaner hesitated, then nodded his head slightly and whispered, "Yes."

Over the next twenty minutes, Mr. Hwong described a thin white man who matched the description of "Ricky" given by Luis Rosario. The man and his thugs had threatened to damage the dry cleaning store unless Mr. Hwong went along with the program. Different men came to drop off boxes of "shirts" and then other men would come in and ask for the boxes, paying large sums of cash for the exchange. The dry cleaner got to keep $500 from each transaction. It was clearly the same operation.

"Why didn't you go to the police sooner?" Jason asked, knowing what the answer was going to be.

The dry cleaner just shook his head. "I either get the five hundred and keep my mouth shut, or my shop burns down. I was not doing anything illegal."

Jason just stared. "Did the little white guy threaten to burn down your store?"

"Not exactly, but I knew that's what would happen. I'm not stupid. That's why I never looked inside the boxes. Maybe they were just really heavy shirts. I don't know. I just handled the boxes and took the money."

"Alright," Jason sighed, sensing that the dry cleaner was getting anxious to leave. "Thank you for coming forward, Mr. Hwong. We really appreciate it when citizens help our investigations."

"Am I going to be in trouble now?" the man said apprehensively.

"I don't think so," Jason soothed. "I'm certainly not going to be arresting you. As long as you cooperate, I think you'll be fine."

The man exhaled and relaxed noticeably. "Okay. Thank you. What do I do if someone brings me a new box?"

"You don't have one now?"

"No. Last one was picked up two weeks ago."

Jason thought about that for a moment before responding. "You just do the same as always, but call me and let me know."

"I don't want to end up dead like Mr. Rosario," the man said, now looking nervous again.

"I get it. We won't put you in any danger. We will follow the man when he leaves your shop and arrest him somewhere else. He will not know that it was you who told us."

"I hope you are right." The dry cleaner stood up and turned to leave, without offering to shake Jason's hand.

Jason went back to his desk in the bullpen and sat for a few minutes, pondering the significance of what he had just heard. Then he called out, "Ray! Meet me in Sully's office, now." He saw Ray wave to indicate that he had heard. Jason needed to brief his partner and his captain before writing up his notes for the case file.

Ж Ж Ж

The next day, an article appeared in *The New York Times* about a young girl who had been found dead floating in the East River. The story was written by Dexter Peacock, a veteran investigative reporter who had been rooting around in city politics and crime issues for a decade. He was known to be a bulldog who would not let go of a story once he got his teeth into it. He also had a history with Mike Stoneman and Jason Dickson. Peacock wrote that the medical examiner, Doctor Michelle McNeill, had raised questions about the cause of death, and the police were treating the case as a homicide, although there was no information available about how the investigation was going. Peacock had obtained the girl's identity, and the story was mostly focused on the hard-luck tale of a young woman who left a small town in the state of Washington and came to the Big Apple, where she met her untimely demise. He linked the case to many other stories of runaway teens and the drug and sex culture into which they were often pulled. It was not an attractive portrayal of New York City, and it did not speak well of the NYPD.

The article caused Commissioner Ward to toss his Times in the trash without doing the crossword puzzle. It caused Captain Sullivan to explode into a series of expletives that made his wife blush. Jason called Ray, then called Mike. The three of them all agreed to ignore the article. Michelle cut out the clipping and saved it, because she was mentioned by name, and she always kept a record of when her name appeared in *The Times*.

Chapter 7 – Recruiting Season

THE NIGHT LOCK-UP IN BROOKLYN HEIGHTS was a buffet of human misery. Drug addicts arrested for possession or petty theft, men slowly sobering up after bar fights, gang members still flexing their muscles, and street people who were glad of a warm night's sleep all huddled together in a space too tight for the humanity squeezed inside.

In sight, but out of reach, was the female cell. Young women arrested for solicitation at one end, keeping their distance from the drug users at the other, a few moaning remorselessly through their withdrawal pains.

Three gray-haired officers sat around a gray steel desk at the front of the precinct house, behind the security door that separated them from the outer lobby and the general public. They had long since resigned themselves to the futility of the system. Most of their guests would be arraigned, charged, and then released back into the dark underbelly of Brooklyn. Their crimes were not severe; they would be no danger to the public if they were released. That was the theory, anyway.

The three cops were huddled around a small television set, intent on the Rangers game. The Blue Shirts were beating the Pittsburgh Penguins with only a few minutes left in the third period. The door buzzed open – it was an unwelcome interruption. The officer in charge looked up. Sergeant Fitzsimmons was a man less than a year away from retirement, who'd taken the night shift desk assignment as a way of avoiding any real police action. He made eye contact with the officer who'd walked through the door.

The man was short, with large, bulging eyes. He was wearing a nondescript beige sports coat and khaki trousers, with his thin black tie hung loosely around his neck. He passed Fitzsimmons, giving him a weary nod.

"Evenin' Sarge," he added in an equally weary voice.

Fitzsimmons nodded back and wracked his brain to identify the man. He'd been buzzed in, so he must be a cop; his clothes said he was a detective, and he strode in with the confidence of a man who knew where he was going. He was familiar, but Fitzsimmons couldn't place him. He shrugged, too tired and too disinterested, and turned his attention back to the hockey game. The Rangers were up by a goal, and were on a power play.

The short man in the beige jacket walked to the back of the holding area, checked in with the duty officer, showed his ID, and asked to talk to one of the female detainees, a young woman named Yolanda Rodriguez. The officer wrote down the visitor's name and ID in the log book. Yolanda looked up on hearing her name.

She rose quickly from the hard bench, balancing carefully on four-inch heels. She had long, dark hair with reddish highlights that hung halfway down her back, cut into bangs on her forehead. Layers of dark blue and black makeup surrounded her eyes, smeared near the corners. She wasn't pretty, exactly, but she was thin, with long legs exposed beneath a short black leather skirt. Her breasts benefitted from a push-up lace bodice, which was covered by a thin black chemise. Her nails were long and painted blood red. She could hardly look more like a hooker, which was exactly what she was, according to the booking report.

The officer escorted her to an interrogation room – a windowless space containing a metal table with grommets where dangerous prisoners were secured with handcuffs. Yolanda was not dangerous. She sat, unchained, and waited. This wasn't her first time; she wasn't nervous. A female social worker would offer her help and make threats about prison if she was caught again. She would be warned about her drug use and how much danger she put herself in on the streets. She'd heard it all before.

The door creaked open and a man in a beige jacket and thin tie sat down in the chair opposite Yolanda. She was surprised to see a man. She was curious – and suspicious. He had no file folder and no note pad – even more suspicious. He stared at Yolanda as if he were evaluating a new car. After two silent minutes, she felt awkward. The pressure mounted. She shifted uncomfortably in her stiff, unyielding chair. This was different.

"Are you happy, Yolanda?" The man spoke in a raspy voice with a heavy New York accent.

"Huh?" she grunted. "Who are you?"

"I'm someone who solves problems, and you have a problem."

"Oh yeah? What problem do I have?" Yolanda crossed her thin arms across her chest and looked defiantly across the table.

"The system," he replied. "You want to party; you want the ice, blow and good booze, nice clothes, good life, comfortable place to sleep at night. You want the police to leave you alone, but they keep busting your ass. You just want to go about your business."

"Man, you don't know nothing about me."

"No? You were born in Buckhead, Georgia outside of Atlanta, graduated high school two years ago, dropped out of community college. You tried Atlanta, but got arrested twice for drugs and once for solicitation. That's when you decided to move your pretty little ass to the Big Apple, ending up with a loser named Taiwan Johnson, a piece of shit drug dealer who shouldn't have assaulted a police officer and is doing five-to-ten upstate. He peddled meth and kept you high as a kite while you were his bitch, but when he got locked up, your supply got cut off. That's when you started turning tricks on your own – and getting busted. Have I got that all about right?"

Yolanda looked at the man skeptically, but didn't contradict him.

"So, you tell me. You got friends now who are taking care of you?"

"Yeah. I got friends."

"Oh, yeah? Where are they? If you got such good friends, why aren't they here bailing your ass out of jail or getting you a lawyer?"

"Man, I don't need no lawyer."

"OK. But when they let you out, where are you going to go, huh? You got family here in New York?"

Yolanda sat passively, not replying.

"I didn't think so. You got somebody you knew from back home? Some friend who was up here when you came north? Somebody you thought you could crash with?"

Yolanda's face contorted into a scowl, but she stayed silent.

"Sure. Everybody knows somebody in New York. But your somebody probably doesn't like you doing drugs in their home, huh? Doesn't want you bringing back men, huh? You have no crib where you can do what you want. Isn't that right?"

"So fucking what?" Yolanda blurted out. "Who the fuck are you coming in here and laying all this shit on me? Like you're gonna adopt me? You wanna set me up with my own apartment or something? What are you, some pervy fucking sugar-daddy?"

The man sat back again in the chair. "No, Yolanda. I'm not going to adopt you, but I can offer you a way to get what you want."

"Yeah?" Yolanda said skeptically, "and what do you get?"

"I'll explain that when you come see me."

"You'll be waitin' a long time, mister."

"Maybe. Maybe not." He reached into his pocket, Yolanda was expecting to see a pack of cigarettes. Instead, he drew out a plastic bag containing a small pile of pale blue crystals. He held it up so she could see it clearly.

Yolanda immediately got the hunger in her eyes, then frowned. "You settin' me up? You tryin' to pin some bullshit possession charge on me?"

The man shook his head gently. "No, Yolanda. Busting you would be easy, but that's not what I do." He reached into his pocket and withdrew a small glass tube with a bulbous end and a hole in the top, along with a butane lighter. He then extracted two of the crystals and dropped them into the ball of the glass pipe. He handed it to Yolanda, along with the lighter. She hesitated for a moment, but then snatched the meth pipe, fired up the lighter, and held the flame under the ball until the crystal liquified and turned to a white gas. She inhaled. She held the vapor in her mouth, closing her eyes as the drug invaded her blood stream, conquering the neural passageways of her brain to induce the euphoria that she craved more than anything in the world. She continued to inhale until the bowl was dry. The man watched. Finally, she set the pipe and lighter on the table and tilted her head back toward the ceiling, reveling in the sensation.

"Now, you see? Me giving you drugs inside the police station, that would be illegal."

Yolanda opened her eyes and looked at him with a half-smile on her face. "So, how about I rat you out and tell those officers out there that you gave me some?"

"Go ahead. I doubt they'll believe you. It's your word against mine."

"You're a cop, right?"

"What I am is not important. What I can offer you is what you need to think about. Here." The man reached into the pocket of his shirt and pulled out a white business card with no name, no logo, just a phone number. "When you get out, call me."

Yolanda took the card, folded it in half, and stuffed it into her shoe. The man stood up, screeching the metal chair leg across the tile floor. As he turned to leave, Yolanda asked, "If I decide to call you, who do I ask for?"

He opened the door and looked back over his shoulder. "Eddie," he said, and was gone.

Yolanda sat in the chair in silence, enjoying the high. Eventually, she was roused by the sound of the door opening. A uniformed officer escorted her back to the holding cell. An hour later, a female officer herded the detainees out of the cell so that they could file across the street to the night court for quickie arraignments, receive their desk summonses, and get processed for release. But as Yolanda reached the cell door, the cop held out her hand.

"You Yolanda Rodriguez?"

"Yeah."

"You go the other way," said the officer, pointing toward the front desk. "Tell them your name and they'll cut you loose."

Yolanda looked at the officer quizzically, then headed for the front door.

Moments later she was free, walking away from trouble. After two blocks, she stopped, stooped, and removed the business card from her shoe. She looked at it, smiled, put it into her clutch, and walked into the New York night.

Chapter 8 – Chasing Shadows

Thursday, Feb. 14

B Y THURSDAY MORNING, Ray and Jason were dragging after working late all week on the Rosario case, but at least they had some progress to show for it. Unfortunately, they still had plenty left to do.

They were huddled at Jason's desk, sipping the morning's first cup of coffee and looking at the Christine Barker file, when Sully walked past and stopped to ask what was up. They explained, causing Sully to stomp on the ground in frustration. "God dammit, you have one case to worry about right now. One! And it ain't a dead drug addict. Now you put that aside, or better yet just close it up, and focus your attention where it needs to be."

Sully didn't wait for a response before storming off to his office and shutting the glass door, glaring back out at Jason and Ray. They knew he was right. Christine Barker, was not a priority in the eyes of the press, the public, or the mayor. There was no need for them to waste time on her. At least for now.

A half hour later, Jason got a phone call. It was Mr. Hwong from the dry-cleaning store in the Bronx. The old Asian man told Jason that he had received a heavy box of shirts on Monday night, and a man had come to pick it up on Wednesday, leaving him ten thousand dollars in cash.

"Why didn't you call me yesterday?" Jason asked, annoyed.

"I was not sure. I am afraid. I am calling now."

"OK, thank you," Jason regained a professional tone of voice. "We will come visit you this afternoon. You told me that the little white guy usually comes to pick up the money on Thursday nights, right?"

"Yes, most times."

"OK. We'll be there in a few hours."

Ж Ж Ж

That evening, Jason and Ray, along with four uniformed officers, were staked out in a perimeter around the dry-cleaning store on Webster Avenue, a few blocks away from the Rosario bodega.

"Hell of a way to spend Valentine's Day, huh?" Ray said as he crushed his empty paper coffee cup.

"It's fine. Not like I had a date lined up," Jason mused.

"Speak for yourself. I had a hottie ready to eat my chocolate."

"I won't comment on that," Jason replied stiffly, before falling back into a tense silence.

They were worried about how close they were to Fordham University and how much foot traffic there was, even after dark on a chilly February night. They were several hours into overtime for the day, but Sully had given them a blank check because of the political sensitivity of the case. There had been nightly vigils at the bodega and chants calling for action by the police, although the attendance at these events had been declining. Al Sharpton and several other activists for the Black and Hispanic communities were keeping up the pressure on the local talk radio programs, and the mayor called Sullivan daily for updates on the investigation.

Ray and Jason were huddled inside a bland brown panel van parked on 195th Street, waiting for the arrival of the man they assumed was "Mr. Ricky." Luis Rosario had worked with a police sketch artist to come up with a picture of the mystery man, which included a scar on his face that should make him pretty easy to identify. They had shown it to the basketball players from Fordham. None of them could say for sure that it was the face of the guy they saw walking past them on that cold early morning, but several of them said it could be. Ray had predicted that Ricky would not show up so soon after the murder, but Jason was betting him a steak dinner that the money laundering business needed to maintain its schedule and that their guy would show up to collect the cash. If Ricky had shut down the operation, his men would not have delivered the package earlier in the week.

The detectives had spoken to several more small-business owners in the neighborhood, but none of them would admit that they had also been victims of the same shake-down. It was pretty clear to both Ray and Jason that a few of them were not being truthful, but beating the information out of them didn't seem good for public relations. Still, they had eyes on several of the local shops to see if there were any other stops on Mr. Ricky's Thursday rounds.

It was a pretty clever scheme. They were not technically extorting money from the business people. It was not exactly a protection racket, although it certainly had the same effect on the store owners. The stores were actually making a little money on the transactions, which most of them probably considered a boon rather than a burden. As long as they never looked inside the boxes, they could claim that if the invoice said ten thousand dollars' worth of Beluga caviar, then that's what they sold, and they made a five-hundred-dollar profit on the deal. Nothing illegal about that. And if there was ever a bust, the only people they could finger were the gangbangers and Ricky. The shop owners were scared of the gangs, so they would be reluctant to ID anyone, and even if the cops could bust one of the gang members, they were notoriously tight-lipped. If this was as organized an operation as it seemed, they would probably lawyer up and say nothing. They would do the time, if necessary, for the drug dealing, and then come out and get a promotion in the organization. Meanwhile, the money got laundered through the stores and came out clean.

At half past nine, a thin white man walked down the Bronx sidewalk, heading in the direction of the dry cleaner, accompanied by three Black youths wearing black pants and jackets. The Black men looked to be well-muscled and as large as NFL linemen under their winter coats. The muscle took up a position outside Mr. Hwong's store, which closed at ten o'clock, while the white guy went inside. The police had quickly installed two very hidden cameras and three wireless microphones inside the shop when they arrived that evening.

Ray and Jason listened through earpieces while Ricky requested payment for his consignment. Mr. Hwong said he would get it and left his cash register for a moment, returning with a thick envelope. Ricky took the envelope and handed Mr. Hwong five one-hundred-dollar bills and a printed invoice. Then, without counting the cash, he turned to leave. He exited the store and nodded to his entourage. The men walked down Webster Avenue toward 197th Street.

"Go!" Jason said urgently into his collar microphone. He and Ray hustled out of their surveillance van and sprinted in the direction of the store while two squad cars, tires squealing, skidded to a stop on the curb. Four officers jumped out with guns drawn, yelling at the four men to get on the ground, while pedestrians scattered in all directions like cockroaches from under a lifted pizza box.

"What the fuck!" one of the large men shouted. He and his two companion linemen turned toward the officers, while Ricky ran the other direction. Jason saw the back of his black jacket as it turned the corner on 197th Street and headed north.

The three big guys stared at the guns pointing at them, then raised their hands over their heads and started walking slowly toward the cops, who yelled at them to stop.

Jason and Ray ran past the scrum on the sidewalk as the four uniformed officers seemed outnumbered by their three larger foes. Jason marveled at the savvy move by the three bodyguards, as he figured them to be. They knew that the cops, while armed, would not fire on unarmed men as long as they did not make any dangerous-looking moves. By the time the three linemen were a few feet from the armed cops, one of the officers lowered his weapon and stepped forward, ordering the big man to get on the ground. The officers were presumed to be capable of subduing unarmed civilians without resorting to gunfire.

While the officers wrestled with the thugs, Jason took off after the man with the ten thousand dollars in his pocket.

Jason leaned into his radio and called for all units to close off 197th street at Decatur Avenue. There were two more squad cars in the area standing by and he hoped they could hem in the runner. Meanwhile, the sleepy television film crews huddled in their vans outside the Rosario bodega came busting out, scrambling to get their equipment ready to film. They had been keeping warm while waiting for the live remotes they were going to do for the early local news shows, about how the dead man's brother had re-opened the bodega just days after the murder. The news crews started getting text messages and calls within a few seconds of the encounter on Webster Avenue. The journalists and cameramen hustled toward the scene, three blocks away.

When Jason rounded the corner, he saw a black and white with its blue lights flashing, parked at the top of the block, and he saw his quarry darting into the alley behind the Webster Avenue storefronts, back in the direction of 198th Street. Ray came skidding to a halt next to Jason, calling out, "Where is he?"

"He's running down the alley!" Jason shouted, removing his gun from its holster and running up the block. "He's a fast sucker." Jason stopped at the alley's threshold, not knowing what he would find around the corner. He held out his gun and motioned for Ray to go ahead of him, ready to put down cover fire. As soon as Ray rounded the bend, Jason stepped out and held his gun ready, but saw nothing to shoot at.

Jason and Ray carefully paced their way down the alley with their guns held in outstretched arms, scanning in all directions for places that Ricky could be hiding. There was no sign of life. Jason called into his microphone for the backup units to fan out and try to seal off escape routes.

The alley ended at a gravel and dirt square where two large trees sprouted from the ground, giving shade to a courtyard with parked cars squeezed into every available space. Ahead, Jason saw a circular structure that looked like a hot tub, and to the left a thin passage ran between two buildings, with more parked cars lining the paved driveway. Jason motioned to Ray to go forward while he went left. When Jason reached the street, he looked left, where the squad car still sat at attention. He turned right and ran down the sidewalk, reaching the next intersection and looking in all directions, but not seeing any sign of their suspect.

At that moment, Jason heard one gunshot coming from his right, then two more shots in quick succession. He ran down the block and saw their suspect, in his black jacket, getting into the rear door of a dark SUV. As soon as the door closed, the window came down; a gun came out and fired off four quick shots back in the direction of the alley where Jason had left Ray. The SUV's tires screeched as it pulled away, with more gunshots coming out as it moved quickly south. As Jason watched, Ray came running out of the alley, firing toward the departing vehicle. A bullet whizzed past Ray's head and pinged against a metal light pole six inches away.

Jason yelled, "Get down, you idiot!" Ray got into a crouch and continued firing at the SUV until his magazine was empty. The car turned left, abandoning the three bodyguards who were still engaged with the officers a half-block away. Jason screamed into his collar that the suspects were in a black SUV heading East on Webster Avenue at 198th Street. He and Ray headed back toward the melee, where they found the news crews frantically trying to set up and get video as the four original officers, aided by two more who had since arrived, tried to get handcuffs on the three big men who had run interference for Ricky. Seeing the camera crews, Ray and Jason stopped and reversed course, heading back toward their parked surveillance van.

"Are you fucking crazy, Ray?" Jason scolded. "You fired, what? Fifteen rounds on a public street where bystanders could be hit, and you stood there in the line of fire where you could have been hit. Do you have a death wish?"

"Fuck you," Ray retorted. "I had a shot and I took it. I didn't hit anybody."

"How do you know?"

"I know."

"You're going to get yourself, and maybe me, killed if you act like that."

"I'll be fine," Ray said dismissively, snapping a fresh magazine into his department-issued Glock.

"Yeah, sure you will," Jason muttered to himself.

Chapter 9 – Distant Connections

Friday, Feb. 15

THAT FRIDAY AFTERNOON, after his physical therapy session, Mike strolled into the medical examiner's office to pick up Michelle. The doctor was sitting at her gray metal desk at the far end of the lab, underneath a large poster of the periodic table of elements. When she saw Mike, she jumped up and walked quickly to meet him before he got halfway across the room. He stopped and waited for her arrival, being careful not to give her a hug or kiss here in her work space. They had an arrangement to be only professional colleagues when in the office – at least when there were other people around. He could see by the look in her eyes and the wicked smile on her face that she had something on her mind. He smiled at her and asked, "Do you want to talk about it here, or over dinner?"

"Talk about what?" she coyly replied, smiling even bigger and bouncing slightly up and down on her toes.

"You obviously have something to tell me, Doctor. Whatever it is, I'm going to suggest that you do it here, before we go out, so that we can enjoy our dinner without the distraction."

"Great," Michelle said, turning on a heel and heading back toward her desk, with Mike trailing behind. He settled into the dull government-issue guest chair and looked across the desk, admiring Michelle's intensity as she gathered up a file, opened the manila folder, positioned it exactly in the center of her immaculate desktop, and then looked up, ready to launch into her report. Mike just smiled and waited.

"I did some digging into the dead woman from the river, Christine Barker. Now that we know who she is, I found some references to her on Facebook. Her page hasn't been updated in a while, but she has a sister named Steph who still lives in their home town of Port Angeles. Steph's Facebook page has a lot of information about Christine.

"Both Steph and Christine had to deal with their brother, Alex, who was four years older. Alex had spiraled into drug addiction. When Christine was just in ninth grade, Alex graduated and moved out of the house. He was arrested, moved back home, moved out again, was arrested again, went into rehab, then fell out, went back to his 'drug house,' and generally made the rest of the family crazy. He went from pot to meth to heroin, and then overdosed. Steph and Christine both dealt with depression. They eventually climbed out of the dark place and seemed to be getting things back together. Then, their father died from cancer, leaving just their mother, who didn't handle all the pressure well. Steph feels really guilty that she didn't do more to help Alex, and hadn't talked to Christine in months."

Mike leaned toward the end of the desk, cocked his head to the side and said, "You got all that from her public Facebook page?"

Michelle grimaced slightly before sheepishly responding. "Well, she contacted me, but after that she sent me a friend request on Facebook and then I could see the private stuff on her page." The doctor looked up at Mike with pleading eyes.

Mike took a moment to gather his thoughts before responding. "So, you contacted a person who may be a fact witness in the case and friended her on Facebook so that you could access her information."

"No, No. She reached out to me."

"How did that happen?" Mike asked, trying to maintain a calm tone of voice.

"She said she read the article in *The Times* about Christine's death. There was a mention about me doing the autopsy and questioning the cause of death, and she looked me up."

"And you figured that you would start snooping into her life?"

"No!" Michelle said defensively. "The point is that I found out a bunch of information that could help the investigation."

Mike looked at Michelle's face, which was begging for some approval. "That's pretty good police work, Doctor McNeill."

Michelle's face lit up with a combination of pride and relief. "Thanks. I'm hoping this will help us. Steph posted that she doesn't believe Christine could have died from a heroin overdose. She says that Christine never did heroin because of Alex. That's consistent with my suspicions about the lack of other needle marks and the general physiology of the body."

Mike held up his hands, palms out toward Michelle. "I believe you that the lack of needle tracks is suggestive, but we can't jump to conclusions. The relatives of the victim never think they could have committed suicide or taken the drugs. That's a common response. It doesn't really prove anything. And you said that this sister hadn't had any communication with Christine in a while, so things could have changed."

Michelle's smile transformed into a momentary pout. "I guess you're right. But it's still consistent with my autopsy report."

"Have you prepared a summary report of your findings?"

"No, not yet, but I could do that easily." Michelle brightened noticeably.

"Good. Please do that and then I'll send it to Jason. You never know when it might come in handy. Now, how do you feel about Mexican food for dinner?"

"Well, Mike, before we go, there's another thing."

"Oh?"

"I did a review of my own files looking for other young girls who died under similar circumstances. I found three cases in the last year where we had girls under age twenty-five who died from apparent heroin overdoses. Yvonne Calderone, age 20, was found in an alley in Brooklyn. Dawn Schneider, age 18, was found on a bench near Citi Field in Queens. Heidi Henniger, age 21, was picked up by an ambulance in Brooklyn and died in the hospital. In all three cases, the autopsies noted the absence of repetitive needle marks but the cause of death was listed as an overdose of heroin."

"Did you do the autopsies yourself?"

"One I did. The other two were while I was out after the – the incident in Queens, so they were done by different doctors. I don't know why I didn't flag the absence of multiple needle marks that time."

Mike was silent for several moments. "Do you have any reason to think that these other girls are related to Christine Barker's death?"

"Not really," Michelle said, her shoulders slumping slightly. "Only the similarity in ages and the absence of track marks."

"It's not much," Mike observed, "but it is suggestive and worth doing some follow-up on."

"I'll keep digging."

"Fine. It can't hurt, and with Sully not really wanting Jason and his new partner to spend time on Ms. Barker, we may be the only ones digging. Now, shall we?" Mike held out his arm and Michelle closed her folder, placed it carefully back in its file drawer, and grabbed her purse.

Chapter 10 – A Day in the Life

THE TALL MAN WITH THE GRAYING DARK HAIR sat at his desk inside the Ninety-fourth precinct house. He was reading a report prepared by one of the members of his team on the activities of people believed to be operating as part of the Gallata crime organization, who were under surveillance. The man was in charge of the task force, which was in turn part of the Vice unit. The report detailed the various suspicious and possibly criminal enterprises in which their targets were engaged, and explained how the most recent observations and accompanying investigatory work were moving their project forward. It also explained why more time was needed before any significant arrests could be expected. It was a masterpiece of bureaucratic water-treading, which would satisfy the district commander and ultimately Commissioner Ward, and would keep his group of officers fully authorized to continue their work without any special scrutiny. This was just the way he liked it.

For someone who worked Vice, the man dressed like a Wall Street banker. He always had a clean and well-pressed suit, a crisply laundered shirt with French cuffs, and black wingtips polished to a high shine. He was solidly built, although as he reached his late 50s there were more soft spots than there used to be. Everyone said he looked "distinguished." If he put on a tuxedo, he could easily pass as a butler for a wealthy estate.

After nearly thirty years on the force, everyone in the precinct expected him to retire as soon as he reached his next work anniversary. His wife of many years had died of cancer five years before, leaving him alone. He had two children, who both lived on the West Coast, and while he was well-regarded by the other cops due to his years of experience and professional manners, there were few in the department who would actually call him a friend. In fact, since his wife died, he had become more and more withdrawn and aloof towards his superiors and the precinct's officers. He also started keeping a bottle of Jamison's in his bottom desk drawer. Nobody paid it much attention, since they figured that the old man would be gone soon. Everyone assumed, by the way he dressed and carried himself, that he would have a job lined up working security for a white-shoe law firm or some multi-national corporation. He had earned the privilege.

At 4:58 p.m., he sealed an inter-office mailing envelope containing the report, dropped it into the outgoing mail basket, retrieved his overcoat and hat from a wooden coat rack near the door, and departed the building for the day. The detectives, who routinely worked until past six, rolled their eyes and secretly longed to have the seniority to leave every day at precisely five o'clock.

Seventeen minutes later, the man emerged from the subway at Atlantic Avenue in Brooklyn and walked along the bustling sidewalk outside the Barclays Center, turning onto a side street and then circling the block before abruptly stopping and entering an old building with an unmarked doorway. A sign nearby identified the place as the Alexander Hamilton Hotel, but you had to look hard to find the sign. Once inside, a man behind a plexiglass security window buzzed the door so that he could walk through. He continued down a dimly lit hallway to the second doorway on the left, where he used a security key card to unlock the door.

After carefully hanging his coat and hat in the closet, along with his suit jacket, he sat down at a wooden desk. He opened the lower left drawer and extracted a cell phone, a ledger book, a pad of paper, and a pen.

After arranging his materials, he pressed a speed-dial button on the phone and waited for an answer.

"Good afternoon, Eddie. Is everything calm today?"

"Sure," came the raspy voice from the other end of the phone. "Very normal. I may have a new girl coming in."

"Very good. I assume you have done your usual background checks?"

"Yeah. She's prime material. Already established in the neighborhood. I sprung her from lockup a few days ago and she made contact."

"Do I need to meet her?"

"Not yet, I think. Let's let her settle in for a week or so first."

"Fine. Let me know. In the meantime, you can send down the afternoon's receipts."

"On it, boss. And I'm sending you a special treat today."

"What?"

"You'll see. I'll come by later tonight."

An hour later, there was a knock at the door. The man removed an ear bud from his right ear, annoyed to miss the climax of the aria, and answered the knock. Before him stood a young woman with long copper hair. She was holding a small box wrapped in brown paper. The box, he knew, carried cash collected by the members of his team who were supplying the local drug distribution operations. The girl, it seemed, was Eddie's special treat.

"I'm Candy," the redhead purred, batting her lashes. "I'm here to deliver."

The man pursed his lips. "Thank you, Candy." He took the box from her outstretched hand, nodded, then closed the door. He carried the package to the desk, re-inserted his ear bud, and returned to his work and his opera.

Chapter 11 – Assignment Priorities

Tuesday, Feb. 19

ON TUESDAY MORNING at 8:45 a.m., Jason stood on the steps outside the precinct house, bracing himself against the cold wind whistling down 94th Street. He was eating the last few bites of a bagel, being careful not to drip any cream cheese on his London Fog overcoat. He waved at Ray, who was climbing up toward the door. "I'm going to be so happy when they let us bring our bagels into the station again," he said with a wry smile.

"Amen to that," Ray agreed.

"Did you see the email from the medical examiner?"

"Yeah, but I didn't read it all yet," Ray replied casually. "It didn't seem really important."

"Here's a tip for you," Jason said sternly, "take everything from Doctor McNeill seriously." With that, he popped the last morsel of his bagel into his mouth and reached for the door handle. Ten minutes later, they were both in a conference room, pouring over a file that had been sent from Central Booking and a group of emails, including the one from Doctor McNeill. Captain Sullivan had given them permission to clear out the case file, but told them he wanted them back on the Rosario murder before noon.

"We have an arrest recorded on November 25," Ray said as he drew a solid line across the center of a sheet of paper and wrote the date down on the left-hand edge.

"If only we had someone to make a list on the whiteboard for us," Jason mused.

"What?"

"Never mind. What's the next date we have in her record?"

Ray flipped through the papers in a file folder, then said, "She was picked up in midtown on December 8 for shoplifting. Processed and sent on her way with a desk summons. Then arrested again on December 21, this time in Brooklyn for drunk and disorderly and assaulting a police officer. Got another desk summons. Then brought in for theft and drug possession on January 5 and released again. Looks like on the last one she was referred to drug rehab."

"Did she show for her first desk ticket?"

"No," Ray said quickly, noting the red stamp on the record. "She is – well was – listed as a fugitive with an outstanding arrest warrant."

"Sure. Her and five thousand others with petty theft and minor drug arrests. Great. That's not going to help us much." Jason got up and paced around the room. "When was her next record?"

"That's it," Ray replied. "End of file. Since then, she managed to avoid any arrests. The next contact was when the EMTs fished her out of the river."

"OK, how about the three other girls the M.E. identified? What do we know about them?"

"Not much. We have the summary from the M.E., but that's it. There's basic intake information on the computer record, but no details and no PDFs of the notes or other documents. Not that surprising. The cases are pretty recent and not high priority, and there's a long backlog in data entry. We'll have to retrieve the physical files to get anything more on them."

"Fine," Jason said. "Send a request for the physical files and we'll see what's in them."

Ray shuffled the papers in front of him and placed them back into the folder, along with the timeline he had been scratching out on his pad. "Dickson, what's the deal with you and Captain Sullivan?"

"What do you mean?"

"I mean, he treats you like you're a twenty-year veteran. He never busts you down like he does everybody else, including me. It's like he's afraid to offend you, even when you give him shit. How did you become the Golden Boy?"

"I'm no Golden Boy, believe me. You never saw how Stoneman treated me."

"Yeah, well, I wouldn't have been here when The Ass of Stone was working with you, now, would I?"

"Careful, McMillan," Jason said sternly, "that's my partner you're talking about."

"I thought I was your partner?"

"You are, for now, but remember who's the professor and who's the student. Stoneman has forgotten more than you'll ever know about being a detective."

"I thought you just said he treated you badly?"

"He treated me exactly the way I deserved to be treated. Maybe Sully doesn't want to say the wrong thing to his one Black detective, but Mike never pulled any punches. So, don't say anything about *Culo de Piedra* while he's in rehab from being stabbed and slashed by a serial killer. Got that?"

"Sure. I got it," Ray replied sheepishly. "Geez – I thought you didn't like the guy."

"What made you think that?"

"That's what some of the other guys say."

"What guys?" Jason said sharply.

"I don't know. You know how it is, you hear things around. C'mon, I'm not gonna call out any of the other guys around here. That can't be a surprise to you, can it?"

"I guess not," Jason conceded. "But don't let me hear you perpetuating that rumor. It's not true. Got it?"

"Fine. Got it. Sure. Should we get back to the bodega murder?" Ray got up from the conference table and walked toward the door. "Maybe we can make some progress there, since we have some actual leads."

"Yeah. It's always helpful to have real leads," Jason said as he followed Ray out of the room.

Chapter 12 – High Hopes

Wednesday, Feb. 20

WEDNESDAY AFTERNOON, when Mike arrived for his rehab session, he saw Darren in the gym locker room. The two detectives agreed to meet up after Mike's session and Darren's workout were over. When Mike went back to the locker room to change, Darren was sitting on a bench looking like he had recently showered. The room was otherwise empty.

"How's the shoulder?" Darren asked.

Mike raised his arm as far as he could manage, which was somewhere between sixty-five and seventy degrees, according to Terry. All Mike knew for sure was that he could not yet get his arm all the way up to vertical. "Eh, it's getting there." He carefully pulled off his workout t-shirt, then turned back to Darren. "I'd really like to come say hi to Marie and the kids."

"Sure. Anytime."

"Really. I'm serious," Mike said. "I want to find a date, soon, when I can come over. I want Marie to make me her chicken parmesan. It's been too long."

Darren smiled. "I miss having you around, Mike."

"Yeah, well don't get all weepy on me, you weak lug." Mike opened up his locker so he could start changing.

"The kids have asked what happened to Uncle Mike."

"What did you tell them?"

"I told 'em that when Daddy goes back to work, they'll get to see Uncle Mike again."

"Is that gonna happen?" Mike asked.

"Sure. It could happen. I'm still on leave."

"Yeah, but what do the doctors say? Is there a real chance for you to get back into shape to return to active duty?"

"I could come back right now," Darren said defiantly.

"On one leg?"

"You've got only one arm. What's the difference?"

"The difference is that I'm ten weeks into a twenty-two-week rehab and I'm making progress toward a full recovery. You're, what, eighteen months removed from those slugs in your leg? Are you any better now than you were six months ago? I know that surgery can do wonders, but is that artificial knee ever going to get you back to full speed?"

Darren was silent. After Mike finished pulling on his socks, his former partner said quietly, "The doctors have to certify that I have a reasonable prospect for recovery in order for me to keep getting the active duty disability payments, and I get checked out every three months. I come in here three times a week and work it. For now, the official report is that there is still a chance, so I'm sticking with that."

"Is Marie working at all?"

"No. She's taking care of the kids. I'm taking care of my family."

"Are you sure you don't need any help?" Mike looked at his friend, trying to keep any hint of guilt or pity out of his voice.

"We're fine. Fine. But thanks, Mike."

"Well, let me know if there's ever anything I can do to help. I know I've been wrapped up in my own shit, and I'm sorry about that. You deserve better from me."

"Yeah, well we all deserve better in general. You don't have to feel guilty, Mike. It wasn't your fault."

"We all make our own decisions, but I could have done things differently."

"Me, too," Darren said softly. "I could have listened to you."

"You were never great at that," Mike said, smiling and reaching out to push Darren's shoulder, sending him off balance on the narrow bench.

"You never could stand a student who didn't do exactly what you said, you old coot."

"Hey, I think that's now a racial slur, so watch it." The two men both laughed. They left the gym and adjourned to a local bar, where they shared a few beers and some memories. Darren picked up the tab. Mike insisted that Darren put an appointment into his phone for Mike to come over for dinner a week from Saturday, when Michelle had a medical society dinner that Mike was anxious to get out of. Darren was happy to give him an excuse.

Ж Ж Ж

The next day, Mike dutifully reported to the Hospital for Special Surgery off of York Avenue and 71st Street for his third post-surgery follow-up appointment with his surgeon, Dr. Frank Cordasco, and his chief physical therapy assistant, who was also named Mike. Stoneman arrived at 3:12 for his 3:15 appointment, checked in with the desk on the second floor of the medical associates building, and sat down in a cushy chair, only to be called two minutes later and ushered into the exam room. It always amazed Mike how incredibly efficient HSS was about getting patients in on schedule and out quickly. It was by far the most on-time medical office he had ever been to.

Mike, the physical therapy guru, manipulated Mike's left arm, had him reach behind his back, had him push down and up against Mike's hand strength, and lifted his arm to test his range of motion. "You're doing great so far," Mike the therapist said. "Keep up the sessions and the exercises and you'll be shooting bad guys again in no time."

Then Dr. Cordasco came in and repeated most of the same manipulations and tests. He smiled warmly at Mike and asked how he was feeling. Mike, who had stared down mob bosses and gang leaders, always felt a little bit in awe of the man who had reconstructed his shoulder and somehow (Mike thought it might have been with a magic wand) put him back together. Mike thanked him repeatedly and they shook hands. The doctor was with him less than five minutes, but he left Mike feeling confident about his prognosis.

On his way down the hallway to Dr. Cordasco's office to make his next follow-up appointment, he passed by the office of Dr. David Altchek, the team physician for the New York Mets. Mike was not entirely surprised to see a very tall, golden-haired figure emerging from that office as he approached. The guy looked like a Norse god, with broad shoulders and an obviously well-muscled body. His long hair was tied into a tight bun at the back of his head. Mike thought hard, then as casually as he could manage, said, "Hey, Thor, shouldn't you be in Florida?"

Noah Syndergaard, starting pitcher for the Mets, turned toward Mike and returned the greeting. "Hey." Syndergaard stared at Mike for a moment with a puzzled look on his face, as if trying to figure out if he knew the guy in front of him. Then, a look of recognition dawned. "I know you. You're that cop dude from the newspaper. I remember – you took out that crazy guy, the . . . the . . . the Righteous Assassin, they called him. Yeah – I remember. Nice job, Sir. I'm sorry, I don't remember your name."

"Detective Mike Stoneman," Mike said, extending his right hand. The pitcher engulfed Mike's hand in his own and gave a firm shake. Mike liked to think he had a strong hand, but this guy's paw was like a rock. "Nice to meet you," Mike said meekly. "I hope you're not here because of any problems – the team needs you this season."

"Oh, no, man. Just a routine check-up. I'm good. Heading back to Port St. Lucie this afternoon."

"Great to hear," Mike said as he extracted his hand and stepped back a pace. "I hear this kid, Alonso, is really good."

"Oh, way yeah, man. He's a beast. And my man Familia is back. Our pen is going to be awesome!"

"I hope so. You deserve to win twenty this year."

"Cool. Well. See you around, Dude," Syndergaard said, then he turned and strode down the hall toward the waiting area and exit, covering the ground with huge strides. Mike whistled softly and marveled at how big the guy looked in person.

Mike made his appointment while looking around at an array of football jerseys mounted in shadow-box frames on the walls. All of them bore inscriptions thanking Dr. Cordasco for repairing the injured players' bodies and allowing them to have successful careers. Mike hoped the same would apply to him, but lamented that not every injury could be fully repaired. Darren's shattered knee had been replaced, but unlike Mike's labrum, it was gone and would never be as good as new again.

Chapter 13 – Lower Decks

Friday, March 1

UNLIKE CHRISTINE BARKER'S DEATH, which was only probably a homicide, the murder of bodega owner Raul Rosario was unquestionably a homicide. And while Jason and Ray had no clear suspects in the Barker case, they knew exactly who they were looking for in the Rosario investigation. They didn't know his real name, or how to find him, but they had witnesses who would recognize him if they saw him again. This was an old-fashioned manhunt, with very little mystery involved. Of course, hunting a man when you have no name or address in a city of ten million people is not exactly easy, even when you have the resources of the NYPD.

Ray and Jason had been working on it for three weeks, without any success. There was an all-points bulletin out for the man, along with an artist's sketch compiled from the joint memories of all the people on the scene in the Bronx, plus Luis Rosario and Manuel Hwong. But, short of a beat cop randomly pulling the guy over or arresting him on some unrelated crime, it was a needle-in-a-haystack chance of stumbling onto him.

Jason and Ray both thought that shaking down local businessmen and using their stores as fronts for the distribution of drugs and for laundering their money sounded like a mob operation. The most likely suspects were connected to the Gallata crime family, which had a hammer lock on that kind of activity, along with prostitution and illegal gambling. The theory was bolstered by fact that the three large men with no recorded employment history who had been arrested after the Webster Avenue shoot-out all had separate lawyers, who were blocking them from providing any useful information. The firm that employed the lawyers was headed by an elderly former judge, reputedly the *consiglieri* for Mickey "Slick Mick" Gallata, the former figurehead of the family. Slick Mick had been abducted and left in the tiger pit at the Bronx Zoo the previous summer. Since then, the organization had been in some disarray, but the various lieutenants and foot soldiers within the Gallata family had kept the wheels turning while the men at the top jockeyed for position. The end game was still opaque to the cops, but the smart money was on Slick Mick's youngest son, Alberto, known as "Fat Albert." The nickname had stuck long before Bill Cosby was exposed as a sexual predator. It was too late to change, unless Alberto decided to lose a few hundred pounds to negate the moniker, which didn't seem likely.

The problem for Jason and Ray was that there were already two separate task forces, one from the NYPD and one from the FBI, investigating and monitoring the activities of the Gallata organization. Two more cops with a separate agenda mucking around in the neighborhood was not a popular idea. The two task forces already had trouble coordinating their efforts without stepping on each other's toes. Jason had circulated the sketch of their guy to the city task force and asked them to ID him. The city cops were supposed to pass it along to the feds. There was more politics involved than police work, in Jason's opinion.

There was not a lot more for Jason and Ray to do on the Rosario case, so they were working their other files. A week later, they were no closer to closing the Christine Barker case than to finding "Ricky."

"I can't believe that this guy's mug isn't pinned to some cork board somewhere," Ray said as he paced around Jason's desk. "These guys have video surveillance on Fat Albert and his goons, and they have diagrams and charts of everyone they think might be part of the operation. This guy has to be up there somewhere, even if he's a low-level bag man."

"I know," Jason agreed. "It makes no sense. If we had another line on the bastard, we'd take it. Did you get the files on the other dead women?"

"No. They never came in."

"That's strange. What did Sophie say about them?"

"Who's Sophie?" Ray asked.

"Never mind. I'll go check on them."

Jason went down to the records room to talk with Sophie Lafontaine. There were other Black cops around the precinct building, but all of them were lower down in the chain of command from Jason. He could talk to them, but he was wary about appearing too cozy with the beat cops just because they were Black. Sophie, however, was different. For one thing, she had thirty years on the force. She didn't give a rat's ass what anyone thought and she pitched the shit to all the higher-ranked officers without regard to their status or race. For another thing, there were seldom any other people down in the records dungeon, so any conversation was confidential and Sophie kept secrets better than anyone. Jason had taken to using her as a sounding board.

"Hey, Beautiful!" Jason called out when he saw her sitting on her high stool behind the records counter. Sophie's face looked like she could be an aging Hollywood starlet. She had high cheekbones that were always well rouged, round lips covered with bright red paint, and oval eyes accented with blue and violet shadow and black eyeliner curved at the edges. Her black hair was pulled into a tight swirl that tilted slightly to her right side. She could change into an evening dress, put on dangling earrings, and pass for a fashion model.

Sophie broke into a broad smile, exposing her perfect white teeth. "Well, lookie here," she boomed, her voice echoing down the empty concrete hallway. She was born in Jamaica, and even after four decades living in New York, she still retained an island accent. "If it ain't the big shot homicide detective coming down to get his shiny loafers dirty."

"Now, Sophie, you know damned well that there isn't a speck of dust down here in your domain."

Sophie laughed. "Well, you got me there, Detective Dickson. So, to what do I owe the honor of your illustrious presence?"

"I need some files and a reality check," Jason said as he strode up to the counter, put his elbow on the ancient wooden surface, and leaned in toward Sophie.

"Well, once I give you the files, I'll lose your attention, so let's start with the other one."

Jason straightened up before explaining the situation. "We have a murder suspect. We have what we think is a very good sketch of the guy. I've seen it and I saw him myself, and the sketch is spot on. We're pretty sure he's associated with the Gallata organization, working as the front man for a shake-down and money laundering operation in the Bronx, so we gave the sketch to the NYPD task force that's monitoring the Gallata gang. We figured it would be a few days and they'd get back to us with his name, but it's been two weeks and radio silence. Does that make any sense to you?"

Sophie looked Jason in the eyes, then furrowed her painted-on eyebrows. "Detective, you're a smart man, right? You're well educated, yes?"

"Yes," Jason replied as if being called upon by his third-grade teacher to recite a simple arithmetic question.

"So, what does it seem like to you, huh? Either the man is not part of Fat Albert's crew, or the cops on the task force know who he is, but they're not telling you. Am I right?"

"That's what I figure," Jason confirmed.

"What do you think is more likely?"

"That they're not telling me, but that doesn't really make any sense."

Sophie took on a disapproving look, as if she thought Jason was missing something obvious. "What would make it make sense?"

"It only makes sense if somebody is trying to suppress the information – trying to protect him. But he's wanted for a very high-profile murder. He's not some kingpin. He's a runner – he's working the street and shaking down the local businessmen himself. He's not high enough in the organization to be worth protecting."

"Unless?" Sophie prompted.

"Unless . . . " Jason started, then stopped. "Unless the shake-down operation is a key part of some current sting and they don't want to disrupt anything until they make a bust. Or something like that."

"Now, Detective, was that so hard?" Sophie folded her arms on top of her bosom and smiled at Jason. "I think maybe without Detective Stoneman, you're losing your magic touch."

"Who ever said I had a magic touch?" Jason asked, genuinely curious.

"I swear sometimes, Detective, you don't see the water when you're standing by the ocean. Don't you know how much Captain Sully sings your praises all the time, like he's the big hero 'cause he picked you and didn't he make such a sensational choice? The mayor says you were the one who sniffed out the Righteous Assassin. He says you were the one who tracked down that white guy who was raping and killing the Black prostitutes. You're a superstar, Honey. Of course, some of us know that Detective Stoneman should take some of that credit, but he's too modest to steal your spotlight. So now, with your mentor on the sidelines, everyone is watching to see if you can keep it up on your own."

"I'm not on my own," Jason responded meekly. "I have a temporary partner."

"Sure, Darlin', but now you're the experienced end of the partnership. You gotta drive the bus now, so make sure you steer carefully."

"Thanks, Sophie," Jason said, turning away from the counter.

"Hold on, there, Mister Genius."

"What?"

"Don't you remember? There was something about some files?"

Jason smacked his palm against his forehead. "Of course. Yes. Thanks. I would have been back before I got to the stairs. It's those files Ray asked for last week. The three dead addicts. They're related – well, they may be related – to the woman we fished out of the river three weeks ago, Christine Barker."

"Right," Sophie said, reaching under her counter and pulling out a large three-ring binder, which she flipped open to a page marked with a bright orange tab. She ran her finger down the page until she found the entries she was looking for.

"You still keep those records in longhand?"

"I enter everything in the computer, too," Sophie said. "I just like havin' my own file. I don't trust those machines. Nobody can hack my book," she said, proudly patting the heavy volume on the counter. "Now, there were three requests here. Two of the files were archived downtown to central storage. Those files were closed. I sent that request down on February 19 and that usually comes back in two or three days, so it should be here by now, but it hasn't come in. I'll call down and check on that for you when we're done. Now, the other one was for a file from the one-hundred-eighth precinct in Queens, so that shouldn't have been a big deal, but I got a note here that the clerk there couldn't find it. She's still looking for it."

Jason frowned. "So, three files requested, and we got zero?"

"It looks that way. I don't know how other clerks manage their files, but I can tell you that wouldn't be happenin' here in my room." Sophie flashed a defiant smile. "Sorry, Honey. I'll keep trying for you."

"Okay," Jason said, slowly turning to leave the area. "Let me know if you hear back on any of those files."

"I'll be sure to do that, Detective."

Chapter 14 – Alla Famiglia

Saturday, March 2

MIKE CLIMBED UP THE THREE STEPS to the porch of Darren's home. The Queens neighborhood was lined with attached houses, each sharing walls with its neighbors, and each sporting a tiny patch of grass between the front porch and the sidewalk. The façade of each home was painted in a different bright color, giving each a distinctive appearance and mood. Darren's house was a conservative tan, with darker brown trim and a natural maple-wood door. A cop's house. An iron railing, painted green, prevented visitors from falling off the three-foot high concrete stoop. As he paused at the doorbell, Mike could smell the sauce simmering on the stove inside. When Darren opened the door, Mike's nose was treated to deep aromas – garlic, tomato, and fresh bread. He started salivating immediately.

"Hey, Partner!" Darren said loudly enough for Marie to hear in the kitchen. "C'mon in." Darren stepped aside to allow Mike to enter.

He looked around at the familiar living room, crowded with chairs, a sofa, and bookcases jammed with photos and mementos of all types.

A faded oriental rug formed a huge circle in the middle of the floor, on which a glass-topped coffee table sat, holding an assortment of magazines and the TV remote control. It was a room very much lived in and looked almost exactly the same as Mike remembered from his last visit, and many before that one. A large crucifix hung on the wall above a fireplace that clearly had not been used for fire in a long time. The mantle was awash in more family photos and a few Christmas ornaments that either lived there year-round or just had not been put away yet.

"Uncle Mike!" Mike's mental inventory of the space was cut short by the excited cries of Tony and Jenny, Darren's kids. Mike marveled at how much they both had grown since he last saw them. They gave him hugs and then hovered a few feet away, waiting to see if "Uncle" Mike had any treats for them. Mike dipped a hand into his jacket pocket and pulled out a handful of individually wrapped caramel candies.

"Now, don't spoil your dinner with those. Save them for later," he admonished. The children each reached out to grab the offerings, spilling several of the candy cubes on the floor, then scrambling after them.

"All right, you little animals. Get washed up for dinner and put those in the candy drawer!" Darren called after them as they hustled around the corner into a narrow corridor that Mike knew led off to their bedrooms.

Mike walked around the side of a half-wall into the kitchen, where Marie was busy over the stove with a wooden spoon dipped into a large pot of sauce. Mike held out his arms and Marie carefully set down the spoon on a paper towel and gave him a lingering hug, then a kiss on the cheek. "It's been too long, Mike. How are you?"

"I'm fine," Mike said as he held his left arm out in front of him, not quite perpendicular to the floor. "I'm on the mend from my surgery and nearly back to normal."

"You look thin, Mike. Have you lost weight?" Marie looked concerned, as if any drop in poundage signaled severe illness or psychological trauma.

"Yes, actually," Mike said, patting his stomach admiringly. "I'm down about fifteen pounds in the last three months."

"Well, we'll fix that right now," Marie said with a smile, turning back to the food preparation. "I'm fixing you a proper meal. None of that cheap restaurant food for you here. We're so happy you could come by."

"I'm happy, too," Mike said as he removed his overcoat, hung it on a familiar hook at the corner of the entrance hallway, and walked to the alcove off the kitchen where a dining table was set up for five. Over the next two hours, Mike was treated to antipasto, a mozzarella and tomato salad, chicken parmesan with a side of spaghetti, freshly made breadsticks, and homemade cannolis. And a bottle-and-a-half of a nice Italian Chianti that Mike had brought along. Over their food, Darren and Marie bragged up the accomplishments of the kids, gave Mike updates on their respective parents and nearby relatives, and grilled him about his relationship with Michelle. They wanted to be the first ones invited to the wedding, but Mike let them know that there had been no discussion about marriage and there would not be any in the foreseeable future. Mike gave a detailed account of his shoulder surgery and his rehabilitation progress. He avoided a discussion about Darren's recovery. By the time he finally put down his fork for the last time, he had to loosen his belt.

"Well, that will put a huge dent in my healthy diet," he said without a shred of guilt. "Marie, that was the best meal I've had in a long time. If I lived here full-time, I'd weigh a ton!"

"No, you would not, Mike, because I'd put you to work and burn those calories right away."

"That may be true, Marie. I really do miss spending time with you and the kids. I can't believe how much they have grown up."

"Before you know it, Tony will be applying to college," Marie said with just a hint of apprehension in her voice.

"So, he'll get a basketball scholarship to St. John's, right?"

"I wish!" Darren bellowed a little more loudly than he intended. "They are great kids, but I don't expect that either of them will be the star athlete in their high school."

"Maybe not, but I bet they can both take care of themselves, being the offspring of a brawler like you." Mike pointed at Darren and made a fist in a mock assault. Darren reached out his hand and engulfed Mike's fist.

As he was getting his coat on and preparing to leave, Mike pulled Darren aside, out of Marie's earshot. "Are you sure you don't need anything? Is there a college fund for the kids? I'd be happy to put in a little contribution."

Darren stiffened. "No, Mike. Thanks. Like I said, I'm doing fine. We're doing fine. I appreciate the thought, but it's not necessary. I'll let you know if that changes."

"You'd better, you stubborn Irish bastard. It's a good thing you married an Italian wife. At least she has some common sense in her."

"I heard that!" came Marie's voice from the next room. "And it's so true!"

Mike laughed and swooped into the room, lifting Marie off the ground in a bear hug before giving her a kiss and letting her down gently. "I'm going to have to walk home to burn off that dinner."

"You be careful out there, Mike. Those streets aren't safe at night."

"I'll be fine, Marie. I promise. I'll just walk to the 7 line."

"Come by any time, Mike," Darren said, extending a hand. Mike took the offered handshake and pulled Darren into a hug.

As he banged hard on the man's back, he replied, "I'm sorry I was away so long. I'll definitely make it a point to get back to visit sooner next time."

"And you can bring that lovely girlfriend of yours," Marie chided. "If you're not scared that we'll tell her the truth about you."

Mike busted out with a huge laugh. "Thanks. I'll consider that. I'm sure Michelle would love you guys."

After one more round of hugs, Mike exited into the brisk winter air. All around the neighborhood, lights were on and the figures of people filled the visible windows. Smoke rose up from several chimneys. Mike shivered slightly, partly from the cold, and partly from a twinge of guilt. No matter what Darren said, Mike would always blame himself for his partner's injury, and the damage it had done to his life. He turned up his collar, dipped his head against a slight breeze, and started off toward the subway stop. He made a mental note to find out about college scholarships that were available to the kids of injured cops.

Chapter 15 – Don't Ask Questions

Monday, March 4

O N MONDAY MORNING, Jason was at his desk sipping a cup of coffee and wishing there was a bagel next to it. He was working the phone, following up on a new case. The stiff in question had been a homeless man well known to the residents of a neighborhood in upper Manhattan, near the George Washington Bridge. He was found in the park area by the river and the autopsy confirmed the cause of death as heart failure, likely triggered by exposure. There was no suggestion of foul play. Jason was trying to track down the next of kin to advise them and make arrangements for the body. It was neither glamorous nor pleasant, but it was unfortunately a frequent part of the job. He was happy to see Ray walk over and wave to him, giving him an excuse to break off the call. After saying good-bye, Jason turned his attention to Ray. "What?"

"We got another arrest record for Christine Barker. This one's for solicitation."

"What? Where did you get that?"

"From somebody named Sophie down in the records room. She sent up a new file."

"You really need to make an effort to get to know Sophie," Jason said.

"Yeah, well, there are a lot of people up here I don't know yet."

"How come we didn't have this in the original file?" Jason asked, not really expecting an answer.

"Because she gave a different name and she had no ID, so they booked her as 'Christine Baker' – B-A-K-E-R – and the record didn't get connected to the correct file. Her prints eventually got matched, but the files were never merged." Ray handed Jason several sheets of paper with the file information about Christine Baker.

Jason reviewed the new file for several minutes at his desk, then called Ray back over. "Hey, take a look at this and tell me if it looks odd to you."

"What?"

"Look at the dates and times. She was brought in at 23:02 on January 9, which makes sense if she was arrested for solicitation. Then, then the next entry is a release two days later, on January 11. No charges. They just cut her loose. Why would they hold her so long and not book her?"

"No clue."

Jason scanned the file. "I also don't see any record of her being interrogated. Wouldn't it be standard practice to talk to the suspect if you're going to hold her that long?"

"I would," Ray said absently, "but who knows. Things get crazy in lock-up. Maybe they just forgot about her. Who knows."

Jason scowled but did not reply. He knew Ray was probably right. He spent the next half hour looking at the file and looking up information in the NYPD database. Then, he called out to Ray, "I think we got something."

Ж Ж Ж

Twenty minutes later, Jason and Ray were sitting in Captain Sullivan's office in the corner of the third floor of the ancient precinct house. The floor had been gutted and turned into open space for desks for the detectives' bullpen. Sullivan's space was enclosed by glass on two sides. The third side was covered floor-to-ceiling with bookshelves, stuffed with books, binders, and dozens of photographs of Sully standing with celebrities and politicians, usually wearing an ill-fitting tux. The fourth side of the office was the front of the building with a window looking out on 94th Street. Sully had blinds on the inside of his glass walls so that he could get some privacy when needed, but for this meeting the blinds were up, giving Jason and Ray the feeling of being in a fishbowl. The spectators in the bullpen could not hear the conversation, but by the redness in Sully's face, everyone could see that he was not happy.

"I told you two knuckleheads to close out this case. Nobody is going to blink if you call it an overdose and drop it."

"Captain, we're happy to drop it as soon as we finish the investigation." Jason was acting as spokesperson, and despite what Sophie said, Sully was not cutting him any slack. "There have been some odd circumstances surrounding the case, one of which is the absence of the files on the three dead girls with similarities in their cases. We're still trying to get those."

"I don't give a shit about odd, Dickson. I care about closure rates and resources and this case is a drag on both!" Sully, whose face turned deep shades of crimson when he got angry, looked like he was going to blow steam out of his ears.

"Fine," Jason soothed. "We now have a lead, so if this one doesn't pan out, we can dump the case without any worry."

"What?" Sully growled, clearly not happy, but unwilling to refuse to listen.

"One of the times that Christine Barker was arrested, she was busted with two other girls, both of whom had multiple arrests for solicitation. One of those girls was later arrested during a drug bust where she was hanging on the arm of a courier known to be a bag man tied to the Gallata crime family."

Sully dropped his head and shook it slowly from side to side. "So fucking what? Half the hookers in Brooklyn work for pimps who work for the Gallatas, we know that. Why should that be significant?"

"It's significant," Ray jumped in, prompting a frown from Jason, "because the theory that somebody pumped her full of smack and dumped her in the river just got more plausible if she was working for some Gallata goon. All she has to do is look at one of those guys funny and they'd off her just for the sport."

Sully stood up from his chair, which seemed to elevate his head only a foot or so. He pointed a stumpy finger toward Ray. "Do not – and I will repeat that for you since you are new around here – DO NOT think that you are going to make a name for yourself by going after the Gallata gang like some federal cowboy. You will NOT take an overdose case and turn it into some crusade against vice and organized crime. Do you understand me, Detective?!"

The volume of Sullivan's tirade was sufficient to penetrate the glass walls and reverberate around the bullpen, prompting every head in the room to turn and watch. The captain sat back down in his chair, his face puffy and a bead of sweat hanging on the end of his bulbous nose.

Jason stepped in, as Ray looked like a dog that had just been swatted across the nose with a wet newspaper. "Cap, we're not going after the Gallatas and this is not a crusade about anything. We just want to ask around and see if we can make contact with any of the other working girls. See if we can get any confirmation about her being a heroin user or whether she was having any problems with any of her, um, handlers. That's it. If it's a dead end, then we're out. Right, Ray?" Jason glared at his partner and nodded his head slightly.

"Sure. Right. Out," Ray said.

"Fine!" Sully shouted. "But I'm making a call downtown first to make sure you two morons aren't sticking your heads in somewhere they're gonna get cut off."

Jason nodded, grabbed Ray by the arm, and headed for the door. "That's great, Sully. Thanks." He hustled Ray to his desk, while every eye in the place watched. Then, he changed his mind about talking in the bullpen and loudly said that he was hungry and since there was no food allowed in the building still, he was going to go find someplace not rat-infested to get a bite. "You're hungry, right Ray?" The two detectives left the mostly silent room.

Chapter 16 – Class in Session

"DETECTIVE MIKE STONEMAN" was written in neat block chalk letters on the blackboard that covered the entire front of the classroom. Mike strolled across the length of the space, his hands clasped behind his back, scanning the faces in the tiered rows. The half-desks were arranged in rising semicircles up to the top of the room, some twenty feet or so higher than the bottom of the pit, where Mike held court.

"Anyone?" he asked with a low, booming voice. He glanced up at the top row of seats and made eye contact with Jason, who was reclining slightly, watching the show. Jason nodded, and Mike returned the recognition with an almost imperceptible incline of his chin. Mike knew that Jason could answer the pending question, but he was looking for one of the young aspiring detectives to answer. The cops taking Mike's class were mostly studying for the detective's exam, but there were also a few veterans in the room looking for a refresher.

"Come now, you've all handled evidence at crime scenes dozens if not hundreds of times. Don't tell me that none of you know how to properly collect DNA samples." Mike had reached the end of the room and turned, keeping his front to the class, and began slowly pacing back the other way. Finally, a female officer with copper-red hair raised her hand. She was sitting in the front row and Mike had noticed her in one of his other classes. She had bright eyes and sat up in her chair, even when she wasn't answering a question. "Okay, Officer Swanson, tell me what you'd do here."

Officer Mary Swanson licked her lips, took a breath, and looked directly at Mike as she started to speak. Mike liked that – someone who looked him in the eye. Even if her answer wasn't perfect, he would praise her confidence and nudge her in the right direction if she started to stray from the correct path. Not because she was an attractive woman, but because she had balls. Good police work often started with a take-charge attitude and self-confidence. People followed instructions if you sounded like you knew what you were talking about – even if you didn't. Mike listened intently, returning the officer's gaze, as she walked him painstakingly through each detail of the process she would use to collect samples from the hypothetical crime scene. She would place each in a plastic evidence bag, seal the bag, place a tamper-proof evidence seal on the bag, initial the seal, and deposit the sealed bag into a pouch for later transport to the crime lab.

"And then?" Mike prompted.

"Then I would continue to patrol the scene, looking for additional evidence."

"And where do you think you might find some?"

Officer Swanson hesitated, but then charged forward. "Next I would check trash cans in the dwelling, looking for material that might contain DNA from the suspect, like a cigarette butt or a used tissue."

"Okay, Officer, let's say you find a tissue in a waste can, what would you do?"

"I would extract the item from the can with the tweezers."

"What tweezers?" Mike pressed.

"I have–" Officer Swanson stopped talking, looked down at her notebook on the half-desk, then continued. "I would have left the tweezers that I used to pick up the hair sample in the evidence bag, so I would need to get a fresh pair from the evidence kit and use that to extract the tissue."

Mike smiled a benevolent, fatherly smile. "Of course you would, Officer Swanson. All of you, I'm sure, have been at a crime scene without a proper evidence collection kit. You have latex gloves in your pocket or in your squad car, but if you don't have a kit and don't have a tweezers, what can you use, besides your hands, to collect bits of evidence without contaminating them?"

Jason watched as the cops in the room called out ideas, while Mike walked to the blackboard and scrawled down the items. When there were a dozen ideas in the list, Mike stopped and let the students argue among themselves about which options were superior to others. He was particularly impressed with one young Asian officer who suggested searching the kitchen drawers for unused chopsticks. "It's an apartment in Manhattan, so there's a better than fifty-fifty chance that there are stray chopsticks in the silverware drawer," he said confidently.

"In the end," Mike said, cutting off the discussion as it was nearly the end of the class, "the point is not which of these options is the absolute best, but what options you have available. If you search the silverware drawer and discover that this is the one apartment in New York with no leftover chopsticks," he paused and nodded at the Asian officer, "you'll have to make do with a different option. Be creative, as you all seem to be," Mike gestured to the long list of items on the blackboard, "and make sure to record your actions or include the item in the evidence bag, unless . . . ?"

"Unless the item might have some other substance on it that could contaminate the evidence," Officer Swanson called out.

Mike smiled, nodded his head, then told the group to study sections three and four of the training manual on evidence collection and chain-of-custody protocol for the next session. As the officers filed out of the room at the top, Jason slid over to the side and walked down the steps to the pit, where Mike was talking to three uniformed officers who had charged up at the end of class like puppies at meal time. Jason waited patiently while Mike answered questions and pointed out to one young officer why nail clippers would not be a good choice as an evidence-collection device. When the last officer had turned to leave, Jason approached Mike and sat down in a front-row seat next to where he was standing. Mike sat in the adjoining chair and faced his partner.

"What brings you to the lower decks, Detective Dickson?"

"I just want to remind myself how much I don't know," Jason said with a playful smile.

"Well, if you still need teaching, then I'm a failure as a partner," Mike retorted. "How's that Barker case going?"

"That's what I wanted to talk about," Jason said, getting up from the chair so that he could take a stroll around the front of the room while he talked. "It's actually kind of a chain-of-custody issue, but involving a person instead of a piece of evidence."

"How so?"

"It's Christine Barker. She was picked up for solicitation a little more than a month before her death. She was brought in and put in a holding cell. Now, normally they would either get the night court judge to issue her a desk summons and cut her loose, or hold her overnight and process her in the morning. But in this case, she was held in the lock-up for two days."

"Maybe they were waiting to charge her with something else?" Mike suggested.

94

"Yeah, could be, but they never did. She sat for two days, then got released without a desk summons or any charges. Just cut loose, free and clear."

"Didn't she have some other outstanding charges?"

"Yes," Jason said, stopping to pick up an eraser and start clearing Mike's chalk scrawl off the blackboard. "She had an arrest warrant outstanding for failing to appear on a prior desk summons."

"Maybe that's why they held her for two days."

"You would think that," Jason replied, "but this is where it gets weird. She was arrested three times under her correct name, Christine Barker. Then, when she was picked up for solicitation, she gave her name as 'Christine Baker' and claimed not to have any ID, so she was processed under that name."

"So, maybe they were holding her until they could verify her identity," Mike suggested.

"That would make sense," Jason responded, "but it doesn't seem that they ever made the connection. They just cut her loose, without any record of an interrogation."

Mike raised an eyebrow. "Nothing?"

"Nope," Jason said. "There's no record of her ever leaving the holding cell. She was never signed out, never questioned, never spoke with a PD, never made a phone call, nothing."

"That's not possible," Mike muttered softly, then looked up at Jason. "Even without the name issue, there's always a record of a prisoner in custody having contact with somebody. Nobody stays in a lockup cell for two days without any contact."

"That's why it's weird. Everything about this case is weird."

"When was she next arrested?" Mike asked.

"She wasn't. That was her last record in the system. After that, she dropped off the map until we found her in the river. That's just one of the things that bugs me about this case."

"What else?" Mike asked.

"It's a lot of little shit. You remember that Doctor McNeill identified three other girls who died from heroin overdoses and she thought they were maybe similar?"

"Sure."

"Well, you would think it would be easy for me to pull those files, but I requested them two weeks ago and they haven't come in yet. They're all lost."

"Curious. But files get lost. It's not like those were important or high-profile cases."

"True, but all three?"

Mike paused to ponder the significance of the missing files. "I guess that does seem particularly unlikely."

"So, you think it means anything?"

"It could," Mike admitted, "but let's not get ahead of ourselves. Those files being missing doesn't mean that somebody is trying to prevent us from making connections between them and Christine Barker."

"But it could," Jason said.

"Yeah. It could."

Chapter 17 – Standing Down

Tuesday, March 5

THE NEXT DAY, Detective Steve Berkowitz grabbed Jason and told him that Captain Sullivan wanted to see him – without Ray. Jason reported as instructed and noticed when he walked to the office that the captain had drawn the blinds. That was generally considered a bad omen. Sullivan, who was on the phone, waved him in and motioned for him to shut the door and take a seat, which Jason did. When he had completed his call, the captain turned to Jason with an unexpectedly friendly expression on his face.

"Dickson, I don't want a problem here, so just listen. I made a call about the Gallata prostitution ring angle you're chasing on that Baker case."

"Barker," Jason said softly.

"Whatever!" Sully yelled, but then composed himself. "As it turns out, there's an ongoing undercover operation involving a prostitution operation in Brooklyn and somebody downtown thinks that your girl might have been involved in it. The district commander wants you to share your information and work with the vice guys on this. Make a

97

copy of all your case notes and forward them to Lieutenant T. Warren Magnan at the Vice unit out of the ninety-fourth precinct. He's in charge of the undercover operation. He'll take the information and make sure that you and McMillian get any leads linking her death to anyone within the scope of their investigation. As far as I'm concerned, you can let them take the damned case and you can stand down. Understand?"

Jason contemplated making a point or two about how he and Ray might leverage the information from the Vice unit to aid in their investigation, but then decided it was futile and just gave up. "I understand, Captain." He slowly rose from the chair.

Then Sullivan had one more thing to say. "You tell McMillan. And tell Stoneman."

"Right," Jason said as he walked out. The eyes of the cops in the bullpen were all fixed on Jason as he exited the captain's office. "What are you all looking at?" he snapped as he walked toward Ray, who was sitting at his desk. Jason motioned him into the conference room and gave him the news.

"When are you going to tell the M.E. that we're going to be standing down on this investigation?" Ray asked.

"I'm not going to tell her," Jason replied.

Ж Ж Ж

"Why do I have to tell her?" Mike asked Jason as they sat at a tiny table against the freezing cold window of the diner at 70th Street and Broadway. Mike liked the place because it had cheap breakfast specials and was a block away from his apartment. The temperature had plummeted down to deep winter levels despite the calendar saying that spring was just around the corner. An ooze of cold air seeped through the cracked caulk as they watched pedestrians,

98

bundled in their heavy parkas, gloves, and furry hats, hurry by outside. Mike was attacking his egg white, onion, and mushroom omelet, with a side of cottage cheese. Not his usual, but he wanted to impress Jason with how healthy he was eating during his rehab. Plus, he had to make up for the huge dinner at Darren's house.

"Because the captain wants to make sure that this has a lid put on it, and the only person who might still push it is Doctor McNeill, and she's more likely to take 'no' for an answer from you."

"That's where you're wrong, Jason. She's less likely to listen to me. She's more likely to try to get me to do what she wants. She'll listen to you. You should do it."

"I'm not going to do it," Jason said flatly. "I'll just send her an email."

"Then she'll call me and ask me about it," Mike said. "Which means that I'll end up talking to her about it regardless, right?"

"Right."

"You're a bastard."

"I know."

"So, you and Ray can still work the case, right? It's not like the whole investigation is shut down."

Jason looked across the table and took a bite from his toasted corn muffin before responding. "Mike, the case is a dead end, the captain wants us to bury it, and we've got the Rosario case to chase, along with all the other incoming stiffs. I'm pretty happy to let the vice guys take the lead."

"I know," Mike said dejectedly. He scooped up the last of his eggs and took a bite of his multi-grain toast, devoid of butter or jam. "Have you checked out this guy, Magnan?"

"A little. He's a lifer. Older than you, Mike. I'm surprised your paths haven't crossed."

"I might have bumped into him a few times, but he's in Vice, so it's another world."

"True enough," Jason said as he drained his coffee mug and stood up. "I need to get to work. Some of us still have to fight bad guys, you know."

"Yeah. You go fight crime and I'll go get a massage."

Ж Ж Ж

Later that day, Mike struggled out of his overcoat, wincing at the pain in his shoulder as he wrenched his arm out of the heavy fabric. He stuffed his gloves and hat into the large pockets of the coat and carried the bulky package in his right arm as he entered the medical examiner's lab. He waved at Natalie, Michelle's Assistant M.E., who waved back with her left hand, which dripped something dark and thick before she returned her attention to a body on the steel table.

Michelle was sitting at her desk, typing on her keyboard with a look of intense concentration. Mike stopped twenty feet away and hopped up onto a high stool next to a counter that was littered with microscope slides, Pyrex trays, and vials of liquids of various colors. He knew better than to interrupt Michelle while she was writing a report. He pulled out his phone and checked his email, which was almost all junk and administrative spam from the City of New York. He felt a wave of melancholy, remembering Jason's dig that he was no longer doing his job and fighting crime. He hated being on leave. Before he could get too morose, Michelle called his name.

"Detective Stoneman!"

Mike hopped down from his perch and walked toward her. "I need to know if you are free for a lunch meeting," he said with a serious, business-like tone.

"Mike, nobody's here except for Natalie. You can just say that you're taking me out to lunch." She smiled and waved toward Natalie, who nodded without interrupting her examination.

"Okay by me, I'm not even a real cop at the moment."

"Mike, don't say things like that." Michelle's face softened and she reached out and touched Mike's hand. They had been dating for more than half a year and were regularly sharing a bed, but he still felt a tingle up his arm at her touch. He smiled and melted.

"I'm sorry. I'm just getting itchy to get back to work."

"You will. You're doing great. Get done with the PT and in ten more weeks, you'll be back bitching about how much you hate filling out reports and sucking up to the commissioner."

Mike laughed and took Michelle's hand. "I promise that I will never complain about writing reports again. I make no promises about the commissioner." Now it was Michelle's turn to laugh.

After Michelle bundled up against the bitter cold wind that was whipping around lower Manhattan, they trudged without much conversation to the Chinese restaurant Mike had picked out for their lunch. They hurried through the flimsy door, grateful for the heat of the interior. After discarding their outer layers, they settled into a small table and ordered lunch specials.

Mike and Michelle had never settled on a restaurant that was "their place." The way eating establishments sprouted up and went out of business in New York City, they didn't want to pick a place and then have it turn into a vegan steak house. Instead, they made it a project to go to every restaurant in Manhattan and they seldom visited the same place twice. They knew they would never get to every place, but it was fun pretending and experiencing different restaurants.

When they had made their orders and the waiter had brought them a pot of tea, a plate of fried noodles, and a saucer of duck sauce, Mike leaned forward and said, "I need to tell you something."

"Me, first," Michelle said excitedly. "I need to tell you what I've learned."

"About what?" Mike asked, happy to delay the difficult conversation.

"I have some more information about Christine Barker."

"More social media posts?" Mike speculated.

"No," Michelle responded hesitantly, looking away from Mike as she spoke, as if the orange Koi fish swimming in the giant tank by the door of the restaurant were suddenly very interesting. "I got the information directly from Steph Barker. She called me at the office. She was really upset about her sister's death and she needed to talk to somebody. The point is that Steph is absolutely sure that Christine would never have voluntarily taken heroin."

"How can she know that?" Mike asked, forgetting about being mildly pissed at Michelle for speaking to Steph Barker and potentially interfering with an ongoing police investigation.

"First, Steph explained to me about Christine's meth habit. She had fallen into a bad group in high school and her boyfriend, Jack, did meth and he convinced her to go to Seattle. He was apparently really bad news, but Christine couldn't see it. But after their brother, Alex, died, Christine and Steph both swore that they would never, ever do heroin. When Christine's boyfriend started using, she left him. That was apparently huge. She refused to see him for the destructive force that he was, but as soon as he started using the heroin, she dumped him.

"Christine contacted Steph after she got to New York and told her that she was sick about the dark place she had been in, but she had pulled herself out of it and she was clean for two weeks. She was making plans to come home, but she had to keep the plans secret from somebody named Eddie. Steph told me that Christine was calling from somebody else's cell phone and she had to hang up very suddenly, and that was the last Steph heard from her."

Mike sat quietly, trying to absorb the information. "How certain are you that Steph is being straight with you and not just giving you her own wishful thinking?"

"Pretty sure," Michelle said, a little bit offended by the question, as if she could be fooled by a nineteen-year-old.

"Okay, we'll assume all the information is accurate. What does it tell us? We know that Christine had run away from Seattle to New York, we know that she was a meth user, and we know that she was turning tricks in Queens."

"What?" Michelle blurted out. "When did we know that?"

"Sorry," Mike apologized, "we just found that out recently."

Michelle looked appropriately chastised. "Fine. Now I know. I wonder whether this Eddie person has something to do with that? It might explain why she had to keep her plans secret, if there was somebody pressuring her into working as a prostitute. We know she got arrested a couple times in New York, so it's possible that she fell into that kind of situation, right?"

"Right . . . " Mike said slowly, thinking about several things at once.

"So, Mike, you'll make sure Jason and Ray get all this information, right?"

Mike froze. "Um, well, Michelle, that's what I needed to talk to you about. You see, Jason and Ray are not going to be actively working the case. The lead responsibility is being transferred downtown to a Vice unit. They have an undercover operation going with the prostitution ring Christine might have been caught up in, and so the captain wants to let them handle it for now. I'll make sure the information gets to the guys in Vice, though." He looked at Michelle's crestfallen expression. "I'm really sorry. I know you were interested in the case."

"It's just–" Michelle started, then stopped herself. "I just feel a connection to these girls."

Mike reached across the table and took her hand in his. "What is it about Christine Barker?"

Michelle took a deep breath in, then let it slowly out through her mouth. It was a relaxation technique that Mike recognized. He sat silently, waiting for her to be ready to speak. "You once asked me why I never got married, and I never told you. I didn't want to scare you away."

"Hey," Mike said, squeezing her hand comfortingly. "You have to know by now that I'm pretty hard to scare."

"I know," she said softly. She took another deep breath, then started talking quickly, as if she wanted to get it all out at once. "When I was in college, I had a steady boyfriend. He never actually asked me to marry him, but I thought that's where we were heading. His name was Dwayne, and he had a sister named Veronica. She was a few years younger and we became close. Dwayne graduated a year ahead of me and while I was prepping for my med school boards, he was foundering. He was a musician, but he couldn't get any good paying gigs, so he was waiting tables and playing in a band on weekends.

"He had always smoked some pot. I did too, back then. But he started doing some harder stuff. We started fighting about it. I wanted him to stop, but he either couldn't, or wouldn't. What was worse was that he got Veronica doing it. They did cocaine and amphetamines and then he started free-basing with coke and heroin. It was awful. I couldn't get him to stop, and I was trying to study and then – then he hit me." Michelle wiped away a tear.

"Did you have him arrested?" Mike asked.

"No," Michelle choked out. "It was a different time. Young women didn't call the cops because their boyfriends smacked them. Besides,

I was still trying to convince him to stop. I still loved him and I didn't want him to get busted. It was just awful. And then Veronica died."

"How?"

"She overdosed. Dwayne said he wasn't there when it happened, but I never believed him. I was devastated. I went to her funeral and Dwayne was there, and he was high. That was it. I totally broke it off and I never spoke to him again. I talked to Veronica's mother a few times, but then I graduated and went to med school and I tried to put it behind me. But when I started to get to know Steph and understand what happened to her sister, I could see myself, and Veronica. It could have been me, hooked on drugs and lying dead in some fleabag hotel." Michelle was fighting back tears. Mike left his chair and went around the table to put his arm around her shoulder while she tried to get herself together. Mike had seen her lose control of her emotions only once before, and that time she was tied to a chair after being kidnapped. Otherwise, she was a rock, but the case of Christine Barker had struck a deeply buried nerve.

"So, after Dwayne, you had trouble trusting men?" Mike asked seriously, but knowing that it was the understatement of the year.

Michelle spasmed with a half-sob and half-laugh and smiled at Mike. "Y-y-yes, Mike, I guess you could say that I had some trust issues."

"I will promise you that I will do my very, very best to never make you regret trusting me." Mike looked into her eyes and made sure she knew that he meant it.

"Aren't you going to–" she sniffed and wiped her nose as she regained her composure, "tell me that you'll never hurt me?"

Mike looked at her seriously. He was on one knee next to her chair, his arm still around her shoulder, which had stopped convulsing. "I can't promise that. I'm a cop, and I could get hurt again, which I know would hurt you. I could even die. I know neither of us wants to think about that, but we both know it could happen. But I can promise that I will protect you as long as I'm breathing and I will never, ever, hit you."

Michelle wrapped her arms around Mike's neck and hugged him tightly until the waiter arrived with their food. He asked if he should come back, but Michelle disengaged, sat back in her chair, and motioned for the server to put down the food. For the rest of lunch, they didn't discuss the Christine Barker case, or any other case. They did talk about Michelle's medical school years, where she found her stride as a student. They talked about her summer internship working for a public health clinic in Baltimore and about patients she remembered helping. That's what she always wanted to do – help people. By the time lunch was over and Mike walked her back to the lab, Michelle had wiped away any remnants of her tears and Natalie did not even ask whether there was anything wrong.

Ж Ж Ж

That Thursday, Mike gave Michelle an informal, off-the-record briefing on the Christine Barker investigation. Ray had sent copies of the file to Lieutenant Magnan and had not heard any updates from the Vice unit. Mike had mentioned the idea of reaching out to the Seattle PD to try to get some more background on Christine, but Captain Sullivan had shot down that idea. Sitting in the living room of Michelle's well-organized apartment, Mike could feel that Michelle was frustrated.

"Mike, while you're on leave, do you have to stay in New York?"

"I guess not, as long as I don't fall too far behind on my physical therapy sessions. Why do you ask?"

"I'm thinking that it might be nice to take a trip. I have some vacation time coming to me. Let's get away for a few days. What do you think?"

"I think it's a nice idea. It's still cold as balls outside; are you thinking about a warm beach somewhere in the Caribbean? Didn't you tell me you knew someone who could get us a deal on a cruise?"

"Actually," Michelle said as she slid over to Mike and slipped her arm behind his back, "I was thinking about visiting the Pacific Northwest."

Mike pulled away slightly and turned his head to look at Michelle, whose eyes were pleading. "I don't suppose that the itinerary for this trip would include a visit with Steph Barker?"

"It couldn't hurt to meet her, right?" Michelle's expression was so pitiful that Mike realized he had two options. He could agree to Michelle's idea and go along with her desire to put a salve on her own mental scars by making a connection with this poor woman who had lost her sister, which would make him a hero in her eyes and solidify his position as her supportive boyfriend. Or, he could tell her that such a trip would be a waste of time and would not bring Christine back from the dead. That would spark an argument that would probably end with Mike agreeing anyway, but only after annihilating any good feelings about the trip, making Michelle feel both guilty about coercing him and angry with him for not being more supportive.

Mike looked at the only woman in the world with whom he would agree to spend six hours in an airplane. "When do we leave?"

Chapter 18 – Searching for the Needle

Friday, March 8

WHILE MIKE AND MICHELLE WERE IN A CAB on their way to JFK airport on a cold morning, a crowd of five hundred or so protesters and community leaders was gathered in the Bronx outside the bodega where Raul Rosario was murdered, along with live remote crews from all the major networks. A makeshift podium had been erected on the sidewalk to give the television cameras a good angle of the flowers and candles that were assembled on the wall outside the store. A parade of community leaders spoke about the tragic death of an upstanding citizen and railed against the general violence and gang culture that the police had been unable to control. There was plenty of criticism of Police Commissioner Ward, but the speakers were careful not to cast blame on Mayor Frederick Douglass, only the second Black mayor in the history of the city. The crowd was whipped into a frenzy by one speaker, who kept repeating that the victim was Latino and the chief suspect was white, and that the police were doing nothing to arrest the man. There were chants and songs and calls for justice.

Ж Ж Ж

Jason and Ray still had no communication from the Gallata task force about their suspect. They had a sketch circulating to all officers, but they had no leads. Sully reported that the district commander overseeing the Vice task force had nixed the idea of going public with the sketch, for fear of compromising an unspecified aspect of the ongoing undercover operation.

"So, the guy is definitely connected to the Gallatas, and they probably know who he is," Jason said to nobody in particular as he and Ray sat in the captain's office. "They don't want him blown, for some reason, which is why they're not telling us who he is. They don't want him to know that *we* know who he is, so they don't want a public viewing of his sketch."

"That seems about right," Sullivan agreed.

"And the commissioner is willing to take the heat from the protesters and the press, who say we're not doing enough to solve the Rosario murder, in order to protect the ongoing investigation," Ray chimed in.

"No," Sullivan responded with great frustration. "The commissioner will not publicly admit that we are standing down on arresting the guy. He's not stupid."

"What about other leads, not connected to the Gallata investigation?" Ray asked. "Are we clear to work those?"

"Like what?" Sullivan asked.

"What about the three thugs who were with our guy? Can we lean on them?"

"No," Sullivan said. "They are presumed to be part of the Gallata operation. Besides, it wouldn't matter. They're not talking and they are lawyered up well beyond the means of gangbangers. But even if they were available for questioning, it's part of the task force investigation. They're off limits."

Neither Ray nor Jason had any other ideas.

"It's not your problem," Sullivan said finally. "Work your other cases."

"Fine," Jason said, getting up and heading for the door, with Ray on his heels.

The next day, the *New York Times* ran a page one story on the Rosario murder. The article, written by Dexter Peacock, criticized the NYPD, and named Detectives Jason Dickson and Raymond McMillian. Peacock noted that the two detectives had failed to make an arrest in the case and that they had allowed the chief suspect not only to get away during the sting operation they had set up, but to remain at large despite so much public attention on the case.

"He's not wrong," Jason said sullenly, sitting at his desk in the bullpen with Ray standing nearby.

"We gotta figure out a way to get to this guy without needing the help of our task force," Ray said.

"That would be sweet," Jason agreed. "Any bright ideas?"

Ray said nothing.

Chapter 19 – Road Trip

I T WASN'T UNTIL THEY WERE THREE HOURS INTO their flight to Seattle that Mike thought to ask Michelle what their schedule was for meeting up with Steph Barker. The doctor explained that she had arranged to call Steph when they reached Port Angeles and they would arrange a time and place for meeting the next morning.

They landed at 1:00 p.m. local time and spent the rest of the day in Seattle, eating at Ivar's Salmon House, taking in the beautiful scenery from the top of the Space Needle, and strolling through the Pike Place market. The next morning, Mike rented a car and they drove it onto a huge ferry that shuttled them across the Puget Sound. After exiting the ferry, they enjoyed the ninety-minute drive along the Olympic Peninsula through old-growth forest land along the rugged coastline, with the snow-covered mountains rising on their left in a series of jagged peaks. Eventually they reached the town of Port Angeles, listed on the sign at the city limit as having a population of 19,872. The outskirts of town looked like any suburban strip, filled with fast-food restaurants, gas stations, small businesses, and lots of billboards.

Mike followed his GPS to the hotel Michelle had booked, the Olympic Lodge.

The place had a rustic-looking interior, filled with rough-hewn logs, stones, and sculptures of elk, bears, eagles, and other fauna of the mountain region. Mike walked up to the front desk and gave his name. A cheery young woman who looked no older than high-school age smiled and asked him whether he would like a separate key for "Mrs. Stoneman." Mike stumbled for a moment and looked over at Michelle, standing a few feet away with their suitcases. "Sure," he replied meekly.

On their way to the elevator, Mike said in a hushed voice, "Did you make the reservation as Mr. and Mrs. Stoneman?"

"It was just easier that way," she said.

Mike tossed his suitcase on one side of the king bed and went to check out the bathroom. When he returned, he stopped and watched in silence as Michelle meticulously unpacked her suitcase, removing perfectly folded clothing and moving each item carefully to one of the drawers in a chest opposite the foot of the bed. When she was done, all her things were neatly arranged. Michelle looked up at Mike. "What are you staring at?"

"Just you and your perfect clothes. Where are your dirties from Seattle, anyway?"

"They are in a separate bag in the suitcase, not that it matters. Now, if you will kindly give me a few minutes in the bathroom, I need to unpack my toiletries."

Mike stepped aside and allowed her to pass by, then came around behind her and stood at the threshold of the bathroom while Michelle arranged her makeup supplies and other personal grooming items on the counter to the left of the sink. "What if I told you that I wanted the left side for my stuff?" Mike asked.

"I'd tell you to use the right side. The left side is where I live."

Mike shrugged. It was the same way in Michelle's apartment, so why should it be any different in a hotel? He wondered if Michelle would be able to put up with him and his sloppily folded clothes. He liked to just toss his dirties in the bottom of the closet and dump them all into his suitcase for the return trip. He placated himself by thinking that traveling together would be a good test for whether they could be compatible long-term. Then he found himself wondering what long-term meant to him. He decided not to ask what it meant to her.

Michelle and Mike took advantage of the remaining daylight and drove up the mountain road to the lodge at Hurricane Ridge, where they got a spectacular view deeper into the Olympic mountains. On the way back down, they were treated to the view back down to the Port Angeles harbor and across the straits of Juan de Fuca to Vancouver Island, part of British Columbia, Canada. They could see a few large tankers and cargo ships on the water far below, and in the other direction skiers and snow boarders were enjoying the snow-covered mountain trails.

"It's gorgeous here," Michelle marveled. She had lived on the East Coast her whole life and while she had traveled, she had never seen a place where she could drive from the ocean to a ski slope in under an hour.

"It sure is," Mike agreed. "I'd love to see it in the summer. But I can also understand how a teenage girl might want to branch out to the big city."

"I know, but it's so quiet and peaceful here. Why would you want to leave and go to the big, noisy, dirty city?"

Mike laughed. "You always want what you don't have, I guess. Plus, don't be fooled by the peace and quiet. You ever hear of Israel Keyes?"

"No, should I?"

"Not really. He was a serial killer. He confessed to killing eleven people, mostly in remote places like this. He committed suicide in a jail cell in Alaska in 2012, but several of his victims were from this area. One was dumped in a deep-water lake just west of Port Angeles. He loved hiking trails and camp grounds where he could find his victims alone and vulnerable. So, don't think that all this peace and quiet means that everything is rainbows and unicorns."

"My, aren't you a ray of sunshine," Michelle said, frowning and slapping Mike's right arm with a good-natured jab.

"Just keeping it real," Mike replied, glad that his surgically-repaired shoulder had not been in the line of fire. "So, we're meeting the sister in the morning?"

"Yes. It will be Sunday, so she doesn't have to work."

"Where does she work?"

"She's an assistant at a rehabilitation facility."

"Really? Can she arrange for me to have a PT session while we're in town?"

Michelle laughed. "I thought you hated them."

"I do, but I'm falling farther behind Dolores."

"Well, let's first talk to her and go from there," Michelle said. "She seems like such a good kid, and she's hurting so much over this. I'm just hoping that we can give her some closure and help her get over it."

"That's not generally in our job descriptions," Mike observed.

"Maybe not, but I'm making it mine for this weekend."

Ж Ж Ж

The next morning, Mike woke up with a stiff neck. Sleeping on his right side to protect his left shoulder was not that bad, but he normally had a soft feather pillow. As they were leaving the building, Mike went to the front desk and asked to get a feather pillow for the next night, but a cheery young woman behind the counter announced that the hotel was "proudly" feather-free. Mike grumbled something about west coast tree-huggers as they walked down the hill outside the hotel to their meeting location.

He and Michelle checked in with the hostess at Joshua's Diner ten minutes before their scheduled meeting time. They were escorted to a booth by the window and offered coffee while they waited for Steph Barker. Mike looked sternly across the Formica tabletop at Michelle. "If this is a police investigation, then let me do the talking. I don't want anyone thinking that you're involved."

"I'm very involved, Mike."

"I know you are, but I don't want anyone else to know. If there is a murderer out there, I don't want him finding out that you're poking around in his business."

"Because he might come after me?"

"I worry about it, yes. After what happened with Ronald Randall, I – I never want you to be put in danger because of one of my investigations again."

Michelle's face hardened. "So, am I not allowed to do my job as medical examiner? I shouldn't testify in court about somebody's cause of death?"

"No, of course not," Mike said, trying to recover his balance. "That's your job. But I don't want to think that you could be a target. Let me take the heat. I'm not sure I could live with myself if anything happened to you."

Michelle's expression softened and she reached out for Mike's hand. "Hey, I had a couple of bad weeks after that night. I had trouble sleeping while you were in the hospital. I told myself it was because I was worried about you, but I had a lot of nightmares. I got over it. Randall is dead, Mike. I'm a big girl and I can handle my own battles."

"I know you are," Mike said quietly. "But what if Jason's right, and Christine fell into working as a hooker for the Gallata organization?

What if one of those goons decides to send the cops a message by hurting you? I can't live with that."

"Listen," Michelle said, getting a little angry, "one of the things I like about being with you is that you treat me like an equal and a colleague. You start holding back and trying to protect me, and I'm going to be pissed off. I'm not going to tell you that I don't think about it. I thought long and hard about whether being in a relationship with you might put me in danger again. It might. But I think you're worth it. If you don't feel the same way, then tell me now."

At that moment, Mike looked over Michelle's shoulder and said, "I do, but right now we have company."

Michelle swiveled her head around and saw a face she knew only from the internet. She jumped to her feet and held out a hand to Steph Barker. She was surprised when the girl gave her a hug instead.

"Thank you for being here," she said, her voice choked up with emotion. Steph was wearing jeans and a pink T-shirt with a large red logo of the band Heart. Her dirty-blonde hair was tied back in a ponytail, emphasizing her slender neck. A pair of small silver dolphins dangled from her ears. She had blue eyes and a small, turned-up nose, giving her a fresh and pretty face, but she was not gorgeous like her sister. Mike thought she looked too skinny. Michelle thought the same.

Mike stood up and introduced himself. Steph asked to see his police credentials, and Mike obliged, pulling out his wallet and badge. He was impressed that the young woman had the poise to ask him to prove his identity. They all settled back into the booth and waited for the waitress to take breakfast orders.

Mike said, in his best sympathetic voice, "We are truly, truly sorry for your loss and we are working to uncover the circumstances of Christine's death."

"You mean murder," Steph said, her fists clenched on the table. "I talked to her. I know what she was going through. I can't bear to think that both Alex and Christine killed themselves." Steph was fighting back tears.

"It would potentially help us if we had a better understanding of the circumstances that led Christine to New York. We also need to have a complete picture of her history. Any small details might help us. I promise you, we don't want to upset you. I hope you can trust us."

Just then, the elderly waitress shuffled up to the table and asked them if they were ready to order. The conversation paused while everyone examined their menus and decided on their breakfasts. By the time the waitress trudged away, Steph had composed herself. Mike took the opportunity to lead the conversation in a slightly different direction by asking about Christine's former boyfriend, Jack. This gave Steph a villain on whom to focus. Steph did not hold back in reviling the boy who had, in her mind, corrupted Christine and spirited her away from home, only to abandon her in Seattle and allow her to run off to New York by herself.

For fifteen minutes, Mike and Michelle pieced together the story from the disjointed fragments coming from Steph, punctuated by curses and condemnations of Jack. Christine had started dating him when they were both juniors at Port Angeles High. He was a star football player and the homecoming king; she was a cheerleader. They were at the top of the popularity pyramid, but then Jack blew out his knee in the next-to-last game. This killed his dream of playing football at the U of Washington and resulted in him getting hooked on oxycontin during his recovery from surgery. He started hanging with the stoners, one of whom was his best friend, and Christine went with him. She still had stars in her eyes about him and felt sorry for him because of his injury. She drove him everywhere because, with his right leg in a brace, he couldn't drive. She got dragged down with him as he started experimenting with meth.

After they graduated, Christine spent the summer practically living with him. He was mostly recovered from his surgery, but he was never going to be a star athlete again and had let himself fall badly out of shape. He got a job working at the bowling alley, but his boss had no patience for his unreliable attendance and bad attitude. He got fired within a month. Then he left town and moved to Seattle, where everyone thought he had a cousin with whom he was living. Steph had been thrilled that Christine could go to the local community college without Jack.

But halfway through the fall semester, he came back to town and begged Christine to take him back. He swore he had cleaned himself up and had a job in Seattle, that he loved her and wanted her to come live with him. He said she could go to college in Seattle and they could be together. Steph was skeptical and told Christine not to give Jack a second chance, but she was in love, or thought she was. She spent the rest of the school year shuttling back and forth to Seattle on weekends to see him.

After Christine finished her first year at Peninsula Junior College, she went to Seattle, intending to enroll as a sophomore at the University of Washington. Steph and her mother knew that she was still seeing Jack, but there was not much they could do to stop it. They had a feeling that something was wrong when Christine didn't come home for Steph's birthday in October. She called to say that she had a lot of work to do, which didn't sound plausible. When pressed for details, she couldn't explain exactly what it was that she needed to do that she could not do from Port Angeles. Then, just before Halloween, they got the call that she was in the hospital. Christine had overdosed on a combination of drugs and alcohol. Steph and her mom rushed to Christine's bedside, where they had a huge fight with Jack when they tried to evict him from Christine's room. Hospital security called the police. When she was released, they tried to get Christine into a rehab facility, but she refused. Since she was over eighteen, they couldn't force her. Christine went back to living with Jack.

In November, Steph tried to engage Christine on the phone and by texts and Facebook, but Christine was not interested in talking much. Then Christine didn't come home for Thanksgiving, and they knew something was very wrong. When Christine called a week later, she asked Steph for money, claiming that she was going to finally dump Jack. When Steph offered to come pick her up and bring her home, she made an excuse. Steph finally had to tell her that if she wasn't willing to come home so Steph could help her, then she was on her own. Steph was crying when she got to this part, tears dripping down into her eggs. "It was so hard to just refuse her," she sobbed. "She sounded so pathetic, but it was just like Alex. If I gave her the money, she'd just spend it on drugs. The only way she was going to get clean was if I said no. I wonder now if she was calling from New York. I guess she really did decide to leave Jack. I wish I'd known that was true." Steph dissolved into weeping.

Mike and Michelle ate their pancakes and omelets silently while Steph composed herself. When she sat back up and dabbed the last tears away, Mike decided that continuing the interview was the best way to go. "Did you hear from her again?"

Steph looked across the table at Michelle, ignoring Mike. "She called in January and told me she was in New York. I was so happy to hear from her, but I was shocked when she told me where she was. She said she had to get away and she was really trying to get herself right, but she didn't have a place to really live. She said she was crashing with a friend she met and she needed money to come home. I offered to send her some Starbucks gift cards that I got for my birthday."

"Did she give you an address?" Mike asked.

"Yeah, she did, and I sent the cards."

"Do you remember the address?" Michelle cut in, then she shrugged at Mike's disapproving look.

"I don't remember," Steph said, prompting a visible sag from Michelle's shoulders. "But I wrote it down. It's at home."

"We'll get that later," Mike said, trying to get back to her story. "Did you hear from her again after that?"

"Sure. The last time. It was maybe a month later. I had almost given up on hearing back from her. I was trying to focus on school, but it was really hard. Mom was depressed. I was depressed. Then she called, and she really seemed like she was better. She was speaking clearly and she said she was clean and was trying to make it home. That's when she told me that she was calling from somebody else's phone and that she had to make sure that somebody named Eddie didn't find out. She said she was going to escape and come home."

"Did she say 'escape?' Did she use that word?" Mike asked.

"Uh huh," Steph nodded. "She seemed really scared, but she wasn't high. I could tell. But that's the last time I spoke to her."

"Do you have any record of those gift cards?" Mike asked.

"What do you mean?"

"Do you have a gift receipt, or copies of the cards or the numbers?"

"I don't know. I think I have the envelope they came in, because there was a card and I kept the card."

"Great. So, at home you have the address where you sent the gift cards, and maybe some record of the cards. We'll want to get those."

"OK. I guess we could go home and I could get that for you. My mom's home, and I don't think she'd want to talk to you, but I could get it."

"We can wait in the car."

"Fine. Then let's get it over with." Steph tossed her napkin on the table and started collecting her things. Mike waved to their waitress for the check and sent Michelle ahead to escort Steph to the door, where Mike joined them as soon as he paid the bill.

Mike and Michelle followed Steph's car, a red Plymouth station wagon that was easily thirty years old. She drove up a residential hill with old but well-kept homes lining the street. They turned into a dead-end lane and parked at the curb as the girl pulled into the garage of a ranch model house with dark brown wooden shingles covering the sides. Mike and Michelle sat restlessly, staring at the vacant lot across the street while waiting for her to emerge from the house. Steph finally came out and got into the back of the sedan.

"OK, I have the address."

Mike extracted a notebook from his jacket pocket and said, "Go ahead."

Steph looked quizzically at the notebook in Mike's hand. "Why don't you just take a picture of the piece of paper?" she said, handing Mike a plain page from a notebook with an address scrawled on it.

Mike handed it back to her. "Humor an old guy and just read it to me, please."

Steph shrugged and read off the paper. "953 Ocean Avenue, Brooklyn, New York, 11226." Mike wrote it down and then read it back to make sure he got it right. "You want the gift cards next?" Steph asked expectantly.

"Yes, please," Mike responded. "What have you got?" Steph handed him an envelope from which Mike pulled out a birthday card, inside of which was a smaller envelope emblazoned with the easily recognized Starbucks logo. Inside that was one plastic gift card and a paper gift receipt, with a bar code. This time, Mike grabbed his cell phone and took a photo of the receipt, needing an image of the bar code in order to try to trace the cards. He fumbled with the camera function on the phone before clicking off three snapshots, then handed the card and envelope back to Steph, thanking her.

"No problem," Steph said. "I only wish I could do more. I know Christine was responsible for herself and it's not my fault that she's . . . gone . . . but I should have helped her when she asked me." Her voice trailed off as she finished.

"Don't blame yourself, Sweetie," Michelle soothed.

"I feel like I don't have anyone I can talk to who understands."

"I understand, believe me," Michelle said softly, "and I'm a really good listener." Then Michelle turned to Mike. "You're going to send that to Jason, right?" Mike nodded, then Michelle got out of the car and opened the rear door.

"Come with me, Honey," Michelle said, holding out her hand to the girl. "Mike is going to have to make a call or two and you and I are going to take a walk."

Mike looked over his shoulder as Steph got out and took Michelle's hand. The two women walked down the sidewalk, toward the dead end down the block where a steel barrier separated the street from an embankment overgrown with bushes and trees. Michelle put her left arm around Steph's shoulders as they walked slowly away from the car. Mike pulled his attention away and swiped his phone to get to his dialer, punching the icon next to the name Jason Dickson.

"Dickson," Mike's partner answered in his usual professional manner.

"Jason, I have a few things for you to chase down on the Christine Barker case."

"I thought you were on vacation?" Jason quipped sarcastically.

"I am. It just happens that Michelle and I bumped into the dead girl's sister and she has some useful information. I'm going to email you some photos." Mike explained what the pictures would be and the potential significance of the records, then hung up, snapped a photo of the page in his notebook with the street address, and attached the image files to an email to Jason. This operation took Mike a solid five minutes and included two failed attempts to upload the picture files. When he finally finished, he looked up to locate Michelle and Steph, but they were nowhere to be seen.

Mike walked around the block, expecting to see the women, but did not. He tried calling Michelle's phone, but it rang twice and rolled to voice mail. He frowned and went back to the car to wait. After twenty minutes, Mike glanced in the rearview mirror and saw Michelle and Steph approaching the car from the direction of the main street. Steph's head was resting on Michelle's shoulder and she had her arm around Michelle's waist. Michelle's left hand cupped Steph's head, holding it gently and stroking her hair. When they got back to the car, Mike watched as the two women hugged tightly for a long minute. As they separated, Steph wiped a tear from her eye. Steph waved one last time as she turned and walked back into the house.

Michelle got into the front seat and closed the door. "Let's go back to the hotel," she said quietly. Mike looked at her and could see in her eyes that she was not in the mood for talking, so he started to drive. He turned on the radio to fill up the silence inside the car. They listened to the DJ read a promo for a local car dealership and a public service announcement about an upcoming charity food drive sponsored by the United Way. He navigated back to the Olympic Lodge and escorted Michelle toward their room, but she stopped suddenly before going through the front door.

"Can we go back up to the mountain?" she asked with pleading eyes.

"Sure," Mike said, turning back to the rental car.

Ж Ж Ж

The next morning, before they started the drive back to Seattle, Mike and Michelle paid a visit to the local hospital. Michelle led Mike to a medical office building across the street from the main hospital building, where the sign read "Rehabilitation and Physical Therapy." When they walked through the door, Steph rocketed from her chair behind the reception desk and gave Michelle a tight hug. When she detached, she looked at Mike and said, "Hello, Detective. I think Hector is ready for you."

"Hector?" Mike said, confused. He glanced at Michelle, who had a mischievous smile and a twinkle in her eye.

"I didn't want you to miss too much PT while we're away."

Mike gave her a kiss. "Thank you. That's very considerate, of both of you." He turned to acknowledge Steph. "Where do you want me?"

Chapter 20 – Worst Laid Plans

Thursday, March 14

J ASON SAT BEHIND THE WHEEL of the beige Lincoln he had checked out of the motor pool, tapping his index finger on the top of the steering wheel. Ray was in the passenger seat, sipping a coffee. They were parked across the street from a gas station in Queens that included a convenience store, which was owned and run by a family from Haiti. The windows of the store had been broken by someone throwing bricks through them. The police report had few details, but it had filtered its way to Jason, who had been trying to track down circumstances similar to the events leading up to the Rosario murder and the Hwong dry cleaner shake-down. He and Ray figured that the only way they were going to find the mysterious "Ricky" was to find one of his active clients. He had been smart enough to abandon the neighborhood around the Rosario bodega, since the police and the press were a constant presence there in the aftermath of the murder and the subsequent melee on the Webster Avenue sidewalk.

The public relations guys were crowing about how the police department had ridded the neighborhood of the criminals responsible, but for Jason and Ray, that just meant it would be harder to catch their guy. As expected, the gang members in custody were not talking. They seemed resigned to doing their time and were not interested in making deals to rat out their bosses. Loyalty among scumbags, Jason called it. When he got the report of the broken windows at the convenience store, Jason figured it was worth checking out. When he and Ray questioned the owner, Francois, he was reluctant to provide any details about who might have been responsible. Throughout the questioning, he shot looks toward his wife, who sat silently with her head down. The daggers coming out of his eyes signaled to Jason that it was the wife who had made the police report and that her husband was not happy that she did. Francois was not at all helpful, but Ray and Jason both came away from the interview convinced that he was not telling them the whole truth.

Although the task force working the Gallata mob clearly did not want to give Ricky up, for reasons that were never explained to Jason and Ray, the commissioner decided that if he got himself arrested in the act of committing another crime, it would not appear that he was ratted out and nobody working undercover with him could be implicated. It helped that there was, in fact, no help coming from anyone undercover. In any case, based on the commissioner's earnest desire to make an arrest in the Rosario murder case – and thereby demonstrate that the department was just as diligent in investigating the death of a minority businessman as it would be for a white victim – Jason and Ray were freed up to stake out the store. Based on the pattern of Ricky's appearances in the Bronx, it seemed that Thursday was collection day in his business cycle. They were hoping that he made the rounds to all his pick-up stations on Thursdays, and so here they were hoping to get lucky. Since this was such a speculative operation, they had no backup from patrol cars, but they had arranged to have some support there within a few minutes if the situation required it.

"I still can't figure why somebody would dump the girl in the river," Ray said. "If you're going to give her an overdose so it looks like either a suicide or just an ordinary OD case, why put her in the river, where it will seem more suspicious?" They had been talking about the Christine Barker case while killing time in the car, waiting for something to happen across the street. The captain didn't want them wasting time or resources on "that stupid case," especially since primary responsibility had been transferred. But since they had time to burn now, they were going over what they had.

"Maybe they were worried that she wouldn't die and would get help, or rat them out before she died," Jason suggested. "They wanted to make sure she was dead, and dumping her in the drink would ensure that."

"True," Ray agreed, "but doesn't it also arouse more suspicion?"

"If the M.E. hadn't flagged it for us, there would have been no suspicion. She would have been buried as a Jane Doe and the file would have been closed as an OD within a week. If I'm the guy doing the killing here, that's what I'd expect. Even if we got an ID on her, she's a runaway drug addict, so who's going to push an investigation?"

"Yeah, I know." Ray tilted his coffee cup up to the roof of the car to drain the last drop. "That's where we should have left it. Of course, if we're assuming that the three others were also killed in the same manner by the same guys, they got away with it three times without anybody raising a flag. You can imagine that they would feel pretty comfortable doing it again."

"But," Jason replied, "none of the other victims were tossed in the river. So why Christine?"

"I dunno. Maybe they were particularly worried that she wouldn't die from the overdose. Who knows. Maybe there was something special about her."

"Mike seems pretty certain that Christine was getting clean and was making plans to go back home," Jason said. "She might have been held against her will, which would make some sense. If she was drafted into service for some pimp, but wanted to get out and go home, the guy might have wanted to silence her rather than let her split."

"Sure, but why be so paranoid that you kill her? I'm sure girls cycle through that kind of operation all the time. I saw some when I was working robbery. They're involved in illegal conduct themselves, they're committing petty crimes to feed their habit, and they're not exactly in a hurry to publicize it to anyone, especially their family. Runaway teenager comes to the big city, gets in trouble, falls in with the wrong guy, ends up turning tricks to survive, then comes to her senses and leaves. It's got to happen all the time, so why kill this one?"

"I haven't got an answer for that," Jason conceded.

"How long do you think it will take for us to get some data off those Starbucks gift cards?"

Jason paused to ponder the question. The truth was that he had no idea. He had turned the information over to the forensic IT guys and asked them to get a trace on the locations where the cards had been used, but since the investigation was not a priority to the captain, they needed to avoid any extraordinary expenses or requests. It could be two days or two weeks, for all Jason knew. But he didn't want to sound clueless. He was supposed to be the more experienced member of this team. "I told the forensic IT team to let me know as soon as they had anything," he said noncommittally.

They had traced the address where Steph sent the gift cards to a church, which also served as a shelter for homeless women. The pastor confirmed that Christine had stayed there a few times, but she was not a regular. Many of the women received mail at the shelter's address, so the pastor could not say for sure whether she had received Steph's gift cards. Even assuming that she did, tracking her movements was not simple. She could have sold them or traded them for drugs, so knowing where the cards were used did not necessarily give them a fix on Christine. But it was all they had.

"If we can get the info, even if it leads us to somebody else who had contact with her, it would help us," Ray said without much confidence. "And speaking of contact with her, I found something reading through the file on her last drug arrest. Before she got her desk summons, she was signed out from the lock-up, presumably for an interrogation. But there are no notes from the meeting, and no summary of it."

"Seems like everything related to this case gets lost," Jason observed.

"Yeah, well, I'd really like to see those notes."

"Was there a name on the sign-out?" Jason asked.

"Just a last name, Curran. I ran a search and came up with seven cops named Curran."

"OK, we can try to track that down the next chance we get. In the meantime – what have we got here?" Jason pointed across the street and down the block, where four figures were approaching on foot.

The conversation ended abruptly as Ray and Jason watched the four men. Two were large Black men, similar to the gangbangers who were arrested during the Webster Avenue chase. One was a tall, skinny Black kid who looked like he couldn't be more than eighteen. The fourth man was the one who made the detectives sit forward in their seats. He was white, wearing sunglasses, a heavy parka, and a New York Knicks knit hat pulled down low over his ears. It was mid-March, and the temperature that day was in the low 50s; not nearly cold enough to warrant the arctic outfit. It was, however, a terrific way to avoid being recognized. Ray took out a camera and snapped some pictures. The detectives slid down in their seats to avoid being seen by the gang, if that was who they were.

As they watched the four figures, Jason radioed for backup and asked for two black and whites to meet them without sirens. The four suspects turned into the gas station and approached the convenience store. When they disappeared inside, Jason and Ray exited the car and crossed the street, releasing the safeties on their service pistols. They took up positions on opposite corners of the small concrete building, sheltering behind the walls and peering around the corner and down the front of the building toward the front door. The plan was to wait for all four of the suspects to exit the building, then come up behind them, pinning them between the detectives and the uniformed officers who would be blocking the sidewalk on both sides with their squad cars. Once they were secure, they would check with Francois to see whether Ricky had just picked up a payment, in which case they would have probable cause to search all the suspects.

Both Jason and Ray scanned the street, waiting for the backup officers and wondering what was taking so long. While they were both looking at the street, the glass door swung outward and the first of the two large guys walked out. Ray ducked back behind the corner, but apparently not fast enough, because the big man turned in his direction and started walking toward the corner. As he did, the second big man came out, then the skinny kid, and finally the white guy, still wearing the sunglasses and parka.

The white guy called out, "Hey, Bo, where ya goin'?"

The first man, whom Jason now figured to be Bo, turned to reply. As he did, he made eye contact with Jason, who was watching from the far corner. Bo called out, "Cop!" and reached for his waistband.

Jason stepped out from his shelter and crouched with his gun held at arm's length. "Freeze! Police!" The other big man, who had been following Bo, spun around and looked at Jason, then dove to his left behind a group of trash receptacles arranged against the wall. The skinny kid reached out and grabbed the back of the white guy's coat, pulling him back toward the door. Jason did not want anyone going back into the store. He took two steps forward, then fired one shot at the ground in front of the skinny kid, hoping that would get him to stop moving. "I said freeze!"

At the same time, Ray sprang out from the opposite corner, realizing that their plan was blown. The suspects had completed their business inside the store quickly and the backup officers had not yet arrived. "He said freeze!" Ray called out.

Bo spun around and pointed a snub-nosed pistol at Ray. When Ray sighted back at him, he saw Jason over Bo's shoulder, in a direct line of fire. Ray hesitated just as Bo fired twice toward Ray's position. Bo was not a good shot, but one of the slugs ricocheted off the cinder block wall and hit Ray, who grabbed his head and fell to the ground.

Jason fired three shots into Bo's back and watched the man fall forward onto his face. Then Jason fired three more shots into the garbage cans where Bo's companion was taking shelter. He heard a groan and the clatter of the man's gun falling onto the cement, but didn't stop to investigate as he ran forward toward Ray. Meanwhile, the skinny kid and the man they figured was Ricky took off running toward the street. They rounded the corner just a few seconds before the first squad car pulled into the gas station. The officers swarmed out of their cars and drew their weapons, covering Jason as he crouched over Ray's prone form. Jason yelled, "Call for an ambulance!"

Two of the officers ran forward to the unmoving body of Bo, while two more hurried to Bo's companion, who was holding his bleeding gut next to the garbage can.

Jason was on one knee next to Ray, who was bleeding from the side of his head. "Stay still, Ray. The ambulance will be here in a minute."

Ray did not respond. Jason put two fingers on Ray's neck and felt a pulse. He wasn't dead. Jason pulled a handkerchief from his pocket and held it against the wound, then took off his jacket and rolled it up, putting it under Ray's head so it would not be resting on the concrete. The blood dripping down from the already soaked handkerchief stained the gray pinstripes, while Jason could do nothing but watch. The ambulance arrived a few minutes later. Jason stepped aside while the paramedics worked to stem the bleeding and got Ray onto a stretcher and into the vehicle. The EMTs were squeezing air into Ray's mouth and nose through an artificial respirator unit as they loaded him in and closed the doors. Jason sat on the curb in front of the store, staring at the empty gas pumps.

Chapter 21 – The Customer is Always Right

BRUNO FALSETTI WAS DOZING while listening to the Rangers' game on the radio. The lobby was empty and it was late enough that he didn't anticipate any more customers. There were three men inside and as soon as they all finished their business and left, he could shut down and go home. He had a girlfriend who was a nurse and worked until 10:00 p.m., so he was looking forward to a late dinner and chasing her around the bedroom. He was jolted from his semi-somnolence by a bang on the security door, which separated the hotel lobby from the interior.

He looked up and saw a man standing at the threshold, a suit jacket hanging over one arm and his dress shirt hanging partially out of his Yves St. Laurent trousers. The man had a pronounced middle-aged paunch and a mop of disheveled black hair. "Open the damned door!" he bellowed.

Bruno recognized the man as one of the three remaining customers and reached lazily for the buzzer that would open the door, but then stopped when he saw another figure running down the hallway. The girl was wearing a thin silk robe that was not entirely tied around her waist. Her auburn hair flowed behind her as she bounded down the hallway on bare feet. "Don't let him leave!" she shouted at Bruno.

"Open the door!" the man hollered again.

"What's the problem, Suzie?" Bruno asked the girl, who was grasping at the edges of her robe, trying to cover herself.

"He stiffed me and ran out," the girl said, sending a withering look towards the man standing at the door.

"Is that true? Did you not pay the lady?" Bruno asked with a thick Brooklyn accent.

"This bitch did not follow my directions, and I am not at all satisfied with the service," the man said with a haughty demeanor.

Bruno rolled his eyes and reached for his phone. "Just wait a minute." Bruno spoke into the phone, "Hey, get down to the front. We got a problem."

"I demand that you allow me to leave, or I will call the cops," the man said, brandishing his cell phone.

"Go ahead, dude," Bruno said. "Call the cops and tell them that you were not happy with the lady's services." That shut the man up for a moment, and then another man walked down the hallway and joined the discussion.

"What seems to be the problem?" Eddie asked as calmly as he could manage.

The man at the door turned to Eddie. "This young lady did not perform up to my expectations and I refuse to pay her," the man said.

Eddie sighed and turned to the redhead. "What did he want?"

Suzie put her hands on her hips and glared at Eddie. "He wanted anal and I told him it was extra."

Eddie turned to the man. "Anal is extra."

"That's ridiculous," the man responded. "I get the girl for my half hour and I do what I please. That's what I was promised."

Eddie dropped his head slightly, not really wanting to deal with this discussion. "I'm sorry that you were not entirely pleased, Mr. Gordon. I tell you what, I have another girl who will be happy to oblige for the same price. Would that be sufficient?"

"It's too late," Mr. Gordon said. "I'm done. I want to go home."

"I'm afraid that I must insist on payment," Eddie said. "What if we call it a half-price evening for you, and I'll make sure that on your next visit we give you a girl who will be more amenable? How about that?"

Gordon scowled, then reached into his pocket and dragged out a large roll of bills. He peeled off four one-hundred-dollar bills and handed them to Eddie with a grimace. "I am not happy about this," he said.

"I can understand that, Mr. Gordon. It is certainly your choice whether to come back, but I hope you do."

Gordon gave a hurrumph and turned back to the door without another word. Eddie gave a nod to Bruno, who pushed the button and buzzed open the door. Gordon pulled it open and walked out, then quickly exited through the lobby door and into the Brooklyn night.

Eddie looked at Suzie. "You couldn't just give him what he wanted?"

"Go fuck yourself, Eddie!" she spat back. "You're the one who told me we should charge the guys extra, so that's what I said and he got all upset and got dressed and walked out. What did you want me to do?"

"Fine," Eddie said dismissively. "Go to bed." The woman spun on her heel and walked back down the hallway. Bruno could not help but watch as she sauntered away, her exquisite ass swaying beneath the thin fabric of her robe.

"The customer is always right?" Bruno asked sarcastically.

"Fuck off," Eddie said, walking away.

Bruno checked off one of his three remaining customers, leaving him with two who still needed to leave before he could call it a night. He hoped that there would be no more fireworks.

Ж Ж Ж

Eddie walked back down the hallway toward room 111, which served as his personal office and home-away-from-home. He let himself in and surveyed his domain. On the downside, the place was a dump, with drab carpeting and furniture, dim lighting, a window that looked out at the back alley, and a pervasive smell of sweat. On the bright side, there were two long-legged blonde women sitting on opposite sides of the bed, finishing up the process of putting on their clothes. They both looked up as Eddie came in. Janice, the older of the two sisters, smiled at him and asked if everything up front was under control. Eddie confirmed that it was, and turned his attention to Sylvia, the younger sister, who was slipping on her heels while generally ignoring Eddie.

"You two should be in a movie," Eddie said enthusiastically. The women just laughed and shrugged. Eddie smiled and turned around, walking back to the hallway and then across to room 108. He used a key card to let himself in, allowing the door to slam behind him loudly before strutting into the main area of the room. "Those two girls from Florida are hot!" he said with a huge smile.

Lieutenant T. Warren Magnan looked up, removed the earbuds from his ears, and sighed. He ran his fingers through the graying hair around his ear and glowered at the smaller man, who had been an officer on his task force for more than four years. "You're cutting into our profit."

"Fuck that!" Eddie said with a grin. "If I can't at least enjoy myself sometimes, what the fuck is the point?"

"The point is to remain professional, achieve our financial objectives, and get out."

"Yeah, well my hour with those two blondes is not going to delay our exit," Eddie replied defiantly.

"You need to keep your focus. What would happen if you said something to one of those girls in the throes of ecstasy that might allow them to compromise you?"

"I'm smarter than that."

"Are you?"

Eddie fumed and clenched his fists. "Fuck you, Warren! I've busted my ass in this operation so I will do what I damned well please."

"Just be careful," the older man said calmly.

"I know. I know. I'm not in any hurry to do any more house-cleaning."

"See to it that you keep that in mind."

"Oh, so you know, Mr. Gordon paid half price tonight. He didn't want to pay extra for anal with Suzie and he tried to walk out without paying, but I handled it. Don't be pissed at Suzie for being short on her cash tonight." Eddie turned abruptly and started to walk out, but then stopped and turned back. "You know, I came along with you on this shit-bag operation because we agreed that we deserved the money and that nobody would get hurt. It's not like I give a shit about these drug addict bitches, but just remember who does the dirty work so you can count the money."

"Noted," Magnan replied flatly, reaching for his earbuds.

Eddie turned once again and left the room, allowing the door to slam behind him.

Chapter 22 – Routine Investigation

Friday, March 15

J ASON STOOD AT THE CONFERENCE ROOM WINDOW, gazing out at the gray clouds that hung low over Manhattan, obscuring the higher floors of the tallest buildings. A cold mist coated the ground with a shimmering wetness, but the temperature remained warm enough that the pedestrians were not sliding down the sidewalk. Jason was wearing his best charcoal suit with robin's egg blue pinstripes, a crisp white button-down shirt, and a multi-toned blue tie bearing a geometric block pattern. His body was tense and the veins on his neck were throbbing silently.

"You should sit down," Mike said calmly from his seat at the conference table. Captain Sullivan had briefed Mike about the shooting by phone. Ray had spent four hours in surgery before the doctors gave up. Sully was handling the notification of his family. Ray was not married and had only his mother, who lived on Long Island, and a sister in North Carolina. Jason had been spared the need to speak with the family; Sully had been concerned about what he might say to take the blame for Ray's death. Jason had already said it to

Sully, and the captain had told him to keep that to himself until after the Internal Affairs inquiry.

Jason was in the conference room with Mike because he was scheduled to meet with an officer from Internal Affairs. There was always an inquest when an officer shot anyone, including a suspected criminal. In this case, the internal investigation would include the circumstances under which an officer was killed in the line of duty. According to departmental protocol and the union contract, Jason was entitled to have a colleague or union representative present for the interview. Mike had volunteered for the duty. He had convinced Terry to squeeze his PT session in early so he could get downtown for the 10:00 a.m. meeting. Jason was glad to have his partner with him.

Before Jason had a chance sit down, the door opened. In walked a sullen-looking man holding a leather folio against his chest. "Good morning, Detective Dickson," the man said curtly. "I'm Agent Lucas Gomez, and I'll be conducting the preliminary inquiry." Gomez was short, probably not more than five-foot-five, with a dark complexion, black hair, and dark eyes. He had a thick scar running down the back of his left hand. Mike guessed him to be in his mid-thirties. "Is this your rep?" he asked Jason.

"Yes. This is Detective Mike Stoneman."

"I am familiar with Detective Stoneman," Gomez replied. Then, turning to Mike, he said, "Do you understand your responsibilities as Detective Dickson's representative during this inquiry?"

"I do," Mike said seriously, trying to get a read on this investigator. In Mike's experience, most of the officers who ended up in Internal Affairs were control freaks and had chips on their shoulders. This was understandable, since other officers viewed them as the quasi-enemy. They were on the wrong side of the thin blue line of solidarity that generally separated officers from everyone else. Cops protected each other, and the guys who tried to accuse other cops of wrongdoing were not appreciated. Mike's own view was that IA served an important purpose in rooting out bad eggs, who gave the rest of the department a bad rap and undermined public trust. But in this case, Mike was pretty certain that Jason was not guilty of any wrongdoing.

"Alright, let's get going. Detective Dickson, please take a seat."

Jason took a chair next to Mike, with investigator Gomez across the table, and assumed a stiff posture as if preparing to absorb a punishment. "I'm ready."

"Fine." Gomez placed a small digital recording device on the table and pressed a button, causing a red light to turn green, indicating that it was recording. "Please tell me what happened at the gas station."

"It was a convenience store," Jason replied simply, trying not to sound defensive.

"Was there a gas station there, Detective?"

"Yes, there was, but the target was the convenience store, not the gas station."

"Does it make a difference?"

"Yes, actually," Jason said. "The problem was trying to get the jump on our suspects after they came out of the convenience store. The plan was to let them exit the store and start walking back toward the street, then move in behind them and pin them between us and the uniformed officers who were supposed to be blocking the entrances."

"Were the officers and squad cars there?"

"No. That was the first problem. We had called for backup and we expected them to be there, but the suspects exited the convenience store before the uniformed officers were in place."

"Why didn't you abort the operation?" Gomez asked in a tone that Jason interpreted to be accusatory, as if he had already reached the conclusion that Jason had screwed up.

Jason bit his tongue and took a deep breath. He looked at Mike, who gave him a nearly imperceptible nod of his head and blew air out of his mouth in a silent whistle, his signal for Jason to stay calm and take his time. Then Jason turned back to Gomez. "We did not have communication in place. This was not an undercover operation. We didn't have earpieces or body mics. I had no way to give a direction to Detective McMillian. But even if I could have, I didn't think that aborting was required. We still had a substantial element of surprise and could come in behind them with our guns drawn. We should have been able to subdue them. This was a very important murder investigation and capturing this suspect was a high priority. I didn't think we needed to abort."

"What happened next?"

"I can't say for sure. I was at the corner of the building. When the door opened and I saw one of the suspects come out, I ducked back behind the wall so that he wouldn't see me. Remember, the plan was to come in behind them after they started walking away, so I planned to watch from behind the shelter of the building until the suspects came into my field of vision. Once they were twenty feet or so away from the convenience store, Detective McMillian and I would both come out with our weapons drawn and approach the group from behind. But I heard one of the suspects shout to Bo, asking where he was going. I could tell that the speaker was facing the opposite direction, so I peeked around the edge of the building to assess the situation. At that point, Bo turned around to respond to his companion, and he saw me. Bo called out 'Cop,' and his companion dove behind a group of trash receptacles lined up against the side of the building. I assumed this man had a weapon and that he would try to fire at me.

"When I turned my attention back to Bo, he had turned toward Detective McMillian's position. I saw Bo fire two shots in the direction of Detective McMillian. As soon as he did, I fired at Bo. I then saw the other man's gun, peeking out behind the trash cans and pointed in my direction. I fired two shots at his position, and I then ran toward Bo to secure him and to secure the other man's gun."

"Where were the other two suspects?"

"They had begun running toward the street."

"Did you make any attempt to apprehend them?" Gomez, who had been looking down at his pad of paper while taking notes, looked up at Jason to watch his response.

"No. My first concern was Detective McMillian, who was down. I needed to secure the other two men and make sure that Detective McMillian was properly supported. I could have fired at the fleeing suspects, but shooting them in the back would have violated departmental protocol." Jason stared defiantly at Gomez, who motioned for him to continue.

"I confiscated the gun from the man behind the trash cans and then the gun from the man called Bo, and then I went to where Ray was down. At about that time, the first black and white pulled up and I shouted to the officer to call for an ambulance."

"When you first saw the scene, before you shot the suspect, did you see Detective McMillian?" Gomez asked, focusing in on the critical part of the story.

"Yes. He was standing at the corner of the building. He had his weapon in his hand and pointed toward the suspect."

"Did Detective McMillian fire his weapon?"

"No." Jason looked directly into the eyes of the Internal Investigations officer. Gomez looked right back, with no anxiety or concern.

"Why is that, do you think, Detective? Why didn't your partner fire at the suspect before the man shot him?"

Mike jumped in before Jason could answer. "Agent Gomez, Jason can't evaluate what was going on in Detective McMillian's mind. It's probably best that he not speculate." Mike looked at Jason with a steady stare, hoping that his partner would get the message and shut up. Jason nodded.

"I can't really say, Agent Gomez." Jason clipped his response short and waited for the next question.

"At that moment, Detective Dickson, were you potentially in the line of fire if Detective McMillian had missed the suspect, or if the bullet exited the man named Bo and continued in your direction?"

Jason knew this was coming. He had spent the night before replaying the scene in his head over and over. Ray had seen him come around the corner. He had been directly in Ray's line of fire. Jason was sure that Ray hesitated for exactly that reason. It was a poor tactical decision to set it up like that, with each of them on opposite ends of the building, but they expected the men to come out and walk away without getting into a fire fight at the door. They wanted to approach the group from different directions in order to have the best angles to fire if they resisted as they were walking away from the store, and block them from running around the building. Jason had not anticipated the situation, and it had cost Ray his life.

"I'm not sure," Jason said softly. He remembered the instructions he had received from several district attorneys about testifying in court: If somebody asks you to speculate about something you don't actually know, say you don't know.

"And do you think that Detective McMillian might have delayed shooting at the suspect because you were in his line of fire?"

"Again, Agent Gomez," Mike cut in, "Jason can't know why Detective McMillian didn't shoot first."

Gomez shot Mike an annoyed look, but pursed his lips and did not speak. He knew Mike was correct, but he wanted to hear what Jason thought. He tried a different tactic. "Detective, do you think it was your fault that your partner got killed?"

Mike kicked Jason's leg under the table, causing him to visibly wince. Gomez shot Mike a withering look of reprobation. Mike just shrugged. Jason replied calmly, "Agent Gomez, that's the point of the inquiry. I expect that you and the others who are responsible for evaluating the facts will make that determination. I will wait to see what you think."

"You have no opinion?" Gomez pressed.

"Would I like to go back and do some things differently? Sure. I wish Ray had not been shot. I feel awful about it. But I can't say that it was my fault. It happened."

Gomez glared at Jason for a full minute before speaking again. Jason sat impassively, looking back, but trying not to show any emotion. Finally, the agent spoke again. "Do you have anything else you'd like to add, Detective?"

Jason paused and thought about it, then said, "No. I don't think so."

Gomez reached out to snatch the recorder off the table and switched it off. He stood up stiffly, said goodbye, and walked out without another word.

Mike immediately said, "Nice."

"What?"

"Nice job staying under control and not giving that asshole anything to hang you with."

"Thanks," Jason said, pushing back his chair and standing up. "Let's get out of here."

Before Jason took a step toward the door, Mike reached out and grabbed the sleeve of his suit jacket. "Hang on just a second."

"What?"

"We haven't really had a chance to talk about it. So, now that this meeting with IA is done, do you want to tell me?"

"Not really. Not now."

"What if we go pound down a few first?"

"Mike, I know you are still on leave, but I'm on duty."

"Fuck duty! Sully gave you the rest of the day off." Mike waved his hand in Jason's direction. "You need to take a few hours, or maybe a few days. Your partner just died. You're on desk duty anyway until the inquest is over, so what important paperwork will you be missing out on?"

"I'm fine," Jason said defensively.

"Like hell you are." Mike looked up at his partner, towering above him. "C'mon, you're coming with me."

"Is that an order?"

"Yes. Consider it a direct instruction, and also a request for a personal favor."

"How's that a favor to you?" Jason asked.

"Michelle keeps telling me that I need to open up more and share my feelings. I think this is an opportunity for me to do that and tell her that I took her advice."

"Oh yeah? So it's all about you, then?" Jason said with a smirk.

"Sure. It's all about me. Now, let's go."

Chapter 23 – Confessions and Connections

A HALF HOUR LATER, Mike and Jason walked into Mike's apartment on West 68th Street. They had stopped in at the deli on Amsterdam to get some sandwiches, which Mike was carrying in a white paper sack. He set the bag down on the table in his small dining alcove, then walked over to a cabinet and extracted two thick glass tumblers. He reached down and fished around in the lower half of the unit as Jason heard the clinking of glass against glass. Finally, Mike withdrew his hands, each of which held a bottle.

"You were serious about drinking, eh?" Jason observed.

"I'm not having this conversation sober, and neither are you." Mike set the two bottles down on the table.

The apartment was a typically small one-bedroom Manhattan affair, with a small bedroom, small bathroom, and tiny kitchen. But it had an unusually large living room area, half of which was partitioned off into a dining area with a table and six chairs next to a window looking out over the front of the building. The blond hardwood floorboards were worn by years of pacing footsteps. On the wall opposite the dining table hung a series of plaques memorializing police department awards and recognitions.

Mike uncorked the first bottle and poured a healthy portion of Johnny Walker Black Label into each glass.

"I'm not really much of a whisky drinker," Jason said, taking the glass and holding it up against the light coming in from the window.

"I know. I've been meaning to do something about that. There are times when being able to participate in the enjoyment of a good scotch will come in handy. There are men in the world who will judge you based on your appreciation for fine cigars and scotch. I've never been able to get into the cigars myself, but I can fake it pretty well. The scotch, however, I have come to appreciate on my own." Mike held up his glass and gave a salute. He said, "Cheers," and took a small sip, allowing the liquid to coat his tongue and fire off the taste buds all around his mouth.

Jason took a healthy swallow and grimaced as the alcohol burned the back of his throat. "Man," he choked out, "I know it makes for a strong drink, but I prefer vodka or tequila. They go down smoother."

"It's not about smooth on the first sip, my friend. But, we'll get there." Mike produced two plates and a pile of napkins and then extracted their sandwiches from the bag. As they ate and sipped their scotch, Mike asked Jason to give him a more detailed run-down on what really happened at the convenience store. Jason gave an accurate recounting, but left out the part when Ray's eyes had locked with his own, just as Ray had hesitated pulling his trigger.

When Jason was done, Mike pushed his plate away, bearing only crumbs and a few stray strands of fat from the corned beef. He downed the last of his drink and poured himself another round as Jason took a bite of his pastrami on rye. They sat in silence for a few minutes before Mike spoke again.

"I know what you're going through, Jason," Mike said with more compassion than Jason had ever heard in his voice.

"You don't know what I'm feeling," Jason shot back, annoyed at Mike's paternalistic attitude.

"That's where you're wrong. I know exactly what you're feeling."

"What's that supposed to mean?"

"Jason," Mike said, pulling back to a more controlled voice, "I never told you about how Darren got injured."

"Darren – that's your old partner, right?"

"Yeah. You've never met him."

"I heard around the precinct that he got shot on the job. He's on permanent disability, right?"

"Not permanent, yet," Mike said. "He's still in rehab, hoping to get back to active duty, but that's not the point. It was my fault that he got injured. He didn't die, but his career is basically over and it's my fault, so I do understand what you're going through."

Jason looked quizzically at Mike. "Ray's death is not my fault."

"Yeah. I know. It's not. But it is, because you were his partner, and you were responsible for him. You were together on the bust and it went bad, and you survived and he didn't. Your fault or not your fault, it's your responsibility. I know. It ate me up for months."

"What happened?" Jason asked, reaching out for the bottle of Johnny Walker Black.

Mike reached out quickly and grabbed the bottle, pulling it away from Jason. "I'll get to that, but for this story we need some better scotch." Mike put the Johnny Black down on the end of the table and reached for the other bottle. It was still sealed, and Mike had to peel back the foil from around the cork before he could remove it. The label was golden and read "The Macallan 18." Mike stood up, went to the small kitchen and returned with two fresh glasses and an 8-ounce bottle of spring water. He poured a small serving of the Macallan 18 into each glass, then added just a few drops of the water. He lifted the glass to his nose and breathed deeply, letting the smell of caramel and vanilla seep into his nostrils.

"Why add the water?" Jason asked.

"The guys who know about this stuff tell me that the water helps open up all the flavor in the scotch. I'm not sure I can tell the difference, but it's part of the ritual. When somebody offers you a really top-shelf scotch, you put a few drops of bottled water – never from the tap – into the glass. And you never add ice. It makes you seem like you know what you're doing."

"What makes this bottle so top-shelf?"

"Well," Mike said as he thought about the question. "First, it smells great, so give it a sniff and see." Jason obliged and nodded his affirmation that the scotch had a very pleasant aroma. "I got it as a gift from a liquor dealer after I finished up an investigation that involved his warehouse. A guy got run over with a forklift and we cleared all his workers of any criminal charges. I accepted this bottle, although departmental regulations probably would not have allowed it."

"Why not?"

"Because it's about a $300 bottle," Mike said simply.

Jason whistled softly. "Is it worth it?"

"Decide for yourself," Mike said, holding up his glass and taking a small sip that he let linger in his mouth for several seconds before swallowing. Jason followed suit, then whistled again.

"Man! That is so much smoother than the first bottle." Jason took another small taste of The Macallan 18 and smiled broadly. "I could get used to this."

"Don't get too used to it, but I'm glad you like it," Mike beamed. "You never start with the good stuff. Your taste buds need to get used to handling the whisky flavors before you can truly appreciate the finer scotch. At least, that's what I'm told. No matter what you're drinking, the second glass is easier than the first. And when the second is really high-quality stuff, then it's really good." Mike took another small sip and made a soft "wooo" sound as he exhaled a long breath.

"Is this the best you have?" Jason inquired.

"Yes," Mike responded. "I've had some even more expensive scotch at a friend's house, and some of it was better, to my taste at least, while some wasn't as good. But this is really good, so it's something I've kept unopened, waiting for the right occasion."

"Is a funeral really the right time?"

"We're not celebrating Ray's death," Mike said somberly. "We're toasting to the life of every good cop who went down in the line of duty. And we're drinking to busting the bastards who made it happen." Each man took another small sip. Mike put down his glass and looked across the table at Jason. "And I'm drinking with my partner, so I need to share the good stuff.

"I've been seeing the department's psychiatrist after my injury, and after I killed Randall. Now, everybody agrees that he had it coming and the inquiry on that shooting was quick and clean, thanks to you." Mike looked at Jason and nodded silently. "You had my back and, in the end, there was no question that the killing was justified as self-defense. Nobody shed any tears over the loss of the Righteous Assassin. But I had to go through the stupid therapy sessions so the psychiatrist could certify me as being mentally fit for return to duty. It's a pain in the ass, but between her and Michelle, they got me thinking that maybe sharing your feelings sometimes and not keeping everything all bottled up inside is healthy."

Jason sat back in his chair. "I'll drink with you, Mike, but I don't think I want to talk about my feelings."

"Fine. Then just listen." Mike got up from his chair and started walking toward the window as he spoke, not looking Jason in the eye. He had his glass in his hand and took a healthy hit of the warm amber liquid. "We were chasing down a double murder that looked to be gang-related. The victims were brothers and their parents told us they were both in with a bunch of thugs who were peddling drugs. It was small-time shit, but the idiots all got matching tattoos, so it was ridiculously easy to identify them. We figured that the brothers had crossed somebody, and the other gang members were the prime suspects or prime witnesses since they basically spent all their time together. We went to their hangout at a bar on the Lower East Side. We weren't there to arrest anyone. We just wanted to take their temperature and get a read on the personalities. It was a public place in the middle of the day. We didn't figure there would be any trouble, even if they were not likely to be very cooperative.

"Darren was a little too cocky and a little too sure of his own prowess with his pistol. We'd been together for about two years. I was working on getting him to be more cautious and to follow protocol in unknown situations. We even talked in the car about how we would handle it if any of the gang members got aggressive. It was my job as the senior detective to make sure he followed the plan and stayed under control. He had a tendency to be a cowboy and fly off the handle at times. He was reckless."

Mike turned around and finished what was left in his glass, then poured himself another, which he lifted and held in his hand as he resumed his story. Jason took the hint and poured himself more of the dark amber scotch and took another sip, savoring the mellow smoothness of this bottle. Mike was right – it was getting much easier to drink it the more he tried, and he was appreciating the complex flavors as he focused on Mike's story.

"We go in and start talking to one of the potential suspects when a little guy comes up to Darren. He couldn't have been more than five-foot-five, but he was chunky, kinda like Sully – a human fire plug, except this guy had about a dozen more tattoos." Jason chuckled at the description. "The little guy taps Darren on the shoulder and says something that I don't hear and the next thing I know Darren and this short guy are going at it. They fall onto a table and then onto the ground, punching and grabbing. I should have stepped in. I should have drawn my weapon and fired one into the ceiling to break it up and restore order. But I didn't. I let him take the guy. I guess I figured if Darren subdued the punk, he would make a point to these thugs and maybe win a little respect. Maybe it would get us some more cooperation. Maybe I just figured that Darren needed to learn a lesson about keeping his head and not getting into a fight in a room where we were outnumbered five to one. Maybe I was just pissed at him for not following my instructions. Shit – I don't really know what I was thinking."

Mike took another drink. He stared out the window at the fountain in front of the apartment building across 68th Street. A middle-aged woman in a heavy coat was walking her golden retriever down the pass-through to 67th Street. Mike could see the dog's hot breath against the still-cold March air. He didn't seem to be talking to Jason as much as to himself.

"The little guy had a gun on him and somehow got it drawn during the brawl without me or Darren seeing it. Darren was on top of him, pummeling his face. I was just about getting ready to step in and call it a TKO when I heard the shot. Darren rolled off the guy onto the floor, holding his leg. I drew my gun, pointed it at the guy, and told him to drop his and freeze. A couple of his buddies made a move toward me and I shot one of them in the foot, which stopped him and got everybody else's attention. I called for backup and an ambulance. The rest of the scumbags ran while I stayed with my injured partner. They all got away, including the guy with the shot-up foot. I sat on the little guy who shot Darren and helped Darren use a tablecloth to wrap up his leg until the EMTs showed up.

"The bullet went in through the back of his thigh, ripping up his hamstring. Then it smashed into the back of his kneecap and lodged there. Poor guy had nerve damage, ligament damage, and loss of muscle tissue after the surgery. He needed a knee replacement and has been rehabbing ever since, but that's just a dodge to keep him on active disabled status. He's not likely to get cleared for duty again.

"I know his wife and kids. They're a sweet group. Darren was a good cop – is a good cop. He was stupid, sure, but I put him in that situation and I didn't step in when I could have. It was my job to train him to avoid putting himself in the line of fire. I should not have let it happen. He didn't die, but his career is over. So, I know a little bit about how you're feeling. You're feeling guilty. You think you shouldn't have let it happen. You think you were supposed to protect your partner and instead you let him get shot. I get it. I think about how I let him down all the time. It eats at me. For a while, it distracted me from doing my job. To tell you the truth, it wasn't until Sully assigned me to work with you that I got back to any sense of focus. I was sure as hell not going to make the same mistakes with you."

Jason took another drink, realizing that he was starting to feel the effects of the alcohol. He let the silence linger in the room to make sure that Mike was done talking, for the moment. "Is that why you were such a hard-ass with me?"

Mike turned around to look at Jason. "Yes. I had my other reasons, you know, but the main thing was that I was going to be God-damned sure you stayed inside the lines and followed procedure. You tried to get creative and I slapped you down. I did not want another partner going down on my watch."

Jason was silent for a minute. He drained his glass and thanked Mike for sharing the good bottle. "Your old partner, Darren, his last name is Curran, right?"

"Yeah, why?"

153

"Nothing important," Jason replied absently, trying to remember the details of the Christine Barker investigation in his alcohol-impaired state. "I saw the name Curran on a file I was reading. It might not have been him."

"Yeah," Mike agreed. "Curran is not exactly a rare Irish name for a New York cop."

For the next hour, Jason and Mike sat in Mike's dining alcove drinking through half of Mike's good bottle of Macallan 18 and talking. The more they drank, the more Jason admitted how guilty and angry with himself he felt after Ray's death. When Jason reached the point that he had trouble putting on his jacket, Mike walked him to the lobby and had the doorman get a cab to take him home. Mike went back upstairs and took a long nap. He dreamed about that day in the bar when Darren got shot. It was not the first time.

Chapter 24 – Early Returns

Monday, March 18

BY MONDAY MORNING, Mike had recovered from the hangover after his scotch binge with Jason. He arrived at the physical therapy room early. When Dolores arrived, she berated him good-naturedly for taking time off from his rehab. She bragged about how much progress she had made while Mike was galivanting around.

When Terry walked in, Mike said seriously, "I have to confess, Terry. I cheated on you with another therapist while I was away."

"Really?" Terry replied, skeptically. "Well, let's see what you got."

Mike did his best to present a positive attitude during the session, and worked as hard as he could to demonstrate strength in his shoulder muscles. But when it came time to be manipulated and stretched on the table, Mike's flexibility and range of motion was not as good as it had been before his trip to Washington. He grumbled, but had to admit that Dolores was well ahead of him and was likely to win their bet.

Ж Ж Ж

After the rehab session, Mike took the subway downtown to the NYPD's weapons range so that he could get in some shooting practice. He knew that he would need to re-certify as competent with his weapon before he'd be cleared for active duty. Fortunately, firing a pistol required only straight-arm action with his left arm and didn't involve lifting the arm over his head, which would be a problem at this point in his rehab. He spent a half hour with his Glock and also broke out a strategic assault rifle used by the SWAT team, just for some practice. His shoulder was aching when he was through, but he was generally pleased with his accuracy. Mike whispered a thanks, for the hundredth time, that it was his left shoulder and not his right that was injured.

When Mike removed his protective gear and retrieved his phone from a locker at the shooting range, he saw a text message from Captain Sullivan. The message just said for Mike to call, which he did as soon as he found a quiet location.

Sully was typically direct. "Stoneman, we've decided to bring you back to active duty sooner than planned because of Detective McMillian's death. You'll be on restricted duty until you're medically cleared, but I want you back with Dickson tomorrow. I'm a little worried about how he'll react to the situation, so having you around should help. He's on desk duty until the inquiry is over, so you two can do paperwork together."

"OK, Captain," was all Mike said in response. "I'll see you in the morning."

Ж Ж Ж

The next day, Mike strolled in to the precinct building, just like he had done for the past seventeen years. He stopped off at the food vendor cart on 94th and Broadway for a bagel and cream cheese and a coffee, and hopped up the four steps to the door with the bag holding his breakfast and his coffee clutched in his left hand. As he reached for the door handle, he nodded to George Mason, one of the other homicide detectives, who was leaning against the side of the building, wearing a down parka and munching on a muffin. When Mike pulled the door open, Mason called out to him.

"Hey, Mike! Nice to see you back. Where the fuck do you think you're going with that bag?"

Mike laughed and smiled at his colleague. "I'm thinking about going inside to my desk."

"What's in the bag?"

"A Cadillac Coupe de Ville, what do you think?" Mike took a step into the vestibule.

Mason reached out and grabbed the back of Mike's coat, holding him back. "Not so fast, Mister Senior Detective," Mason called out playfully. "We're still operating under a food ban."

"Oh, Christ. The rats. The no food thing is still a thing?"

"Yep. The exterminators have been in twice, but until we're cleared out there's a strict no-food policy in the building. Leave it outside, bro."

"Oh, that sucks!" Mike exclaimed. He took a step back from the door and handed Mason his white paper bag. "Here, knock yourself out." He took his coffee cup and went into the building, leaving Mason on the stoop, munching his muffin and holding Mike's bagel bag. Mike walked in and took the stairs up to the bullpen on the third floor. He was greeted warmly by the officer behind the intake desk on the first floor, and by several officers on the stairs, and by nearly everyone on the third floor. He had been back in the precinct to visit while he was out on disability, but everyone knew that this was his actual return to work. Mike smiled broadly as he waved to his colleagues. One of the beat cops he knew flashed him a "V" for victory sign with two fingers. Fellow homicide detective Steve Berkowitz wished him "Mazel Tov." Jason got up from his desk and walked over to Mike's space to shake his hand and welcome him back.

Mike and Jason barely had time to let go of each other's hands before Captain Sullivan appeared at the door to his office and bellowed out, "Dickson, Stoneman, I'd like to see you both. Now!" Sullivan disappeared back into his lair. Mike and Jason exchanged resigned glances, shrugged, and shuffled off toward the captain's office. Mike still carried his coffee cup.

Jason sat down in the one chair in the office that wasn't covered with debris. Mike stood behind him, calmly sipping his coffee. "I see that you haven't cleaned up in here since I've been gone," Mike observed casually.

"Don't start pitching me shit already, Stoneman," Sully responded gruffly, but couldn't help cracking a smile for just a second, before regaining control of his facial expression. "Listen up. I got a call from IA today and the inquiry over McMillian's death is finished. Jason is clear to return to full active duty." He paused to look at Jason, who nodded, but said nothing. Mike patted Jason's shoulder encouragingly.- "Now, Mike, you are not yet cleared for full duty. You can't carry a weapon until you get recertified. You can go out into the field, but let's try not to get into any fights or situations where you're going to reinjure yourself before you're fully recovered. Is that clear?"

Mike opened his mouth to respond, but Sully cut him off. "No bullshit, Stoneman. I mean it. If I hear about you doing anything stupid out there, I'll revoke your permission to be in the field and you'll sit at a desk until I have a doctor's certification. You got that!?"

Once again, Mike opened his mouth, ready to give the captain an affirmative response. Before he made a sound, Jason piped up, "I'll make sure he doesn't do anything stupid, Captain."

"Thanks," Mike said sarcastically. "It's good to know that somebody will be looking out for me."

"That's it," Captain Sullivan said dismissively, looking down at some paperwork on his desk. Mike and Jason knew the drill. Jason got up and led the way out the door and back into the bullpen. They walked to Jason's desk.

"Can I borrow your gun?" Mike deadpanned.

"Fuck you," Jason shot back with a chuckle.

A half hour later, Mike and Jason, along with Steve Berkowitz and George Mason, were in the conference room off the bullpen along with a stack of folders and two cardboard boxes. The cases that Jason and Ray were working at the time of Ray's shooting had been redistributed to other detectives, but mostly to Steve and George on the assumption that they would be sent back as soon as Jason cleared the Internal Affairs inquiry. Now, George and Steve handed back the files that were still active, and the four detectives haggled about trading off two dog cases for one easy-to-close case file. When they were done, Berkowitz and Mason left, leaving Mike and Jason to review the files.

"We haven't had much of a chance to talk about the Christine Barker case," Mike began. "I told you about our meeting out west with Christine's sister. We're pretty sure that this overdose was not voluntary and that Christine was murdered."

"We?" Jason said, raising his eyebrow as high as it would go.

"Yeah, me and Doctor McNeill."

"Is Doctor McNeill your partner now?"

"You know what I mean."

"I do, but I'm not sure that the M.E. should have authority to determine how we investigate our cases."

"Of course not," Mike protested, "but it was Michelle who noticed the irregularities in the autopsy and called it questionable. She has really been interested in this case."

"Why is that?"

"It doesn't really matter. I'm as convinced as she is that this was no accidental overdose, and it wasn't a suicide. I know that the case got reassigned downtown to the Vice unit, but I think we should try to get it back."

"Not likely," Jason said simply. "When Sully told me to send them copies of our files, it was pretty clear that the order came from way over his head. He's not going to have the authority to give it back to us."

"We may be able to change that," Mike offered. "Were you able to get any information on the locations where Christine spent the Starbucks gift cards that her sister sent her? If we know where she was buying coffee, that might help us."

"Sure. It might," Jason said without conviction. "Or it may just tell us where she was getting her coffee without leading us anywhere else. Or she could have sold them to somebody or traded them for drugs and we'd end up chasing down some schmuck who likes coffee. What are we going to do, initiate an unauthorized investigation and start interviewing baristas about whether they recognize her and can tell us where she went after her visits?"

"Don't joke about it or I might make us do it."

"That will be hard since you can't drive."

"You're a bastard."

"I know. Until you get cleared, I've got the keys and we go only where I drive us."

"We could take the subway."

Jason paused. "I don't think the captain would want you to be that exposed. You might fall down the stairs and dislocate your shoulder." Jason reached over and planted a soft punch on Mike's left arm.

"Ow," Mike protested. "Be gentle with a cripple."

"You're such a bullshitter," Jason scolded. "I saw you carry that file box into the room with your left arm. I know you're fine."

"Fine. I've still got more PT sessions, but you're right about that. So don't treat me like I'm broken. We need to work this just like always. I'm back, so let's make some progress on this dog."

"There was one thing," Jason said, pausing to make sure Mike was focused. "I may have mentioned this to you last Friday. In the file on Christine Barker, we found a reference to an unusual interrogation. She was in the lock-up after being arrested for drug possession. Normally she'd get cut loose the same night, or maybe first thing the next morning. It was a nothing bust, with no extenuating circumstances. But she was held overnight. The next day, she was signed out of the lock-up for an interrogation. The name on the sign-out was Curran."

"I remember." Mike said. "I wonder how many cops there are on the force named Curran?"

"Ray said he checked and found seven," Jason said. "The thing is, there's no record of the interrogation. No notes, no summary of what she said about where she got the drugs. The file is empty. It looks like whoever it was wanted to lean on the girl without leaving behind a record."

"That would mean a cop," Mike observed.

"Yeah. I know. It would mean that somebody within the department was involved and didn't want his involvement to be recorded."

"We'll need to keep an eye on that angle," Mike said. "Were there any irregularities in the records from Christine's prior arrests?"

"No. Nothing that stands out. But you remember I told you about the unusual circumstances of her last arrest, too. The files don't make sense."

"Yeah. Not much about this investigation makes sense," Mike agreed.

Chapter 25 – Public Relations

Wednesday, March 20

THE NEXT DAY, MIKE WAS BACK in the bullpen after his PT session, still without a bagel. He was making calls to line up witness interviews in a case on which Ray McMillian had been taking lead. It was fairly routine, although Mike always said that no homicide is ever routine to the families – or the victim. In this case, the dead guy had allegedly picked a fight in a SoHo bar that had a tough reputation. He and another man ended up in the space between the bar and the adjoining building, where he fell, or was pushed or thrown, and split his head open against a fire hose stand pipe. He was dead before the EMTs arrived. Amazingly, not a single person at the scene knew who the other guy in the fight was. Mike had placed a half-dozen calls to employees of the bar and witnesses who had been identified by the officers who had responded to the scene. He was waiting for call-backs from several of them when his desk phone rang.

"Detective Stoneman," he said in a moderately friendly tone.

"Detective! Very nice to speak with you again. This is Dexter Peacock from *The Times*. I know how willing you are to work with the press on important issues and I wanted to arrange a time to speak to you and Detective Dickson."

Mike held the receiver away from his face and scowled. Mike had exploited Peacock's willingness to be fed information during the investigation of the Righteous Assassin and had allowed the reporter to break some key facts in the story, when having those facts in the public domain was helpful. Peacock had developed an annoying sense of entitlement about calling to mine for information during the rest of that case. Mike suspected that he had been champing at the bit during Mike's absence from active duty, waiting for his next opportunity to take advantage of the relationship he thought he had. As much as Mike would love to shut him down, there was also the possibility that he might want to use this backdoor into the press in the future. So, he resisted the urge to hang up.

"Mister Peacock," Mike said in a friendly voice, "nice to hear from you. You know that I'm only just yesterday back on active duty, right?"

"Yes, I heard that, Detective. Very nice that you're back earlier than expected. Was that because of the tragic death of Detective Ray McMillian?"

"I don't think I'm going to comment about that," Mike said as calmly as he could manage while seething.

"Well, that's fine, Detective. But part of the reason I'm calling is that a source of mine told me that the internal investigation has cleared Detective Dickson of any negligence or wrongdoing in his partner's death. I was hoping that, now that the investigation is over, he might be willing to give an interview and tell the story of the heroic actions of Detective McMillian. It's a story people want to hear and, so far, we've been unable to get any details. Well, now that the investigation isn't ongoing anymore, I think it's time the real story gets told. Don't you agree?"

Mike again removed the receiver from his ear and took a deep breath, steadying himself before responding. Mike had to hand it to Peacock; he almost believed for a second that the reporter was seriously interested in writing a positive story about a heroic cop cut down in the line of duty. Mike dismissed the idea as impossible and put the phone back to his face. "Mister Peacock, I appreciate your interest, but I don't think Detective Dickson is going to be giving an interview about that, at least not for a while. I'd appreciate it if you would not try to contact him directly."

"No, no, no, of course not," Peacock soothed. "I would not do that during such a sensitive time. That's why I called you, and I certainly appreciate your position. If you or Detective Dickson change your mind and want to get that story out, you know you can count on me to be sympathetic and supportive. And speaking of that, I've also been thinking about the story of your rehabilitation after your serious injury, inflicted by Ronald Randall, and your triumphant return to duty. That would also be a spectacularly interesting story that New Yorkers would love to hear. And since it seems you have been pressed back into active duty sooner than expected due to Detective McMillian's untimely death, I see all kinds of intriguing human-interest angles here. Do you think that I might have the opportunity to speak with you about that?"

"I'm flattered, certainly," Mike responded in what he hoped was an appropriately encouraging voice. "Right now, I'm very busy trying to get back into the duties of a detective and I really don't want to distract myself from that process at the moment."

"Well, I understand, Mike."

Mike flinched and grimaced at the oily reporter's attempt at familiarity.

"Perhaps after a few weeks back on the job you'll be ready. I'm absolutely sure that the reading public would be fascinated to hear your story, including perhaps some of the never-before-disclosed details about your personal confrontation with the Righteous Assassin."

Mike wondered if Peacock actually believed his own bullshit, because he was remarkably convincing. "Thanks. I appreciate the offer. I will reach out to you if I decide that the time is right."

"Fine, fine. Thank you for your time, Detective. I'm sure we'll be talking again soon, and you feel free to call me any time there are issues you think the public needs to know." Peacock disconnected the call, depriving Mike of the pleasure of slamming the receiver down on him. Mike sat in his chair, staring at the handset and fuming about the conversation until the phone rang again and he punched the flashing button to answer.

"Stoneman!" he barked, then immediately apologized to the witness who was returning his call.

Later, when Mike and Jason were both getting a coffee refill, Mike told his partner about the call from the reporter. "I hope you don't mind that I stonewalled him on your behalf," Mike said.

"No. You can shut down that asshole for me anytime."

Chapter 26 – Strange Bedfellows

Monday, March 25

THE FOLLOWING MONDAY, JASON AND MIKE went down to the basement records room to have a chat with Sophie. She was so happy to see Mike in the building that she actually got off her stool, came around the counter, and gave him a big hug.

"Careful, now, Sophie. You can't be squeezing that shoulder too hard or I'll never finish my rehab," Mike scolded her playfully.

"Oh, go on, you old goat. Nothing can slow down an old mutt like you," she said with her Jamaican accent, which Mike always thought sounded like someone who was British, but lived in New Orleans. She slapped him hard across his left arm as she finished. Mike flinched, but didn't outwardly acknowledge the stab of pain he felt in his shoulder. He did make a mental note not to miss his next PT appointment. He had blown off the last one on the pretense that he was too busy with the transition back to active duty, but that pain made him remember that he was not fully recovered yet.

Jason took a step to get close to Sophie and asked, "Can a brother get some of that?" He gave her a hug, while turning his head and

167

winking at Mike. When he broke away, he said, "You remember those files that Ray and I were looking for?"

Sophie's big smile instantly disappeared. "Oh, that's such a shame about Ray. I didn't know him, in fact I don't think he ever came down. But still, such a shame."

"Thanks, Sophie. It's a tough one."

"How are you managing?" the older woman asked with motherly concern. Sophie felt like she was responsible for all the younger officers, but in particular she acted like a surrogate parent to the Black and Hispanic cops.

"I'm getting along fine," Jason replied. Then he added, "Mike here has helped."

Mike cocked his head, surprised that Jason would share that, and marveling at Sophie's ability to get others to open up and talk to her. That's why she was the queen of workplace gossip. "Detective Dickson is handling the situation very professionally," Mike said.

"Well, ain't no one ever handled losing a partner without some sleepless nights, Honey, so don't you worry if you got some nightmares. You come down and talk to ol' Sophie any time."

"Thanks, Sophie. The department has a psychiatrist, but if I need somebody who really knows what they're talking about, I'll be sure to come down here." He smiled warmly at Sophie, who beamed back at him as her smile returned.

"Now, what about those files?" she said as she walked back behind the counter and sat back down on her stool. She muttered something that Mike and Jason could not hear as she tapped keys at her desktop computer. "What was the day I said I put in that transfer request?" She asked Jason.

"You said it was February 19," Jason responded. Mike and Jason stood like statues, waiting for Sophie.

"That's so very odd," she mumbled, reaching for her mouse and tapping additional keys. After a minute, she threw up her hands in disgust and turned toward the two waiting detectives. "I can tell you that those files are probably not coming," she said, obviously annoyed.

"Why not?"

Sophie frowned at her computer screen. "The two files that were supposed to be in Central were signed out to archiving to be scanned into the electronic file system. Well, archives says they can't find the files, and after archives finishes with files, they burn them so that the confidential information doesn't get thrown in the trash where somebody could find it. So, if they say they can't find them, we may never see them."

"What about the other one," Jason asked, "the one from the precinct in Queens?"

"The records clerk there said she couldn't find the file, and that was two weeks ago. The most recent note was from three days ago, and it says that they've exhausted all avenues and the file is irretrievably lost."

They all exchanged looks of frustration, but nobody offered any options. Mike thanked her and he and Jason went back up the stairs. Mike muttered something about the perils of undue reliance on technology. Jason just said that Mike sounded like an old fogie.

"There is another possibility," Mike said as he climbed the first flight of steps.

"Yeah, I know," Jason said, keeping his breathing regular despite the exertion of the climb. "It's quite a coincidence that the files on these three allegedly unrelated overdose deaths suddenly all come up missing. It's like somebody is hiding them and covering their tracks, but that would mean that the people involved are inside the department."

"Yeah," Mike said, panting slightly and trying to suppress his heavy breathing. "That would be a problem."

When they reached the third floor, Mike stopped at the landing to catch his breath.

Jason asked, "If these other cases were somehow related, and the perps are covering their tracks, why were we able to get Christine's file?"

Mike drew in a deep breath before trying to speak. "Well, none of those other cases were identified as homicides." Mike had to pause again, but then continued. "It's possible that they just didn't have a chance to expunge or hide Christine's file yet."

"So, the good news is that it's possible to get ahead of them," Jason said. "Now all we have to do is stay ahead of them."

"Let's not jump to any conclusions. There might not be any 'them'."

"Yeah, I know. But then again, there might be."

Ж Ж Ж

Later in the day, Mike made a call to the sergeant in charge of the lockup at central booking in Brooklyn. The sergeant, named O'Neill, did not immediately recognize the name Curran. O'Neill speculated that it might have been someone visiting from another district. He said a lot of detectives from Manhattan came through talking to their detainees.

At the end of the discussion, Mike asked O'Neill to pull the electronic records of badge swipes in the security system for the relevant date so that they could get an ID number for the mysterious Officer Curran. O'Neill agreed, but let Mike know that since the date was more than thirty days ago, pulling the data off of the archive server would take some time. Mike thanked him and said that it was not a priority matter that required a rush on the archives. There was no need for anyone to contact Captain Sullivan to inquire about it.

Ж Ж Ж

The next day, Mike's desk phone rang. The LED readout said "number blocked," but he answered anyway, hoping it was not some kind of junk call. "Stoneman," he said gruffly into the receiver.

"Detective Mike Stoneman?" the caller asked.

"Yes."

"This is Agent Lucas Gomez, from Internal Affairs. We met a few weeks ago, when I was interviewing Detective Dickson."

Mike paused, wondering why the IA investigator was calling him now. Was he looking for some comment about Jason? "I remember you," Mike said warily. He did not want to engage in any small talk with this guy.

"Good. I'm calling because of a request I reviewed for information about another officer. I understand the request came from you, regarding Detective Darren Curran."

Again, Mike paused. He had not specifically inquired about Darren – only about the identity of the cop who was signed in as Curran at the lockup. "Why do you ask?"

"Detective, any time there is a request for private data about a police officer, it gets reviewed by Internal Affairs. Can I ask why you're seeking this data on Detective Curran?"

"I didn't actually request information on Darren," Mike said, trying not to show any particular emotion, although he was apprehensive. Had Gomez already checked the electronic records and determined that his old partner's ID was used to log out the prisoner? How could that be possible? Darren had not been on active duty for eighteen months, and certainly would not have had any reason to interrogate an inconsequential detainee in Brooklyn.

"Detective Stoneman, I'm curious, really more than just a little curious, why you are looking into these records. I know that Detective Curran was your partner before his injury. I've looked into the case file for that matter, and it seems strange that Detective Curran would be engaged in any police activity, since he's still out on a disability leave."

Mike paused, trying to put together the pieces of this puzzle in his head. "Agent Gomez, I'm as confused as you are about how the record could show Darren Curran as the one who signed out this detainee. It makes no sense. I'm going to look into it, but until you just told me, I didn't know the record was for him – I assumed that it had to be another officer named Curran."

"Well, Detective, now you know. We're going to have some work to do if we're going to unravel this little mystery."

"We?"

"Yes. You will be assisting me with my investigation," Gomez said in a matter-of-fact voice. "I trust that will not be a problem?"

"No. No problem at all," Mike said flatly.

"Good. In that case, please meet me tomorrow morning in my office. I find that when I show up at a precinct, silly rumors start to fly around. It's more distraction than it's worth."

"Sure," Mike agreed, "I understand that perfectly. Detective Dickson and I will meet you in the morning."

"Fine. I look forward to working with both of you." With that, Gomez terminated the call, leaving Mike holding his receiver and staring at it as if it were a hostile reptile.

Chapter 27 – Facing the Inevitable

Tuesday, March 26

THE NEXT MORNING, MIKE AND JASON walked into the Internal Affairs office at police headquarters in lower Manhattan. Even the act of walking through the IA doors could result in gossip within the department, but they were both resigned to the necessity of the situation. Agent Gomez personally came out to the cramped entry foyer to meet them and shook hands warmly with both detectives.

"I trust that there are no hard feelings after my role in the investigation into Detective McMillian's death," Gomez said, looking up confidently at Jason's eyes.

"Not at all," Jason replied graciously. "You were just doing your job. If you had found that I was at fault, I'd have a different attitude."

"Fair enough," Gomez said with a slightly forced laugh. "Now, let's get down to business." Gomez led Mike and Jason inside the suite of offices and to a long table in the middle of an open space. He sat down and gestured to Mike that he should sit in the adjoining chair.

"We're going to talk about this out here in the open?" Jason asked.

"Detective, this entire office handles confidential internal investigations. There is no worry about secrecy and discretion."

Jason sat across from Mike and both detectives stared at Gomez, waiting for him to direct the discussion. They were hesitant to volunteer anything, even in the absence of a pending investigation. Just being inside the IA sanctum made them nervous. The apprehension was based more on the general dread of being under investigation than on any actual sense of guilt or fear. The Inquisitor didn't need actual evidence of wrongdoing to ruin a cop's career.

Gomez opened up a very thin laptop and input a password. After navigating to the page he wanted, he looked up at Mike. "Tell me, Detective Stoneman, why you were searching the records of the detainee log-out involving Detective Curran."

"Since we're working together on this, can we drop the formality and use first names?"

"Sure. I'm Lucas."

"Thanks. So, like I told you before, we didn't know that it was Darren Curran. We just had the name Curran and we were tracking it down."

"Why was it important?"

Jason cut in. "My partner – my former partner – Ray, was the one who flagged it, Lucas. As part of our investigation into the Christine Barker homicide."

"Have you concluded that the Barker girl was murdered?"

"We're working on that assumption," Jason said tersely. "There's enough evidence to warrant working under that theory until it's proven wrong. We were examining the file on one of her arrests and we noticed an unusually long period of detention, and then an interrogation that didn't make sense and for which there was no record. We wanted to talk to the officer or detective who interrogated her."

"Why would Detective Curran interrogate this girl?" Lucas asked.

"He didn't," Mike responded. "Darren Curran is rehabilitating from major knee surgery and has not been on active duty for eighteen months."

"I know," Lucas said calmly. "But he's still in active status with an active identification card, so it is possible that he did go to the lock-up to talk with this girl."

"Possible, but it didn't happen," Mike said firmly.

"How can you possibly know that?"

"Because Darren was my partner. I know him, and I've seen him recently at the gym working on his rehab, and there is simply no possible way that he was involved in any investigation."

"I know that he was your partner, Detec – Mike. I know that you think you know him, but please put aside your personal relationship with him and focus on the facts. His ID badge was used to access the secure area at the station and his name is in the log-out book. How else would you explain those facts?"

"I can't explain it," Mike conceded, "but if someone else had Darren's ID card, he could have swiped in with it and put Darren's name in the book."

"Why would someone do that?" Jason asked, drawing a quick stare-down from Mike as if Jason was not supporting him.

"To hide his identity," Lucas offered.

"Right," Mike agreed. "And if someone was hiding their identity inside the station, and if that person is a cop, then we've got something very fishy going on."

"Was there anything unusual about Miss Barker, other than that she was later found dead?"

"There was," Jason said. "The last time she was arrested, she had an unusually long stay in lock-up. That time, there was no record of anyone speaking to her, which is also odd. Then, she was cut loose with no charges, despite an outstanding warrant. In that case, she gave a false name, but that doesn't seem to explain what happened."

"So, now that you have the information about the swipe-in and log entry for Detective Darren Curran, what would be your next line of inquiry?"

"I suppose I would want to check the department's records to see if there were any other swipe-ins by Darren's ID, to see if there were any patterns." Mike looked at Jason, who nodded his agreement.

"I agree," Lucas said. "I have already asked our IT team to run a report on that ID card. I expect that we'll have it very soon. In the meantime, can I offer you a donut?"

"You have no idea," Jason said, smiling.

Ж Ж Ж

An hour later, Mike and Jason had mostly put away their apprehension about Agent Gomez. They talked through the Christine Barker investigation and all the possible angles that they could still investigate. But they always came back to the fact that it was the medical examiner's observations about the body that originally raised the suspicion of homicide, and the other three similar cases were their best leads. The case files for the women were still somehow lost. Lucas said he had encountered cases before where someone had tampered with files. He had seen dirty cops try to cover their tracks by falsifying records, but he did not recall entire files being spirited away. Three files related to the same case all turning up missing was definitely suspicious.

When the discussion started to peter out, Mike decided to take a few swings at the hard outer shell of Agent Gomez. "You sound like a native New Yorker," Mike prompted.

"Yeah, that's right. Born and raised in the Bronx. I practically grew up at Yankee Stadium."

"I won't hold that against you," Mike quipped good-naturedly. "How did you find your way to Internal Affairs?"

Lucas hesitated, as if assessing how much he wanted to share with these two relative strangers. "I was never comfortable in my assignments. I got pushed around for several years after making detective. I always felt like I was held back because I'm Latino. I finally got fed up and when the chief from IA came to see me, I figured that if other cops were going to treat me like shit, I might as well give them a reason."

"When did you make detective?"

"I was twenty-eight. I got to IA just after my thirtieth birthday, which was five years ago now."

"Are you looking to get out?" Mike continued to press.

"No. I think I've found a good spot here. It's not just an assignment, it's more like a calling. Are you a religious man, Detective Stoneman?"

"Not really."

"I didn't think so. I remember taking one of your procedure classes when I was studying for the detective exam. You made a comment about a cop needing to be objective and not to let emotion or prejudice or superstition cloud his judgment. You seemed to have little use for faith."

"I suppose that's true," Mike conceded.

"Well, I was raised Catholic and I am still devoted to the faith. We are taught that there is good and evil – right and wrong. The good must fight to overcome evil every day. That's why I think I'm in the right place. I fight for the right. It reinforces my faith."

"Don't you think there are times when right and wrong are ambiguous?" Jason asked. "I mean, there's a lot of gray out there in the world."

"Not for me," Lucas said confidently. "There is always a line. If you cross the line, you break the code and the oath you took as a police officer. You do that, and I will root you out and make sure that the light of truth shines on you."

Mike and Jason exchanged an extended glance. Then Mike said, "Well, I will agree to disagree with you on that one, Lucas. In my career, I have experienced moments of moral ambiguity."

"That is because you lack the clarity of faith, Detective."

Before they could continue the existential discussion, a small bell tone sounded from Lucas' computer and he looked down. "Ah, we have the report in."

Lucas downloaded a spreadsheet as Mike and Jason crowded around the small screen. The top of the sheet said "Curran, D" and had Darren's badge number and eight-digit NYPD ID. Below were columns of data, which Lucas immediately started sorting and manipulating. He hid several columns and added grid lines. After less than two minutes, Lucas sat back and gazed at his handiwork.

"Here is the log-in at the lockup when Miss Barker was interrogated," he said, pointing to a line part-way down the page. "I assume you tried to pull the video from the interrogation room for that day?"

"Sure we did," Jason quickly responded. "There wasn't any."

"Another odd fact, eh?" Lucas observed.

"Yes. But we were told that it isn't uncommon for the officers to use their interrogation rooms for lawyer conferences because of a lack of meeting space. So, they have the video system turned off as a default and they turn it on when they have an interrogation."

"Makes sense, but it's very convenient for our mystery cop."

"So you're coming around to the notion that someone was using Darren Curran's ID?" Mike asked.

"Yes, based on this," Lucas said, motioning to the spreadsheet on the computer screen. "This shows a dozen instances of Detective Curran's ID. You see these?" Lucas pointed to one of the columns of numbers.

"Are those precinct numbers?" Mike said, only half as a question.

"Indeed. I recognize most of them, and the ones I know are all in Brooklyn and Queens. Look at the dates. Months apart, different precinct houses. Never the same one twice. This is not the pattern of an officer working in any normal way."

"What does it mean?" Jason asked.

"I don't know," Lucas said softly, looking intently at the screen. "But this data will lead us there."

Over the next three hours, the three detectives pored over the information they could find in the electronic files. Darren Curran's ID had been recorded on exactly thirteen dates over the past year. In some cases, there were multiple records on the same day in the same place, indicating that the ID card was used to access multiple doors that required sensor swipes. Each swipe had a time stamp and a code corresponding to the specific door. In other cases, there was just a single line of data in the spreadsheet. There was no record of when the person carrying the ID left the buildings.

"We are going to have to get the data to show us which door corresponds to each code, but more importantly, we'll need to pull the detainee records to see if the person signed anyone out of the lock-up, like we saw with Miss Barker."

"How long will that take?"

"We're not going to get it today," Lucas said, getting up and stretching his back. "I'll put in a rush request to the four locations with the most separate swipes. Why don't you two go back uptown tomorrow and we'll plan to meet back here on Thursday."

"That's probably a good idea," Mike agreed. "There's one other thing, Lucas, since we're working together. We have another case we're working. You've probably heard about it – the Raul Rosario murder, the bodega owner in the Bronx."

"Sure, I know about it. Has some racial overtones."

"Yeah, and that doesn't help matters. The thing is, we have a pretty good sketch of the principle suspect, and we're pretty sure that he's connected to the Gallata syndicate. But when we sent the sketch down to the task force working on the Gallatas, expecting to get an ID on our suspect, we got nothing. Does that seem strange to you?"

Lucas sat in silence for a minute before responding. He looked at Mike, then at Jason, seemingly pondering how much he wanted to share. "Have you received any word back that the task force guys don't know who he is, or is it just silence?"

"Silence," Jason said. "I've sent a half-dozen emails down to them and I get no replies. It's like they're ignoring us."

"Well, one thing I would recommend that you not do is go up the chain of command. There's no point in trying to pressure these guys. In my experience, they are so insulated that they think they can do whatever the hell they want and that they don't answer to anyone except the commissioner. Have you tried contacting the feds on this?"

"We sent the sketch to the city task force. They were supposed to share it with the FBI guys. We're supposed to work through our guys."

"Sure, that's the way it's supposed to work, but sometimes going around the protocol can get you some answers. Do you have any contacts at the Bureau you could use to get a little off-the-record intel?"

Mike looked up at Lucas with a smile on his face. "I just might."

Chapter 28 – Look What I Found

Wednesday, March 27

T HE NEXT DAY, Mike arrived at the precinct house early before heading to his PT session. He had a fax to send. He knew that he could take a picture of the sketch of "Ricky" and then send an email, but he preferred not to leave an electronic record. The night before, Mike had made a call from his home landline to FBI agent Everett Forrest, the FBI field director he had worked with the prior fall during the Ronald Randall investigation. Forrest had been leading a surveillance operation that was monitoring an arm of the Gallata syndicate, which had been smuggling drugs and foreign women into the country. The main operation had been shut down after the key front man, Justin Heilman, was boiled alive in a hot tub, but the underlings were rebuilding the supply lines and Forrest had expanded the scope of the surveillance to include some new targets. Forrest had checked in on Mike during his shoulder rehabilitation. He always said that if Mike ever needed any help from the Feds, he should feel free to call. True to his word, when Mike explained the situation, Forrest said he would try to help if Mike could send him a copy of the sketch.

After sending the fax, Mike generated an activity report from the fax machine, which printed out six pages of data. Nobody had cleared the cache in the old-school communications device in a while. He carried the printout to the shredder and then headed for the door. He would easily be on time for his physical therapy session.

Ж Ж Ж

On Thursday, after a morning of phone calls and paperwork in the bagel-less precinct building, Mike and Jason went back downtown to the IA office. They found a row of boxes lined up on the work table where Agent Gomez was sitting with his laptop computer, a legal pad, and a full box of Krispy Kreme donuts.

"Why so much?" Mike asked, gesturing toward the file boxes.

"Getting the records clerks to dig through boxes to find one particular document is more difficult than getting them to send you the archive box that, presumably, includes the document. So, there we are – we dig ourselves."

Each man took a box and, by referencing the computer records of the badge swipes, tried to find the particular binder containing the log-out list for the relevant date. The process immediately became a race to see who could find their record first. Lucas won. His sheet was dated September 14, 2018 and showed a detainee named Connie Sykes signed out and then signed back in twenty minutes later. Lucas looked her up in the department's computer records.

"Arrested three times, all for drug-related misdemeanors. Nineteen years old. Address unknown. No other information. I'll run her name though the national database and see what I get."

Jason was next across the finish line. His records were computer printouts. Curran, D. signed out a detainee named Donna Shore on December fifth. She was recorded back into the lock-up a little over an hour later. "Our guy spent some time with this one. What do we have in our system about her?"

Lucas put Donna Shore's name into the NYPD database and waited for the results. "Twenty years old. Four arrests. Two for possession and two for solicitation. Sound familiar?" Mike and Jason both nodded. "Address listed in Minnesota. Another kid from out of town comes to New York, gets in trouble, and gets a visit from our guy. Nothing else in our system on her. No other arrests after this one. I'll add her to my national search."

As Lucas was tapping the name into his laptop, Mike held up a sheet of paper he had extracted from the binder he had been reviewing. "You're last," Jason said with a smile.

"Good things come to those who wait," Mike responded. "You don't have to put this one into the computer."

"Why not?" Lucas asked.

"Because I know this one."

Jason raised an eyebrow and asked, "One of our three dead women?"

"Bingo. Yvonne Calderone. She was signed out for fifty-three minutes on September seventh."

Jason gave Lucas the rundown on the information available on Yvonne Calderone, which he knew well from repeated viewing. "She was from St. Louis. Nineteen years old. Her mother reported her missing but since she was of age, the New York police couldn't force her to return home, although they sent a report back to St. Louis to let the cops there know that she had been located. She was arrested six times for shoplifting, drug possession, disorderly conduct, and solicitation. Three months after her last arrest, she was found dead in an alley behind a strip club in Queens. The cause of death was listed in her file as a drug overdose. Dr. McNeill identified her as having similar characteristics to Christine Barker – lack of track marks, no physical symptoms consistent with heroin addiction, and bruises indicting physical abuse. That's all we know, because her physical file is missing."

"Where was the file?" Lucas asked.

"She was arrested in four different precincts, so the file was sent to central booking," Jason responded.

"Alright, so we have a person who either is a cop, or is impersonating a cop. He identifies young women from out of town who have multiple arrests. They are vulnerable and are not likely to have much of a support network in New York. They also may not be excited about running back home. Do we think they're all on drugs of some kind?"

"Yes, all of them," Jason replied.

"OK, young women who are already on drugs. Maybe that's what he has to offer them – a supply."

"And maybe a warm bed," Mike said.

Lucas nodded his affirmation. "He meets with them in the lock-up and they drop off the map – no additional arrests. Then they turn up dead months later from heroin overdoses. Why? He's not raping them and then killing them, so what's happening?"

"Could be sex trade," Mike suggested.

"That would make sense," Lucas agreed, "but why kill them? And why use a drug overdose as the method?"

Neither Mike nor Jason had an answer.

Jason frowned and looked at Lucas. "Miss Barker had a long stretch in lock-up after her last arrest, but there's no record of any sign-out. How does that match up?"

"Maybe our guy, when he can get away with it, talks to his targets without leaving a record of the sign-out," Lucas suggested. "Lots of precincts get a little sloppy with the sign-out process."

"So, he might have had even more contacts than we have records of," Mike observed. "Is there any way to check video or other security records at the lock-ups to see if we can figure out who this guy is?"

"I'm on it," Lucas replied. "I'm hoping we can pin him down, but it will not be easy. In the meantime, you probably need to talk to Darren just to make sure that it wasn't him."

"I know," Mike replied without any enthusiasm. The last thing he wanted to do was interrogate his former partner. But he knew it was necessary.

Chapter 29 – Anticipation

Thursday, March 28

WHEN MIKE AND JASON LEFT THE IA OFFICES, still puzzling over what they had learned, Mike called Michelle's cell phone. He motioned for Jason to go ahead without him and then diverted to Canal street to pick up some Chinese food. Twenty minutes later, he arrived at Michelle's apartment building. He input the code to open the front door and quickly found himself knocking on the door of apartment 7-H. Michelle greeted Mike with a warm smile and a quick kiss.

"May I come in?"

"You'd better."

After consuming their sesame chicken and bean curd Szechuan style over pleasant small talk, Michelle asked, "When is your next rehab session?"

"Tomorrow," Mike said as he swallowed his last dumpling. "That will be fifteen weeks, which means seven to go."

"You're going to lose your bet to Dolores, so you'll owe her fifty bucks, right?"

"It's only twenty, but yeah. I got that covered." Mike slid down off his chair and dumped the empty food containers into the trash bin. "I am looking forward to being done with the PT, though."

"You'll still need to do your exercises, you know?"

"Yeah, yeah, I know. Terry keeps telling me. Even the doctor told me the same thing. After my last session I go back to the doc so he can sign off that I've completed the rehab, and sign my card so I can get my gun back."

"What is it with you cops and your guns?"

"It's a security blanket, like Linus from Charlie Brown. I sleep better when I have my Glock under my pillow."

"Then you're not sleeping in my bed!"

"I'll make an exception where you're concerned," Mike said with a suggestive raising of his eyebrows.

"You're barking up the wrong tree there, Mister. Your big gun does not turn me on in the slightest."

"My gun isn't that big."

"I'll restrain myself from the obvious response," Michelle said with a laugh. "If you play your cards right, you might convince me to help you service that weapon of yours later, but right now I want you to tell me about developments in the case."

"Which one?" Mike asked innocently.

After Michelle punched Mike lightly in his uninjured shoulder, he explained that they had connected one of the three other dead women to Christine Barker through her interview with "Darren Curran."

"Isn't that your old partner?"

"Yeah. Well, it is, but we're pretty sure that it wasn't Darren who interrogated Yvonne Calderone."

"How can you be sure?"

"Well, he hasn't been on active duty, so it couldn't have been him."

"Have you asked him?"

"I'm going to talk to Darren tomorrow, after PT. We have a date to celebrate me getting to fifteen weeks."

"A man-date?"

"Sure. A man-date. Why not? We're going to meet at the gym and then go out for a beer."

"How is that different from any other day you two have spent together?" Michelle asked seriously.

"It's not. But since it's a special occasion, maybe we'll order imported beer."

"Nice. And speaking of dates, did you get the tickets to the Hero's Ball?"

Mike nodded. He had been hoping that Michelle might forget about the upcoming event, although he knew it was not likely.

"I'm so excited about that," Michelle said, bouncing up and down slightly. "I've been shopping for a new dress and Rachel already has hers."

"Rachel?" Mike tried to access his memory of prior conversations with Michelle to identify Rachel.

"You remember. We met her at the outdoor concert downtown last month? She's an EMT – really tall?"

"Oh, sure," Mike said, only vaguely recalling the concert, let alone a person he had been introduced to after several beers.

"I would have expected you to remember her. Her name is Rachel Robinson, and you're such a baseball fan. Plus, she has a little thing for Jason, so I arranged for them to come together, since Jason didn't have a date."

"Aren't you the match-maker."

"Well, why shouldn't everyone be happy? Anyway, I have a great dress and I'm looking forward to you seeing me in it."

"You always look good," Mike said.

"That's why I like you, Mike. You make me feel beautiful."

Chapter 30 – The Needle Has A Name

Friday, March 29

O N FRIDAY, MIKE ARRIVED at the rehabilitation center ten minutes early for his appointment. He sat in an uncomfortable chair in the waiting area and watched through the glass doors while Terry finished working with another patient – a female officer who was rehabbing a knee injury. While he was watching, Dolores arrived.

"How you doin', Mike?" she said with her usual cheer.

"I'm pretty good. I've been doing my rubber bands at home every day and I think I'm going to show a lot of improvement today."

"We'll see," Dolores smirked.

Once inside, Terry ran Mike through his exercises and manipulations. When Mike couldn't take the pain anymore and begged for mercy, Terry congratulated him on getting to 78 degrees. Mike beamed and went to work on the bands while Terry put Dolores on the table. She was at 83 degrees and wasn't even uncomfortable, or so it seemed.

After dressing, Mike walked out to the general gym area and looked for Darren. His old partner was sitting at a leg exercise machine, straining to lift his left leg from a bent position up into a straight-leg posture. Mike watched as he grunted and strained through five reps. When Darren allowed the machine to slam back into its resting position, Mike called out. "Hey, Curran, is that all you got?"

Darren flipped Mike a good-natured middle finger as he leaned down to pick up a small blue-and-orange workout towel and wiped the sweat off his face. "Did Dolores kick your ass again today?"

"I'll meet you in the front lobby," Mike said, ignoring the question. "It's freaking cold out today, so I'll stay inside. How much time do you need?"

"I'll meet you there in fifteen," Darren called as he walked toward the locker rooms.

Later, the two cops sat in a booth back at the One-Ten Pub. Darren insisted on shots of Jameson's to go with their beers, and they both ordered sandwiches and lingered over their food. When he ran out of small talk and speculation about the prospects for the Mets, Mike had to deal with the difficult part of the meeting.

"You remember I told you about the woman we fished out of the river last month? Well, we've had a pretty interesting development that I need to talk with you about."

"Yeah?" Darren said, interested. "How can I help?"

"Well, you see, Darren, we identified another girl named Yvonne Calderone. The medical examiner thinks Ms. Calderone may have died under similar circumstances. There's a strange thing about her file. She was in the lock-up in Brooklyn after she was picked up for solicitation. But instead of being processed and released, she was kept for several hours. During that time, she was signed out and interrogated for nearly an hour, but there is no report in the file about that interrogation." As Mike recounted this history, he watched

Darren's facial expressions carefully for any sign of recognition, or a guilty conscience. He saw nothing.

"Sounds to me like you should talk to that detective and find out what he talked to her about," Darren suggested.

"That's why I'm here."

"What do you mean?" Darren asked, looking genuinely confused. "Do you think I know the guy?"

"The guy is you, Darren. According to the records, it was your ID that was used to sign her out, and your badge number is on the log-out sheet." Once again, Mike watched carefully as Darren's face went through stages of confusion. Mike saw no sign of recognition, but also saw no sign of Darren being angry about somebody using his identity without his knowledge.

"Mike, I don't understand. Are you telling me that somebody used my ID and my badge number?"

"That's what it looks like." Mike paused and cleared his throat. "I have to ask, Darren. Did you speak to that girl on September seventh?"

Now Darren looked upset. "Hell no, Mike. I haven't been in a lock-up since – well, since the shooting. I haven't interviewed anyone. I haven't had any cases. You know that."

Mike nodded. "I didn't think so, Buddy, but you know I had to ask. Do you have any idea how somebody got your ID?"

Now Darren's face changed to a look of deep thought. "When I was in the hospital, after that day, somebody from the department came in to see me and asked me if the hospital staff had returned all my personal effects, including my badge and ID. I didn't know, so the woman looked through the drawers in my hospital room and we found my uniform shirt, my belt, and my holster. You took my gun back to the precinct house, I remember. I guess they had to cut off my pants, so they were gone, along with my shoes. We didn't find my badge or

ID card, which would have been in my shirt pocket, so she ordered new ones for me. I got the replacement ID maybe a week later."

"Do you have it now?" Mike asked.

"Sure. I need it to check in and out of the rehab center." Darren reached into his pants pocket and withdrew his badge and ID card, which were both encased in plastic in a small, flip-open leather case. He passed the identification case to Mike, who opened it and glanced at the contents. They looked like just about every other officer's credentials. Mike handed it back.

"So, is it possible that somebody has your missing ID and is using it to impersonate you?"

Darren's face went blank. Then he said, "No. No, I don't see why anyone would want to do that. Besides, wouldn't our IT folks have canceled my lost ID card?"

"Well, it seems that somebody is using it, so I guess it's not deactivated. We need to figure out who it is."

"I have no idea who would do that," Darren said.

"Well, I understand. Think about it, and if you think of anything, please let me know."

"Sure," Darren responded blankly. "No problem. Do you have any other leads on the identity of the guy?"

"Not much. We're trying to look for video from the locations of the ID swipes, but so far no luck."

"You think there's video inside the lock-up that would show him?"

"Maybe. We're looking for it." Mike did not mention the involvement of Internal Affairs. Darren went silent for a minute, but didn't say anything else about the case. Mike figured that he was a little insulted about being implicated.

They didn't talk about the case anymore that afternoon. After another round, Mike gave Darren a slap on the back and headed off South toward his apartment, while Darren headed the opposite direction, toward the garage where his car was parked. On his walk, Mike thought about how he was going to report his conversation to Jason and Lucas.

Ж Ж Ж

When he got to his desk, thoughts of his conversation with Darren were driven from Mike's mind by the message slip on his desk from "John Woods." This was the fairly obvious pseudonym Agent Forrest said he would use to contact Mike if he had to leave a message. Since their communications were off the record, they didn't want to use Mike's cell phone, which would leave an electronic trail. Mike moved to the conference room, picked up the handset on the old desktop phone, and returned the call.

"You in a good spot?" Forrest said as soon as Mike said hello.

"Yeah. I'm in a conference room."

"Great. Here's the quick scoop. First off, my guys say that they had never seen that sketch before, so it looks like the NYPD boys never sent it over. Second, I was able to get an ID for you. Your boy is on the bottom of the pyramid, but he's on the chart. He's known as 'Ricky the Runner'."

"Because he's a bag man?"

"Well, yes, but also because he's apparently an actual runner. Some kind of track star in high school. Claims to be able to outrun any cop."

"Well, he outran Jason, so I'll give him that."

"Whatever. His real name is Richard Spezio. He's a local boy from Coney Island. We don't have an address for him, but he's a pretty regular visitor to Fat Albert's headquarters."

"Where's that?"

"I can't tell you that, Mike. And you can't go busting in there anyway or it would fuck up the Bureau's operation. But if you can track

193

the guy down on your own and bust him for the Rosario murder, my boys say they won't care and that Fat Albert will hardly miss him. Of course, the fat man will ice him without batting an eye if he thinks Ricky is a potential liability, so keep that in mind."

"OK," Mike said as he scribbled down the name, asking Forrest to spell it for him. "Thanks. I owe you, buddy."

"No problem, Mike. Just don't tell anyone you got it from me."

"Roger that," Mike said, hanging up the phone and scuttling back to his desk. He would tell Jason the news the next time they were alone.

Chapter 31 – Human Resources

T. WARREN MAGNAN WAS ANNOYED when he heard the knock at his door. It was close to one in the morning and he was wrapping up the accounts for the night. As had been the case in the past three months, the cash revenue from drug sales exceeded the flesh fees. This did not make him happy. He never intended to be a drug dealer. The drugs, mostly crystal meth, had been used to entice and control the girls. They had a ready supply from their Gallata contact, who was happy to provide. When some of the girls wanted cocaine, his source was eager to fill the order.

Tina, the first woman he and Eddie had recruited, handled most of the distribution. Eddie knew her from several prior busts and liked how business-like and practical she was about her trade. He had offered her immunity from additional arrests and a bigger cut of the fees if she would help him recruit other girls and serve as the madame of the house. She was happy to apply for the job. She brought in young women who wanted protection, and most of them were induced to be cooperative with a little product. Tina was smart.

With such an ample supply of a variety of pharmaceuticals, Eddie had suggested that they diversify a little and start selling the drugs to the local population. They cleared the idea with their Gallata contacts. Magnan knew that the Gallatas normally never let anybody siphon off their profit margin, but this was a special case. Before long, there was a stream of regulars coming in to pick up their daily fix. The johns also kept coming at a steady pace, both those referred by the few officers who were aware of the arrangement and took their cut, and those the ladies brought in on their own. Everyone was happy, and the cash flow was ample. But Magnan grumbled. Somehow the sex trade didn't bother him, but selling drugs made his skin crawl.

But here he was, tallying up the daily receipts and calculating how long it would be until he and Eddie could retire from the sordid enterprise and turn in their badges. Soon, he thought. Maybe another six months.

The knock on the door worsened his already dour mood. He reluctantly got up from the spartan chair and crossed the dimly lit room to the door. Through the peep hole he saw the face of His Honor, Judge Malcom Snell. The judge's presence puzzled, but did not alarm him. The judge was a regular customer, but this was the first time he had come to visit since the first time he had arrived seeking some female companionship. The jurist being at his door was unlikely to be a good development.

"Good evening, Your Honor," Magnan said as he opened the door. "What can I do for you at this late hour?"

"May I come in?" the judge replied. Magnan was hoping this would be quick, but he graciously stepped aside and allowed Snell inside.

"I'm sorry to say that I don't have comfortable accommodations here, Malcom," Magnan apologized as he motioned for the judge to sit on the crisply made bed and rolled the desk chair away from the closed laptop computer. All the day's cash had been packaged up and sent off to the night deposit bin at the local Citi Bank, so Magnan was not worried about any incriminating evidence being in plain view.

"Not to worry, Warren. I won't be staying long. I just wanted to let you know that you may want to watch the little Asian girl I was with tonight."

"Why is that?" Magnan inquired, suddenly more interested.

"She was asking me a bunch of questions about who I am and what I do, and whether I have any contacts with the police."

"You think she's looking to turn snitch on us?"

"It's possible. She was very attentive to me, and it was afterwards that she got inquisitive."

"Thanks," Magnan said, standing up and hoping that the judge would do the same. "I'll make sure that this is not a problem for you, or for me."

"See that you do," the judge said as he folded his overcoat across his arm and walked to the door. "I'm relying on your discretion."

"And I yours," Magnan replied, closing the door. He listened for the buzz from the security door at the end of the hallway that indicated the departure of Judge Snell. He really didn't need this problem. He pulled out his cell phone and punched a speed dial button.

"Eddie, I need you to pay a visit to Jade up in 313. She was asking her last customer a lot of questions and wanted to know if he knew anybody in the police department. She needs an attitude adjustment . . . No, I don't think so, just a refresher course on loyalty. It's a good lesson for the rest of them . . . No, let's not get drastic yet. I want to maintain a lower profile for a while . . . Thanks. I'm going to wrap up, you can give me a report tomorrow."

Magnan stuffed his laptop into a leather briefcase, turned out the light, and left the room. The hallway reeked of sweat, weed, and beer. He scowled as he walked to the door, cursing himself for ever letting things get to this point, but at the same time vowing that he would end his purgatory soon.

Ж Ж Ж

Eddie held up a tiny plastic bag with several blue-green crystals languishing in the bottom. The baggie swung slowly back and forth in his hand. "You ready for your dessert, Jade?"

"Mmhmm," the woman said, sitting up in the disheveled bed and tossing away a faux-satin sheet. She had an eager, hungry expression in her eyes. The left side of her red lace teddy dropped down over her shoulder, exposing the top half of her shapely breast, but Jade was oblivious. She crawled on all fours across the bed as seductively as she could manage, letting Eddie know that she would do anything – anything – to earn her dessert.

"Did you take good care of your customer tonight?"

"Of course I did," Jade said with a wide smile.

"That's good. You know we need to keep the regulars happy."

"Mmhmm," Jade purred, reaching out a slender hand and lightly stroking the crotch of Eddie's blue jeans, hoping not to get a reaction. She got one, but it wasn't the one she was expecting.

Eddie reached down and grabbed Jade's wrist with his left hand, pulling it away from his pants and twisting as he pulled upwards. Jade lost her balance and spun, falling onto her back on the bed as she cried out in pain. "You think you're pretty fucking smart, eh?"

"Wh-what?" Jade squeaked out, whimpering as Eddie continued to twist her arm painfully.

"Don't play dumb, bitch!"

"Owwww!" She contorted her body, trying to relieve the pressure on her elbow. In the process, the red teddy bunched up, exposing her smooth buttocks as her long black hair spilled down onto the sheets. "Get off!"

"You'd like that, huh?" Eddie growled as he stretched out his right hand, still holding the meth baggie and slapping Jade across the side of her face. "You gotta cut the chatter with the customers. You got that?" Jade could only groan in response. "You talk to him about the police again and I'll make sure you sleep with the fishes. You get me?"

"Ahh, okay!" Jade screamed as Eddie increased the pressure on her twisted elbow.

Eddie gave her arm one last turn, causing Jade to scream even louder. She fell off the bed in a heap as he released her. He held up the bag of blue-green crystals and waved it toward her as she sobbed softly. "You get no juice tonight, sweetheart. You get some when you behave."

"No! Please!" Jade pleaded, reaching out with her uninjured arm.

"You come see me tomorrow. We'll talk again. Now get that sweet ass down to your room. Tina will be around in a little while to check on you." Eddie turned and walked out of the room, a satisfied smile on his face.

Chapter 32 – Black Tie Affair

Saturday, March 30

T HAT SATURDAY AT 6:00 p.m., Mike and Michelle arrived in a Lyft car at the Metropolitan Museum of Art on Fifth Avenue. It was bitterly cold and starting to sleet as they arrived. The area in front of the main stairs was cordoned off by police, who were allowing limos and cabs in to drop off passengers. Flood lights bathed the white marble steps, which had a red carpet running up to the Corinthian columns that flanked the main doors. The Hero's Ball was one of the social events of the season, and a phalanx of photographers and video teams surrounded the drop-off area to get pictures of the arriving celebrities, officials, business tycoons, donors to the Met and to the mayor's re-election committee, and honored guests.

Michelle stepped out of the car, allowing her black dress to ride up over her knee and show off a toned thigh, covered in dark nylon. She planted her silver sequined Jimmy Choo sandal on the red carpet at the curb and allowed a tuxedo-clad valet to help her out to a standing position, where her best diamond earrings sparkled in the bright lights. She had her hair styled in an alluring curve around her cheekbones. She was smiling – beaming, really – as she gazed around at the spectacle. She took three steps forward along the red carpet before turning suddenly and looking back for Mike, who was still struggling to climb out of the car. Mike waved off the valet's offer of assistance and got out. His hair was slicked back and matted down with styling gel, which Michelle had insisted would make him look dignified and would keep his hair in place for all the pictures. In his rented tux, Mike felt like an extra in a bad gangster movie.

But when Mike saw Michelle's smiling face and how fabulous she looked in that new black dress, he had to just shrug and tell himself to go with it. He had told Michelle repeatedly that he did not like big public affairs like this. Michelle had insisted that it was a great honor for him to be invited by the mayor to get a medal of honor for his heroism, and besides, she had always wanted to go to one of these big swanky New York City gala events. She was acting like it was the Academy Awards and she was nominated for Best Performance by a Medical Examiner. He had to shake his head and chuckle, looking at her with a valet holding a huge umbrella over her head. He offered her an arm and escorted her up the red-carpeted stairs.

He really didn't think he deserved to be recognized as a hero. He had not felt much like one after he nearly got Michelle killed and barely escaped the ordeal with his own life. Not dying was hardly a reason for accolades. But the mayor and the police commissioner had insisted that the city needed it, and they wanted Mike and Jason to get some glory. Jason, as a Black detective, would look great in photos standing next to the mayor. That much Mike understood.

Inside the monstrous building, they were escorted to a large, open room with a three-story-high ceiling, which had been transformed into a ballroom for the occasion. A string quartet played Mozart in the far corner. The setting looked like a royal mansion in Vienna more than the middle of Manhattan. The place was not yet fully packed with guests, but Mike could immediately see that there were not nearly enough chairs around the small circular tables lining the walls to accommodate even the current population of the room. He was going to be doing a lot of standing.

Mike looked around for Jason, whose six-foot-three frame normally stood out in crowds. With most of the men wearing tuxedos in the dimly lit space, however, Mike could not find him, assuming he was even there yet. Michelle had wanted to be on the early side so that she could enjoy the whole evening. She glided across the marble floor on Mike's arm. Mike marveled at her ability to balance herself on the four-inch heels she was wearing, but he did love the way she looked and didn't mind the illusion of her being a little taller. They both plucked glasses of champagne from a silver tray being passed around by a waiter. Michelle clinked her glass against his.

"I'm loving this, Mike," she said with a dreamy look in her eyes. Mike leaned down and gave her a light kiss, just next to her mouth so as not to smear her lipstick.

They found a tall, round table covered with a black tablecloth. There was a single votive candle burning in a glass enclosure and casting a pathetically dim glow around the center of the small, otherwise empty space. There were no chairs, but at least the little table gave them a place to put down their glasses. Mike glanced around again, scanning for Jason, his eyes stopping on each couple. The women were dressed in as much glitter, gold leaf trim, and lace as Mike could ever recall seeing in one place. Every woman seemed to be trying to upstage every other woman and garner the center of attention. Mike looked back at Michelle and smiled at her. She looked great. Her dress was tasteful and elegant and not at all flashy. It suited her.

Mike told Michelle to guard their table while he made an assault on the appetizer tables along the far side of the massive room. When he returned with one plate of finger food and one plate piled high with veggies and fruit, he saw that a small crowd had gathered around Michelle. He immediately recognized the back of Jason's head, sprouting up from his tuxedo jacket. Next to Jason, Mike saw the backside of a tall woman in a deep purple gown, her black hair piled up on top of her head in an elaborate arrangement. The dress had a plunging open back that exposed her dark skin and the outline of her spine down to a dangerously low point.

Mike set his plates down proudly on the table, just as Jason noticed him. "Hey, Mike," Jason said with a broad smile, showing off his perfect, white teeth. "You know Rachel Robinson, don't you?"

"Sure I do," Mike said, taking her hand and stretching up on his toes to give her a kiss on the cheek. She really was tall, and probably wearing heels to boot. Jason didn't tower over her like he did with most women. "I'm guessing your father was a baseball fan."

Rachel giggled softly, causing her sequined dress to shimmer all around her well-curved body. "Yes, well, it was more my grandfather, who was a die-hard Brooklyn Dodgers fan. He made my father promise that if he ever had a son, he'd name him Jack. Well, he had me and had to settle for Rachel. Oh!" Rachel exclaimed, reaching for a sequined clutch purse that closely matched the color of her dress. "Wait, I need to get a selfie with you."

Rachel pulled out her cell phone and put an arm around Mike, stretching her long arm out in front of them and posing for a photo. "I have to get a shot with the big hero."

"I can assure you, Jason is more of a hero than I am," Mike said.

"Oh, yes!" Rachel squealed. "Jason, Jason – come here!" She pulled Jason towards her and made him pose with her and Mike for another picture. Rachel was radiating happiness. She then gathered Michelle into the group for one more shot before Michelle reached out and pulled Mike away.

Michelle directed Mike to a group of guests standing around the other side of their little table. She immediately grabbed the arm of the man standing next to her.

"Oh, Mister Zemeckis, this is Mike." Then, turning, she grabbed Mike's arm and pulled him toward the man. She was glowing. Zemeckis had a jovially round face featuring round, wire-rimmed glasses. He was about Mike's height and looked to be in his late sixties, with graying hair swept back from his forehead. His tuxedo looked a little worn and was obviously not a rental. He flashed a practiced smile and thrust out his hand toward Mike. As they shook, Michelle made the introduction. "Mike, this is Robert Zemeckis, the film director and producer."

Mike did a double-take, muttering, "I'm glad to meet you," as he struggled to remember what movies he could associate with the familiar name.

"We were just watching *Who Framed Roger Rabbit* last week, Mr. Zemeckis. It's one of Mike's favorite films, right Mike?" Michelle nudged him with her elbow.

"Yeah, oh, yeah," Mike stumbled, disengaging his handshake with the director.

"Good to meet you, Detective Stoneman," Zemeckis said. "A friend of mine tells me that he's working on a project involving your last big case. Are you consulting on that?"

"No," Mike said quickly, "I'm not involved."

"Well, that's too bad, Detective. It's a hell of a story. It'd be a shame if they get it wrong."

"I'm sure they'd get it wrong even if I were consulting," Mike replied, making eye contact with Jason.

Jason turned to Rachel and Mike got his first good look at the front of the purple dress. The neckline in the front did not plunge as far as the back. Mike found himself staring at her chest and quickly looked up at her face. She was made up with a bit too much color for Mike's liking, but he had to admit that it matched her gown remarkably well.

Mike was not keen on jumping back into the conversation between Michelle and Robert Zemeckis, nor did he want to do anything to keep her from enjoying the moment with a celebrity. He popped a cheesy puffed pastry into his mouth and looked out over the expanse of guests without really focusing on anyone in particular. Then, a shrill voice caught his attention.

"Oh, my gaawd! I can't believe it!" the voice exclaimed in a distinctive New Jersey accent. "There he is! Allan, you have to – Allan!" she yelled out, scoldingly, as if admonishing a young child to keep up in the mall. The woman wore a red dress wrapped in horizontal pleats around her shapely body. The fabric shimmered in the dim light. At its strapless top, the dress encased the woman's enormous breasts from both sides, pressing them together into twin mountains of cleavage that mesmerized Mike momentarily. When he looked up at her face, below a bee-hive of blonde curls, his mind sparked a hint of recognition that he could not quite tap into fully. She had blue eyes surrounded by so much shadow and mascara and such huge false eyelashes that it was hard to focus on her actual pupils. She was dripping in diamonds on her ears and around her neck. The skin on her face was stretched tight and covered with a glossy sheet of makeup, and her lips were plastered with a thick coat of lipstick that exactly matched the color of her dress. She wobbled up to the little table as if having trouble balancing on her high heels, but then Mike saw that the bottom half of the red dress was wrapped so tightly around her thighs that she could barely move her legs to walk. She held out a hand toward Mike, palm down. Mike immediately saw the large diamond protruding from her ring finger – so big it belonged behind a glass case at the Museum of Natural History.

Mike took the offered hand and pantomimed a kiss without actually allowing his lips to touch her skin, still puzzling over who she was and why she seemed familiar. A pace or two behind the woman came a man in a tuxedo. His shirt collar was a little too tight, causing the fatty skin of his neck to bulge out over the edges. He was short – much shorter than the woman, even allowing for some extra heel-height, with thinning black hair combed over his scalp and slicked down with oil of some kind. He had a haggard look about his round face, which was otherwise pleasant enough if not very memorable, with dark eyes and a distinctly well-fed appearance. His bow tie was askew and Mike immediately sensed that, like himself, this man really didn't want to be here. The man was totally unfamiliar to Mike, so he turned his attention back to the hand of the woman, which he was still holding. He dropped his own arm down, releasing her hand in the process, and decided to drop all pretenses and just ask her.

"That's a lovely dress," Mike began, hoping to segue into an introduction. But he never got the chance.

"Thanks, Detective Stoneman. Oh, yeah, I remember it's Detective. I never forget a face, you know. I have a photogenic memory."

Mike raised an eyebrow, but didn't try to correct the woman, who was clearly a rolling freight train that would not be stopped.

"And I know I called your partner 'officer' and he made sure to correct me. I remember. Allan!" she called out impatiently, looking behind her and holding out her other hand, even as she kept talking. "Allan – I met these two detectives after my scumbag ex-husband was killed. The best thing that ever happened to me." Then she turned to Mike again. "Detective, I want you to meet my new husband, Mr. Allan Rosen, who I will say is far more financially secure than that scum-sucking worm Nick DiVito, who I know you never actually met, until he was dead, I mean, but I told you what an asshole he was so it's almost like you knew him. But look at me now!" she said as her voice went up even higher. She raised one arm above her head in a kind of Marilyn Monroe pose as she turned to the side. "I found a man who really appreciates me." She looked down at the still uncomfortable-looking man and motioned for him to step forward. "Allan! Say hello to one of the honorees of tonight's ball, Detective Mike Stoneman, the man who took out the Righteous Assassin."

The man took a step forward and offered Mike a firm handshake. "Nice to meet you, Detective. Helene has told me about how she helped you with your investigation."

Mike smiled and said, "Thank you. It's nice to meet you, Mister Rosen." By the time Mrs. Rosen had finished talking, his memory was fully refreshed. The woman was previously married to Nick DiVito, the first victim of Ronald Randall the prior April. Jason and Mike had interviewed her in August as they began their investigation into what turned out to be six related murders. The former Mrs. DiVito had made it abundantly clear to the two detectives that she was not at all disappointed that her husband was dead, although she was quite upset that she had not inherited much money out of the deal.

Before Mike could plan a strategy for extraction from the conversation, the woman turned her attention to Jason and loudly announced to the group, "And I remember you, too, Detective Jason Dickson!" She stepped past Rachel without so much as a "pardon me" and extended her bejeweled hand toward Jason, who took it lightly in his fingers and just gave it a small squeeze before releasing. "I want you all to know that it was *this man* who was in charge of that investigation. He was the one who figured out that my ex had been the first victim. He was the one asking all the questions last summer. I know he didn't kill the bastard, but he was just as responsible, don't you think?" She pointed at Jason proudly, as if she were the first person to solve a mystery.

It wasn't clear to either Mike or Jason whether the former Mrs. DiVito was directing a question to them, so both of them left it alone. Mike decided to try to steer the conversation in a different direction. "So, Mrs. Rosen, what brings you and your husband here tonight for the ball?"

"My Allan is a big supporter. Allan is in the hedge fund business, which I don't really understand, but he makes a boatload of money and he's on the mayor's committee for public housing. So he's helping to do good things for the city and he's always hanging out with the mayor and his boys. So, tonight I get to come along, which is so fun, don't you think so?" Her voice reached a pitch at the end of her question so high that Mike worried that the crystal would shatter.

"That's great. Really. Great." Mike reached out for Mr. Rosen to shake his hand again, catching the man by surprise. "Very glad to have you as a benefactor for the city, Sir. You really have found an extraordinary woman here," Mike motioned toward his wife, who had stopped talking momentarily and was now taking a large drink from a champagne glass that had materialized from some unknown waiter's tray.

"Yes. Certainly. I'm a very lucky man." Mr. Rosen said, raising an eyebrow.

"I can only imagine," Mike replied. "Or maybe I can't even begin to imagine." The two men exchanged a chuckle. "I hope that you enjoy your evening." Mike turned away from the Rosens and tried to rejoin the conversation that Michelle was still having with the film director. Before he could interject himself into that discussion, another hand reached out toward him and a deep voice called out.

"Detective Stoneman! Glad I found you." The voice, and the extended hand, belonged to someone Mike actually recognized. Keith Harris was an Assistant District Attorney, with whom Mike had worked on several murder prosecutions over the years. Harris was about Mike's age and had made a career out of being a prosecutor, which Mike respected. So many ADAs did their time in public service and then moved on either to higher political office or into the private legal sector, where they traded on their contacts within the criminal justice machine to get a big payday. Mike didn't begrudge the people who cashed in after years of working on a public servant's salary and getting little if any thanks for their hard work. But he had a special admiration for the guys like Harris who stayed put doing the important work of prosecuting criminals and directing the younger attorneys. Harris was definitely one of the good guys, in Mike's view.

"Harris, nice to see you here!" Mike called out warmly, and not just because it gave him a diversion from the assault by the former Mrs. DiVito. Mike always referred to the ADA as "Harris." Never Keith. It was just one of those things that grew up between them. Harris was wearing a very nice blue business suit, one of the few men in the room not decked out in a tux. He was comfortable with himself and his position and was not there to impress anyone. Mike wished he had made the same wardrobe choice.

"I didn't want to miss you having to make a speech after everyone tells you what a big hero you are."

Mike turned a little pale at the mention of the speech. He taught classes of cops all the time, but getting in front of the microphone tonight was not something he looked forward to. He didn't like talking about himself. "Thanks for reminding me," Mike said sarcastically. "Maybe I can appoint you my spokesperson for the night. Are you up for it?"

"Not me," Harris responded quickly. "It's your party. I'm just here for the free booze. So, is it true that you're back in the saddle?"

"Yeah. I'm back working with Dickson."

"Any more serial killers on your radar?"

"Not exactly," Mike responded. This caught the ADA's interest and he pressed Mike for details. Mike gave him a quick summary of the Christine Barker case, happy to talk shop for a few minutes. They stepped away to an alcove under a huge oil painting and Mike said that they were not getting much help from the Vice guys. Harris was intrigued and suggested that Mike talk to one of his assistants, who had a case involving a Vice task force in Brooklyn. Mike agreed that it was worth a call and told Harris to have his guy give Mike a ring.

As Harris walked away, Mike saw that Michelle was no longer talking to Robert Zemeckis, who was nowhere to be seen. Mike headed back toward her, but he was intercepted by *New York Times* reporter Dexter Peacock. "Detective Stoneman – Mike – can you tell me what case you were discussing with District Attorney Harris?" Peacock was wearing a standard tux. Without his usual brown tweed jacket and derby hat, Mike hardly recognized him.

"Do you just skulk about all the time waiting to eavesdrop on people?"

"Not at all, Detective. I'm here covering the gala and I just happened to be walking by. It looked like you two were having a private discussion, which means you were probably talking about a case. It doesn't take Sherlock Holmes to figure it out."

"Congratulations," Mike said sarcastically. "Now, since you already know it's private, what makes you think that I would tell you about it?"

"Because we have a special bond," the reporter responded without any hint of irony or humor.

"Well, I'm glad you feel that way, Mister Peacock, but I must decline in this instance. When I have something public to say, you'll be the first person I call."

"I'll hold you to that," the reporter called out as Mike walked away.

After making it back to the little table and reuniting with Michelle, Jason, and Rachel, Mike managed to accept congratulations and good wishes from a dozen more gala-goers with good-natured smiles and genuine thanks. No more Hollywood stars wandered by their table, but just before everyone was ushered out of the hall (which turned out to be only the pre-event reception area) Mike and Jason got a visit from their host.

Frederick Douglass was the second Black mayor of New York, and he was determined to leave his mark on the city. He had initiated plans for an overhaul of the public housing system, thrown support for a significant increase in the minimum wage, advocated for many other programs to aid poor and underprivileged citizens, and had only barely disguised ambitions for higher office. The Hero's Ball was not only an opportunity to honor New Yorkers whose contributions to public welfare were laudable, it was also a fundraiser for the mayor's pet programs, a time to make political connections, and a chance to see and be seen. The mayor's public relations office invited not only the big papers but also the gossip columnists, entertainment networks, and fringe internet publications.

When he walked over to Mike's and Jason's table, the mayor was accompanied by an entourage of people, including Police Commissioner Earl Ward. Ward was his usual dapper self, sporting a European-styled all-black tux with a silk vest. There were also two photographers and several members of the press orbiting around the mayor.

"Detective Mike Stoneman," Douglass said, somehow still keeping the focus on himself.

Mike stepped forward and shook the mayor's hand, then stepped aside so that Jason could do the same. The flashes from the cameras were significantly brighter during this encounter, as the mayor threw an arm around the taller detective and mugged for the photographers.

It was a rare chance for him to be seen in a tux along with a similarly dressed, Black, hero cop. His PR people salivated at the prospects for such pictures to appear in the New York papers and on the 11:00 news. The mayor said a few words praising Dickson and Stoneman, although Mike could not hear most of them. After a quick wave good-bye, the mayor and his procession continued to the next table of guests.

Later, when it was time to recognize the guests of honor, local weather man and master-of-ceremonies Irv Gikofsky, better known as "Mr. G," introduced Mike and Jason together. He praised the "hero cops" who had doggedly investigated the case of the Righteous Assassin, and brought the now infamous Ronald Randall to justice, preventing more murders in the Big Apple. Mike was happy to let Jason take the microphone to express his thanks to the mayor and the commissioner, and to praise the efforts of all the officers and other detectives who helped in the investigation. When Jason stepped aside, Mike was able to add his thanks to the FBI and Special Agent Angela Manning, who was the Bureau's key resource during the four months that their joint task force had tracked the elusive killer. With that, Mr. G. stepped in, shook their hands again, and proceeded to the next award recipient's introduction.

Mike and Jason walked down from the improvised stage, waving at the photographers and carrying their medals in decorative red-and-black cases. Michelle and Rachel met them at their front table with kisses and hugs. Rachel insisted on one more group selfie with the newly-minted heroes and their medals. Mike exhaled and relaxed for the first time all evening.

Later, as they were sharing a cab, Rachel pulled out her cell phone to show Michelle all the photos she took during the ball. When she got to the selfie she had taken of the four of them during the cocktail hour, Michelle asked to see the phone. "Look," she said, pointing to the background of the photo, "I think that's Robert DeNiro." They all looked and all agreed that it was, in fact, the actor.

"You see," Rachel beamed, "you never know what you might get if you take enough pictures."

Chapter 33 – New Directions

O N MONDAY, AFTER MIKE FINISHED UP his "Physical Torture," he and Jason went to meet with Keith Harris and his colleague, David Zimmerman, at the district attorney's office downtown. They left Lucas back at Internal Affairs, since there was no particular reason the DA should know that IA was involved. Zimmerman was a bookish-looking lawyer with a thin, wiry frame, steel-rimmed glasses, and tussled black hair. He was wearing a drab, dark suit with a thin black tie and a white shirt. Jason thought he looked like a wannabe extra from a *Men in Black* movie. But once they started talking, they discovered that his unassuming appearance masked a fiery prosecutor.

Zimmerman explained that he had a case that was connected to a team of NYPD Vice cops in Brooklyn. They had been trying to gather evidence on an organized prostitution operation run by Robert Sawyer, who was connected to the Gallata crime family. The investigation had been derailed after Sawyer and Slick Mick Gallata were murdered. But after Fat Albert Gallata took over the organization, the sex ring was back in business.

"You can't keep a business down when they have a product that people want to buy," Jason observed.

"You got that right," Zimmerman agreed in his Long Island accent. "The case that bothers me involved a woman we prosecuted in November. She was picked up for solicitation and drug possession. She resisted arrest and slashed a cop with a knife, so she got booked on assault, too. She told us the men who ran the sex business told the girls that if they got out of line or tried to run away, they would turn them over to the cops and have them sent to prison. She said that the bosses were not afraid of the cops. Of course, she didn't have a lot of credibility. So, we tried to see if we could get her to identify the bosses, but she refused to name names or wear a wire unless she got a deal."

"That sounds pretty standard," Mike said.

"Yeah. You would think. We were ready to cut the deal and send her back in with a spy cam hidden in her purse, but the cops on the task force didn't want to work with her. They said she was unreliable and too strung out to be a good witness. The cop who was slashed insisted on pressing his charges and demanded that she do some serious time. It didn't make much sense to me, but our hands were tied. We were ready to run it up the chain of command to see if somebody higher up would overrule the boys on the task force. But before we could do it, our witness got herself killed in Riker's Island."

"Really?" Mike said. "What was the cause of death?"

"She was supposed to be in isolation, but they sent her to shower and there were some other detainees there. There was only one female guard, apparently. There was a fight, and our witness ended up with her skull split open. There's no video in the shower, of course."

"Do we think it was a setup?" Jason asked.

215

"It's quite a coincidence. We tried looking into it. There were a few different guards and shift supervisors who could have been involved, but regardless of that, our potential witness was toast."

"It's certainly possible that there might have been cops involved," Mike suggested. "Cops who had a motive to protect the scumbags running a prostitution ring. Cops who would have access to inside police information. Have you shared this with Internal Affairs?"

"We did," Zimmerman said, "but they didn't seem very interested in a hooker arrested for assaulting an officer who kicked it before she could go to prison."

"Tell me, who was the head of the Vice task force involved in this situation?"

"A lieutenant named Magnan. He's been around since the Pilgrims. I spoke with him a bunch of times and he seemed to be fully in charge. I never seemed to tell him anything he didn't already know. I have no reason not to trust him, but I have to tell you, Detective, I don't trust him."

"I think I know someone in IA who might be interested," Mike said, looking at Jason, who gave him a silent nod.

Ж Ж Ж

Mike and Jason stopped in at Internal Affairs to brief Lucas on their discussion with ADA Zimmerman. It turned out that he had news as well. After much digging, Lucas had tracked down the security video from the precinct in Brooklyn where Connie Sykes had been interrogated by the mysterious Darren Curran. The archive had been deleted.

"I thought they retained those tapes for six months," Mike said.

"They're supposed to," Lucas agreed. "But the tape for September was apparently used to record the video for last month, instead of being saved until April. It's a clerical mistake. Nothing suspicious, right?"

"Like Hell," Jason exclaimed. "I don't believe in those kinds of coincidences."

"Regardless," Mike said, "if it's gone, then it's gone. We can speculate all day about what the tape would have shown and who might have arranged for it to disappear, but it won't help us."

"If I were a corrupt cop," Lucas mused, "I would cover my tracks."

"But if the guy was using a false identity, why worry about the security tape?" Jason tossed the question out.

"Because he's very careful," Mike responded, "or because he's feeling some heat."

Lucas stood up and pressed both palms onto the conference table around which they were all sitting. "If these guys are that aware and that paranoid, they are going to be very hard to catch."

Ж Ж Ж

That evening, during dinner, Michelle said that she had an idea about their suspect, Ricky the Runner. Mike and Jason had been trying to track him down using conventional methods, but without success. They were able to rule out all but one of the known Richard Spezios with New York roots based on their driver's license photos and their birth dates. The one remaining Richard Spezio did not seem to have a driver's license, which was not entirely unusual for residents of New York City. He had two credit cards, but neither one had been used in the past year and both were listed with a P.O. Box as the billing address, which was consistent with somebody who was living off the grid. They had a social security number, but he had not filed any taxes, ever, and had no current employer they could track down based on tax withholdings. There were no images of him on the internet that they could find. They continued to work other city records, but had been striking out. The unknown Ricky had no criminal record. Jason joked that he must have outrun all the officers trying to bust him.

"I told Rachel about the runner, and she asked whether you had checked the NYC Runners website."

"What's that going to tell us?"

"Well, Rachel runs in all the big New York City races – the 10Ks and half-marathons and whatnot. She even ran the NYC Marathon last year. She's a wonder. But anyway, those races are organized mostly by the NYC Runners. They keep track of all the names of the runners, and they take photos of all the runners when they cross the finish line." Michelle watched as Mike absorbed this information and a spark of recognition passed over his face.

"So we could ask the running organizers to share the names and photos."

"You don't even need to ask, it's all on their website." Michelle beamed with satisfaction for being able to give Mike an idea he had not thought of.

"OK. We can look for his photo, assuming that he hasn't been running in a disguise. Do you think he used his real name?"

"You never know."

Mike paused to take a bite of his pasta primavera. "Could it be possible for us to wait for him to cross the finish line of a race and arrest him?"

"Why not? The New York Half-Marathon is coming up next Sunday. If the guy is a real runner, he'll be running that one."

"It's certainly worth looking into. Tell Rachel that I'm very grateful for the suggestion."

"Oh, I will certainly tell her," Michelle smiled. "I think that she'll be giving the same suggestion directly to Jason."

"Really?" Mike said, raising an eyebrow. "Are they seeing each other tonight?"

"She said that they had a date planned. I'm really hoping that they get together. She's such a great woman and I think they'd be really good together."

"Are you sure you want that responsibility?"

"Just call me a Yenta," Michelle said with a smirk.

Chapter 34 – Early Collections

Friday, April 5

T. WARREN MAGNAN WAS NEARLY FINISHED with the day's bookkeeping when his cell phone vibrated on the desk next to him. There were only a few people who would call him on this line at this hour, and he was not shocked to see that it was Bruno at the front desk who was ringing him.

"What?" he barked into the phone, after tapping the speaker button so that he could keep working while he talked. Bruno was a decent security man, and he was as loyal as he was strong. But he was not a rocket scientist and could not be counted on to do any deep analysis or logical thinking.

"Mister M, sorry to bother you, but Ricky is here to see you."

Magnan stifled a groan. He thought about sending the man away but decided that the headache of dealing with that was worse than just getting his visit over with. "OK, buzz him in and send him back to me."

A moment later, Magnan heard the distant buzz of the security door at the front entrance, and shortly after that, a knock on the door to his room. He closed his ledger and stood, cursing his aging knees for popping and for the pain they inflicted every time he got up after sitting for a long time. He pushed down on the latch handle and pulled the door open, turning around and heading back inside the room without greeting his guest, who followed without a word.

"I'm here for the receipts," Ricky said in the high-pitched and slightly scratchy voice that Magnan detested. Richard Eugene Spezio was in his mid-twenties. He was not particularly tall, but he was thin as a rail, which made him seem taller. His legs and arms seemed too long for his torso. He was a cocky kid who had no attention span and was always rocking back and forth like he was in a hurry to get somewhere. Magnan had heard the stories about how Ricky had been some kind of big athlete, and he had lean muscles and quick reflexes, but Magnan was never impressed. The kid did not respect his elders.

Ricky had a thin scar running along his jaw from his right ear to the corner of his mouth, which he wore with pride and the origins of which he told anyone who would listen. The knife fight was two years ago, but it was Ricky's claim to fame, since the other guy ended up dead. Magnan was not sure how Ricky had obtained his position of favor in Fat Albert Gallata's organization, but he detested the punk.

"Friday is tomorrow," Magnan said as non-sarcastically as he could manage. "Are you drunk, or just confused?" Magnan had returned to the desk chair and his ledger and was trying to ignore the other man's presence in the room.

Ricky took a step forward and let out a high-pitched laugh. "It's after midnight, and I got plans t'morra, so I'm gettin' my rounds outta the way early. The boss don't care as long as I get the cash in the bank, so let's have it. Ya don't wanna keep Fat Albert waitin'.'"

It annoyed Magnan that Ricky always made a point of mentioning Fat Albert's name in their conversations. Magnan suspected that Ricky was recording them in order to blackmail Magnan someday, or at least hold it over his head to keep him in line. Ricky, although not a well-educated kid, was savvy enough to know that this was his one and only point of leverage, so he used it frequently.

"Doesn't it worry you, Ricky, that you're talking to a police officer? How do you think Mr. Gallata would feel about you dropping his name and implicating him in a criminal enterprise? Hmmmm?"

Ricky snarled and opened his mouth to say something, but then couldn't think quickly enough to figure out what to say. He just closed his mouth again like a fish trying to breathe on a beach. After a few moments of thought, during which Magnan ignored him, Ricky went back to his typical hard-ass approach. "Listen, wise guy, you just hand over the boss's cut so I can get outta here."

Magnan looked up and gave Ricky a bored expression, then removed a key from his belt, unlocked the bottom right drawer of the desk, and pulled it open. He extracted a metal box, which he unlocked with a different key, removed a thick envelope inscribed with the letters "AG" in cursive handwriting, and handed it to Ricky, who had taken three steps forward so that he was hovering directly above Magnan. Ricky shoved the envelope into the pocket of his coat and, without another word, turned and walked back toward the door. After he heard the door slam shut, he let out a sigh and mumbled to himself, "I can't believe I have to put up with a putz like that."

Chapter 35 – Closing the Noose

Monday, April 8

MIKE AND JASON SPENT THE NEXT SEVERAL DAYS working the Rosario murder, which was just what Sully wanted. They enlisted two rookie cops and one IT tech to review the finisher photos from the past several races staged by the NYC Runners. They had checked the names of the runners and determined that if Ricky Spezio had run any of them, he had done so under a different name. That did not surprise Mike or Jason, figuring that a career thug, who seemed to be living off the grid, would not make it that easy for the authorities to identify him. They figured he would have a fake driver's license that would easily allow him to register for the races. Jason had run a few 5K races and knew that the security at bib pick-up was not exactly the airport TSA.

Without a name to look for, they enlisted face-recognition software to screen out women, children, and older men. Even narrowing it down with these parameters, there were still several thousand faces that had to be scrutinized, looking for a potential match for an artist's sketch. It was slow work, but after a pile of overtime hours, they had identified eight possible matches.

By cross-referencing the bib numbers of the finisher photos against the roster of runners, they got names for their eight possibilities. The website listed each person's city or country, but no address. The team was able to find seven of their eight faces at easily available addresses, only two of which were in New York City. All of the seven checked out clean and had solid alibis for the nights of the Rosario murder and the Webster Avenue chase.

That left one face, which corresponded to the name James Ryun, listed as New York, NY. Mike immediately got the joke – Jim Ryun was the first high-school runner to break the four-minute mile. That had to be their guy. They referenced prior races staged by the NYC Runners and found that James Ryun had run in several of them, including the NYC Half-Marathon the previous year. He finished in an impressive 1:15:53, placing him among the first 150 finishers. He was actually pretty fast, even over a long distance.

The NYC Runners club was happy to confirm that James Ryun of New York, NY was registered for the upcoming NYC Half-Marathon, and that he would be wearing bib number 10023. The bib had already been picked up, so it was not possible to catch him when he showed up to claim his entry credentials. They would have to get him on the day of the race. Jason wanted to send in a bunch of uniforms just before the start of the race to storm the mass of runners in the first wave and pluck their man out of the crowd. Mike, however, was not excited about trying to pick Ricky out of a tightly packed group of runners, and he was worried that their rabbit would run on them. With all the people at the Brooklyn starting line for the race, he might get away. Mike's preference was to nab him as soon as he crossed the finish line. There, the runners would be spaced out, Ricky would be hemmed in by the barriers that surrounded the Central Park finish line, and he would be exhausted from running 13.1 miles. Sully liked Mike's plan best, since it would require minimal uniforms and had the highest probability of success.

Ж Ж Ж

On Sunday morning, 24,000 runners left the starting line and began their journey from Brooklyn toward Central Park. Mike and Jason were sitting on cold metal bleachers just beyond the balloon arch that marked the finish line. The timer clock was clicking its way past forty-nine minutes. Two officers were staking out the point where the runners would turn north from the fountain near Columbus Circle and wind their way over the undulating road toward the finish line a half-mile away. They radioed to Mike and Jason that the lead runners would be coming past within the next ten minutes. They were tracking the progress of "James Ryun" on the NYC Runners app and he was still twenty-five minutes away, in all likelihood. Two more beat cops were stationed on Fifth Avenue, where the runners first entered Central Park. The lead runners had passed their location, but they had not spotted their target.

Mike and Jason both got up and stretched. Mike pulled his wool hat down over his ears, while Jason adjusted the imitation fur ear muffs that matched his black pea coat. The warmth of the prior weekend was a distant memory. Jason had his service pistol in a holster at his side, under his coat, and two extra magazines of ammo in his pocket. Mike was still not cleared to have a gun, so he had an old-school Billy club in the inside pocket of his overcoat, just in case.

Mike checked in by radio with the two teams of uniformed officers who were assigned to assist with the arrest at the finish line. He thought it was overkill to have so many officers, but they wanted to be sure not to miss the guy. The area around the finish line was lined with metal crowd-control barriers on both sides of the park drive, keeping family members and friends from jumping onto the course to run the last few hundred yards with their loved ones. The barriers extended beyond the finish line for the next several hundred yards, where the runners were handed their finishing medals, water bottles, bananas, bagels, orange slices, and Mylar blankets. Inside the barriers, there was no place for Ricky the Runner to run, and the cops would be able to cuff him and lead him away to a waiting squad car. Jason suggested that they should let him get his medal before they busted him, since it would be one more thing the cops could grab onto if he tried to resist. Mike liked the idea of strangling the guy with his finisher medal.

Ж Ж Ж

While Mike and Jason moved one of the metal crowd barriers aside so that they could get inside the finisher area, a man wearing heavy gray sweatpants and a gray NYU sweatshirt exited a cab on Fifth Avenue and hurried into the park, carrying a small black pull-cord backpack. His given name was Horacio, but everyone called him Harry "the Spoon." Harry liked his pasta, and he had an extra-large silver soup spoon that he carried with him to assist with his spaghetti spinning. Harry was no runner, although he was dressed today as if he were planning a jog in the park.

Harry approached the inner roadway, where a trickle of the leading runners whooshed past. This point was about three miles from the finish. There were no crowd barriers here, and a smattering of spectators lined the road, some with encouraging signs and some with bells or other noisemakers. They cheered and clapped as the fastest runners passed them. Harry the Spoon carefully scrutinized the runners. He chose a spot where there was a long flat stretch of road, followed by a curve and a slight incline. The runners would slow down slightly at that point. Harry reached into his black bag and extracted a dark red windbreaker, allowing the black bag to fall to the grass.

After waiting for five minutes, Harry stepped forward toward the roadway. He had spotted the runner he was looking for, wearing blue shorts, a thin white tank top, and bib number 10023. As the runner approached, Harry stepped out into the road and ran as fast as his thick legs would allow, glancing back over his shoulder. When the runner in the blue shorts came up on his left to pass him, Harry veered suddenly. He grabbed the man around the torso and pulled them both off the road and down onto the cold grass and mud next to the curb.

The runner cried out, "Hey, what the fuck?" Harry looked him in the eye and held one finger over his mouth in the universal signal to keep quiet.

"You been made," Harry said quickly. "You just twisted your ankle. You're comin' with me. Try to limp." Harry tossed the windbreaker at Ricky the Runner. "Put this on and let's get out of here." Harry got up and jogged back across the road, then started walking in the direction of Fifth Avenue.

Ricky panted out three long breaths, trying to slow his heart rate. He pulled on the windbreaker and then limped at a trot to catch up with Harry. He looked back over his shoulder longingly at the other runners, who were closing in on the finish line. "I was on a pace for a personal best," Ricky lamented.

"Tough break, Kid," was all Harry said before he hailed a cab and got inside, leaving the door open for Ricky.

Ж Ж Ж

As the race clock ticked past 1:35:00, Jason and Mike were pacing back and forth just beyond the finish line, watching the runners come through. The lead women had finished, and the line of runners was getting thicker, making it more difficult to pick out individual runners and their bib numbers. The two cops near Columbus Circle reported that they had not seen Ricky the Runner. Jason checked the app on his phone. It had been more than 45 minutes since their prey had crossed the last checkpoint. He picked out a random runner wearing a tank top emblazoned with a charity sponsor's logo, "Team McGraw 45." He noted the bib number and punched it into the app. The Team McGraw runner had crossed the last checkpoint fifteen minutes after bib number 10023.

"Where the fuck is he?" Mike asked nobody in particular.

"Maybe he got hurt – pulled a muscle or fell down?" Jason offered without enthusiasm.

Mike picked up his radio and instructed two of their backup units to move into the medical tents and to start reverse-walking the course from the finish line toward the last check-point. They spent the next hour looking for any sign of Ricky the Runner, while more and more runners flooded the roadway, making it difficult to see any individual person. The officers reported back that there was nobody lying injured on the side of the road, and nobody in the medical tents fitting Ricky's description.

"You think somebody warned him to duck out before the finish line?" Mike asked Jason.

"The only people who knew this was happening were cops."

"Yeah. I know."

"Lucas is not going to like this," Jason shook his head.

"I don't like it either," Mike responded.

After another half hour, they finally gave up and released the officers to go back to their normal shift duties. Mike and Jason walked west toward Mike's apartment, trying to come up with a scenario where Ricky had not been tipped off by a dirty cop. They did not come up with any plausible alternate possibility.

Chapter 36 – An Unexpected Arrival

Monday, April 15

T HAT MONDAY, MIKE AND JASON spent most of the day trying to figure out what had happened on Sunday. They had no idea how Ricky the Runner had figured out that he needed to leave the course somewhere in Central Park. The NYC Runners tracking system confirmed that James Ryun never crossed the finish line. They kept coming back to the same conclusion – he had been tipped off. Since the only people who knew about the operation were cops, that meant that either a cop had tipped him, or a cop had told someone else who tipped him. Agent Gomez felt the same way, and he was keen on tracking down the cop with the loose lips. But they had no leads. They interviewed all the officers who were part of the operation, and a few admitted telling other cops about the plans for Sunday. By the end, it was clear that the intra-departmental grapevine could have leaked the information to virtually any cop on the force. They had failed to make it a confidential operation, and it cost them.

On Tuesday, Mike got a call from Michelle in the middle of the day. She told him that she had received a call from Steph Barker. While that was surprising, the real shock was that Steph was calling from the Port Authority Bus Terminal in Manhattan. Michelle didn't have any idea what Steph was doing in New York, but she had arranged to meet her. Michelle suggested that Mike should meet them. Mike agreed and said he'd meet her and Steph for lunch at the Nom Wa Tea Parlor in Chinatown. The little dim sum place was one of Mike's favorites and one of the few places that they returned to often. He hopped a ride in a black and white downtown and arrived only a few minutes after the time he and Michelle had set.

He exited the squad car at the corner of Canal and Mott and walked to Doyer Street, which curved around between Bowery and Mott for only a few hundred yards. The tiny street had a lot of history, its "Bloody Angle" having been the site of several high-profile crimes. The little tea house near the middle of the curve was itself semi-famous, after a Kevin Bacon movie used it as the setting for a major shoot-em-up scene. But Mike had known the place since it was so obscure that the menu was available only in Chinese. Now it was more upscale, and even took credit cards. But it had good memories.

When Mike walked through the door, he was smiling and reminiscing about coming to the little place with his cousin Lou. He waved at the little Chinese woman at the counter in the front and scanned the expanse of small mismatched tables and chairs for Michelle and Steph. He spotted them at a table near the back. The girl was dressed casually in jeans and a red off-the-shoulder top. She was staring at Mike and looked nervous. Mike tried to plant a neutral expression on his face and walked without hurry toward the table, trying to get a read on the situation from Michelle's eyes, without success.

"Well, this is certainly a surprise," Mike said with as much enthusiasm as he could muster, reaching out his hand to Steph. "Miss Barker, it's good to see you. What brings you to our fair city?"

Before Steph could respond, their waiter appeared and asked for drink orders. Mike asked for tea, as did Michelle. Steph ordered a Diet Coke. When the waiter left, Mike prompted, "So, there's a story?"

"Yes," Michelle cut in, "it's really interesting. You see, since we visited Port Angeles, Steph and I have been exchanging emails. She asked me how the investigation has been going so I told her about how you and Jason had tracked Christine's movements to Brooklyn and you had a theory about how she might have been taken in by the prostitution ring, but that you were having trouble finding any additional information."

"You told her all that?" Mike said. Mike had shared that information with Michelle because she was a government employee and because they worked together and spent so much time together. Sharing information with a civilian was a complete breach of regulations and could get both of them in a lot of trouble.

"Well, not all at once," Michelle said, sheepishly.

"It wasn't her fault," Steph piped in. "I made her tell me. I feel so bad that I didn't do more for Christine. I didn't reach out to her enough. I didn't go try to help her in Seattle. If I had done more, she wouldn't be dead now." Steph was fighting back tears by the end of her little speech.

"You can't know that," Mike soothed. "You can't beat yourself up about not preventing what happened. I can tell you from experience that it does no good. People make their own choices. You can give advice but you can't live their lives for them. Nothing you could have done would have made a difference."

"That's not true!" Steph snapped back, between sniffs. "I know it's not true. Now I just can't live with myself if I don't help you catch whoever killed her. I just have to."

Mike stared at Steph with a puzzled expression, then turned toward Michelle with the same what-the-Hell-is-she-talking-about look.

Just then, a server appeared next to the table rolling a metal cart piled high with plates, tins, and bamboo steamer baskets filled with dim sum. Mike and Michelle picked out an assortment. Steph said she would eat anything so they should just choose for her. They arranged the plates on the table and ate steamed buns and dumplings with chopsticks for several minutes. Finally, in between bites, Michelle continued with the story.

"Well, Mike, I told Steph the same thing — that she should not feel guilty about Christine's death. But she really wanted to help. So, I encouraged her to look for more information on her end that might help with your investigation. I didn't disclose any confidential information, but we brainstormed about what facts about Christine's life might help us trace her movements after she came to New York. She couldn't really think of anything, but she told me that she wanted to come to New York and try to retrace Christine's steps — to see if she could help us find the people who killed her."

"What?" Mike exclaimed, breaking into Michelle's narrative.

"I told her she could not do that," Michelle quickly added.

"But I could!" Steph said excitedly, putting down her chopsticks. "That's why I'm here."

"Could what?" Mike said, not entirely following the confusing story.

"Go undercover," Steph said confidently.

"Undercover? We don't — there's no undercover operation."

"But I could do it."

Mike paused to compose himself. "Miss Barker, I think you've been watching too many TV cop shows. We can't run any undercover operation here, for reasons that I really can't go into, and even if we could, we could never have a civilian involved. That's crazy."

"I'm not crazy," Steph said defiantly. "And don't be mad at Michelle. She told me it wouldn't work and she told me not to come but I don't care. I'm going to do something to help Christine."

"Christine is dead," Mike said as comfortingly as he could manage. "There's nothing you can do for her."

"Then it's for me," Steph shot back. "I'm doing it for myself. To make me feel better. I know that. I have to do this."

"Do what?" Mike asked rhetorically.

"Help you by going undercover."

"No. That cannot ever happen."

"Now, Mike, I know that, of course," Michelle broke in. "I told Steph that. But she just kind of showed up here today and I didn't know what to do so I wanted you to come and help talk some sense into her." Michelle reached out and squeezed Mike's hand.

"We can just put her on a plane home and that should take care of it," Mike said as if that ended the discussion.

"I took the bus," Steph said, "and I'm not going back. You can't force me. Even if you don't want me, I'm going to do something."

"What?" Mike said, not really intending the question to be answered.

"I can find out who killed Christine. I can go to that shelter in Brooklyn, where I sent her the Starbucks cards, and let those guys find me. I can imitate a meth addict. I've seen them up close for long enough. I can fool anyone. I'll get them to give me some information that will help you and then I'll tell you and you'll get 'em and they'll pay for killing Christine." Steph finished with her balled-up fist hitting the table.

Mike looked at Michelle. "Did you tell her that the address was a shelter?"

"No, she didn't," Steph replied before Michelle could speak. "I Googled it."

Mike sucked in a deep breath and tried not to make it a sigh. He put on his best soothing, fatherly advice voice. "Steph, I really appreciate that you want to help. You are loyal to your sister and I get that. But, this is a police investigation, and it could be dangerous. We could never allow a civilian to be put in harm's way. You're not trained, and frankly it would get me in a ton of trouble. I love your desire, but it's just impossible."

Steph was quiet for a moment. Mike wasn't sure if she was about to scream or cry. "Michelle told me you'd say that. She said that same thing. It's too dangerous. I don't know what I'm doing. Well let me tell you that I don't give a shit. Christine didn't know what she was doing either."

"And it got her killed," Mike snapped.

"I know – I'm her sister!"

"Steph," Michelle broke in, trying to keep a lid on the emotions. "You have already been so helpful. Really."

"Then I'll just have to go find that reporter from *The New York Times* who wrote that story about Christine before. I'm sure he would want to write about how a civilian tried to take down a prostitution ring."

"What do you mean by that?" Mike asked.

"Just what I said. I've been thinking about it. If you won't let me help the police because I'm not a cop, then fine. I'll just do it as a private person and get *The Times* or somebody to cover it and write a story about it afterwards. If they don't want to, then I'll just write a blog about it myself."

"They could be writing about how you got killed," Michelle said with true worry in her voice. Michelle was not a mother, but Mike thought she sounded just like one.

"Why should I care?" Steph shot back defiantly. "I've got nothing. My family is in shambles. I can't even think about college. My mom is a wreck already. Maybe I don't care if I get killed, as long as I'm doing something worthwhile. You can't stop me."

"Listen to me, young lady, I will have you arrested for obstruction of a police investigation."

"Fine! Put me in jail. I'm sure that will make a good story for the papers, too." Steph stuck out her chin and looked Mike right in the eye. He had to give her credit – she had balls.

"Let's just slow down," Mike said, sitting back in his chair after noticing that he had been leaning forward. "Let's not rush into anything. Where are you staying?"

Steph looked at Michelle, who looked at Steph awkwardly. "Um, well, I'm not sure. I didn't really make plans for that. I was hoping to stay with Michelle."

"What?" Mike looked dumbfounded as he stared at Michelle. "Is that true?"

"Well, I did offer to put her up if she ever visited," Michelle said reluctantly.

"We can get her a hotel room."

"I don't want to stay in some hotel. I want to stay with someone I know."

"What about you, Michelle? Is that what you want?" Mike tried to remember what plans he and Michelle had made for the next few nights. They had been playing it very spur-of-the-moment each day, but Mike had visions of sleeping alone while Michelle had a visitor.

"I guess it's okay with me," Michelle said. "I'd rather have her with me than off somewhere else in the city alone. I can look after her."

"Great. Fine. Let her stay at your apartment while she's here."

The waiter approached the table with their lunch check, which Mike snatched from his hand. The group gathered up their things and Mike walked to the front counter to pay the bill and tell owner Wilson Tang that the food was wonderful, as always. When they got outside, Mike pulled Michelle aside. "You realize how much trouble I'm going to be in if the captain finds out that I shared confidential information about this investigation with the victim's sister?"

"You didn't share it, Mike. I did."

"That's not going to matter. You heard it from me, so it's my ass on the line. If that girl goes and gets herself killed, there will be hell to pay. We have to convince her – you have to convince her – to give up this crazy idea."

"I'll try."

"Use your most persuasive voice," Mike said, as he kissed her on the cheek and walked away to grab the subway back uptown.

Ж Ж Ж

Later that afternoon, as Mike was on his way back to his apartment after the end of the work day, his cell phone rang. It was another cold day and it was raining, so Mike had hitched a ride in a squad car that was heading that way.

"Mike, she's gone!" Michelle's voice was frantic.

"What do you mean, gone?"

"I mean I went out to get some supplies so I could make us dinner and when I got back Steph was gone. Her backpack is gone, too, so I think she's not coming back."

"Did you speak with her about . . . the situation?" Mike said, not wanting to be specific in front of the uniformed officer who was driving the car.

"Yes."

"So, how did it go?"

Michelle hesitated and Mike's stomach did a back flip. "I really tried, Mike. I explained how much trouble we would be in, but she is so stubborn. She said that she was going to do it with us or without us.

I told her to calm down and we'd talk more over dinner. Then she split."

"Did she say anything about where she might be going?"

"No. But I'm assuming Brooklyn."

"Great. OK, listen. You contact her by text or phone or whatever and try to get her to come back. Tell her that I'll come down there and talk to her again. In the meantime, I'll see what I can do to find her." Mike hung up and told his driver, Officer Matt Barsal, that his plans had changed and that he wanted to get to Brooklyn as fast as possible. Meanwhile, he called dispatch and asked for units in lower Manhattan and Brooklyn to be on the lookout for Steph and gave her description, based on what she was wearing when he had seen her at lunch. She might have changed clothes, but he had to give something to the beat cops.

An hour later, after fruitlessly cruising the area around the shelter in Brooklyn where Steph had sent her Starbucks cards to Christine, Mike had officer Barsal drop him at Michelle's apartment building. Jason met him there, after Mike had filled him in on the day's events.

"You're shitting me," was Jason's reaction to the idea that this 19-year-old civilian was going to charge into harm's way on an ill-conceived "undercover" mission without any support or backup.

"How are we going to stop her?" Mike asked.

"We may not be able to," Michelle said dejectedly. "I spent all afternoon trying to make her understand, but she wouldn't listen. She is fixated on this idea that she let her sister down and that she needs to make up for it or die trying."

"Great. You got a magic wand that can control unruly teenagers, Jason?"

"Don't look at me. You're the father figure here."

"Thanks. I'll have to get you back for that remark, you know."

"What if we just let her do it and protect her?"

Mike and Jason turned toward Michelle with matching perplexed expressions. "Are you insane?!" Mike offered as a response.

"Hear me out," Michelle said, holding up her hands, palms out, to indicate that everyone should calm down. "We can't throw her in jail or tie her up and put her in my closet. But we can give her a GPS tracker and let her go out on the street and talk to some of the working girls while you guys watch her to make sure she doesn't get into any real trouble. After a day or two she'll realize that it's not going to do any good. She'll be tired and hungry and ready to say that she tried and then she can go home. Just a couple of days is all it should take, right?"

"Why can't we put her in jail for interfering with a police investigation?" Jason asked.

"Because she told us that she'd contact Dexter Peacock at the fucking *Times* and tell him her sob story, which will probably include the fact that Michelle leaked confidential information about the case to her."

"I see the problem," Jason conceded. "But how would we even run a support operation without telling the captain? And if anything goes sideways, the shit we'll be in will be so deep we'll need a new wardrobe."

Mike looked out the window of the apartment. "Nothing will matter unless we get her back first."

At that moment, Michelle's cell phone buzzed and she hurriedly answered. "Hello? . . . Oh, thank God . . . Is she alright? . . . Where are you? . . . OK, that's great. I'll meet you at the door." She hung up. "That was an officer. She has Steph in a squad car and was calling from her phone. They're on their way here to drop her off."

"Good. Let's see what we can do to get her to go home if we let her spend some time on the street first."

"You sure, Mike?" Jason asked.

"No, but I have no better ideas."

Ж Ж Ж

When Steph arrived, escorted by a uniformed officer, she was wet and shivering, but also defiant and angry that she had been forced to come back. She calmed down only after Mike and Jason tag-teamed to convince her that they were ready to let her participate in their investigation, as she had suggested. Steph agreed to accept their assistance and support, rather than go charging into the New York sex trade on her own. After a half-hour of discussion, Mike promised to be back the following afternoon to brief her about the "operation," after he had made some arrangements.

When he left Michelle's apartment, he called Everett Forrest. Mike always said that the FBI had the best toys, and he needed to borrow a few. Everett had always said that if Mike ever needed anything, he just had to ask. It was time to ask.

Ж Ж Ж

The next day at the scheduled time of 2:00 p.m., Mike arrived at Michelle's apartment. Jason was already there, chatting with Steph and Michelle. Mike and Jason had already discussed how they wanted this to go.

"Alright, we're going to run this as operation CB," Mike started his official "briefing" for Steph's benefit. "Stephanie Barker has volunteered to be our eyes and ears on the ground to see if we can gather any information from the girls on the street about Christine Barker's murder. I have secured this," Mike held up a slender black device that looked a little like a stapler. "This is a sub-dermal GPS transmitter, on loan from our friends at the FBI. Steph, we'll inject a

239

tiny transmitter chip under your skin in the back of your neck, just around your hair line. It will be totally undetectable and invisible, and you can just forget about it. We will be able to track your location no matter where you go. We'll also install some software that our FBI colleagues have sent to me on a burner phone. When you activate the app, your phone will silently connect to my phone so that we can listen and record anything that's happening. The open call line will suck battery life from the phone, so you should only activate it if something important is happening. If anyone looks at your phone, it will not seem to have a call in progress – it all happens behind the scenes. It will even be active when the phone appears to be powered off."

Mike continued, "Tomorrow, we'll take you down to Brooklyn to the neighborhood where somebody used the gift cards you sent to Christine. Your job is to hang around the area – go to the Starbucks, walk around the neighborhood, and keep your eyes open. See if you can find a hooker and ask if she's willing to sell you some meth. Pretend to be a user. We'll get you some clothes from the Goodwill down on Canal Street. Don't shower or wash your face or hands today. Get into character. Got it?" Steph nodded, clearly paying close attention and thrilled to be getting instructions instead of objections from Mike.

"One of us will be in position somewhere around you, keeping tabs. You will not know where we are and you should not look for us. If we do this properly, and we will, you will not know that we're there, and neither will anyone else. If we see you in any trouble, we'll move in and get you. If anything happens, you drop to the ground or hide somewhere and get out of sight. We'll know where you are based on your tracker, and you can activate the phone app and just say that you need help and we'll move. You got that?" Mike finished with the harsh question, like an army drill sergeant.

"Yes." Steph said, her voice cracking a little bit.

"Are you sure you really want to do this?" Jason asked her sternly.

"Yes," Steph managed with more enthusiasm. "I have to do this for Christine."

"Fine," Mike said, as if ending the briefing. "Michelle will handle the insertion of the subdermal transmitter. Jason and I have some prep work to do. We'll meet back here at 10:00 a.m. tomorrow. You understand that this is not going to be fun. It's going to be uncomfortable for you." Mike looked sternly at the young woman as he made his last-ditch effort to scare her into abandoning her Quixotic quest. "You're going to have to live on the street. The people you will come in contact with will be addicts and hookers and homeless people. There's a chance someone could get violent with you. As much as we're going to take precautions, there is a good chance you will come out of this with some scars, both physical and emotional. Are you sure you really want to do this?"

Steph returned a defiant, "I'm sure."

Everyone nodded their affirmation and understanding. Mike motioned to Jason to follow him out of the apartment. He smiled at Michelle and gave her a wink, then turned and left. Mike and Jason were going to Brooklyn to scope out the area where they would be sending Steph and establishing surveillance positions. They had much to do to make this look realistic, so that Steph would think she was really operating undercover. They talked about all the ways that things could go wrong, but agreed that none of them were likely. Mike mumbled under his breath, "Sure, what could go wrong?"

Chapter 37 – A Matter of Trust

Wednesday, April 17

MIKE AND JASON SPENT TWO HOURS touring the Brooklyn neighborhood where they planned to send Steph, then circled back to Manhattan and stopped in at the Internal Affairs office to see Agent Gomez. After several visits to the office, their appearance was becoming routine and did not arouse any special interest. The staff there knew that Stoneman and Dickson were working with Gomez on an investigation that was peripheral to a murder case. Mike picked up a box of donuts and three coffees on the walk from the car into the building and Lucas met them at their usual conference table.

"Thanks for the snack," Lucas said as he hovered his fingers over the assortment, trying to decide which to select.

"It's really our pleasure," Jason replied. "We can't have them up at the precinct, so this is an opportunity for us to indulge."

"Still have the rat issue up there?"

Stoneman nodded. "They pulled a dozen of the suckers out of the traps this week. They say it's good news that they're still catching them, but I'm starting to wonder whether the supply is infinite."

Lucas chuckled, but Mike and Jason did not laugh with him. After he chose a chocolate frosted and took a healthy bite, he asked, between chews, "So, why did you want to talk today?"

Jason took the lead on the explanation. He and Mike had decided that since Mike and Michelle were seeing each other, they didn't want it to seem like Mike's idea and they wanted to keep Michelle's involvement mostly out of it. Making Jason the spokesman seemed to be the best way to accomplish those goals. "We're staging a mock undercover operation in the vicinity of the activity that we think is associated with Christine Barker's murder."

"Mock?"

"Yes. It's not real, but it will have some of the characteristics of a real operation. Since we think we have a mole somewhere in the department, we want to keep it very hush-hush so that nothing makes our potential suspects think that it's a real sting. We're telling you so that you know in advance, just in case things end up leaking or the facts come out later. We don't want you to think we were acting behind your back. As far as we're concerned, you're part of our team on this. Are we right?"

Lucas finished a bite of donut and took a sip of coffee very slowly, obviously pondering the situation and stalling for time. Jason and Mike indulged him gladly. "How much can you tell me?"

"We'd like to tell you as little as possible. The less you know, the less you have to tell your bosses. We don't know where the leak is. It could be inside IA."

"It's not here," Lucas shot back indignantly. "I can promise you that."

"Well, you're probably right, but it's best if we keep the whole thing very low-profile. It's not going to amount to anything."

"Then why are you doing it?" Lucas raised one eyebrow, which curled into the shape of a fish hook against his forehead.

"It's a long story that we'd best not get into, Lucas. It's only going to be a day – maybe two. Call it a training exercise."

"How many people are involved?"

"Just Mike, me, and the trainee."

"I don't suppose you want to tell me who the trainee is."

"No, that's probably not a good idea. But when this is behind us, we're thinking that we should make it known that we're planning a real undercover gig and see if anyone jumps. It might be a good way to put dye in the water and see where it leads."

Lucas pondered this idea, which Jason hoped would distract him from their "mock" operation. "It's an interesting idea. Plant a false lead and see if it pops up somewhere that might give us a clue where the leak is. I like the concept. Let me think about how we could do that."

"Great," Mike broke in. "That sounds like a plan." Both Mike and Jason grabbed donuts and ate them without fear of crumbs as the three of them talked about possible controlled leaks. A half-hour and half a box of donuts later, Mike and Jason walked out of the building, retrieved their car, and headed back to the precinct. Mike reported that they had spent the day making observations about the suspected crime scene area in Brooklyn, which was essentially true.

When Mike was ready to leave, he stopped by Jason's desk. "Any second thoughts?"

"Many," Jason responded without emotion. "But no better ideas."

"OK. We're go for tomorrow. I'll meet you at 10:00 at Michelle's place."

"We could use another member of the team," Jason suggested.

"Yeah, I know. Just the two of us may be a little short, especially since we can't really call in backup."

"Any ideas?" Jason asked.

"The only one I can think of is Darren."

"Can we trust him?"

Mike paused a moment, then responded forcefully. "He was my partner. He has my back. I can trust him."

"But can I trust him?"

"Yeah, I think so."

"OK, Mike. I trust *you*, so if you're good with the guy, then I'm good."

"I'll give him a call." Mike turned to his phone and Jason walked away. Mike wondered whether it was wise to pull his disabled ex-partner into the operation, but it wasn't a real operation, so what was the harm? Darren would probably enjoy a little fake action. What could go wrong?

Chapter 38 – Operation Undercover

Thursday, April 18

WHEN MIKE ARRIVED AT MICHELLE'S APARTMENT the next morning, he scanned the rooms looking for Steph. He knew that the girl was supposed to be sleeping on Michelle's couch, but there was no bedding or pillow in sight. "Where's Steph?" Mike asked, hoping that she had changed her mind about the undercover operation and was in the shower.

"She's on the balcony," Michelle replied, gesturing toward the sliding glass door that Mike knew was behind the white lace curtains in the living room. The door led to a small outdoor space with a view up Third Avenue, where Michelle and Mike sometimes sat in the two small plastic chairs that mostly filled up the area. Mike estimated that the balcony was no more than ten feet wide and four feet deep, surrounded by a four-foot-high metal railing. It was barely above freezing outside.

"What's she doing there?"

"Sleeping," Michelle responded, again gesturing toward the sliding door as if to invite Mike to take a look.

Mike opened the curtains and peered out. The two chairs had been turned to face each other. In between the seats, Mike saw a bundle of blankets without any clear explanation for what was keeping them suspended above the concrete balcony floor. Steph was somewhere under those blankets, still asleep at ten in the morning. "Your idea?" he asked Michelle.

"Nope. Hers. She said that if she was going to have to sleep on the street tonight, she might as well get used to it. Plus, she thought it would help get her into character as a homeless person."

Mike whistled softly and nodded his head slightly. "I have to agree with her. Damn! I was hoping she would change her mind. You think sleeping outside last night might nudge her toward abandoning this thing?"

"Doubtful," was all Michelle could say.

Mike opened the sliding door and called out to Steph, who stirred under her mountain of blankets and then eventually emerged, shivering slightly. She was wearing gray sweatpants and a bright red sweatshirt with a cartoon image of a fox on the front. She looked a good twenty pounds heavier than Mike remembered, which he guessed was a byproduct of wearing two or three layers of clothing. Her feet were covered by large hiking boots, which were not laced up, revealing black-and-white checkered stockings. Her hair was pulled back in a pony-tail, but it lacked its normal sheen and instead looked dull and sticky. She rubbed her eyes and said, "Morning!" with a forced smile.

"OK," Mike said, clapping his hands loudly together, "let's get this show on the road."

Ж Ж Ж

247

A few hours later, Steph struggled up the stairs from the C train at Clinton Avenue in Brooklyn, pulling a wire basket with oversized wheels one step at a time. The basket was stuffed with spare clothes purchased from the Goodwill shop, two reusable plastic bottles filled with tap water, and a heavy wool blanket that was already dirty from the night spent on Michelle's balcony. She looked the part of a street dweller, with her clunky hiking boots, two pairs of sweatpants, mismatched sweatshirt, bulky scarf, and a man's overcoat draped over her shoulders. She squinted into the morning sun, trying to get her bearings on the unfamiliar street. She pulled the bill of her dirty black baseball cap low over her eyes and wished that Michelle had let her bring along her sunglasses. She looked left and right, then began walking slowly east on Fulton Street. The early spring sun was out, taking the bitter edge off the air, but it was still in the low 40s and the perpetual breeze off the water in Brooklyn chilled her down to the clean white panties she had allowed herself to wear despite the otherwise grungy clothes.

After two hours of walking the neighborhood, dragging her little cart up and down curbs, she ducked into an alley behind a diner and opened the top of a dumpster, searching for something that would serve as breakfast, or lunch. She had intentionally not eaten before she boarded the subway in Manhattan. At Mike's suggestion, they had decided that Steph should assume a different name for her assignment, so she left her wallet at Michelle's apartment. With no ID, she could claim to be anyone, and since she had never been arrested or in the military, even her fingerprints would not yield her true identity. Mike had provided a burner cell phone with no identifying information – and the special FBI app – with her new name along with a fake home number with a Denver area code. Michelle had uploaded a selfie that Steph had taken at the beach a few years earlier to be the wallpaper for the burner phone. As far as anyone in Brooklyn was concerned, her name was Dani LaBlonde, which was the actual name of one of Steph's high school classmates. Steph would be able to remember her new name easily, along with a backstory if she needed one.

She knew that there wasn't likely to be much action for her until the late afternoon at the earliest, but she wanted to establish herself in the neighborhood. She smiled at any men who made eye contact and said "hello" to any women who looked like they could possibly be hookers. Most importantly, she kept her eyes out for anyone who looked like a user or a dealer.

After a nap in a bus shelter and two hours nursing one cup of coffee at Starbucks, Steph was being ushered outside by a burly barista when she saw three women walking in together. They were dressed like they were on their way to a nightclub on a Saturday night rather than to a Starbucks at 5:30 p.m. on a Thursday. They all had their hair down and were wearing thick makeup. She could smell the mixture of their various perfumes as they passed her. One of the women was Black, one looked vaguely Asian, and one was white with blonde hair. Steph made eye contact with the blonde and tried to give a pathetic, pleading kind of look, as if asking for help. The blonde gave her a puzzled expression.

Steph lingered outside the Starbucks, waiting for the group to come back out, and then followed them up the street, keeping her distance. The three hot women in tight dresses under puffy jackets were not hard to follow even through the crowded rush-hour sidewalk. They stopped on a side street near the Barclays Center, the arena where the Brooklyn Nets played basketball and the New York Islanders played some of their home games. Tonight, there was a rap concert on tap. The three women balanced on their heels as they drank their coffee and watched the pedestrians go by. Steph crossed the street and sat down on a pile of empty boxes that had been set out with the trash next to a liquor store. She tried hard not to look around to see where Mike and Jason were hiding. It was not difficult for her to look rather pathetic.

By a quarter to seven, the sun was low in the sky, the temperature had dropped a few more degrees, and the commuters were mostly gone for the day. The crowd of concert-goers, however, had started to gather. The bars and restaurants were hopping with pre-concert diners and drinkers. The liquor store where Steph had squatted was also busy. Laughing groups emerged with small bottles, which they were probably going to try to get past security. The women across the street had discarded their Starbucks cups and were working the crowd, getting the attention of the men walking by toward the arena. As Steph watched, the Black woman, who was wearing a red dress and a leather-colored jacket, took the arm of a large Black man and escorted him around the corner. The other two kept up their discourse with the passing men until the Asian one also made a contact. After several minutes of talking, she also walked away in the same direction.

With only the white hooker left, wearing a black leather skirt that was cut mid-thigh, Steph decided to make an approach. She waited until she was not engaged with any passing men, then walked up to her. "Hey, you got any ice?" she said in a hushed voice.

"Fuck off!" the girl said dismissively, turning away from Steph and trying to make eye contact with two passing guys wearing Jay-Z hats.

"Hey, c'mon. Gimme a break. Where can I get some product?" Steph hunched over slightly and spoke roughly into the woman's waist.

"I said, fuck off!" she said, louder than before.

"Sure, I'll go. I don't want to get in your way. Hey, I know about working. That's cool. But, where should I go? Gimme a clue, you know? I'm not from here. I need some." Steph was breathing in shallow gasps. She licked her lips repeatedly and shifted her gaze from the ground up to the woman and back again. She looked up and pleaded with her eyes.

She looked down at Steph with suspicious eyes. "You a cop?"

"Fuck no," Steph replied with as much indignity as she could muster. "Are you?"

"Shut up. Get the hell out of here. I'm workin' and got no time for you."

"C'mon. Give a sister a break. I can help you out. I can work, too. I just need a source." Steph scratched at her arm, a typical behavior for meth users.

The blonde still looked skeptical, and annoyed that this homeless girl was interrupting her efforts to score some business. "Look, Bitch, you stay out of my way until after the show starts. Then we'll get some down time until it lets out later. You got a watch?"

"I got a phone."

"Whatever. Just get the fuck out of here. Come back at 8:30 and I'll think about it."

Steph took a step back and smiled. "OK, OK, that's OK. Hey, well, where can I go around here to stay warm and maybe get some food?"

"You figure it out, fool."

"OK, OK, I'm goin' and – hey – what's your name?" Steph had backed up a few more steps.

"It's Tina, now go!"

"Cool, Tina. Yah, cool. I'm Dani. So – I'll see you later." Steph turned and walked back toward the liquor store, pulling her cart.

The pile of boxes she had been sitting on was actually a pretty comfortable spot, and she could keep an eye on Tina from there in case she tried to run off without her. She reclaimed her perch and started panhandling the guys coming out of the store, asking for a drink and some food. To her surprise, several guys stopped and gave her hits from their bottles, she collected twelve dollars in singles, and one guy offered her twenty bucks to give his buddy a blow job. She laughed and asked for a hundred, which generated a barrage of insults and laughter. Steph did not look very attractive, and she knew it.

The volume of people rushing into and back out of the liquor store increased as concert time approached. The show started at 8:00, but the acts everyone wanted to see would not be on stage until 9:15. Still, as soon as the official show time came and went, people started hurrying toward the Barclays Center. The crowd right outside the arena got thick, while the sidewalk in front of the liquor store thinned out. In between begging to the men coming out of the store – she avoided talking to the women who were with them – she kept an eye on Tina and two other women who had rejoined her. They were still working the crowd across the street.

Chapter 39 – Working Girls

JASON PLUNGED HIS LARGE HANDS DEEPER into the pockets of his cashmere trench coat and hunched his shoulders, trying to force his collar up higher onto his neck. He realized after the first hour that he should have worn a scarf, but the relatively mild afternoon had lulled him into complacency. From his location in the plaza outside the Barclays Center, he could see Steph sitting on a pile of garbage outside a liquor store, where she had been for the past forty-five minutes. As the patrons of the hip-hop concert siphoned themselves into the arena, Jason's position became more and more exposed, but there were still plenty of folks wandering about and he blended in.

"Excuse me, Sir, is this the Barclays Center?" The voice coming from behind him was high-pitched and sounded shy and embarrassed, but it didn't fool Jason.

"Yes, Mike. It's the Barclays Center. Do you know the name of the artist performing here tonight?"

"No clue," Mike said in his normal voice as he took up a position next to Jason, but not looking directly at him. "Where's our little birdie?"

"Two o'clock, across the street next to the liquor store."

"Got it," Mike responded without appearing to look. He turned to the side and stared up at the huge electronic sign that flashed advertisements for upcoming events at the arena. "Any activity?"

"Not much. She made contact with three ladies working the crowd on the back side of the arena. You can't see them from here, but they seem to be pretty standard-issue hookers. She hasn't turned on the surveillance app yet."

"OK. Great. Where's Darren?"

"He's down the block, last I heard."

"Fine," Mike said blankly. "Why don't you walk down there and check in?"

"That's fine, I'm going to circle around past the working girls and check them out."

"You don't think they're actually connected, do you?"

"Not likely. I know we don't want her to really get anywhere with this whole farce, but just in case those women try to take advantage of her, I want to get a good look at them."

"Sounds reasonable. Check in with me when you make contact with Darren."

Jason strolled casually around the side of the huge building, skirting around the swirling crowds gathered around the entrances. After several minutes, he emerged on the far side of the venue and saw three women standing together on the sidewalk across the street. He crossed over and walked by them.

"Hey, Baby, you're looking good tonight," the Black woman called out to Jason.

"Mmm, that's some good-looking man there, Sheryl," the white one said. "Hey, Babe, you wanna get nasty?"

Jason slowed down and looked toward the group, taking mental notes about their appearance. He spotted Darren standing in an alcove next to the door of a building across the street, within sight of Steph's location. Jason stopped and nodded to Darren, receiving a low wave in response. Then he resumed walking.

"Oh, Baby, don't walk away," Sheryl shouted. Jason kept walking. He crossed back over the street and circled around the arena to a subway entrance. He glanced at Mike, still standing in the same place where Jason had left him, but did not make any further contact.

Mike had been following Jason's movement, but there was no point in additional conversation. They were trying to keep a low profile, and they didn't want Steph to spot them.

As the clock edged toward 8:30, most of the concert-goers had entered the arena. The plaza outside was empty save for the vendors, who were either packing up to leave or hunkering down until the after-concert rush in a few hours. Mike was thinking about moving to a location where he would be less visible now that the cover-crowd had abandoned him, when Steph made the decision for him by getting up and moving from her garbage heap.

Steph wheeled her pathetic little wire cart back across the street to where Tina and her two companions were standing, although their potential clients had diminished to a trickle. The crowd that might have been interested in a brief diversion before the show was basically tapped out. Steph approached slowly, then called out when she was about ten feet away.

"Hey, Tina. It's Dani, remember? You said you might have a line on a supply?" Steph was slightly hunched over, still holding onto the handle of her cart, and looking up with as much hunger and

255

desperation as she could manage. She twitched her left eye and scratched at an imaginary itch on her left hip.

Tina looked at her skeptically. "Sheryl, you think the boss would want to talk to this bitch?"

"I dunno," Sheryl replied without enthusiasm, "She looks like shit. Probably ain't got no money neither."

"I got some money!" Steph broke in, acting more excited than was warranted. "Really, I do. I can pay."

"Oh, yeah? Show me some cash," Tina shot back.

Steph looked confused and glanced down at her cart, then back at the women. "Well, I'm not gonna wave it around here on the street. I'm not stupid. But I got some, so whatever you can do for me, hey, I'm good. I just wanna buy some and go. I ain't no trouble."

Tina squinted her eyes at Steph and then fixed her attention on the little cart. "What'cha got there in the trolley?"

Steph took a step back away from Tina. "My stuff. Just my stuff. Nothin' nobody would want but me, so you just leave my stuff alone."

"Well, I tell you what. We're all goin' back to the hotel to rest up until the show lets out. You follow along and we'll see what the boss says." With that, the three women blew right past Steph and her cart with a few long-legged strides. Steph turned herself around and dragged her cart after them, keeping a respectful distance. They crossed two streets, then made a left and walked down a deserted sidewalk until they abruptly turned into the entrance of a drab building, with no awning or other marker that Steph expected to see at a hotel. When Steph drew even with the door, she saw a dim neon sign in the window advertising "Rooms for Rent" and a small painted sign identifying the place as The Alexander Hamilton Hotel.

Steph hesitated at the door. This was clearly not going to be a safe space. She reached under her bulky clothes and pulled out her burner cell phone, tapped a four-leaf clover icon on the screen, then shut off the power and returned the device to an inner pocket of her overcoat. Then she took a deep breath, pushed open one side of the double-doors that marked the hotel entrance, and slid herself and her cart inside.

Mike watched the screen of his phone, which displayed a map of the local streets and a blue circle indicating the position of Steph's subdermal tracker. Then, an alert message popped up and a ping advised him that Steph had activated her phone's clandestine broadcast function. Mike was walking along the sidewalk a block behind Steph. He stopped to fit an earbud into his left ear and connect it to his phone. He knew where Steph was, and he could hear what she could hear. The plan was seemingly working fine, although Mike would have been happier if she had spent the whole night on the pile of boxes outside the liquor store and never made contact with the three hookers.

Chapter 40 – The Alexander Hamilton Hotel

STEPH IMMEDIATELY THOUGHT that the lobby of the Alexander Hamilton Hotel looked more like the waiting room of a long-neglected doctor's office. In the cramped space to the left of the door was a line of worn chairs, with a similar line on the opposite wall about ten feet away. At the end of the row of seats, a forlorn potted palm tree sagged against a grimy window. A television mounted eight feet high in the corner displayed a baseball game for the benefit of the three men who occupied the space. All of them looked homeless and strung-out. Each of them was dressed like Steph, with mismatched layers of dirty clothing and clunky boots. Two were white and had unkempt beards and long, stringy hair. The other man was Black and had a shaved head. None seemed that interested in the game.

To the right of the door, a plexiglass partition separated the lobby area from a man who was leaning back in a chair and smoking a cigarette. The plexiglass ran the length of a ten-foot desk, at the end of which stood a large door bearing a sign that read "Wait for Buzzer." As Steph stood there, trying to take in these strange surroundings, she was startled by a loud clang, followed by an even louder buzzing noise coming from behind the door. A man emerged. He was Black, and looked very much like the three men sitting in the waiting area. He glanced at Steph and then hurried out the front door toward the sidewalk beyond.

While Steph was trying to figure out her next move, the man behind the plexiglass leaned forward toward a series of holes in the barrier and shouted, "Gus! You're up!"

One of the two white men in the lobby jumped to his feet, faster than Steph thought possible given his bedraggled appearance. He shuffled toward the desk, then turned and faced the door, which buzzed again almost immediately. Gus grabbed for the handle and pushed it open while it was still buzzing. The noise stopped and the door slammed shut.

"Can I help you?" the man behind the plexiglass shouted at Steph, who was still standing a few feet inside the door, clutching her cart of belongings with her left hand. She startled and turned her head towards the man, looking confused.

"I – I – I'm, I was following Tina."

"Right. You Dani?"

Steph looked at the man with a blank expression, before remembering her alias. "Yeah, that's me."

"Take a seat," the man instructed, pointing toward the chairs.

Steph walked to the nearest chair and pulled her cart up alongside it. She sloughed off her coat and jammed it into the basket, trying to make room around the other contents. She took off her hat and gloves also, stuffing them into the pockets of the overcoat, covering up her cell phone. She waited twenty minutes before anything happened.

The buzzer sounded again and Steph's head shot back in that direction. Another man emerged, this time much better dressed and looking like an executive running late for a meeting, rather than a homeless drug addict. The man behind the glass shouted, "Yo, Dani!"

Steph jumped up, grabbed the handle of her cart, and hurried toward the desk. As she approached, the buzzing sound startled her again. She went to the door, grabbed the metal handle and pushed it open, dragged her cart through, then allowed the heavy door to slam closed behind her. On the other side, a hallway stretched out in front of her, with dim light bulbs set into ceiling fixtures that were probably elegant fifty years earlier, before they were covered with grime. On her immediate right, near the edge of the hallway, she saw a large door with a small, rectangular window in the middle and a red EXIT sign glowing dimly over it. She could see a concrete stairway through the window and wondered if she should go up. She wasn't sure, so she stood there.

Just as Steph was about to turn around and try going back to talk to the desk attendant, a door opened down the hallway and Tina emerged. She waved toward Steph, motioning her to come forward. Steph walked slowly down the dimly-lit hall, past two elevator doors. When she reached the door to room 108, which Tina was holding open, she looked up at the taller woman with a frightened expression. "It's cool," Tina said calmly. "You come on in and see the boss and he'll fix you up. I told him you were OK."

Steph hesitated at the threshold to the room. Then she inched forward and peered inside, but could not see much aside from the bottom end of a bed and a floor lamp in the corner. There was no sign of the other two hookers. Steph walked in slowly, still hauling her wire cart behind her, its wheels squeaking. When she crossed the threshold, the door closed behind her with a joltingly loud slam. Steph looked back, but Tina was not there – leaving Steph alone with whoever was inside the room. She almost panicked and thought about turning around and running back out the door, but she wasn't sure that she would be able to get through the buzzer door. She pressed forward with a few hesitant steps.

Steph then heard a deep voice call out, "C'mon in, Dani. I don't bite on the first date."

When Steph reached the corner of the short hallway that led into the room, she finally saw the whole space. It was fairly large, but shabby, with maroon wallpaper and a grayish carpet that looked like one big stain. A made-up bed sat in the center of the room, with a night-table and lamp next to it. Beyond the bed a man sat in a low chair in front of a desk under the glow of a high-intensity lamp. The glare from the lamp made it hard for Steph to see his face as she squinted into the bright light. He had an earbud in one ear. The other bud hung down from its cord and lay on the desk. His outline was imposing. He was thickly built and wore a white button-down shirt with a crisp tie. A dark jacket hung neatly on a nearby chair. The man, who she assumed was the boss, was smoking a cigarette. "Tina says you're looking for a room, is that right?" the coarse voice asked.

"What? No, not – I mean, I told Tina I wanted to score some meth."

"And Tina told you that I'm the man who can get you some?"

"Um, yeah, that's right," Steph choked out, far more scared than she thought she would be, considering that this was the exact plan she was supposed to follow. She was so nervous that she completely forgot that her telephone was broadcasting the events back to Mike and Jason. It did not occur to her to narrate what was happening by talking to the oddly scary but well-dressed man.

"You got money?" the man asked.

"Sure, I got some. How much you askin' for and what are you selling?"

"Selling? Young lady, I don't know what you're talking about. This is a hotel. We rent rooms. You want a room?"

"I'm – I mean, I don't – wait, is there stuff in the room? Is that how it works?"

"We've got lots of different rooms, Miss. Some folks want to get a room so they can fuck. Some people just want to take a nap. Some people aren't feeling so good and need some meds. Is that what you are? Somebody who needs some medication?"

"Oh, sure. Yeah. That's right."

"Do you have a prescription?" the man asked.

"Huh?"

"A prescription. From a doctor. Do you have one?"

"Uh, no," was all Steph could manage.

"Well, I don't think we can provide any pharmaceutical products without a prescription." The man stared at Steph, as if waiting for a response, but she had none. "But I think there's a doctor in the house who might be able to take care of you. I can send you up to his room and you can ask him for a prescription. Would you like to do that?" The man leaned forward, and as he did, his head blocked out the bright desk lamp, allowing Steph to see his face. He stared at Steph with probing eyes.

"Um, sure. I could do that."

"You'll have to pay the doctor for his services."

Steph hesitated again. "How much?"

"That depends on what you want him to do for you. If you want a week's supply, it might cost more. But maybe you want just a day – something to get you through until morning."

"Yeah," Steph said quickly, remembering the part she was playing. Her sister used to say that she just needed one more hit – just enough to get her through until tomorrow, then she would quit. It was never true, but Steph remembered how sincerely she always said it. "Just need to get to tomorrow. When can I get it?"

The man sat back in his chair, allowing the bright light to shine back into Steph's eyes. "You go up to room two-twenty-two. You ask for Doctor Smith, and he'll take care of you. Then you come back down here to see me and we'll talk some more."

Steph turned to leave, having trouble maneuvering her cart in the cramped space.

The man called out to her, "You can leave that here, Sweetheart. I'll look after it for you."

"I'd rather take it with me," Steph replied.

"It's not a request," the man said sternly. "You leave it here. The doctor doesn't like folks bringing things into his office."

"But I need my money," Steph pleaded.

"Fine. You get your money and then you go upstairs."

Steph pawed through the cart, moving a blanket and an old sweatshirt aside and pulling out a battered black purse. She strung the long leather strap over her shoulder and then moved the cart against the wall. "Two-twenty-two, right?"

"That's right. You go ahead now and I'll watch your stuff for you."

Steph hesitantly turned, walked back to the door, and exited into the dim hallway. Once there, she unzipped her purse and looked inside. Her heart sank when she realized that she had left her cell phone in the pocket of her coat, which was in the wire cart. She quickly reached back for the door handle, but it was locked. She thought about knocking and asking the scratchy-voiced man for her phone, but she couldn't think of a good enough reason why a meth addict would need her phone before getting her drugs. She turned and walked to the elevator.

Ж Ж Ж

When Steph emerged from room 222 clutching a zip-lock bag, she stood motionless in the hallway, trying to figure out her next move. She had played the part of the desperate meth addict as well as she could have during her five minutes in the room with the "doctor," who had written her a prescription on a pink pad and accepted her cash. He had suggested that Steph could get a discount if she provided a blow job, but Steph had claimed to need her hit so badly that she couldn't wait. The small bag had cost her all the cash she had, but she was happy to take it and run. The doctor said she should go back downstairs to talk with the boss when she left. But Steph did not want to have anything to do with him, even though he was holding her cart of stuff, including her burner phone.

She took the elevator back to the ground floor and then turned right toward the door leading to the lobby. She remembered the buzzing sound that signaled that the door was available to be opened. She considered seeking out the attendant from behind the plexiglass, but he might not let her out without calling the boss first. Maybe if she waited, she thought, she could sneak out. She looked around and saw a short hallway around the corner from the big door. The hallway had no doors, but at the dead-end about twenty feet away, there was a wood-framed square in the middle of the wall. She stuffed the bag of meth into her purse and examined the structure. There were two buttons, like elevator call buttons, just to the side of the square, which was made of wood with a bronze knob at the bottom. She tried the knob and was happily surprised that it lifted up and the door opened, revealing a cubby-hole of space with wooden sides and a hard, white bottom. The cube was about three feet on each side. Steph had never seen a dumbwaiter in her life and had no idea what it really was, but she could fit inside, so she climbed in and slid the door down.

The light from the hallway was blotted out by the closing door. Steph was breathing rapidly and her heart was pounding in the total darkness. She wished she had her phone. She hoped that someone would come through the buzzing door and that she would have a chance to pop out from her hiding place and scamper through before anyone could stop her. It seemed like a good plan. She tried to position herself with her ear to the door. She tried not to focus on the futility of her efforts to track down Christine's killer. At that moment, she could not remember how that had seemed like a good idea. All she could focus on was how scared she felt. She was no cop. She took a deep breath and slowly exhaled through her nose, trying not to cry.

Chapter 41 – Waiting Game

MIKE STARED AT THE SCREEN OF HIS PHONE. When it dimmed, he swiped his finger across to keep it from going into sleep mode. The map of the neighborhood stared back at him, along with a small, blinking dot, which had been in the same spot for the past half hour. At one point he thought he detected some movement, but then the dot settled back into its familiar spot. According to the Google map, the location was occupied by the Alexander Hamilton Hotel, which he had never heard of. He tapped the telephone receiver icon (which always made him smile, since so few people used telephones with such old-fashioned handsets) and punched the "last" option to dial Jason. They had been exchanging calls every few minutes. Mike was standing on the corner of Atlantic Avenue, a few blocks from the hotel. Jason was on the other side of the location, also about two blocks away. With the GPS locator on her, they were not likely to lose track of Steph, but they didn't like to entirely trust the tech, so they kept their eyes on all the pedestrians. Darren was across the street from the front entrance, watching the foot traffic go in and out of the place.

"Anything, Jason?"

"No. Nothing coming this way, Mike. It's pretty deserted on this side."

"OK." Mike punched the END button and dialed Darren. When the phone connected, Mike didn't waste any time with small talk. "Any action?"

"Plenty of traffic," Darren responded. "Just the one group of ladies I told you about before. The rest of the guests are a mixed bag. Mostly men. A few look like businessmen, but a lot of scraggly folks. Nobody has a suitcase, so I doubt there's much overnight action. I'm starting to see a few people come out who I saw go in; seems like about a thirty-minute turn-around."

"OK. Stay alert."

"Mike, you know that she's on the street for the first time, and this is a kind of hotel. Maybe she's just found a place to crash for the night."

"I don't think so," Mike replied, then paused. He and Jason had decided to keep the FBI tech they had to themselves. The fewer people who knew that Agent Forrest had made an unauthorized loan of the Bureau's toys, the less chance there was of him getting called out. But Mike hated holding back from Darren, especially at this point, when it mattered. "Darren, you need to keep this strictly on the QT, but Steph's phone is wired with some sneaky software that lets us listen in even when the phone is turned off. She activated it forty-five minutes ago. If she was hunkering down to sleep away the night, she would have turned it off and probably would have said something to let us know that she was safe."

"Any chance she's just scared and nervous and forgot about it?" Darren suggested.

"She's pretty smart and pretty calm, so I'd say it's possible but not likely. We need to work on the assumption that she's engaged inside. We heard an unidentified male tell her to go upstairs to see the doctor to get a prescription. I never worked narco, but that's a pretty clear drug buy, which is part of her cover. If she's smart enough, she'll make the buy and get the hell out of there. She left the phone behind when she left the room – probably in her cart of crap – so the phone is transmitting silence, which is not helping us."

"Well, then I guess there's nothing to do but wait, unless you want to go in and extract her."

"Nah," Mike responded. "This is an unofficial gig. Breaking in on an organized drug dispensary is not likely to be a smart move. There's no telling how well-armed they are inside."

"Roger that," Darren agreed. "I'll sit tight and let you know if she comes out." Darren punched the END button on his phone to make sure the call was disconnected. Then he dialed a different number and turned around, facing into the doorway in which he was lurking. When the call connected, he spoke softly and quickly. "Hey, you're not with TW, are you? . . . Good, listen, I may want to come by tonight, you know, to relax a little . . . Yeah, so maybe I'll see you later . . . OK." He disconnected and turned back around to watch the entrance to the Alexander Hamilton Hotel.

Ж Ж Ж

A half-hour later, Mike looked around, trying to develop some kind of plan. He kept coming back to the conclusion that waiting was their only option. There was not much chance that Steph had stumbled into a truly dangerous situation. Drug dispensaries like this one were fairly common and they didn't have a habit of harming their new customers. They would want her back for more. He knew that Steph had some cash with her, so she would be able to make a buy pretty easily. He had instructed her to let her cash go without a fight if she were robbed. She was not likely to be in any real danger, and they didn't have any good options. Mike still had an earbud in his left ear that was picking up the transmissions from the stealth phone, but it had been quiet for a long while now.

He stretched his back, reached down toward his toes, and then rolled his neck a few times. He seemed to have more kinks to work out these days. He rotated his left shoulder and raised his arm up to a point parallel to the ground, held it there for five seconds, then slowly lowered it to his side. He repeated this exercise ten times, trying not to groan as the pain grew with each repetition. Terry would be proud of him for remembering to do his exercises. He wanted it to stop hurting just to raise his arm, but he knew that it was just a matter of time and effort. He turned up his wrist to look at his watch, and that sent a twinge of pain down his arm. He grunted and let out a soft, "Damn."

Chapter 42 – Revelations

EDDIE SWIPED HIS KEY CARD and walked into room 108, closing the door quietly behind him. He went directly into the bathroom for a piss. He knew that the sounds of the flush and of washing his hands would get Magnan's attention. The lieutenant didn't like being startled, and he worked with earphones blasting opera most of the time. Getting his attention without making him jumpy was an art form that Eddie had been forced to master. He was starting to wonder if the profits of the operation were worth the aggravation of working for Magnan, and dealing with his domineering attitude. When Eddie emerged from the bathroom, he closed the door loudly behind him and called out "Hey," as he walked into the light of the desk lamp.

Magnan pulled the buds out of his ears, allowing the piercing high note of a singer to leak out into the otherwise silent room. "What?" he growled. "I'm working on the books. You want your cut, let me work in peace."

"Yeah, I got that, but I just came in and Bruno asked me what I thought about the new girl and I had no idea what he was talking about. What's the story, Warren? I thought I was in charge of the girls?"

"Tina picked up a stray over by Barclays tonight. Said she looked strung out and asked where she could get some product. I gave her a look and she had some potential, so I sent her up to see the doc. There's her shit over there," Magnan said, gesturing to the wire cart still resting on the dull carpet next to the dresser and the flat-screen TV.

Eddie walked casually over to the pile of blankets and plastic bags and pawed through the top layer and down to the hidden stores. He pulled out a sweatshirt and gave it a sniff. "This has been washed, so the girl's not complete trash." He tossed the gray blob back on the pile and kept digging, when he felt something hard inside a coat pocket. He pulled out a cell phone, holding it up so Magnan could see it.

Magnan frowned and pulled his finger silently across his neck, indicating that Eddie should not say anything in case the phone was hot. Eddie examined the phone, then pushed and held the power button so that the unit fired up. Its screen showed a happy selfie of a cute girl-next-door making an exaggerated duck face, with the ocean in the background across a rocky beach. He pressed the button again until the "power off" option appeared. He pressed the off button and watched the screen go dark again as the phone emitted a sad bleep and a brief buzz of vibration. "It's fine," he said, "it was off when I picked it up. It wasn't recording anything."

"It wouldn't matter; I never say anything I might regret when the customers are in the room. I'm more careful than you."

Eddie bristled. "Fuck you, Warren. I'm plenty careful, but I'm startin' to get tired of all this bullshit. I'm tired of vetting the whores and worrying about which one will make friends with some cop we don't have on the team and try to rat on us. And I'm tired of keeping tabs on fucking Stoneman, who won't just give up on that stupid bitch they fished out of the river. Jeez, you'd think he and his partner, Shaft, would just let it fucking go."

"Shut up, Idiot. I told you to always assume there's a bug in the room." Magnan turned back to his desk, then spoke without looking at his companion. "Keep it together for another month and we'll both have seven figures in the Merrill Lynch accounts, on top of the pensions waiting for us. Now go find the new girl – I think Tina said her name was Dani. She probably snorted the whole bag and passed out somewhere. She can't get out the front door unless Bruno lets her, and Don is on the back door. You check her out and send her on her way. If she comes back tomorrow looking for more, we'll see how much she wants it. Take that fucking cart of shit out of here and don't bother me again unless the place is on fire."

Eddie scowled and flipped his middle finger at Magnan's back, then reached out and dragged Steph's cart, its wheels squeaking loudly, out into the hallway. He cursed under his breath and started walking the hallways, looking in each doorway and around every corner for the missing girl.

Ж Ж Ж

Mike took the earbud out of his left ear and pulled out his phone, punching the speed dial button. Seconds later, Jason answered. "Are you listening to this?"

"Yeah. I heard. Are we fucked here?"

"We are unless we can get her out."

Chapter 43 – Storming the Castle

MIKE AND JASON CONVERGED on Darren's location, across the street from the hotel. They were still worried about being made as cops because they didn't want the guys inside to take hostages, including Steph. They were standing deep in a shadowed doorway, out of the illumination of the street light that glowed twenty feet farther down.

"Options?" Mike asked his current and former partners.

"I can go around the back and try to find a way inside," Jason offered. "Then you two can go in the front once I'm in and we'll meet in the middle."

"We don't know what's in there," Mike cautioned. "And we've got no backup except each other. I don't want to take any stupid risks here." Jason and Darren both stared at Mike without speaking. The death of Ray McMillian was fresh in Jason's mind. Mike figured he knew exactly what Darren was thinking as he glanced down at his old partner's surgically reconstructed knee. "Are you sure you're up to this?"

Darren nodded. "I'm good, Mike."

"You both know that if this goes sideways, we're probably all going to get fired if not prosecuted. This was supposed to be simple surveillance on a dummy assignment, not a raid on a drug dispensary and whorehouse. I'm committed here, but you two can still have plausible deniability. I can go in alone."

"Shit, Mike. You can hardly lift your arm up and you have no gun!" Jason said dismissively.

"You could loan me your gun," Mike said, seriously.

"Like Hell! Just what we need, another reason for Sully to bust your ass and mine."

Darren then suggested that Jason should go in first by himself, because he looked the least like a cop and not because he looked the most like a drug user. Mike would follow in the front, while Darren volunteered to go around to the back of the building to see if he could find a way in. It wasn't Mike's first choice for Darren – to be on his own without any cover or backup – but Darren persuasively argued that covering the rear would be the job least likely to encounter any active resistance.

They were truly the walking wounded, between Mike's shoulder and Darren's knee. They connected their cell phones on a conference call with an open line and, while Jason attempted to frumpify himself, Darren walked around the block to an alley behind the hotel. After five minutes, Darren confirmed that he was in position and Jason started shuffling across the street, trying to seem as much like a strung-out drug buyer as he could manage while wearing Brooks Brothers khakis. He kept an earbud in his left ear and stuffed the other bud, along with the microphone for his phone, down his shirt. Mike watched as Jason disappeared into the interior of the hotel lobby, listening to the feed from the conference line in his right ear. He had Steph's stealth phone still in his left, but it had been quiet for some time.

Jason glanced around the lobby as nonchalantly as possible. There were two people sitting in the shabby chairs, neither of whom paid him any attention. He quickly noticed the plexiglass partition near the heavy-looking metal door that presumably led to the interior of the hotel, and the bored-looking man reclining in a desk chair behind the barrier. He hesitated, wondering whether the protocol was to take a seat and wait to be called, or to check in. He opted for the latter, partly so that he could have a conversation that Mike and Darren would hear. "Hey, man," Jason called into the grouping of small holes drilled through the thick plexiglass.

Bruno Falsetti looked up from something he was watching on a screen that Jason could not see from his angle. He was obviously annoyed at the interruption. His black hair was plastered against his semi-bald dome by his sweat, which beaded up on the exposed skin. He had a thin black moustache and a cigarette dangling from his lips. He frowned at Jason as if trying to recognize him. "What?" he barked.

"Hey, man, I'm lookin' for a buy."

"Who the fuck are you?"

"I'm Joe. One of the bitches over by the Barclays told me I could get some here." Jason twitched his right eye and tried to make his left hand shake a little bit as he stood, slightly hunched over.

"Let's see some ID," Bruno snapped.

"I ain't got no damned ID!" Jason shot back, indignant. "What do I look like, a fuckin' investment banker?"

"No ID, no service, my man. I don't know you, so you gotta get the fuck out of here!" Bruno sat up in his chair and pointed toward the exit door.

"That's bullshit, man!" Jason shouted. "These dudes ain't got no damned ID, I bet," he gestured toward the two disheveled bodies sitting in the tattered lobby chairs. Both of them looked up as he pointed toward them, as if just now noticing the altercation. Jason figured it was unlikely that either of them could produce an ID if their life depended on it.

"Tough shit, motherfucker! I know these pieces of shit. I don't know you from Jack, so take a fucking hike." Bruno pushed his face up next to the plexiglass in a menacing gesture, but then he backed off and looked to his right, toward the interior of the building. He nodded silently at whomever he was looking at, then reached his right hand under the counter in front of him. Immediately, a loud buzzing sound filled the lobby and the big door burst open with a metallic clang.

"I wanna speak to the boss!" Jason said as he quickly lunged toward the now-open door, pushing it farther open. A startled woman in a tight dress with a slit up one side all the way to her belt line pulled away from the door handle and glared at Jason. She quickly scuttled past him as Jason hurried through the heavy metal door toward the interior. As he moved, he reached into the pocket of his overcoat and extracted the heavy rubber case that normally housed his cell phone. He had removed the case in order to better conceal his phone in the waistband of his pants during the operation. Now, he jammed the case into the crack between the door and one of the heavy hinges, hoping that the obstruction would prevent the door from re-closing. "I'm going through the interior door," he said into his chest, hoping that the message would get to Darren and Mike without being audible to anyone else.

Ж Ж Ж

Steph huddled in the dark, cursing herself for not keeping the phone in her purse or in her pocket. Mike knew her location because of the GPS tracker, but she couldn't communicate, and Mike couldn't get inside because of the security door. She needed to get out to the street. She didn't need her little cart, she just needed to get through that buzzer door. Maybe she could get the guy behind the plexiglass to open the door for her.

Just then, the jarringly loud buzzer sounded again. Steph reached for the bottom of the little wooden door to pull it up, then heard a voice shouting.

"Hey! Asshole!"

She pulled her hand back, afraid to be seen even cracking the door. She closed her eyes, unable to slow her breathing. Her pulse pounded out a fast beat in her ears. "Keep it together," Steph whispered to herself. "It's just like a volleyball game. Score tied, match point. Deep breaths, focus." She heard the heavy door slam shut with a loud clang. Steph told herself to wait and be ready for the next time.

Ж Ж Ж

When Jason went through the buzzer door without permission, Bruno Falsetti called out, "Hey! Asshole!" Bruno reached out and smashed his hand against a red plunger-button on the counter. Immediately, a high-pitched siren screamed out two short bursts of sound louder than a Rolling Stones concert amp. The two people waiting in the lobby jumped up, holding their hands over their ears, and then quickly gathered up their belongings. At that moment, the front door burst open and Mike rushed in. He did not hesitate more than two seconds to assess the configuration of the lobby before darting for the interior door, which had closed only about half way before catching on Jason's phone case.

"I'm inside!" Mike shouted, trying to make sure Jason and Darren could hear him over the blaring siren. "Darren, what's your twenty?"

"I'm inside," came Darren's short response. "First floor back hallway. I'm going to try to link up with Jason."

Mike rushed into the inner hallway and crouched against the left-hand wall as he reconnoitered his surroundings. A bead of sweat trickled between his left eye and ear; he could feel the pressure of each heartbeat in his temple. The warning siren was still blaring out two staccato bursts every five seconds. In the interior hallway, strobe lights flashed at five-second intervals. To Mike's right, a short hallway ended at a dead end with a wooden square situated three feet off the ground. Mike speculated that it might be an old dumbwaiter system, but certainly nothing that presented a threat. Opposite the dumbwaiter, another short hallway without any doors ran into a blank wall. The main hallway stretched out a good hundred feet, with doorways spaced every twenty feet or so, except for two elevator doors. At the far end, there was a window shrouded with thin lace curtains, and it looked like the hallway continued both on the left and the right. Mike wondered what the floorplan of the place must be – it looked like a giant I-beam. There was no movement or activity inside the hallway; just the deafening blare of the warning siren.

"Darren! Jason! I'm in the front hallway, first floor. Who has a location on Steph?" He got no reply. "Give me your location, Darren!"

There was no reply.

Ж Ж Ж

Steph pressed her hands against her ears, trying to block the intrusive blasts of sound coming from the siren in the hallway. She couldn't hear anything else and was terrified by the din. She had told herself that she would be brave, but right now she just wanted to be curled up in her bed back in Port Angeles with her favorite stuffed unicorn with the sparkly rainbow mane. She sat on the floor of the cramped, dark space, her knees aching to stretch out. All she could see was a sliver of light peeking through the gap under the little door. "Mike will find me . . . Mike will find me," she whispered to herself.

Chapter 44 – Bullets Without Backup

MIKE WAS FROZEN IN PLACE against the wall of the long hallway, not sure where to go, but knowing that the guy behind the desk who had set off the alarm when Jason barged in would not sit still. "Jason!" he called, hoping he would be heard either through the cell phone or just by the shout. Mike yanked the earbud from his left ear; Steph's stealth phone wasn't going to be much help. His partner's voice came back through his other ear.

"I'm in the back. I can't find Darren."

"He's not answering on the phone line," Mike stated the obvious. "His last check-in said that he was inside in the back. Any other movement on your end?"

"Nothing. It's like the place is empty. Does your tracker have a fix on Steph?"

"It says I'm standing on top of her, but she could be five floors up, or in the basement. I don't know how accurate this thing is."

"What's the location?"

Mike looked at the screen again to make sure the blip on the little map had not moved. "Looks like it's in the front of the building. I'll try the door of the first room here, see if you can find Darren and meet me here in the front."

"I'm on it."

Mike slid his back along the wall until he got to a cut-out about four feet wide. A worn sign identified the room as number 102. Mike pressed his ear to the green door, but could not hear anything on the other side. He gently pressed against the lever-style handle, which did not yield. Kicking down the door did not seem to be a particularly likely method of entry. A hotel door, even an older one, would resist his solo efforts. That left knocking and seeing if anyone answered. If Steph was in there, and she could cry out, that would give him much better probable cause to try to break down the door or get Jason to shoot the lock. It would also alert anybody else in the room to his presence. He decided to go with a variation.

Mike slammed his fist against the door three times as loudly as he could. "Hey, we gotta go!" he yelled urgently, hoping that he might sound enough like the guy from the front desk that any bad guys inside would think that they were being advised to evacuate. He stood, listening as best he could amid the continuing screaming of the alarm. He took a step back, giving himself some distance in case somebody burst through the door. Nothing happened. No sound of movement, no scream, and no change in the blank exterior of the door.

Then the alarm suddenly stopped blaring. The absence of the intrusive noise hung in the air like the resonance from the last chord of *A Day in the Life*. The unexpected silence was accompanied by a ringing in Mike's ears.

"Steph!" he called out, having no better option. Silence was his only response. But then he heard something.

"Mike!" It was very faint, like it was coming from behind a door. He thought it was coming from inside the room in front of him, so he banged on the door again.

"Steph – are you in there?"

Again, he heard, "Mike! I'm here!" but it seemed to be coming from behind him. He took a step back and turned toward the front of the hallway just as he heard a loud crack, followed by the ping of a bullet ricocheting off the far side of the doorway – right where he had been standing a moment before.

Mike instinctively crouched and threw himself against the other wall. The shot had come from the front. From his position, he could see partially down the hallway toward the back. Remembering that his phone was still live, he spoke softly into his front pocket, "Shots fired front hallway. I'm pinned down. Need–"

Before he could finish saying "backup," another shot rang out in the hallway, this time coming from the rear. Mike could not see the second shooter, but he guessed it was Jason. "Jason!" Mike said in a sharp whisper into the phone, "I'm going to run across the hallway in front of you to get the shooter's attention. When he fires at me, you make a run at him."

Two seconds later, Mike jumped out from his hiding place and dashed across the hallway and into the cut-out of another doorway on the opposite side. As he expected, a shot rang out just as he reached his shelter. He had been counting on the shooter being late with the shot, and likely not all that accurate, since criminals seldom spent much time at the practice range.

A second after the shooter's bullet embedded itself in the drywall, Jason rushed down the corridor. As he moved forward, a figure peeked out from around the corner. Jason wasn't sure whether it was the guy from the lobby, but it didn't matter. He was holding out a pistol in his hand. Jason dropped to one knee, raised his weapon with both hands, and pulled off two quick shots, aiming for the man's half-exposed torso. At least one shot found its mark as the man spun backwards, his gun flying from his hand as he uttered a guttural "Ummph."

ЖЖЖ

When the siren stopped, Steph thought she heard Mike calling her name. She reached for the door of her cage and lifted up. When the door was half-open, she saw the back of a man's semi-bald head about ten feet in front of her. She wasn't sure if she recognized the man as the guy from the front lobby. She was absolutely certain, however, that he was holding a gun in his right hand, pointed at the ceiling. He was standing at the corner of the little side hallway as if he was peeking around it. As she watched, the man leaned forward, lowered his gun, and fired with a deafening blast. Steph quickly re-closed the door, plunging herself back into darkness. She sobbed quietly.

Chapter 45 – Out of the frying pan

MIKE JUMPED FORWARD, quickly looked both directions to determine that there were no other people in the narrow hallway, then grabbed the shooter's gun, which had fallen to the floor. While Jason covered him, Mike sprang toward the prone figure lying on the grimy carpeting. He was face up, his left hand pressed against his right pectoral. Mike thought that he looked like the guy from behind the counter, although he had only seen him for an instant on the way in. The man was grimacing and moaning softly as the blood from his chest wound seeped past his weakening fingers. Mike could not tell for sure if he had been hit once or twice, but he wasn't taking any chances. He rolled the man over onto his stomach, ignoring the cries of pain, and planted his knee into the man's lower back, keeping the gun ready.

When the man rolled over, a white rectangle of thin plastic, like a credit card, caught Mike's eye, dangling from a hinged clip on the man's belt. Mike grabbed it and pulled. The card came away from the clip, attached to a thin filament of black thread. When the wire reached the end of its length, Mike yanked and the card detached from its clip, which snapped back to its base. Mike pocketed the card, then pulled on the clip again to extend the wire. He grabbed the man's right hand, which was lying limply on the floor, encircled his wrist several times with the wire, and tied it off in a simple knot. It wasn't as strong as a set of handcuffs, but it would be difficult for him to go anywhere, even if the gunshot wound in his chest didn't keep him down.

Jason stationed himself with his back to Mike, pointing his gun toward the empty hallway. "Hallway looks secure for now," he panted, having just sprinted its length, checking each door along the way. "All the doors are locked."

"I'm hoping this is a key," Mike said, reaching into his jacket pocket and extracting the white plastic card.

"Is it ever that easy?"

"Sometimes."

"We gotta call this in now, Mike," Jason said with his gaze firmly fixed on Mike's eyes. "Shots fired. Man down. We have to call for backup and an ambulance for this guy, or he'll bleed out and Sully will have our asses."

Mike dropped his head a fraction of an inch and nodded. "No way we'll explain bringing Darren into this shit-show. Tell him to get the hell out of here after you call it in. No need for him to get wrapped up in our mess."

"Roger that." Jason stood up and reached for his cell phone when both men heard a muffled, high-pitched voice cry out.

"Mike!"

They both looked around, trying to determine the source of the voice. The door of the dumbwaiter slid up, revealing Steph's cramped form. "Steph!" Mike and Jason shouted at the same time.

"Jesus!" Jason exclaimed, as he rushed to the end of the short hallway to help her extricate herself from the dumbwaiter. She groaned as her cramped legs unwound. She let Jason half-carry her

285

out of her hiding place and set her on the ground, where she stood on wobbly legs, holding on to Jason's elbow.

"You call this in, I'm going to get Steph out of here," Mike said, taking a step forward and extending his right hand. Jason reached for his cell phone, but then stopped when he heard a voice from behind them, back in the direction of the main door.

"Freeze right there, Motherfuckers! Drop those guns right now or so help me I will blow your brains all over that wall!"

Chapter 46 – Hard Choices

MIKE AND JASON BOTH HAD THEIR BACKS to the voice. Mike shot a quick glance out of the corner of his eye toward his partner and saw Jason shake his head slightly. Mike nodded. They both shared the same thought. If the voice seriously had a gun and they tried to spin around and take a shot at him, they would certainly suffer casualties. But if the voice was bluffing, then when they dropped their guns and turned around, they would still be able to fight hand-to-hand. Mike dropped Bruno's gun straight down so that he could reach for it quickly if the opportunity arose. Jason tossed his gun off to his left, to a spot he hoped to jump towards later. They both turned around slowly, raising their hands. Steph whimpered softly, trying to stay behind Jason.

When they finished turning, they looked at not one but two men, both holding pistols and standing in the middle of the main hallway, just in front of the security door. Mike recognized the taller, older man as T. Warren Magnan. The other man was short and thin and Mike did not know him.

Mike relaxed his shoulders and smiled, lowering his hands halfway. "Well, I'm certainly glad to see you, Lieutenant. For a moment we thought we were in trouble." Mike took a step forward but stopped short as a shot rang out and plugged into the carpeting three feet in front of him, fired by the thin guy.

Magnan spoke next. "I'm very sorry, Detectives, that you have wandered into this situation. It seems that you know that young lady. We've been conducting an undercover operation here. At this point, I don't think our cover is completely blown, so I'm going to ask you to please accompany us down the hall where we can talk in private. We will maintain the appearance that you are our prisoners in case anyone sees us, so please walk ahead of us with your hands raised. Go down the hallway to room 108, on the left. We'll be able to talk freely there." Magnan smiled at Mike and Jason, then waved his pistol barrel in the direction for them to walk.

Mike and Jason exchanged skeptical glances, but nodded to each other and started walking with their hands up. When they got around the corner and were ten feet or so ahead of Magnan, Eddie retrieved the dropped guns, then hurried forward ahead of the prisoners and opened the door to room 108. He trained a gun on them as they walked in, with Magnan trailing behind. Once in the room, Magnan motioned for the two men to stand next to the bed. Eddie grabbed Steph by the arm and pulled her away from Jason. He shoved her toward the corner of the room, where she sat on the floor, fighting back tears and breathing heavily.

While Magnan covered them, Eddie frisked Mike and Jason, removing their cell phones – both of Mike's phones – and satisfied himself that neither man had any other weapons or electronics. Magnan then had Mike sit on the floor several feet away from Jason.

Mike said slowly, "You're not undercover and you're not letting us walk out of here. You're the one we have on tape talking about the whores and the drugs with your buddy here, aren't you? My advice is that you give up and not add murdering two police officers to your list of offenses."

"He's full of shit!" Eddie cried out.

"Quiet," Magnan said calmly. "Let's presume that we are, in fact, under surveillance, although I can't imagine how. We are guilty of nothing and we are engaged in a legitimate police operation. The question is how to extricate ourselves from this situation while maintaining our cover. I would love to discuss this in depth, but time is short. Eddie, I think we will need to restrain the detectives. Do you have some cuffs?"

"I got one pair on me, but I can get another," Eddie responded.

"Warren, stop!" Darren's voice came seemingly out of nowhere and caused everyone to freeze and look up. Darren was standing at the edge of the room, next to the short hallway that led to the door. He faced Magnan, holding his Glock in both hands.

"What the fuck, Curran?" Eddie called out and redirected his aim toward Darren, leaving Magnan to cover both Mike and Jason.

Magnan glanced to his right, in Darren's direction, and said in a remarkably calm voice, "Stay out of this, Curran. Go home. You don't want to be here."

"It's over, Warren," Darren said in a quavering voice. "It's time to stop and walk away. We can all just walk away right now."

"Like hell we can!" Eddie shouted. "You're such a schmuck, Curran."

"Fuck you, Eddie! I'm done. I'm out."

"Fuck me?" Eddie said with a wry laugh. "You're just as fucked as we are. You're not done. You can't just walk away. You're as deep in the shit as we are, Asshole."

"I'm not. I didn't do anything illegal. I'm still clean. I can deny any knowledge of your whores and your drugs. All I did was let you steal my ID card."

"That's all you did?" Eddie shot back, still pointing his gun at Darren. "You snorted more meth than the whores, and you had your fun with them, too."

Mike turned his head toward Jason, while the three men holding guns continued their Mexican standoff. He silently mouthed to Jason, "What the fuck?" Then he turned to Steph, who had a confused and terrified expression on her face. Mike raised his eyebrows to get her attention, then mouthed to her, "Be ready to run."

"Don't kid yourself, Curran," Magnan interjected, still aiming his gun at Mike, but turning his head to speak to Darren. "You took the money; you knew what was happening. You can rat us out, but you're just as guilty. The DA isn't going to grant you immunity if you're an accessory to murder, so grow a pair and face reality. Grab that gun on the desk, it belongs to Bruno. He'll take the fall here, and we'll be heroes for taking him down. You and Eddie will back me up. And why the fuck are you here, anyway?"

"I came in for a hit and a fuck."

"Who else knows you're here?"

"Nobody."

"What about them?" Magnan asked. "Who knows they're here?"

Darren hesitated. "How the fuck should I know?"

"Then we're clear," Magnan said. "We need to make this look plausible right now. These two came storming in, Bruno took them both out, then we shot Bruno. Put down the damned gun, Curran!"

"I can't let this happen," Darren said, his gun shaking in his hand. "There has to be a way. I'm telling you we can all just leave, right now."

"You think these two are just going to turn their backs and let us walk out of here? Pretend they were never here?"

"Yeah, I do." Darren kept his gun pointed at Magnan, but glanced at Mike with pleading eyes. "Mike, you gotta agree. You're in deep shit here. We all are. You walk away with Steph, I walk away, they walk away and never come back to this shithole, and we all just keep our mouths shut. It's a solution for everybody." Darren looked at Jason. "Dickson, you're in, right?"

"Sure," Jason answered, "that's a whole lot better than the ending I'm looking at."

"What about you, Mike?" Darren pleaded.

"I'm in, Darren. Let's just all put down our guns and walk out there into the hallway." Mike looked at Magnan. "Warren, you and Eddie here are working undercover, right? So, you had a problem tonight. An addict came in and you found out that the guy at the front desk was selling drugs. The addict busted in and Steph here, who had run away in search of her sister's killers, got in the way and we came in and Jason shot the guy when he pulled a gun. You guys were upstairs running your surveillance operation. You came down to support us after you heard the gunshots. Darren will go out the back like he was never here. We'll all file reports and nobody downtown will care about some scumbag drug dealer who got shot. You dump this sleazy operation and we'll all play dumb and keep moving toward retirement. I'm good with that."

Eddie had stopped listening as something Mike said sank into his brain. "Sister's killers? Are you fucking kidding me? This bitch is the sister?" he shouted. Then he turned to Darren. "And how did you know her name?"

Magnan said, "I'm going to solve this problem right now," and reached for the gun on the desk.

"Stop!" Darren shouted.

Magnan grabbed Bruno's gun with his left hand, still pointing his own at Mike with his right. He looked at Curran, whose eyes were wide and whose brow was sweaty. Magnan saw the desperate expression on Darren's face and smiled. "Or what, Curran? You going to shoot me?" Magnan raised Bruno's gun.

The room exploded with the sound of the gunshot. Magnan screamed in pain and crumpled to the floor, Darren's bullet having torn through his right hip and shattered his pelvis. A moment later, a second shot reverberated in the small space, making Steph cover her ears with her hands as she screamed. Darren was spun around by the impact of Eddie's bullet in his right shoulder. His gun flew from his right hand and a searing pain ran down his arm.

Mike lunged for Darren's gun, while Jason threw himself toward Eddie. Before Eddie could re-aim, Jason collided with the smaller man's knees, sending him toppling over as the two men became a tangle of arms and legs. Mike secured the fallen gun and rose to a kneeling position, taking aim at Eddie, but he had no clear shot. Eddie's body was intertwined with Jason's as the two men struggled on the floor. Then Mike heard a grunt and turned his head. He saw Magnan lying on his side on the floor, still holding a pistol in his right hand, pointed toward Mike.

"Don't!" Mike shouted, but Magnan just sneered and pulled the trigger.

The flash of the muzzle came a split second before the deafening bang. Mike involuntarily closed his eyes, just as he saw the large shadow fall in front of him. Darren groaned as the bullet entered his chest cavity just north of his third rib, glanced off the bone, and deflected downward, exiting through his lower back. Darren slumped onto Mike's legs just as Mike pulled off three shots toward Magnan, who rolled onto his back and lay still. A pool of blood formed on the carpet next to his torso.

Mike looked up to see Jason pummeling Eddie's face.

Seeing that Jason had Eddie well under control, Mike turned back to Darren. He bent down and put his face next to Darren's. He was listening for breathing, and got a grunt in his ear.

Darren's eyes opened as he sucked in a tortured breath and winced with the pain. He saw Mike's face close to his, and moved his mouth, slowly at first. Then he croaked out his last words. "Take care . . . of . . . Marie."

Chapter 47 – Surprising Reunion

OR SEVERAL SECONDS, Mike sat on the floor with Darren's lifeless head resting on his lap. He knew on a logical and conscious level what had just happened, but his brain refused to acknowledge it. He started working through the stages of grief, but got stuck immediately on denial. Maybe Darren was not actually dead – maybe he was just unconscious. If the paramedics got there quickly, maybe he could still be saved. He knew it was a fantasy, but it gave him something to focus on. Mike reached for a pillow from the nearby bed and gently rested Darren's head on it. Jason had handcuffed Eddie to the leg of the desk, which hardly seemed necessary given the man's extreme state of unconsciousness.

Jason retrieved his cell phone, which Eddie had thrown onto the bed, and dialed 9-1-1. He asked for police and multiple ambulances to respond, noting that they had officers down. "We should have EMTs and backup here in a few minutes," Jason said, panting slightly after expending his effort pummeling Eddie.

Mike reached into his suit jacket and extracted a latex glove. After putting it on, he carefully picked up Magnan's gun, a department-

294

issued Glock, from where it had fallen on the floor. He stuffed it into his waist band, keeping Darren's gun in his right hand. He also grabbed Bruno's gun from Magnan's dead hand and laid it on the bed, along with another glove for Jason, who had already acquired Eddie's gun. Jason looked around for his own Glock, but couldn't locate it. He donned the glove and put Bruno's gun in his coat pocket. Mike looked in the corner of the room where Steph was huddled, looking more frightened than he could ever recall seeing anyone look. She was staring blankly forward, not focused on anything. "Steph!"

She startled and turned her head quickly. "Nnnmmm," was all she could manage to intone.

"You're alright," Mike said in his soothing grandfather-cop voice. "We're all going to be fine. We're going to get you out of here in a minute." Steph just sat on the floor, knees hugged up against her chest. She nodded several times, fighting to keep from crying. Mike suspected that the loud gunfire inside the enclosed space had damaged her ear drums, which were certainly not accustomed to such abuse.

"Jason, let's secure this location."

Jason got up, planting a last kick into the side of Eddie Goddel's unconscious body. "What are we going to do with Steph?"

"I'm thinking that we get her out the back before the cavalry arrives."

Jason looked at the frightened girl and nodded his head. "I agree, let's get her home."

"Right. Go out into the hallway and make sure that security door is still open for our backup and the EMTs and prop open the door to this room so they can get in. And check the douchebag in the front hallway to make sure he's still down."

Jason, who looked even more rumpled than when he had entered the building, walked towards the door. Mike reached for Steph's hand, intending to help her to her feet, but his attention was diverted by the sound of a gunshot in the hallway. Mike stood up quickly and yelled out, "Jason, talk to me!"

Jason's faint voice came back, "Hostile in the hallway! Unknown location!"

Mike turned back to Steph, then spun around quickly, scanning the room. He spotted an umbrella leaning against the wall in a crack of space next to the desk. He grabbed it and returned to Steph. "Listen, you will be safe here. That guy is out cold and handcuffed to the desk, but you take this," he handed her the long black wand, with its steel tip, "and you smack him if he wakes up." Steph nodded blankly and took the umbrella, which she held across her knees with both hands. She was shivering and Mike suspected that she was in shock, but he had few other options. He couldn't give her a gun, and he needed to get out into the hallway to back up Jason.

Mike sprang toward the doorway and peered out. Jason had grabbed a towel from the bathroom and stuffed it under the door to prop it open. Mike eased out into the doorway, keeping his back against the narrow wall of the doorway cut-out, holding Darren's gun in front of him with his elbows pressed against his chest. He looked right and could see Jason in a similar posture, in a doorway across the hall. Mike could feel his heart pounding in his chest and took two quick breaths – in through his mouth, out through his nose – to steady himself. He made eye contact with Jason, who pointed toward the front door. Mike gave Jason a hand signal that he would lay down cover fire so that Jason could emerge from his sheltered spot and take a shot at their assailant.

Mike darted across to the opposite side of the doorway and put his back against the wall there, giving him a better angle to shoot down the hall. He stuck his right arm awkwardly across his body, eased out to his left, and fired off five shots blindly down the corridor, spaced out about three seconds apart. The bullets were not designed to hit a target, but to encourage anybody down the hall to take cover. Mike stuck his head out after the second shot to get a look at his possible targets and to allow him to provide better cover fire for Jason.

Mike waved a hand to Jason, who spun from his cover into the hallway, crouching down with Eddie's gun extended in front of himself and scanning the space for their attacker. The hallway was deserted, the odor of gunpowder hanging in the air. Jason waved to Mike to fall in behind him. The two men advanced down the hallway, slowly, as they inspected each doorway while keeping their eyes on the end of the hall. Was it possible that their shooter or shooters had turned and run out through the security door? Mike squinted forward and saw that the heavy metal door was still slightly ajar.

When they were past the last doorway, both Mike and Jason snapped into shooting posture as they saw a flash of movement at the very corner of the hall, to the right of where Mike had left Bruno lying on the ground. The point of a shoulder peeked out, then a head and a torso lurched from behind the corner. Mike and Jason both opened fire, sending multiple bullets into the man. Mike exhausted his magazine and reached into his pocket for a spare, but immediately remembered that he did not have his own gun, or any spare ammunition. The man who had emerged from behind the corner had been blown backwards by the impact of the bullets and was now lying on his back on the floor. Mike took a few steps forward, then threw himself up against the right-hand wall and yelled out to Jason, "It's a dummy! That's Bruno, not the shooter!"

Mike motioned to Jason to move to the opposite wall, on the left, and forward, while Mike slid along the right wall toward the corner. Mike, who had extracted Magnan's gun from his waist band, got to the edge and stopped. Jason stopped also, unable to see what was around the corner. Mike took a step back away from the wall and then, as quietly as he could manage, took off his jacket. He winced as pain shot through his left shoulder due to the awkward angle, but he clamped down on his jaw to avoid any sound seeping out. Then he took his jacket in his right arm and motioned to Jason that he was going to throw it. On a silent count of three, Mike whipped the jacket around the corner, drawing an immediate barrage of gunfire.

At the moment the hidden shooter was putting four holes in Mike's jacket, Jason moved forward like a panther, crouched, and fired three rounds, aiming low. The shooter let out a bellow of pain and rage and stumbled backwards, a bullet lodged in his left kneecap.

Mike rushed around the corner and jumped on the man, while Jason came up behind, training his pistol on the fallen figure. Mike took the gun from the man's hand and put a knee on his right arm, pinning him to the ground. Within seconds, Jason jumped in and put his knee into the man's chest and pointed the gun at his head, shouting "Stay down!" The man's face was contorted in pain as he lifted his head to look Jason squarely in the eye.

Jason froze as recognition dawned on him. He had seen this man before. He was the bag man – the man known as "Ricky" to Luis Rosario and Manuel Hwong. He was the white guy who had entered the convenience store in Queens, along with a big guy named Bo. He was the guy whom Jason and Ray McMillian were trying to capture the day Ray was shot and killed.

"No fucking way," Jason said softly.

"What?" Mike asked, as he patted down the man to make sure he didn't have any hidden weapons.

"This is Ricky the Runner."

"You're shitting me."

"I'm not. This is the guy."

"Then," Mike said, then hesitated, "this bastard is responsible for Ray."

Mike and Jason locked eyes. A siren blared in the distance, getting louder, as their backup and an ambulance approached the hotel. Mike got up, comfortable that Jason had the man fully pinned and that the blood spurting from his knee made him a non-threat.

Mike turned his back to Jason and said, "I'm going to go get Steph out of here. Remember, Partner, I've got your back." Mike then disappeared around the corner, back in the direction of room 108, leaving Jason to deal with Ricky. He hurried down the corridor, pushed open the door, then paused. His stomach turned a somersault. He would rather have faced a dozen drug dealers with guns than go back into that room and see Darren Curran's dead body on the floor. But Steph was still in there, and he thought about how awful it was for her to be stuck with two dead guys and another one unconscious. She was just a scared teenager. He was a veteran cop. "Suck it up, Stoneman," he whispered to himself. Then he forced himself forward into the room.

The smell of death had not yet permeated the space, but the acrid, metallic stench of spilled blood was strong. Mike tried not to look at the bodies, and instead looked immediately into the corner, where he had last seen Steph. She had not moved in his absence; still huddled on the ground, her knees pulled up against her chest, braced by the black umbrella. She was still in a state of semi-shock, but when Mike looked at her and smiled a comforting smile, she dissolved into tears. Steph jumped to her feet and ran to Mike, throwing her arms around him and sobbing. Mike gave her a hug and then pushed her away and held her by the shoulders. He said sternly, "Listen to me, Steph. We need to get you out of here. Now! Follow me – we're going out the back way. Darren came in that way, so there's some kind of door back there. Can you get yourself back to Michelle's place?"

She nodded silently. Mike dug into his pocket and pulled out his money clip, peeling off two twenties and shoving them into Steph's hand. Steph looked at him blankly, then shook her head slightly, as if breaking out of a trance. "Um, yeah, I think so."

"Then we need to go now," Mike said, as soothingly as he could. "You go back to the Barclays Center and get a cab. Go to Michelle's and I'll meet you there a little later. You understand?" Steph nodded again, then Mike took her hand and helped her to her feet.

Mike and Steph hurried towards the door and went out into the hallway without hesitation. They turned left and walked quickly to the far end of the hall. To their right, another hallway led to a dead end, so Mike turned left. There were windows now on their right, reflecting their images as they scuttled along. Mike made out a dim street light somewhere beyond the window, perhaps in an alley. When they rounded another corner, Mike stopped short, grabbed Steph by the arm, and pulled her back around the bend. He had seen people in the hallway.

Mike drew his weapon and peered around the corner. He saw a door on the left side, halfway down the corridor. As he watched, three young women burst through the door, wearing an assortment of night clothes, robes, and winter coats. They turned left, ran down the hall, and exited on their right through another door with an EXIT sign glowing in red above it. When they had departed, Mike took Steph's hand and pressed forward. Just as they reached the door on the left, which turned out to be a stairway, it suddenly opened again, this time for two more women and an older man. The man was wearing a heavy black overcoat. He had graying hair and rimless glasses hanging on the edge of his nose. He stopped as soon as he saw Mike with his drawn gun. He looked about ready to vomit, then put his hands up, while the women just stood and stared.

Mike surmised that this guy was a john, here for a session with one of the ladies – or maybe with both of them. Mike lowered his gun and waved the three of them towards the exit door, then pushed Steph after them. When they got to the door, Mike stopped Steph so he could ensure that it was safe. When he opened the door, he saw the figure of a large man lying on the gravel, his hands bound behind his back. The man wasn't moving. Mike smiled at Darren's handiwork – neutralizing the guard at the back door. Then he looked at Steph. "Go. Get to Michelle as fast as you can."

Steph looked up at Mike with frightened eyes, but she seemed more herself after their trek down the hallway. "I won't let you down, Mike," she said, then gave him another quick hug and dashed for the door. Mike watched until she was safely outside, then turned and hurried back toward the front of the hotel.

Ж Ж Ж

Within a few minutes, the first patrol car and an EMT crew screeched up to the curb in front of the Alexander Hamilton Hotel, and their occupants spilled out and rushed toward the front door. Mike met them and advised the EMTs to head down to room 108 and to tend to the man on the floor with a pillow under his head first. Mike took his time leading in the officers. He banged on the big buzzer door three times with the flat of his hand, then pushed it open and led the officers to the spot where Jason was still kneeling on Ricky's chest. The man's face was bloodied and his head lolled to the right, his eyes closed. Jason got up and turned him over to the uniforms. He and Mike walked back to room 108, where the EMT crew was working on Eddie Goddel's wounds as best they could, given that he was handcuffed to the desk. One paramedic was crouched down over Darren Curran's prone form, but he was not working urgently. Mike caught his eye and the man shook his head.

When three more uniformed officers came into the room, Jason told one of them that the key to the handcuffs was probably in Eddie's pants pocket. He told the officers that the handcuffed man was a cop, but that he was also under arrest and they should treat him as a suspected killer. Mike motioned to Jason to leave the room with him, and they walked out into the hallway.

The scene was now becoming chaotic as more officers and another EMT team scurried around the hotel, checking to make sure that nobody else needed medical attention and confirming that there were no more potential shooters. Mike handed one of the officers the plastic master key and suggested that she start clearing the building. The officer called for more backup and assembled a team to get started. Mike and Jason stood off to the side, watching the activity.

"There will be a detective team sent in soon," Mike observed.

"I guess we should hang out until then," Jason responded calmly.

"So that guy, Ricky – looks like he'll survive his gunshot, but he'll probably need to do some rehab before he runs any more races, huh?"

Jason looked at Mike and smiled, then said, "I guess so."

"You almost feel like it would have been a better outcome if the scumbag had been killed."

"Yeah, well, sometimes it's better if the guy is available to be interrogated. Maybe the Feds can get him to flip on his bosses, or at least get some useful information from him."

"You're probably right," Mike agreed. "What was he doing here?"

"Beats the hell out of me, Mike."

"Maybe our guy, Eddie, will help us out on that one."

"You think he'll rat out the Gallatas?" Jason asked, raising an eyebrow.

"If it's the only way to save his ass from prison, he might. Bad cops don't tend to do well on the inside."

"Let's hope," Jason said as he started walking back down the hallway.

"Where are we going?"

"I'm tired, Mike. I'm going find a chair to sit in." Jason continued down the hall through the big door, which was now propped wide open, and took a seat in one of the ratty chairs in the lobby. Mike plopped down next to him. He stripped off the latex glove he had been wearing and tossed it toward a trash can, missing badly. Jason pulled of his glove and lobbed it into the can. "Swish," he said with a smile. Then he turned to Mike and said, "You should call Michelle and tell her we're OK."

Mike looked at his partner and nodded. "You got a cell phone on you?"

Jason let out a quick laugh and handed Mike his phone.

Chapter 48 – Fallout

Monday, April 22

THE FOLLOWING MONDAY MORNING, the day after Easter, Mike and Jason sat quietly in the two most uncomfortable chairs on the planet – the ones in front of Captain Sullivan's desk. The captain had already read the reports from the officers who responded to the scene in Brooklyn, as well as the report from the responding detectives. He had also read the article on the front page of *The New York Times*.

The article included a quote from Commissioner Ward, which was more entertaining in the video version on the paper's website. Standing in front of a podium emblazoned with the seal of the City of New York, Ward sent a message to any cops who might think about straying from the straight and narrow. "Today, those who swore an oath and then betrayed it have felt the consequences of that infidelity. The people of this department are rightly held to the highest standard, and should they fail to meet it, the penalty will be swift and severe."

What *The Times* didn't have was the full picture of the carnage inside the Alexander Hamilton Hotel. Bruno Falsetti, who was identified as a low-level hood with a lengthy rap sheet, was found very dead in the front hallway. T. Warren Magnan was found dead on the floor of Room 108, just a few feet away from Darren Curran. Both men had succumbed to gunshot wounds to the chest. Meanwhile, Officer Eddie Goddel was found unconscious with a severely beaten face and two broken ribs. Eddie was taken away to the hospital before any of the responding officers could question him.

Mike and Jason were thrilled when Steve Berkowitz and George Mason showed up at the crime scene. Mike and Jason explained that they had been investigating the Christine Barker murder with Darren and had followed a group of hookers into the hotel on a hunch, since they had visited the same Starbucks where Christine had made purchases with her gift card. When they arrived, Bruno behind the desk confronted them, which led to the shootout in the hallway. Magnan and Eddie had been in the building because they were involved in the prostitution and drug operation, and they confronted Mike, Jason, and Darren, leading to the shoot-out in room 108. They didn't mention Steph. While she was certainly a material witness to the events, Magnan and Bruno were dead, Steph had never seen Ricky the Runner, and Mike and Jason could testify about Eddie's involvement, including the fact that he had shot Darren. They also left out any mention of Darren being anything other than part of their investigation team.

The story had satisfied the responding detectives. Captain Sullivan, however, was not as easily placated. "So, Detectives, is there a reason why you two were running a night-time operation in Brooklyn – on overtime – chasing down this phantom murder case without telling me?"

"Sir, it was a murder, not a phantom," Mike couldn't keep himself from blurting out a defense of their investigation.

"I don't give a rat's ass whether it was a murder or a petty theft, you pedantic jerk! What I care about is that two of my detectives were out there naked without any backup on a fly-by-night operation where two cops got killed. Now I'm facing an inquiry from Internal Affairs and I'm caught with my dick in my hand because I had no idea you two cowboys were even out there. I want an explanation, because you're usually a by-the-book guy, Stoneman, and this was a fucking shit-show. So please tell me what the hell happened to get your former partner shot and killed." Sullivan stood behind his desk, both hands resting on the faded wood as he glared down at the two detectives.

"Sully, there's nobody on the planet, save for Marie and the kids, more sorry than I am that Darren went down. I blamed myself for him getting shot the last time. I'm sick about this. So, I'm going to do something really stupid here and tell you the truth. The actual, complete, truth."

"Mike–" Jason interrupted.

Mike held up his hand toward Jason. "No, Jason. I know what I'm doing. It's time I took responsibility here. If there are consequences, then I'll take them. It was my operation. It was my call. You should not take any heat for this."

"I was right with you, Mike," Jason said softly, looking at Mike with eyes that pleaded for him to be careful.

"I know you were, and I appreciate it. You've been a good partner. You were there because I needed you and because I asked you. You put your ass on the line for me, and I respect that and thank you for it. But you shouldn't get a black mark on your record because you were backing up your partner." Mike turned away from Jason and faced Sully. "It was my fault, Cap. Give me a few minutes and I'll explain everything."

Over the course of the next half hour, Mike came clean about nearly everything. He explained how he and Michelle had traveled to

Washington State and met Steph, how Steph had shown up in New York unannounced, and how she had run away and gone off by herself to Brooklyn. He explained that Steph insisted that she was going to track down her sister's killer and that Mike and Michelle felt responsible for her and needed to prevent her from doing something stupid. He told the whole story about the mock operation that wasn't supposed to be anything but a way to get Steph to give up and go home. He explained that he had mentioned the operation to Darren at the rehab center, and that Darren had insisted on helping out. And he told the whole story of what happened inside the Alexander Hamilton Hotel, including that he had let Steph leave the crime scene. He left out the part about Darren admitting his involvement with the prostitution ring, which he and Jason did not know about until they heard Goddel, Magnan, and Darren talking about it in room 108. Instead, Mike made sure to emphasize how Darren had saved their lives and sacrificed himself. When Mike was finished, Sully looked at Jason with piercing eyes. He asked no questions. Jason nodded his head to confirm that he agreed with Mike's story.

"Get the fuck out of here, both of you. You're both suspended pending the Internal Affairs inquiry. No desk duty – just get out and don't let me see your faces until I call you back. And make sure you both call the union and get some counsel."

Mike and Jason both left silently, gathered up their things, and exited the bullpen without speaking to anyone. They walked over to the Amsterdam Avenue watering hole where the cops tended to hang out after work and had a few drinks without talking much. As they were settling up the bill, Mike said, "Thanks, Jason."

"For what?"

"For backing me up, and for not being pissed at me for exposing you to discipline by telling the truth."

"I'm glad you did, Mike. I'm not sure I could have lived with it if we had lied to Sully."

"Well, I didn't lie, but I also didn't give him the whole truth."

"Yeah, but you took the responsibility. It's plausible that you would not have known about Darren being involved in Magnan's little skin den."

"Well, don't get too comfortable with the truth. You repeat any of that to anyone and we're both fucked."

"True that," Jason agreed.

Chapter 49 – Farewells

Tuesday, April 23

THE NEXT DAY, MICHELLE TOOK A PERSONAL DAY and she and Mike took Steph for a walk along the High Line on Manhattan's West Side. Spring was finally starting to make an appearance and they only had to wear light jackets to enjoy the April sunshine. Steph talked about her sister, and repeatedly thanked Mike and Michelle for all they had done. The young girl had a backpack containing all the clothes she had brought with her on the impromptu trip to New York, along with a few additions provided by Michelle. When they reached the end of the walking path, they continued to the mammoth structure of intertwining stairs known as the Vessel, situated behind a new shopping and residential complex. Steph was impressed. Mike thought the thing looked like a LEGO tower.

They walked across 34th Street to the Port Authority bus terminal. As they waited for the bus to Seattle to board, Mike asked, "Are you sure we can't change your mind and take you to the airport?"

"No, thanks. You've done so much for me, I can't take any more from you. I'd rather take the bus." Steph turned to Michelle and then lunged forward to give her a lingering hug. When they finally detached, Michelle promised to stay in touch. Steph then turned to Mike and repeated the hug. She had a tear in her eye when she stepped back. "I love you guys. I'll miss you." She wiped away the tear, turned, and climbed up the stairs into the bus.

Michelle laughed, grabbed Mike's right arm, and drew him close to her as they walked back out to Eighth Avenue.

Ж Ж Ж

While Mike and Michelle were walking toward the subway, Captain Sullivan, Police Commissioner Ward, and Mayor Douglass were in the mayor's office in City Hall, deep in a heated discussion of how to handle the "Hamilton Hotel incident." The Internal Affairs team, aided by the FBI, had already rounded up six other cops who were implicated in the prostitution operation, thanks to T. Warren Magnan's careful financial records. The mayor had his public relations people working on a press release announcing the arrests and decrying the breach of public trust committed by these men, who had sworn to protect and serve and instead had exploited the innocent. He was going to use the opportunity to call for a full house-cleaning of the police department and a complete overhaul of all undercover vice operations. The mayor had hoped for a chance to pull cops off of victimless crime operations and focus more on violent crimes and street-level policing. This was a political windfall for him and he did not intend to miss it.

"What about the misconduct of Stoneman and Dickson?" the commissioner asked. "We can't let them walk away unscathed here."

"Well, we can't tell the public that two recently decorated heroes put a civilian into an undercover operation without authorization or backup, and that she was nearly killed. I'll tell you for damned sure that's not a story I want in the papers." The mayor stared at the two other men, looking for affirmation. He got a quick nod from Ward, and a grudging one from Sullivan. "The story they told the detectives on the scene is plausible. Magnan and Goddel were involved in the murder of that other young woman. Goddel will take a plea if we don't charge him with murder. He's already told the DA that Magnan killed her, along with the three others."

"He's probably lying," Sullivan pointed out.

"Sure, but it makes sense, and it plays well on TV. The dead guy is never going to say anything else. Goddel will do enough hard time, and we'll see if the feds can get anything useful from him about the Gallata gang."

"What about Curran?" Sully asked.

Ward answered before the mayor this time. "Curran is a hero cop who was injured in the line of duty. He was there backing up his former partner, and he got killed protecting Stoneman and Dickson. That's all true. Even if he was involved in Magnan's operation—"

"He was involved," Sully interrupted. "Magnan's records listed payments to Curran. I can't say for sure whether Stoneman and Dickson knew that or not, but I doubt it."

Ward said, "Besides, even if he took some money and let Magnan use his ID and shit, there's no reason to think he was involved in any of the murders. There's no reason to besmirch Curran's reputation. No reason to take his pension away from his wife and kids. Let's just let that one lie."

The Mayor agreed, and Sullivan did not object.

"What about the witness?" Sullivan finally said after a few moments of silence.

"What about her?" Ward asked rhetorically.

"Do we need to tell the public that she was involved?"

None of the men spoke for a full minute. "I guess not," the mayor finally said. "I hear she went back to Idaho."

"Washington," Sullivan corrected.

"Wherever!" Douglas yelled, exasperated. "She's gone. Nobody knows she was ever here. She's a non-issue."

"Fine," Ward said.

"Fine," Douglas agreed.

"Done," Sully said, standing up and walking toward the door.

"Make sure your detectives keep their damned mouths shut," the mayor called out to Sullivan.

"Don't worry, Mr. Mayor. They know that their asses will be pinned to my bulletin board if they don't."

Chapter 50 – After Effects

TWO WEEKS LATER, Mike woke up on a sunny Sunday morning in Michelle's apartment. He stretched out in the bed and noticed that Michelle was not there, which was not unusual; she was an early riser. Mike pulled on a t-shirt over his gym shorts and walked out into the bright living room, then padded off to the kitchen to start a pot of coffee. He surmised that she had gone out for bagels, fresh fruit, and the Sunday *Times*, which was their normal routine on such days. He stopped himself and smiled at the thought that he and Michelle had established a Sunday morning routine. His role was to make the coffee and set out the plates, knives, and forks on the little dining table so that when Michelle returned, they could split up the sections of the paper and dig into the food without delay.

Later in the day, the plan was to hit a little Mexican restaurant that had recently opened, to see if their Cinco de Mayo party was up to the many banners and balloons that the owners had put up during the prior week. The coffee had barely stopped dripping when Mike heard

The apartment door open and close. The heavy deadbolt locked with a loud *ker-chunk* and Mike called out, "Welcome home, Doctor."

Michelle walked slowly into the kitchen, dropped a brown paper bag on the counter, and handed Mike the *New York Times* without a word. Mike took the paper with a puzzled expression, but when he glanced at the front page headline in the upper right corner, he stopped, then sat down and started reading.

The article was titled, "Teen Escaped Brooklyn Death Trap." There was also a subtitle, "Dirty Cops Ran Prostitution Ring Where Three Died." The byline identified the reporter as Dexter Peacock. For the next ten minutes, neither of them spoke. Peacock's article went into detail about the Brooklyn prostitution operation run by the corrupt cops. This was not really new ground; the story had been all over the local papers since the mayor made his announcement and identified Magnan, Goddel, and six other cops as disgraces to their uniforms. The lead was the story of "Sara," who was identified as a young girl who was there the night that T. Warren Magnan and Darren Curran had died in the Alexander Hamilton Hotel. Peacock acknowledged that Sara was not her real name and that her identity was being shielded to protect her from retaliation from the Gallata family.

Sara, the story went, had come to New York from an unnamed town in the West to search for her sister. Peacock described the unnamed sister's struggles with drug addiction and how she had come to New York and became ensnared in the corrupt cops' prostitution ring. The article implied, without providing any proof, that the cops were also selling drugs out of the hotel. Sara says that she was hiding in a closet when the gunfire broke out, and that Detectives Stoneman and Dickson saved her life. There was no mention of Darren Curran, and no suggestion that "Sara" had gone into the hotel as part of an unauthorized undercover operation.

"Wow," was all Michelle could say.

"Wow is right," Mike agreed. "How the hell did he get this?"

Before Michelle could answer, Mike's cell phone rang. He answered and then listened without speaking for several minutes, uttering only an occasional "uh huh." He eventually punched the END button while Michelle sat at the table, nibbling on a bagel and looking on intently.

"So?"

"So, that was Dexter Peacock."

"What?"

"Yep. He called to tell me that he got the story from Steph. She told him everything, including that she had gone to the hotel undercover with my help, but he left that part out at Steph's request. He also left out any mention of Darren because Steph asked him to. He said he hoped that I would appreciate him leaving out the embarrassing details, and he hopes that someday I will return the favor. Can you believe that shit?"

"I believe it, coming from him," Michelle said, reaching for a strawberry.

"When could he have spoken to Steph?"

Michelle paused and thought deeply. Finally, she said, "Steph first reached out to me after she read the story in *The Times* about Christine's death. That article was written by Dexter Peacock, so she would have known to contact him if she wanted to tell her story."

"Yeah. Maybe. Whatever. We can't control what she does, but I'm disappointed and a little pissed off that she didn't keep her story to herself. I guess she wanted Peacock to write another story about her sister, to clear her name so to speak. But the douchebag wrote it more about her. You can't trust the press."

"Well, at least he kept out the details that would get you in trouble."

"Hmmff," Mike grunted. "I'm sure he'll hold that over my head forever."

Chapter 51 – Facing the Music

Monday, May 6

T HE DAY AFTER *THE TIMES* RAN PEACOCK'S STORY, Mike and Jason returned to work, having been cleared by Internal Affairs of any misconduct. Lucas Gomez had been the investigating agent and he pushed the process through quickly. He told Mike, privately, that he would have come along as backup for the operation if Mike had told him more about it in advance. The corrupt cops were all dead or in custody, so Lucas was satisfied that justice and right had prevailed. He was also comfortable that Mike and Jason had acted out of innocent and good intentions.

But before Mike reported to the precinct, he had a final appointment with Terry in physical therapy. He was amused to see Dolores sitting in a plastic seat outside the therapy room when he arrived. "You're still not finished?" Mike chided playfully.

"Oh, hell yeah," Dolores retorted with a big smile. "I finished up a week ago. I'm just here to rub it in and collect on our bet." She stood up and laughed, then followed Mike into the therapy room. Terry greeted him warmly and then ran him through his stretching and weight work while Dolores watched and shouted out good-natured taunts. Mike stood against the wall and extended his left arm to its full height, pressing his left side flat against the gray paint and letting out a sigh and a low moan as his ligaments fully stretched out. He did twenty reps with a seven-pound weight and then Terry did a full extension manipulation on the table, without any screaming from Mike.

When he had finished, Terry said, "That's it, Mike. You check out at full range of motion. I'll certify you as achieving maximum medical recovery."

"Good. I hope I never see your ugly mug again," Mike quipped with a playful smile.

"The feeling is mutual," Terry responded, slapping Mike on the back and stepping away to grab a towel. "I have other patients who need my time, so you can stay the hell away."

"Gladly," Mike said, turning and offering his hand to the therapist. They exchanged a firm shake, and then Terry drew Mike into a hug. Mike walked over to his jacket and pulled out a gold gift bag, designed to hold a bottle of wine. Inside was a bottle of The Macallan 18, which Terry accepted with enthusiasm.

"What about me?" Dolores asked. Mike strode over to her and gave her a bear hug, then dug out his wallet and extracted a twenty-dollar bill with a bow of his head. "You got me," he said.

"You're damned right," she said. She then walked over to Terry and handed him the bill. "That's for you, Honey. You got me there ahead of this schmuck. Thanks."

They all exchanged a good laugh before Mike had to excuse himself to get to work.

Ж Ж Ж

When Mike walked into the bullpen, nobody was at their desks, but he could hear loud laughter and talking coming from the conference room. Mike walked over and peeked inside. The entire detective staff was inside and almost everyone was holding a donut.

"I guess the ban on food is lifted?" Mike asked rhetorically.

"Yeah," replied George Mason, the corner of his mouth showing a trace of powdered sugar. "The exterminator was just here and gave us a clean bill of health. No sign of recent rat droppings and nothing in the traps. We're clean. He suggested that we might want to avoid food inside the building for a few more months, but we told him to go fuck himself."

"No doubt," Mike said with a laugh.

"You want one?"

"No, thanks," Mike said, "I'm trying to watch what I eat."

"Don't kid yourself, Stoneman. The lovely medical examiner will never mistake you for a stud."

"Yeah, well maybe that's right, but I'll keep trying to fool myself."

After the donut orgy broke up, Mike and Jason adjourned to the fifth floor conference room to work on their paperwork to wrap up the Christine Barker investigation. The probable murderer, T. Warren Magnan, was already dead. No further arrests were likely and the case could be closed as "solved." They sorted through the documents and weeded down the file to the bare minimum. Jason volunteered to walk it down to Sophie in the file room.

"Sure," Mike said, "you make sure that you stay on her good side. She's a valuable resource."

"Amen to that."

"Did the vice guys take care of all the women in the hotel?"

"I think so," Jason said, looking up from the file box. "I spoke to one of the uniforms from Brooklyn and they took them to a local women's shelter that specializes in rape victims. They should be in pretty good hands."

"Good. Sometimes we forget about the living victims. The dead ones can't get hurt anymore."

"Have you heard from Steph?"

"Michelle is in contact with her. We're not happy about her reaching out to that douche, Peacock. But she posted some things on Facebook about how she's happy that Christine didn't really OD and while it's sad that she was murdered, Steph is glad that it's resolved. It's funny how she was so offended by the idea that it was an overdose, as if that's a worse way to die. Anyway, she seems fine. Michelle told me that the kid is thinking about enrolling in college in the fall."

"That's good. She could use a fresh start." Jason picked up the file box, tapped on the lid, and headed toward the stairs.

A few minutes later, Captain Sullivan called Mike into his office. After the story in the *Times*, the commissioner suggested that Mike and Jason should take some time off – so that they could get out of town while the story faded into the oblivion of the 24-hour news cycle. The commissioner and the mayor were concerned that Dexter Peacock or other reporters would dig further into the story and they both wanted Jason and Mike to be unavailable for comment. Although Mike protested that he was just back to work, it was clear that Sully was not going to take no for an answer. Mike said that he would talk to Jason about it and make some arrangements.

Ж Ж Ж

Later that day, Mike visited Marie and the kids. They had exchanged hugs at the cemetery, but this was an opportunity to really talk.

"I'm so sorry," Mike said, unable to articulate his feelings more specifically.

"Don't worry, Mike. Darren was depressed because of his injury and he knew deep down that he wasn't going to get back to active status. On some level, I'm sure that he's happy he went out shooting and protecting you. The kids and I will be alright."

Mike just nodded. He made sure Marie knew about some of the foundations and charity groups like the Steven Siller Tunnel to Towers foundation and the New York Police and Fire Widows' and Childrens' Fund, which provided money for mortgage payments and college tuition for the families of fallen heroes. "He really was a hero," Mike said.

"I know," Marie said, wiping away a tear. "Will you come by sometimes so I can make you a proper dinner?"

"Absolutely," Mike responded with a smile.

Ж Ж Ж

That night, Mike walked back to Michelle's apartment with her after they had been to dinner at a jazz club in Greenwich Village. "You really need to start leaving more of your stuff here," Michelle suggested.

"Hey, I have a toothbrush and a change of clothes," Mike retorted. "What more do I need?"

"How about a work suit and a few clean shirts?"

"If I did that, you'd start expecting me to be here all the time."

"I could get used to you being here," Michelle said, wrapping her arms around his neck and looking up into his eyes.

"I agree," Mike said, giving her a tender kiss. "But I don't want you to have to do my laundry for me."

"I hate laundry, but I won't mind folding your shirts."

"Well, let's talk about comingling our dirty laundry in the morning."

"I spoke to Rachel about the idea of taking some time off together. She has an Aunt who works for a cruise line and can get us a discount. She's going to talk to Jason about it."

"Great. I kinda like the idea of being in the middle of the ocean and unable to be reached by email or cell phone."

They undressed and Mike deposited his clothes in Michelle's hamper.

Michelle shed her robe and climbed into bed. They turned out the light and pulled up the covers. Michelle snuggled into the crook of Mike's left arm. "I'm glad you have two working shoulders again."

"So am I. Believe me. So am I."

The End

Note from the Author

Thank you for reading *Deadly Enterprise*. As an independently published author, I rely on word-of-mouth recommendations to help generate interest in my books. So, if you enjoyed it, please pass along your recommendation by posting a review on amazon.com, Goodreads.com, and/or BookBub.com. And tell your friends! You can also post notes and comments on the Mike Stoneman Thriller Facebook group at www.facebook.com/groups/MikeStoneman. You can also contact me directly at my website, www.KevinGChapman.com. I'm happy to talk about the book, and if you noticed any errors, typos, or incorrect information, I'm happy to hear from you so that I can correct the next edition. (If you are the first person to point out a typo, I will thank you by sending you a free autographed copy of one of my other books – or this one if you'd like a special copy.) I'm currently working on book #3 in the Mike Stoneman Thriller series. If you want to get previews, or if you want to be a beta reader of the manuscript of the new book, contact me at the website and I'll get you on the list of my super-fans – the "White Board Squad." (If you don't understand what the White Board Squad means, then you haven't read *Righteous Assassin,* so you really should do that right away.)

BookBub members: Please follow me and help me get to 1000 followers at https://www.bookbub.com/authors/kevin-g-chapman. You will receive notices from Bookbub when I have a new release, preorder, or discount!

Again, thank you for your time, which I know is valuable, and please keep reading independent authors – we need you!

--KGC -- November 2019

Acknowledgements

As always, first and foremost I thank my wonderful wife, Sharon, who is more invested in the characters of the Mike Stoneman series than any other reader, and in some cases even more than the author. Sharon helped brainstorm plot ideas, character development, and the broader story arc of the series. She also read early drafts and made dozens of helpful suggestions.

I also owe huge gratitude to my excellent editor, Samantha M. Chapman www.SamanthaChapmanediting.com, who picks apart my writing without mercy – exactly what I want in an editor. Her contributions are too numerous to count. Any independent authors who think it's well-edited (as I do) should consider hiring Samantha.

I am also grateful to my beta readers, especially J.B. Holeman and Buzz & Beth Baradyn, who provided amazing insight and helped point out gaps and inconsistencies in the drafts and got me to tighten up the story.

Finally, many thanks to my cover designer, Peter O'Connor from Bespoke Book Covers www.BespokeBookCovers.com. Following up on a marvelous cover design for *Righteous Assassin,* Peter outdid himself for this book and I am thrilled with the result. Special mention here to Ryan McGrady, the photographer from Brooklyn who took the original picture of the lower Manhattan skyline and the Brooklyn Bridge that Peter turned into the finished product.

I also need to acknowledge that gathering accurate information about the inner workings of the Internal Affairs department of the NYPD, as well as some of the other technical details about the internal security procedures of the department, proved difficult for me when writing this book. To the extent that any of the details here are inaccurate, the fault is entirely mine. If you noticed, and you know better, please contact me – I'd love to have you as a consultant on a future book!

I also will extend my apologies to the runners reading this book who know that the NYC Half-Marathon was on March 17, 2019, not exactly in line with the book's timeline. Since the race referenced here was organized by the fictional NYC Runners and not the NYRR, I'm taking a bit of poetic license about the fictional date of this fictional Half-marathon. But, if you said "wait! That's the wrong date!" I congratulate you for paying attention.

And, for anyone reading this book who is thinking that it's not plausible that members of the police department would be running a prostitution operation, please see the next few pages, which are excerpts from actual news reports of the events that inspired this story.

Finally, for readers who have not yet read book #1 in the Mike Stoneman Thriller series, *Righteous Assassin,* keep reading and you will find a preview of the beginning of that book.

--KGC

APPENDIX

(Truth is sometimes just as strange as fiction . . .)

Former NYPD Detective Ran $2 Million Prostitution Ring, Aided by Officers.

September 13, 2018

Retired New York Police Department Vice Detective Ludwig Paz used his experience investigating prostitution rings to run his own brothels, aided by seven active police officers. The Brooklyn and Queens operation netted more than $2 Million. Paz was arrested this week and charged with promoting prostitution and enterprise corruption, according to the Queens District Attorney's Office. He is also accused of paying off active officers to protect the operation.

Deputy Commissioner of Internal Affairs Joseph Reznick said all of the officers charged in the case had sex with the prostitutes, while on and off duty. "If a book was ever written about this case, I would probably name it 'Loyalty,' or 'Disloyalty Versus Friendship' because that's what it came down to," Mr. Reznick said at a news conference. Brooklyn South Vice Detective Rene Samaniego, 43, Sgt. Carlos Cruz, 41, and Detective Giovanny Rojas Acosta, 40, allegedly tipped off Mr. Paz on investigations. They face enterprise corruption charges. The officers worked in units based in Queens and Brooklyn, including a Vice squad investigating prostitution in South Brooklyn, an official said. Another officer, Giancarlo Raspanti, provided confidential information from department computers in exchange for discounted sex from the prostitutes, prosecutors said.

Commissioner James O'Neill said Thursday that the suspects "tarnished the NYPD shields they wore." He went on to say that, "Today, those who swore an oath and then betrayed it have felt the consequences of that infidelity."

In May 2017, a retired NYPD officer was sentenced to 15 months in prison for running a multimillion-dollar online escort service. Another former NYPD officer was sentenced to 66 months in prison that September for conspiring to engage in sex trafficking of a minor.

(Consolidated from news reports, September 13, 2018.)

For any Readers who have not yet read Book #1 in the Mike Stoneman Thriller series, *Righteous Assassin,* here's a taste of that book. If you want an autographed paperback copy, you can order it from my website at www.KevinGChapman.com.

RIGHTEOUS ASSASSIN (Mike Stoneman Thriller #1)

Chapter 1 – It's a Jungle

July 29

C RIME SCENES IN NEW YORK CITY are often bloody, regularly bizarre, and occasionally fascinating to the homicide detectives who are jaded to all but the grisliest circumstances. Detective Mike Stoneman had seen them all in his twenty-four years on the force. Stiffs in swimming pools, stiffs tied up in basement dungeons, stiffs with various parts of their anatomy removed, and stiffs fished out of the Hudson river with their eyeballs eaten away by aquatic creatures. This one, however, was a new variation – what he referred to as a "unicorn." Eaten alive by tigers is not a cause of death often registered by the New York City medical examiner. Mike knelt down next to what was left of the corpse's foot and examined the remnants of duct tape that had bound one ankle to the other. The tigers had left the tape mostly uneaten. Discerning palates, apparently.

"Just another routine murder in the Big City, eh, Mike?"

Stoneman looked up, squinting against the morning sun, and saw Detective Jason Dickson towering over him. Jason was six-foot-three, with broad shoulders that tapered down to a slim waist. Even wearing a suit, it was obvious that he was in great shape and had well-defined muscles across his entire upper body. He was a mountain compared to Mike's five-foot-ten and slightly paunchy frame, even when Mike was standing. On this morning, Jason was wearing a blue pin-striped suit with a starched white shirt that contrasted sharply against his dark brown skin. His red-and-blue silk tie was expertly knotted and held in place with a gold tie bar, giving him an especially dapper appearance next to Mike's rumpled jacket, wrinkled shirt, and scuffed loafers. Even at 9:00 a.m., the July humidity made Mike sweat as the temperature started its unstoppable rise toward too-damned-hot, but Jason seemed impervious.

Mike looked up at his young partner and smiled, which was a rare occurrence. "What? Never seen a stiff partially eaten by wild animals before?"

"Oh, sure," Jason parried, "just not this early in the morning."

Mike turned his attention back to the remnants of the body. The crime scene team was nearly finished, but the photographer was still taking shots all around the area. Normally, Mike would be worried about people walking around and contaminating the evidence, but in this case the press had been relegated to the spectator area above the tiger enclosure and the zoo security team had not allowed anyone but NYPD into the pit. The whole Bronx Zoo was closed for the day. Mike could hear the faint thumping of a chopper's rotors somewhere overhead, but he ignored it. "Did we get a positive ID on the corpse?"

"Yes, we did," Jason responded with his usual perfect diction. "You were correct, Mike. It's Mickey Gallata. The family has not reported him missing, but his son confirmed that he left home yesterday evening and did not come back. I guess he's not going to make it."

"No," Mike said without emotion. "Slick Mick will definitely not be having supper with his family ever again. It's funny, you know. We've been trying to pin a conviction on him for what, a dozen years? And now, somebody has taken care of all that for us. I guess we should thank them."

"When we figure out who's responsible, I'll send a fruit basket." Jason walked away to talk with the uniformed officer who was patrolling the perimeter of the tiger enclosure looking for anything out of place. Mike was pretty sure that the beat cop from the South Bronx was not going to know whether anything he saw in the replica jungle was out of place or not.

Mike stood up and squinted again as he gazed out of the pit and saw the television news crews positioned along the black iron fence that normally kept the zoo visitors from getting too close to the edge. They had jockeyed for position as soon as the cops had let them in an hour earlier. At the time, the low sun had made the left side of the enclosure the prime real estate for live remote shots. But now, as the sun rose a little higher in the sky, the crews were repositioning, staking out spaces and camera angles with the best backgrounds and lighting. Signs all along the bars reminded the public not to feed the animals. These particular tigers would not need feeding again for a few days.

Several minutes later, Mike and Jason walked together to have a talk with the director of zoo security, Maurice Walker, who was understandably both pissed off and embarrassed by the situation. Walker sported a jacket that could have been navy blue or black, depending on whether it had been cleaned recently. He wore light grey slacks with an elastic waist band that hugged the bottom of his belly, which was spilling slightly over his black belt. His dark sunglasses and open-collared dress shirt made him look like an extra in a gangster movie. He had been working security at the zoo for thirty years and had been promoted up the ranks. This was his home, and it had been violated.

In a thick Bronx accent, Walker explained to the two detectives that there were no security cameras inside the animal enclosures, but there were cameras at the zoo entrances. Jason asked him to provide copies of the recordings so that he could have someone review them as soon as possible. Walker said he would have the tapes sent over.

"Tapes?" Jason asked incredulously. "You mean disks, right?"

"Nah," Walker responded. "This is a City-run operation. C'mon. You know how it goes. We installed this security system twenty years ago. Ya think City Hall is springing for the latest tech for the fucking zoo? Ha! We got VHS machines and big-ass cassettes. But looking at tape's a waste of time. I know where the scumbags broke in, and there're no cameras there."

"Where's that?" Mike asked.

"Over on the wall, a few hundred yards," Walker said, pointing toward the brightly sun-lit space overhead and to the right of the tiger enclosure.

"What about the route from there to here?"

"Well, there are a couple cameras, but they're only turned on during the day when there are people here. We don't run them twenty-four hours a day. No reason to record darkness."

Stoneman looked at Dickson and shrugged. "It only matters when it matters. Can we see the entry point?"

Walker led the two detectives out of the tiger pit and up a long ramp past the news crews, who scurried to grab their equipment, thinking that the appearance of the two NYPD detectives might signal something worth recording. When Mike waved them off and kept walking, they set down their cameras and went back to their territories. Walker guided Dickson and Stoneman to the perimeter wall that separated the zoo grounds from the surrounding city. It was made of concrete blocks that were arranged to mimic stonework, like a medieval castle. Every few hundred feet along the wall, there were steel gates secured with a deadbolt lock and a separate chain-and-padlock combination. Walker explained that the gates were there to allow access for trucks bringing in supplies and large items that would not fit through the public access entrances. They had occasionally had kids climb over the wall and commit acts of vandalism, but nobody had ever broken through the gates before. Walker stopped in front of a gate that was obviously no longer locked. Yellow police tape was strung across the threshold. Its broken padlock lay on the ground, the metal twisted where it had been cut.

"Even with vandalism issues in the past, you didn't keep the security cameras running at night?" Mike was trying to keep a professional demeanor, but his annoyance with the absence of potentially helpful evidence seeped into his voice.

Walker shrugged. "It wasn't my call, Detective. It was a budget decision made by the managing director."

Mike pursed his lips and said nothing. At first, he could not imagine how running cameras could be a budget issue. But, when he thought about the eight-hour maximum duration of a VHS tape, which would need to be changed during the night, he figured it out. No reason to pay somebody to sit in the security office and swap out tapes all night. He examined the broken lock and severed chain lying on the ground. It would have been simple for anyone with some basic equipment to cut the padlock and chain and drill out the deadbolt. "Aren't you worried about somebody stealing valuable animals?"

Walker shook his head. "The only animals here that are really worth anything outside the zoo industry are so poisonous or dangerous that nobody with a brain would try to steal them. And they're all tagged with permanent identification that makes them pretty much impossible to sell."

Stoneman nodded, then asked, "How did they get Slick Mick into the tiger enclosure without being attacked themselves?"

Walker paused. "Why do you think it was more than one person?"

Mike smiled at Walker's perception. "You're right, Mr. Walker. I shouldn't make that assumption. It's just that, in my experience, one person generally has a hard time dragging a full-grown man around, and it's particularly hard to get someone into a spot like that even if he's unconscious."

Jason interjected, "If this was a mob hit, there were probably multiple goons involved."

Mike frowned. "We're making a lot of assumptions now, Detective Dickson."

Jason bit back a response and nodded. "Right, Detective Stoneman. Stick to what we know for sure, not what we think."

Mike nodded back. "Right. We'll figure out how the facts fit together later." They walked slowly back to the tiger enclosure, tracing the probable route of the killer or killers and looking for anything out of place, but saw nothing they could perceive as out of the ordinary. At the bottom of the sloping ramp that ran along the side of the tiger pit, they came to a door they had come through before, marked "zoo staff only." The three men paused while Mike examined the broken lock. "Why isn't this door secured with a better lock?"

Walker shrugged. "Who in their right mind wants to break into the tiger pit?"

Mike nodded and said nothing. They walked through the door into a dark corridor, then through another door, with no lock, back out into the pit and the mid-morning sunlight. Mike squinted while Jason smoothly extracted sunglasses from the front pocket of his suit jacket. Jason asked, "Where were the tigers when the killers dragged Gallata out here?"

Walker didn't hesitate. "The animals all stay in their interior cages during the night. We release them each morning, but they're never out here after dark."

Mike nodded again. "Once the perps were past the staff door, was there anything blocking them from releasing the tigers out into the pit?"

"No," Walker replied. "Just a sliding bar on the access door. No lock."

"Pretty easy gig," Jason opined. "Tie the guy up, either ahead of time or when you get here. Cut him a little to get some blood flowing, then release the tigers and walk away."

"Yeah. Very creative," Mike deadpanned. "Jungle Book meets Goodfellas."

Mike walked back into the middle of the pit, scanning the lush foliage and the large rocks hewn from some upstate granite quarry. A small artificial stream meandered across the jungle-scape, ending in a deep pool where the tigers could cool off on hot days. The mangled corpse had been removed while Mike and Jason had been away, leaving only a series of pins in the ground and blood stains to mark the place where Mickey Gallata had met his end. Jason sidled up to Mike as he stood there, contemplating whether this apparent mob hit was worth any time investigating, and kept silent and still for two full minutes. "Good," Mike commended. "That's the longest I've ever seen you keep your mouth shut."

"Thanks. I have two thoughts."

"Great, Kid. Tell me both of them."

Jason paused, frowning down at Mike from his six-foot-three perspective, but he kept his annoyance in check. "First, do you remember what they used to call Slick Mick before he became the boss, back when he was just a goon for the old man?"

Mike smiled and nodded his head slightly. "Oh, yeah. I remember. 'Mickey the Animal.'"

"Kind of poetic justice, don't you think?"

"Sure. Somebody's idea of a sick joke. What's the other thing, Junior?"

"I thought you weren't going to call me that?"

"Sorry. Habit."

"What I was going to say," Jason said softly, "is that last night was the last Saturday of the month."

"Yeah," Mike responded blankly, "I thought about that. This one seems pretty obviously not connected, don't you think?"

Jason turned to his partner and took off his sunglasses, revealing his dark eyes. "Like you always say, Mike, no matter what we may think, what we know is the evidence. What we know is that there was a murder with unusual circumstances on the last Saturday of the month. It could be a coincidence, of course, or it might not be."

"Yeah," Mike grunted, wiping away a trickle of sweat from his eyebrow with the back of his increasingly dirty suit jacket. "Let's see what happens."

To continue, order your copy of *Righteous Assassin* at
https://www.amazon.com/dp/B07JJDZZC1

Made in the USA
Middletown, DE
13 December 2019

80635111R00205